8-11

W9-ANY-481

NEB

WITCHLANDERS

WITCHLANDERS

LENA COAKLEY

Atheneum Books for Young Readers
NEW YORK   LONDON   TORONTO   SYDNEY

ATHENEUM BOOKS FOR YOUNG READERS

An imprint of Simon & Schuster Children's Publishing Division

1230 Avenue of the Americas, New York, New York 10020

This book is a work of fiction. Any references to historical events, real people, or real locales are used fictitiously. Other names, characters, places, and incidents are products of the author's imagination, and any resemblance to actual events or locales or persons, living or dead, is entirely coincidental.

Copyright © 2011 by Cathleen Coakley

All rights reserved, including the right of reproduction in whole or in part in any form.

ATHENEUM BOOKS FOR YOUNG READERS is a registered trademark of Simon & Schuster, Inc.

For information about special discounts for bulk purchases, please contact Simon & Schuster Special Sales at 1-866-506-1949 or business@simonandschuster.com.

The Simon & Schuster Speakers Bureau can bring authors to your live event. For more information or to book an event, contact the Simon & Schuster Speakers Bureau at 1-866-248-3049 or visit our website at www.simonspeakers.com.

Book design by Sonia Chaghatzbanian

The text for this book is set in Goudy Old Style.

Manufactured in the United States of America

First Edition

10 9 8 7 6 5 4 3 2 1

CIP data for this book is available from the Library of Congress.

ISBN 978-1-4424-2004-5

ISBN 978-1-4424-2006-9 (eBook)

YA F COA
  1611 3824   08/26/11   NEB
Coakley, Lena, 1967-

Witchlanders

adk

LeRoy Collins Leon Co
Public Library System
200 West Park Avenue
Tallahassee, FL 32301

To the memory of Agnes "Mardi" Short

Smith Collection ©
Property of L. Smith
Summer 1999
List Price $9

ACKNOWLEDGMENTS

This book took many years to write, and in that time I have received the support of many wonderful writers and readers. Much of the first draft was written on Aino Anto's dining room table, while she wrote twice as much in half the time and then made me tea. Patient readers of early drafts were: Karen Krossing, Richard Ungar, Cheryl Rainfield, Karen Rankin (twice!), Anne Laurel Carter, Georgia Watterson, Wendy Lewis, the students in Peter Carver's writing class, and Peter Carver himself. Hadley Dyer was kind enough to use my manuscript in her Ryerson University courses on children's publishing, and her students gave me some very useful comments. Most importantly, my writing group— Hadley Dyer, Kathy Stinson, and Paula Wing—read this book so many times they could probably recite it with me. Thank you all.

But even with all that help, this book would have been so much less without my agent, Steven Malk of Writers House, and my editor, Caitlyn Dlouhy. Thank you both. If this book sings at all, it is because of you.

I'd also like to gratefully acknowledge the City of Toronto, who gave me a grant to complete this novel through the Toronto Arts Council at a time when I needed it most.

And finally I'd like to thank my family, especially my late grandmother, Agnes Short, who read me so many books as a child that I still have her voice in my head when I read to myself. This book is for her.

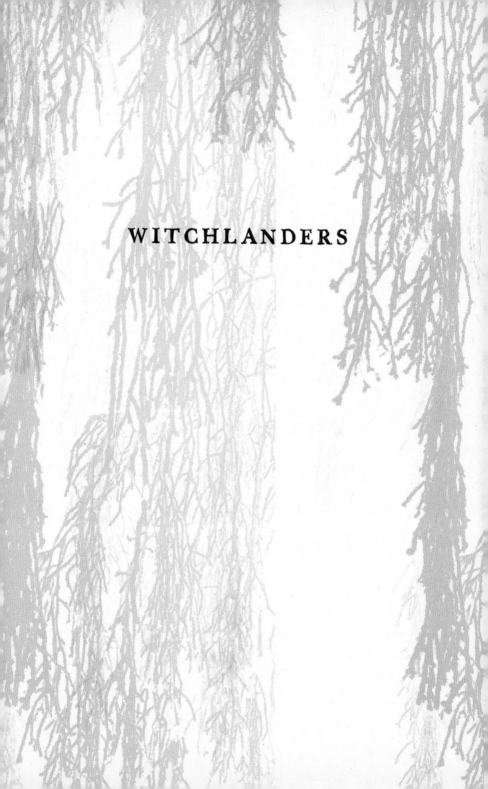

WITCHLANDERS

PART ONE

The Great God Kar sings the world into being. He is singing even now. If he stopped, everything from the mountains to the oceans to the ink on this page would disappear.

Kar's magic comes from harmony, and yet the God is alone, singing with his many mouths and tongues, watching mankind with his thousand eyes.

Once, all men could hear his songs. They joined their voices with their brothers, imitating the harmonies of creation, until they made a magic that rivaled even Kar's.

And so the jealous God sealed up their ears to his music. He created war and discord. Now few can hear his songs —and those who do, find that their brothers are scattered to the winds.

—The Magician's Enchiridion

CHAPTER 1

FLOWERS AND BONES

Ryder woke to the sound of clattering bones. A red curtain separated the sleeping area from the main room of the cottage, and he could see the faint flickering of candles through the fabric.

"Skyla," he whispered.

Even in his sleep he'd known there was something wrong. A feeling of dread lay heavy in his stomach. Next to him in the long bed, Ryder's two younger sisters were quiet. Pima, the little one, lay diagonally with the covers bunched up around her. Her mouth was open, and she was snoring gently. Skyla was pressed into the corner.

"Sky . . . ," he began again.

"I know," she said. There was nothing sleepy about her voice. He wondered how long she'd been awake.

"Why didn't you do something?" Ryder flung off the bit

of tattered blanket that covered his legs. "Why didn't you wake me?"

The dirt floor was cold under his bare feet. He'd grown tall in the past year, too tall for the low door frame that led to the main part of the cottage, and he hunched a little as he peered around the red curtain.

Mabis, his mother, was squatting on the floor, picking up bones. A goat's femur, a horse's rib. They were dark with age and etched with thin lines. She placed each one into a wooden bowl as large as the wheel of a donkey cart.

"Tell me who it is," she murmured. "Tell me." Smoke from the fire hung around the room, making rings around the candles.

Skyla slipped in beside Ryder, and together they watched as their mother rose from the floor. Mabis looked furtively around, squinting toward the sleeping area, but they were well hidden in the shadows. She seemed to satisfy herself that she was alone, and staggered to the lit fireplace, grabbing an iron poker.

"Did you check the fireplace?" Ryder whispered. "I told you to check the fireplace."

"I did," Skyla insisted.

Mabis climbed onto a wooden chair and up onto the large table their father had made. She was wearing her reds. It was the traditional costume of the mountain witches— loose-fitting pants and a quilted tunic with embroidery along the edge. Ryder had seen his mother wear reds only a few times before. They had a dramatic effect on people that Mabis liked to keep in reserve. Usually they were packed carefully at the bottom of a wooden blanket chest; now the tunic was buttoned up wrong, and there was a greasy stain down the side of her leg.

Her sleeves slid down her brown arms as she reached up with the poker. From the rafters fell a cloth bag tied with string. Ryder cursed inwardly. He'd thought he knew all her hiding places.

Mabis knelt on the tabletop and set down the poker. Greedily she opened the bag. A shower of black flowers, each the size of a baby's fist, fell to the table.

"Maiden's woe," Skyla breathed.

Ryder nodded, noticing the black stain on his mother's lips; it wasn't the first she'd had that night. Maiden's woe was a river plant whose flowers bloomed in the shallows. Ryder had pulled up all he could find, but the plants grew like weeds this time of year; if he missed even the smallest bit of root, they came back twice as thick. As he watched, his mother pushed two of the black flowers into her mouth and grimaced.

"She promised," Skyla whispered.

"Promised," Ryder muttered as if the word were a curse. He started forward, but Skyla grabbed him by the arm.

"Wait!" she said. "Just . . . wait." Ryder frowned but

held back. His first impulse was to confront his mother, but Skyla's judgment was usually sound; perhaps she had some reason to suspect a second hiding place.

Mabis had left the table now and was kneeling over the great bowl, shaking it with both hands. She could do this half the night, Ryder knew: stir the bones, shake them, mumble at them, then pour them out onto the floor and pretend to read like some ancient witch doing a casting.

When Ryder's father was alive, Mabis threw the bones only for customers. Telling the future was something she did for money. Of course, the villagers in the valley knew that she was not a real witch, not anymore. She didn't live in the mountain coven, devoting her life to the Goddess and studying the teachings of Aata and Aayse; she had given that up long ago. But real witches didn't concern themselves with the daily problems of the village, and Mabis's prophecies were full of common sense, if vague, and so she had a tidy business.

What villagers never saw was how Ryder's father would frown when the door closed behind them, how Mabis would laugh, jingling their coins in her hand. Any fool who believed a pile of bones could tell the future didn't deserve to keep his money—that was what she used to say.

Yet here she was—holding a bowl of bones over her head. She shook it one, two, three times, then spilled its contents onto the floor with a loud clatter. The room fell silent. Mabis looked toward the sleeping area and cocked her head, listening, but Ryder and Skyla stayed quiet. Ryder glanced back at Pima, but his littlest sister was still asleep.

Finally Mabis turned back to the bones, circling them like an animal stalking prey. Skyla seemed to hold her breath; she lifted herself up on her toes, craning her neck. Ryder could see his sister was trying to make out the pattern the bones made on the floor, but what did she think was there? After a while, Mabis moved back to the table and popped two more of the dark blooms into her mouth.

"I've seen enough." Ryder stepped forward again, and again Skyla pulled him back. "What in Aata's name is wrong with you?" he hissed. "There's always another hiding place, Skyla. We can't just watch . . ."

His sister looked up at him with somber eyes. Her pale eyebrows stood out against her brown face, and even in the dim light, her hair glinted like polished metal.

"You can't go now. You're not supposed to interrupt a witch's reading once the bones are thrown."

"What witch? What reading?"

Those eyes again. His sister looked like Fa sometimes with that wise look. "Maybe . . . maybe she really can see the future. Maybe something bad is going to happen. Shouldn't we know?"

Ryder swallowed his annoyance. He knew all he needed to know: Throwing the bones was just his mother's excuse for taking the flowers, and the mad visions she had afterward were not the future, just the inside of her own bewildered mind.

"You really are getting gullible, Sky," he said, and before she could stop him again, he strode into the main room of the cottage.

Mabis's head snapped up when he entered. In spite of himself, Ryder was taken aback. Her yellow hair was loose and tangled, and her eyes glittered strangely in the firelight. His recriminations died on his lips.

"Do you see it?" she asked, gesturing to the casting. Her voice had a kind of fragile hope, as if pleading to be believed. "Someone has arrived. There's a stranger in the mountains."

"Go to bed now," he said. "Please." His mother just stood there, swaying slightly.

The walls of the cramped cottage seemed to lean in on him. No one had put the cheese away, he noticed— good market cheese he'd bought for a treat, not their own homemade. Dirty wooden plates were stacked by the door, waiting to be washed in the river. Mabis had sent her children to bed insisting she would clean up, and Ryder had been so tired from his other chores that he'd decided to believe her.

"Mabis," he said firmly. "Listen to me—we need you

now. The hicca will freeze on the stalks if we don't get it harvested." He crossed toward her. "I can't do everything. The chilling could come any day."

"Watch your feet!" Mabis took his elbow. "Watch out for the bones." She gestured to the floor. "Try to see it, Ryder. Just try. Start with the anchor bone—the small one—that's the key. See how it touches the shadow man? Place the pattern in your mind and the vision will come."

"Mabis, you're talking gibberish." She never did this, never tried to teach her children how to read, though Skyla had often asked to learn. Mabis had always said the witches made it all up, so why bother to pass it on? "Don't you understand? If you don't help with the harvest, we might not have enough to eat this winter."

"The stranger in the mountains is just the beginning. Terrible things are coming."

"Stop it! Stop it now. You sound like a madwoman."

She turned away from him in disgust. "Your father would have believed."

Ryder frowned, stung by the bitterness in her voice, as if he were the one disappointing her. Could it be that she really saw something? He let himself consider the idea for just a moment before shaking his head.

"No," he said firmly. "If throwing the bones were real—which it isn't, you've told me a hundred times—but if it were, then there would be witches in the coven doing it right now, doing it better than you. And if there was something terrible coming, they'd tell us—they'd have told us already. Isn't that why they're up there? Isn't that why we pay our tithes? So they can guard the border and keep us safe?" Mabis had stopped listening to his argument and was looking blankly into space. "Mabis?"

Her eyes startled him when she looked up; they were so bright and blue and wild. "I see the future," she whispered. "I'm seeing it right now."

"You're not." His voice quavered a little. "Stop it. You're not even looking at the casting."

"A great witch doesn't need bones. I can see the future written in the flecks of your eyes." She touched his face with cold hands, holding him by the chin. "Stay still. I almost have it all."

Worry stabbed through him. She was like a feral creature gazing out at him from a deep wood, seeing and not seeing. It frightened him. He should have gone to the river every day and made sure every bit of that weed was gone.

"An assassin is coming." She seemed alarmed now, afraid. "An assassin in the mountains. Right across the border. He mustn't succeed!" His mother's gaze left his face and slid to the table by the fire. "Just one more flower and I'll know everything."

"No," Ryder said, stepping away from her. "No. This is nonsense." In three long strides he crossed the room and gathered up every one of the black blooms.

"What are you doing?" Mabis stumbled forward and bones scattered. Ryder looked around the small room, flowers in his hands. His eyes lighted on the fireplace.

"Don't!" she shouted. Lunging forward, she lost her balance, bones under her feet. She fell heavily onto one knee. Ryder seized the opportunity and tossed the maiden's woe into the fire. The black trumpets hissed and popped, sending sparks up the chimney.

Mabis struggled to her feet and ran toward him. "I need them!" she pleaded, sounding desperate. Just in time, Ryder grabbed her wrist and stopped her from plunging her hand into the flames. Mabis turned on him. Her face, lit by firelight, was twisted with rage. Before Ryder could do anything, she slapped him across the cheek. Hard.

Silence.

Skyla rushed in from behind the curtain. "Mabis, stop it!" she cried. But by then there was nothing to stop. Mabis was leaning against the fireplace, avoiding their gaze, her breath coming in shallow gasps.

"Do you see?" Ryder hissed at Skyla. "This has nothing to do with the bones, with the future."

His sister's eyes were wide with fright. From the sleeping area, Pima's voice came loud and shrill.

"Maba, I want Maba!"

"Just go help Pima, will you?" Ryder told his sister.

"I'll go," said his mother. Her voice was small, and she still didn't meet his eyes.

"No! Pima can't see you like this."

His mother winced. Skyla took a breath and nodded, then went off to comfort the crying four-year-old. When she was gone, Ryder turned to his mother. "This has got to stop."

"I'm so sorry," she said. She sank to the floor with her back against the wall.

"Sorry," he repeated, putting his hand to his cheek.

He dropped down next to her on the floor, and for a while neither of them spoke. Outside, trees creaked in the wind. The stones of the fireplace were warm against his back. He tried to hold on to his anger, but as he sat there he felt it slipping away from him, leaving a hollowness in his chest. Skyla was singing softly to Pima in the other room—a lullaby of Fa's—and without warning, a feeling of loss pierced him. He'd become used to it since Fa died, surprise attacks of emotions that came out of nowhere, left him breathless. But he realized it wasn't his father that he was missing so painfully at this moment. It was his mother. His mother as she used to be. Mabis had been like iron once. She'd been like stone. Nothing could break her. And he'd felt entirely safe.

Slowly Mabis got to her knees and reached for something under the table. One of her bones, the smallest one, had skittered there in the scuffle. She tossed it into his lap before sitting heavily back down.

"What's this?" he said.

"You're right. It's got to stop." Her eyes were already beginning to clear. Maiden's woe gave Mabis a burst of frenzied vision, but the effect soon dissipated, leaving her moody and tired—until she took more and it all started again.

Ryder picked up the fragment of black bone. Unlike the others in the set, this one had no marks scratched into it. It was a piece of vertebra most likely, but it was so worn he couldn't tell from what animal it had come. He'd never noticed it before, had never cared enough about his mother's bones to distinguish one from the other, though they'd sat on the high shelf above the kitchen pots all his life. His mother had always been so quick to deride them, to belittle anyone who believed they had something to reveal. "I don't understand. Why are you giving this to me?"

"It's the anchor bone," Mabis explained. "It's very old. A casting wouldn't work without it." She pressed his hands around the small black knob. "You keep it for me. Without it, I won't be tempted."

The meaning of his mother's words began to dawn on him. Could it be that simple? Could hiding this little thing really keep his mother away from the maiden's woe? He should have thought of it before. He would have tossed the whole set of bones into the river if he thought it would stop her from taking the flower.

"And you were right about something else," she said. "The witches in my coven, they must see the assassin too. I've got to speak to them about it. Ryder, we've got to build a firecall."

"What? Tonight?"

"Please, I won't be able to stop thinking about it. . . ."

Ryder was about to refuse. He knew the witches wouldn't come, wouldn't allow themselves to be summoned by the village fortune-teller. But then, maybe being ignored by the witches was just what his mother needed to bring her back to herself. He glanced at the shuttered window for any sign of light slipping in between the cracks. As yet, dawn hadn't reached them, but he was beginning to suspect he wouldn't sleep again that night.

"And if we build this call and the witches don't come, will you promise to stop all this? Will you face the fact you can't see any visions in the bones?"

Mabis smiled, and Ryder could see the black stains on her teeth. "I'll promise anything you like," she said. She pulled herself up from the floor, brushing the dust off her dirty reds. "But the witches won't ignore a call from me."

* * *

On the other side of the border, Falpian Caraxus watched the column of greenish smoke rise up over the shoulder of the mountain. Dawn was breaking. Behind him, his father's men hovered around cooking fires, rolling up blankets or talking softly over last cups of steaming tea, careful not to disturb his thoughts. Some had already taken their leave with a nod or a silent bow and were leading their horses down the steep path.

Falpian stood in the dewy grass on the edge of the plateau. The mountains were a stunning sight. The zanthia trees had changed their color, turning every peak to crimson.

"The witches are in their reds," he said to himself. Here, so close to the border, it was easy to see how the Witchlanders could believe in Aata and Aayse, the witch prophets. Even the red trees seemed to honor their customs.

Bron, his father's kennel master, came up quietly beside him, his great shadow spilling over the lip of the plateau. "Firecall," he grunted, frowning up at jagged peaks.

Falpian hadn't considered that. At first he'd thought the rising smoke must be a funeral pyre, but then he remembered that Witchlanders didn't burn their dead; they buried them in the ground, or worse, preserved them in dank catacombs.

"Black for war, green to gather, red when the coven is under attack," Falpian recited. He turned to Bron. "Some witch calls for a gathering with that smoke. Do you think they know something?"

Bron took a moment to answer. "What is there to know?"

"I'm not a fool."

After another pause the kennel master said quietly, "It's always best to assume the witches know every move we make. And every move we're going to make." He turned to Falpian now, as if to use his face to make the point. Falpian was used to the cruel scars that slashed from left to right across Bron's features—souvenirs of war—but seeing them now made him flinch. Witchlanders were a vicious people.

"Maybe I should just go home with you," Falpian suggested hopefully. "These are dangerous times."

"Are they?"

Behind them on the plateau, some of the others had noticed the smoke and were murmuring and pointing. They were young men mostly, too young to be veterans of the war like Bron, too young to remember when the fire-calls all burned black.

"It's all right!" Bron shouted, but his words were for Falpian as much as for them. "I expect a call's a common enough thing in these parts!" In a lower voice he went on, "There's nothing to fear. The witches won't break the treaty."

"I don't want to go back because I'm afraid," Falpian snapped. Bron raised an eyebrow at Falpian's tone. Although a servant of Falpian's father, he demanded respect from someone so young. "I'm sorry, Bron. It's just . . . I should be home. I should be training with the others."

"Others?"

"Why do you pretend not to know what I'm talking about? There wasn't a spare bed the day we left—there were even boys sleeping in the stables."

"Men have always sent their sons to your father to learn their battle skills."

"Never so many sons as this year."

Bron pursed his lips and stared out at the scarlet mountains as if he enjoyed the view. *He must be under orders,* Falpian thought. *He'd tell me if he could.*

"We'll await you in the gorge," someone said to Bron, and the last of the men and horses began to make their way down the path.

Falpian watched the last horse disappear and felt a weight settle over him. Soon Bron would leave as well, and Falpian would be alone, alone at Stonehouse for a hundred days with only the dog for company—and even Bo's company couldn't be counted on. He was off chasing rabbits now, enamored of his new freedom.

Of course, Falpian would want for nothing during his stay. His father had sent crates of poetry, bags of flour, jars of honey, barrel after barrel of dried fish—everything he'd need and plenty of things he wouldn't. Somehow the man could make even bounty seem like a slap in the face. In the old days he would have told his son to live by his wits, that hardship would make him strong; he would have scoffed at the idea of reading poetry and insisted Falpian study logic or military history. Now he didn't seem to care.

"I can't be completely useless," Falpian said to Bron. "Surely there's something I can learn to do." He pointed to the smoke over the mountain. "I hate *them* as much as everyone else. If there's another attack planned. If it's war—"

"Shh!" Bron warned. The men were gone now, but he looked to the mountain's crooked peak as if, from their high covens, red witches were listening. "You are in mourning, child. This is a time of grief for you—a time of meditation and prayer."

Falpian waved his words away. "There are a dozen retreats where I could spend my mourning season. But Father sends me as far as he can, for as long as he can. Am I being banished?" He bit his lip, remembering how cold his father had been when they parted, barely taking the time to say good-bye. "*You* don't have any magic in you either, but at least my father can stand to look at *you*." This was the heart of the matter, Falpian knew. His lack of magic. "All those men and boys back home, how many of them will have the gift? One or two, if any? But he doesn't treat the others as if they've disappointed him just by being alive. He puts a sword in their hands and teaches them how to use it."

"I seem to recall your father giving you many lessons in swordcraft."

Falpian blushed hotly. Neither he nor his brother had ever excelled with weapons. "I thought," he stammered, "I thought I would have other skills." He paused, steadying his breath. The last thing he wanted was for Bron to see him cry, and report what he had seen to his father. "I shouldn't have assumed."

The kennel master set a thick hand on his shoulder. Falpian shrugged away his touch, but at least Bron wasn't like his mother, constantly telling him that he was a late bloomer, that his magic would come. Falpian was grateful for that.

"Perhaps your father has a reason," Bron said, still speaking in hushed tones. "Did you think of that? A reason for sending you so close to the border, in these . . . uncertain times."

"What do you mean?"

Bron's eyes were suddenly brighter, and the torn corners of his mouth turned upward to a grin. There was a leather pack at his side, and from it he pulled a metal cylinder that glinted dully in the sunlight. Falpian recognized it as a container for a scroll.

"I was supposed to wait until the last moment to give this to you," Bron said, "and I suppose that time has come."

All at once, Falpian was reminded of a day years earlier—the day he'd been given his dog, Bo. He remembered the kennel master holding the trembling ball of fur cupped in both his hands, that same glad brightness in his eyes: It was something special, this scroll. Falpian looked again at the cylinder. He'd never seen it before, but he recognized the Caraxus family mark etched over its surface: the words DUTY, HONOR, SACRIFICE coiled together in the ancient Baen script.

"Is it . . . from my father?" Something like hope fluttered in his chest. "But if he had a message—"

"Not a message," Bron interrupted. "A mission." He smiled again. "I wish you could have heard him. Your father did not confide everything in me, but he did say your presence here was very important, that *you* were very important."

"Very important? Me?" Try as he might, Falpian couldn't picture his father saying the words. "Important for what?"

"For what's to come."

Later, when Bron too had gone, Falpian stood at the edge of the plateau clutching the metal cylinder tightly in one hand, delaying for a moment the pleasure of opening it.

He had a mission. A reason to be here. His father had not banished him after all. The red mountains had been just a pretty picture before; now they were strangely thrilling, as if his destiny were hidden somewhere amid the rocky crags.

Nearby, a stand of zanthias shook their branches, and a cloud of seedpods floated down on him like fat red snow-flakes. Without thinking, Falpian pulled one out of the air. It was soft and feathery. He'd read somewhere that Witchlanders made wishes on them.

"Let me do this well," he whispered, "whatever it is. Don't let me disappoint him again."

Falpian blew a soft breath over his palm, and the seed-pod floated down on a current of air, disappearing into the gorge.

He'd rather die than disappoint his father again.

CHAPTER 2

THE SKIN OF THE SEA

The song Ryder sang in the hicca fields rose and fell, inventing itself. He had always sung while he worked, not because he was happy or because he wanted to, but just because mindless labor always seemed to bring the strange, wordless melodies to his lips.

"Ryder!" his sister shouted from the base of the planting hill. He ignored her. "I know where you are!"

Ryder stopped singing and ducked a little lower. It was early morning, but already he'd been picking for so long that his hands were raw and his shirt was damp with sweat. All around him, rows of golden hicca swayed stiffly in the breeze.

"Fa prayed every day at harvest time," Skyla called. "And you haven't done it once!"

"Is that you, Skyla? I can't hear you!" He turned back to his work, but he knew he couldn't get rid of his sister that easily.

The hicca plants were tall and straight with an earthy, fruity smell. Ryder grasped the nearest one just below the tassel and slid his hand down the plant, knocking off the hard brown berries that grew close along the stalk. On the ground, an open sack caught the berries as they fell. It was rough work—his fingers would be blistered by sundown—but a Witchlander who wore gloves in the hicca fields couldn't show his face in town.

"If we start right away, we'll be finished in time for breakfast." Skyla's voice was closer now. He could hear her coming toward him through the rows. "We should thank the Goddess for her bounty."

Ryder bent down and gathered up the few berries that had missed the sack. "Bounty! We'll be lucky if we get a fortyweight this year."

"Even so . . ."

Ryder straightened up. His sister was standing behind him, panting a little from the climb. She wore a pair of Fa's old leggings, tied in a knot at the waist to keep them up.

"Performing Aata's prayer will take up half the morning," he argued. "You and I and Mabis tilled the soil, planted the berries, weeded. What did the Goddess have to do with it?"

"Everything," Skyla said firmly.

Ryder snorted. "You don't really believe that."

Something behind him caught her eye, and Skyla

pushed past, frowning. At the top of the hill, the lucky man—a scarecrow they had made that spring—stretched out his stick arms, watching over the crops.

"Look," she scolded. "You've let him get all bent over." She grasped the pole that formed the scarecrow's body and began to twist it deeper into the dirt.

Ryder threw up his hands. "Yes, the Goddess and the lucky man. They're the ones responsible for this harvest. I might as well go back to bed."

Skyla shot him a glare. She'd been in a mood all morning, and Ryder knew he wasn't helping. Normally he'd be happy to appease his sister by praying for a little while. It was Mabis he was really annoyed with. This morning she had refused flat-out to help with the picking, saying that she had to tend the firecall. It had been burning for three days now without a word from the coven. Of course the witches weren't coming—anyone could see that—but Mabis kept adding herbs and grasses to color the smoke, kept feeding it the good logs Ryder had split for winter. He realized now that he should have put a time limit on their agreement. Mabis had promised that things would go back to normal if the witches didn't come, but she didn't say how long she was prepared to wait.

Ryder followed his sister to the top of the hill and looked out over the tops of the hicca plants. From there, he could see down past the cottage, past the neighboring planting hills, past the bend in the river, all the way to the village in the valley. Theirs was the highest farm, the last of the green foothills before the mountains turned red with zanthias and began their climb into witch country.

"We do these things for Fa," Skyla said softly, without turning around. She was adjusting the head of the lucky man, an old helmet from the war. "He taught us to till and plant and weed. And pray. We'd be ignorant as blackhairs if it weren't for him."

Ryder was still staring into the valley. "Farmer Raiken's got his whole bottom field done."

Skyla gave a frustrated hiss. "A beautiful view and that's all you see? It's not a race—our crops are always the last to ripen up here."

"But it *is* a race, Skyla," he said—it was maddening that he was the only one who could see it. "The chilling might come tomorrow, or the day after that. And we've still got to take the hicca to the miller, cut and dry the stalks for the animals, fix the cottage roof—then there's the vegetable garden . . ."

"Villagers wouldn't let us starve if worst came to worst."

"Charity?" Ryder could hardly believe what he heard. "Fa would cry out from his grave—"

"Maybe," she interrupted. "Maybe we'd be better off living in the village."

She inclined her head slightly toward the column of

greenish smoke that rose up below them from the cottage. Every once in a while, the wind would change, and Ryder would catch its bitter smell—like burnt herbs and sour milk. Skyla meant Mabis—Mabis would be better off in the village. "Or perhaps the coven would take us in," she added softly.

"The coven." He laughed. "Can you imagine us living there? Anyway, Mabis is fine."

He put his hand to his chest and felt for the little bone his mother had given him. Day and night he kept it with him, safe in a leather pouch that he wore around his neck. He hadn't told Mabis where it was, but she knew—he caught her looking at the pouch sometimes.

"She hasn't been near the flowers," he added. "I go every morning to check the river."

"So do I," said Skyla. Ryder hadn't known that.

"Anyway, the more we talk, the less we do." He started off down the hill, but Skyla pulled gently at his sleeve.

"Ryder?" Her voice was soft, almost shy, and when he turned back, her pale blue eyes were clear as glass. "Haven't you ever . . . wanted something else?"

"Else?"

"You used to talk about going to sea." The words made something tighten deep in his chest. Why was she bringing that up?

"What I want," he said, more sharply than he meant,

"is for us not to starve. What I want is for us to get this hicca in. That's how we honor our father's memory, Skyla, not by bowing and bending on the prayer hill."

"And what do you think I want?"

She was serious, he could see that, but he'd never thought of Skyla wanting anything more than what was right here under their feet. He was the one who wanted more—not that he'd ever get it now.

Ryder shrugged. "What do you want?" His mind was a blank. "How should I know? To get married, I guess. To some boy. Have babies and nice dresses."

"By the twins, how can you be my brother and know nothing about me?"

"Well, what *do* you want, then?"

He was baffled by the tears that were suddenly glistening in her eyes. For the first time, he noticed how tall and wiry his sister had grown in the past year, how womanish she was looking, even in her too-big men's leggings.

"Are you angry because I wouldn't let you buy that cloth for a new set of prayer clothes?"

Skyla's cheeks went crimson. She looked at the sky as if there were someone up there who could witness his stupidity. Then she turned on her heel without answering and stormed down the hill, her long braid flicking back and forth behind her.

"Now what did I do?" he yelled.

Skyla turned again and shouted up to him. "You know, Ryder, you talk and talk about 'honoring our father,' but I remember how it was. Every time he told one of the old stories, every time he spoke about the Goddess, or about Aata and Aayse, it was all you could do to keep from laughing out loud."

"That's not true," he sputtered. "I never laughed at Fa."

"You and Mabis loved to sit up there on your high perch and laugh at everyone below you. 'How stupid people are to believe in things. How much better we are than everyone else.'" Skyla put her hands on her hips. "Well, Fa was one of those people and so am I. And now so is Mabis! You're all alone on your high perch, Ryder. Enjoy the solitude!"

Ryder went back to working the hill, up one row and down the other, but his usual songs didn't come to him now, and he couldn't get Skyla's words out of his mind. Girls were irrational creatures. You never knew what you did to make them angry, and they never just came out and told you.

Above him on the prayer hill, Skyla and Pima were stretching out their arms, beginning the sun position, the first part of Aata's prayer. From a distance, one looked like a miniature version of the other, with their long, skinny limbs and hair the color of the fields.

"Prayer hill," he muttered. "Next year I'll plant hicca up there. Get us five more sacks of flour."

Pima saw him looking and waved, jumping up and down in the grass. "Hey, Ry-der!" she yelled.

He thought of yelling back—that would really annoy Skyla—but instead he smiled and put a finger to his lips; Aata's prayer was supposed to be silent. Pima put her hand over her mouth, remembering, then stretched her arms out and bowed low, lifting one wobbly leg behind her. Next to her, Skyla's pose was as steady and graceful as a statue in the village shrine. It was a pretty sight, Ryder had to admit. Behind the girls, the jagged mountains rose up dramatically, scarlet with zanthias in seed.

The witches are in their reds. Ryder thought he had heard the expression recently, but he couldn't remember where. With a sigh, he turned from the view and went back to work.

A year ago Ryder had been just days away from leaving home, days away from setting out for Tandrass or one of the other port cities. Somehow he'd always known he wasn't meant to be a farmer like his father. He was supposed to do something else, be something else. He could never put his finger on what, exactly—but he'd resolved to go to sea to find it. Then one afternoon he came back from a trip to the village to find his father in bed in the middle of the day. There was something wrong with his face—only half of it was working. Mabis sat in a chair beside him, staring straight ahead. She had a jar of dried herbs in her lap, but it was unopened. Pima lay next to Fa, trying to push the slack side of her father's face up into a smile. *What's wrong, Fa? What's wrong, Fa?* she kept saying until someone shushed her quiet.

Fa had seemed so ordinary when he was alive, but everything held together then. He would have pulled a sixtyweight out of these rocky planting hills, Ryder thought. He would have known what to do about Mabis. For one brief moment, it didn't seem silly to bow and bend to the Goddess or believe that the lucky man guarded the fields. Skyla had a connection to their father that he would never have.

When he came up to the top of the hill again, Ryder saw the lucky man differently, as something almost precious, an artifact of his father. The helmet at the top had tilted to one side, giving the figure a quizzical look. It was an enemy helmet, with one long slit for the eyes and a perfectly round hole for the mouth. Ryder had never thought to ask his father if he had killed the soldier who wore it.

"I never laughed at Fa," he said to the lucky man. "He didn't really think I did, did he?"

"Do you think he can answer?"

Ryder wheeled around, startled.

"The bone. Give it to me." Mabis stood in front of him. Her dress was clean, and her hair was brushed and braided, but there was something greedy in her eyes. Ryder looked for the telltale stain of maiden's woe on her lips and fingers, but he found nothing.

"You told me not to." He glanced up to Skyla on the prayer hill, but his two sisters couldn't see him. They had begun the earth position and were kneeling in the grass with their foreheads touching the ground.

Mabis grabbed him by the wrist. "I want to ask the bones why the witches don't come," she said. Her grip was surprisingly strong. "You can watch me. You can make sure—"

"No!" He clutched the pouch to his chest and stumbled backward into the lucky man. It fell over, and the helmet went bumping down the hill, disappearing into the rows. "There goes our luck."

He said it as a joke, but when the words came out of his mouth they seemed ominous. He backed away farther, rubbing his side where the pole had scraped his skin.

"I need it," Mabis insisted. She was talking about the bone, but was that really what she craved, or was it the flower?

Again, Ryder felt that strange feeling of loss for his mother, although she was standing right in front of him. Her disdain for witches and their prophecies had always been such an important part of her. Who was she now that it was gone?

"It's time to put out that fire, Mabis," he said, suddenly feeling awash in frustration. "The witches didn't come because you have nothing to tell them. It's all nonsense. There's no stranger in the mountains, no assassin. You're just a farmer's widow gone mad on maiden's woe!"

Mabis stepped back, her face crimson, and Ryder winced, knowing he'd gone too far. He braced himself for an angry torrent of words, but his mother pushed past.

"Mabis!"

Without looking at him, she fled off toward the cottage, hicca tassels brushing her arms as she went. *First Skyla, now Mabis,* he thought, shaking his head. And all he wanted to do was get the crops in.

He found his mother in the clearing between the cottage and the barn, tending to the fire. In the past three days, Ryder had grown to hate it. The bitter smoke seemed to permeate everything. He tasted it at the back of his throat, smelled it in his hair. Yellowhead didn't seem to mind, though. The family horse was so old he had lost his sense of smell, and he stood not far from Mabis, happily tearing up mouthfuls of grass.

Mabis didn't turn around as Ryder approached, just tossed another bundle of herbs into the flames. For a moment the pale, gray-green smoke that rose up over the trees darkened to viridian.

"My coven has forgotten me. I'm the sister of Lilla Red Bird, and they've forgotten me," she said, her voice wretched.

Ryder sighed. "Who knows what witches remember?"

As he came up beside his mother, he could see she was blinking back tears. There were dark circles under her eyes. She had been fighting her craving for three days now, and it was taking its toll. Most people said she looked too young to have children nearly grown, but today Ryder could see that she was starting to show her age. There were thin, spidery lines on her forehead, and her cheeks seemed drawn.

"I was so sure," she said. "So sure I'd seen something in the bones."

"Mabis, all my life you've told me that there is no magic in the world, that witches have only fooled themselves and everyone else into thinking they can predict the future."

"I know."

"So . . . why? Why change your mind now?"

It took his mother a long time to answer. When she did her voice was so quiet he had to strain to hear her over the crackling of the fire. "He was lying sick, Ryder. Lying sick in the fields all morning. If Farmer Raiken hadn't come along . . . Even then it was too late."

She was talking about Fa, of course.

"Nothing anybody could have done about that," Ryder said firmly.

"Are you sure?" She turned to him with shining eyes. "If I hadn't turned my back on the coven, if I hadn't thrown away everything I ever believed, I might have known. I might have predicted it."

"No! Mabis, throwing the bones isn't real. You've always believed that. Can't you see? It's only that—that plant that's made you doubt yourself."

"Maybe." She turned away. "Probably. But if something happened to you or one of the girls and I didn't do anything . . ." Her voice trailed off. "I should go up to the coven myself, just to be sure."

Ryder wondered why she hadn't gone already. But then, she never went up there, not even to take the tithe. "The witches are too proud to listen to the prophecies of a villager."

She shook her head. "There are other covens. I could go to them. They'd remember me from the war."

"Do you really think it would make any difference?" he asked gently. Mabis didn't answer.

Yellowhead ambled up behind them, poking his head between the two as if he wanted to be part of the conversation. Mabis wiped the corner of her eye and laughed as the horse rubbed his forehead against her shoulder.

"You're right," she finally said. "Of course you're right. It's all a lie, witchcraft. No one knows that better than me."

Ryder wasn't convinced by this sudden change of heart, but he stroked Yellowhead's neck and didn't question her words. The horse tossed his head with the pleasure of the attention. He was lazy with wisdom, more a family pet than a work animal. Ryder loved the stubborn old creature, but today all he saw was the gray around Yellowhead's muzzle, the bluish film that was beginning to mask one of his eyes: Everything on this farm was falling apart.

"I think you've aged a hundred years since Fa died," Mabis said, as if she'd been able to hear his thoughts. "You're a good son—taking on this farm. I know what you've given up to stay."

Ryder gave a short laugh. *No*, he thought. *No, you don't.* He wished Skyla hadn't reminded him about how he'd once wanted to go to sea. It was easier not to think of it, easier not to be reminded of how much his world had shrunk down to this small farm, to the four walls of their bare cottage.

"Here," she said quietly. "Give me that bone. I know exactly what to do with it." Ryder's hand went to his chest. "Trust me." His mother smiled with her hand outstretched. "It is mine, you know."

The greedy look had left her eyes, but still Ryder hesitated. Slowly he took the leather pouch from around his neck and, holding it out by its leather cords, placed it into his mother's palm. Mabis's eyes didn't leave his. Without even glancing toward the fire, she tossed the bone, pouch and all, into the flames.

"Mabis!"

A log shifted, and a cloud of sparks rose swirling into the air like a swarm of burning bees. Yellowhead whinnied with alarm and stepped back.

"Oh," said Mabis as she followed the sparks with her eyes. "Look at that."

"But . . ." Ryder stepped toward the fire. In the depths of the flames, he could see the leather pouch blackening and curling around the bone inside. "You told me it was special."

"Yes. Very special. It's been in our family for a long time. The way the witches tell it, my sister won us the war with that bone." Mabis frowned.

"It's not too late. A stick . . ." He looked around wildly. "I need a stick. I could pull it out."

"Don't," she said sharply, grabbing his arm. "Do you see now what I would do for you? Do you see how strong I am? Stronger than any plant." Ryder wondered who she was trying to convince, him or herself.

"Don't worry," he told her. "I've pulled up all the maiden's woe. Even if the craving overcomes you, you won't be able to find any."

His mother dropped his arm. "It is my *will* that has kept me away from the river, Ryder. My own *will*. If I wanted a flower, I assure you I could find one."

"I don't think so. I've searched downriver all the way to Raiken's farm."

Her face turned stony. "And what about upriver?"

This made Ryder hesitate for a moment as he wondered if there really was a way for her to climb up there. "It's too rocky," he answered slowly. "You know that. If there was any maiden's woe upriver, you'd have to walk on water to get it."

"What makes you think I can't? When I was a witch I used to walk on water all the time."

Ryder snorted. "I'll believe that when I see it."

Mabis pursed her lips and stared into the flames. After a while she took his arm again, gently this time. "You know, Ryder," she said. "There is a lot more to the world than what you can see. Sometimes I think it was very wrong of me not to teach you that."

No one could walk on water. But the idea must have stayed on Ryder's mind, because that night he dreamed of it. Something was calling to him. Something was singing to him—a strange muttering, humming song. He followed it to the sea. Ryder had never seen the sea before, but in the dream it was familiar. Far offshore, on a surface smooth as glass, two little girls held up their skirts and stepped daintily, laughing at their new skill, ripples circling out from satin slippers.

"Careful," Ryder called from the beach. "You're too far."

The girls looked up. "Hello? Is someone there?" Their voices were strange, someone else's. *They shouldn't be so reckless,* he thought. *They will ruin their best clothes, and Father will be angry.*

Ryder stepped out onto the sea to fetch them, not wondering how it was done. The water was clear and deep, and he held out his arms for balance as he walked. A large fish, like a triangle with a tail, loomed up from the depths, pale and slow, then withdrew into blackness. Ryder shivered with delight.

This is easy, he thought. It was the song that held him up, the song that was coming from the sea itself. Ryder found himself humming, then singing, repeating the melodies like a lesson.

"The sea is a lullaby," he said, when he'd reached the girls. "I never knew that." In his ears, the song of the sea thrummed and whirred.

"He wants to go there," one said, laughing.

"But he doesn't know the first thing . . ." The other giggled.

Ryder gasped, and the music of the sea turned sharp and dissonant. He didn't know these girls. What made him think he had? Their pointed little faces were ghostly white, and they stared up at him with ink in their eyes.

"Blackhairs," he breathed.

The girls started to cry. Underneath his feet the sea grew rough, lifting him up on a hill of water. Little hands clutched his clothes. "How could you be so cruel?"

"I don't believe in this!" Ryder shouted to the darkening sky. "This is a dream, and I don't believe any of it."

"Now he's done it," said one of the girls through her tears. All at once the music stopped, and Ryder plunged through the invisible skin of the sea. The water around him was cold and black and silent.

"I can't swim," he sputtered, breaking the surface for a moment. The girls looked down at him with fear in their dark eyes.

"Hello?" said one.

"Is someone there?" said the other.

Ryder slipped under the waves again. As he sank to the bottom, the white faces of the girls were like twin moons, receding and receding and receding.

CHAPTER 3

THE WHITE WITCH

"You had a nightscare."

The room was dark. For a moment Ryder thought the small, cool hand on his face belonged to one of the eerie children in his dream. But it was just Pima.

"Go back to sleep, Sweetlamb," he said, yawning. Instead she climbed on top of him, sharp knees poking his thigh. "Ow!" Pima landed on him with a thump. "Get off," he said, laughing. "I have to pee." Her breath was warm against his neck.

"I'm coming with you," she whispered into his ear. "I'm going wherever you go."

Ryder groaned. The hay in the mattress had shifted into lumps under his back, and his muscles were sore from picking.

"I'm not going anywhere," he said. "Just the fields." He pulled her to him and stroked her hair, finding sticks. Pima had been running wild lately, but she didn't seem to mind. "You smell like barn. I'll make you sleep with Yellowhead and the goats if you don't take a bath."

"I don't believe in washing," she informed him. She wriggled out of his hug and sat up, straddling his chest. "You were singing in your sleep again. La, la, la!" She bounced on him, singing tunelessly. "Lolly, lolly, lolly la."

"Shh! I do not sound like that. You'll wake the others."

"Maba isn't here."

Ryder looked over. Skyla was a lump swathed in blankets—but Mabis was gone. *She's started the picking,* Ryder told himself. *Or the milking.* But he knew he'd check the river first. Maybe she was walking on water.

Ryder sat up, adjusting Pima on his lap. "I guess I should get up too."

Pima threw her arms around his neck, squeezing him tight. "I told you I'm coming with you."

"Why don't you climb on Skyla instead?"

The lump of covers stirred. "No," it croaked. "No climbing on Skyla."

Ryder sighed. "If you come with me, you'll have to work. When I was little, Fa would give me a sack and send me through the fields to look for missed berries."

Pima thought about this for a moment. Then she pulled a corner of Skyla's blanket over her head. "I can't do work," she said. "I'm still asleep."

He was pulling on his boots by the door of the cottage when Pima slipped around the red curtain and called out to him.

"Ry-der!" He looked over at her in the dim light. Her short nightgown showed her bare legs. "Are you sure you're not going away?" He could hear the worry in her voice.

"No, Lamb," he said softly. "Of course not."

"Maba says bad things are coming. She says . . . that we won't all be together much longer."

Ryder gave a faint gasp. "She was wrong to say that," he said sharply. "It's not true. Besides, she's . . . changed her mind now."

He wanted to go back to Pima, swing her up into his arms, but she was already reassured. She gave him a wide grin, then popped back behind the curtain. A moment later, Ryder heard Skyla's voice:

"Pima! Get off me!"

Outside, the moon was still up. Ryder's breath came out in clouds. He trotted around the side of the cottage to the out-house, crossing his arms in front of him to ward off the cold. *It won't be long,* he thought, and he glanced at the sky for any sign of the strange, low clouds that signaled the coming of the chilling day. Nothing yet. There had been years when the hicca froze in the fields, but so far, his luck was holding.

It wasn't until he came out of the outhouse and was

starting toward the river path that he noticed he wasn't alone. A person, silvery in the moonlight, was stirring the dying embers of the firecall with a long stick. At first he thought it was Mabis. Then he stopped.

It was a witch.

A mountain witch—it had to be!

Ryder had seen witches before. A few times a year they came down to the village shrine to lead prayers, and for the past two harvests he'd gone with Fa to take the tithe up to the coven. The witches did no farming themselves but relied on villagers to give them one-quarter of all the hicca farmed. As far as Ryder was concerned, they did little for it. He didn't intend to act impressed, or give this girl any more respect than she deserved.

She was about his age, fully as tall, and slender as a hicca stalk. When her eyes met his she froze, then smiled and continued to poke through the mounds of white ash and dimly glowing coals. She reminded him of a snowcat—a beautiful, dangerous thing from a cold, high place. But was she a witch after all? He noticed that she was wearing white—a quilted tunic and loose-fitting pants. It certainly looked like the traditional costume of witches, but he thought they always wore red.

"Are you from the coven?" Ryder asked. The girl looked surprised to be spoken to. She made a movement over her mouth, a gesture for quiet. "Well, are you?"

The girl frowned and ignored him. Yes, it must be a witch. Only one of *them* could be so arrogant. Briefly he considered just asking her to go away. He didn't like to think what Mabis would do when she found out her call had been answered. He knew he should probably make the traditional greeting, the witch's bow, but the idea of bowing to someone on his own land galled him.

The girl moved around the edge of the dying fire, intent on something she saw in the ashes. Suddenly she made a flicking motion with her stick, and a small, knoblike object leapt out of the pit in a spray of sparks. *It couldn't be the bone,* Ryder thought.

He bent to pick it up, but the witch touched him on the shoulder and shook her head. She unwrapped a white sash from around her waist and bound her hand to protect it from the heat. Ryder's eyes widened. The thing she picked up *was* Mabis's bone.

"That's my mother's," he told her. She wrinkled her forehead. "You should give—"

The witch wouldn't let him finish. Her other hand darted forward, and with the tips of her fingers she gently squeezed his upper and lower lips together. For a moment Ryder was too surprised to move, and he could only stand there staring into the girl's face, feeling her touch on his lips. He couldn't quite tell in the dim light, but she seemed to be smiling at him.

Slowly she withdrew her fingers.

"I don't understand," he snapped. "Am I not good enough to speak to you?"

The smile, if it had ever been there, left her face. She gave a little huffing sound and turned away.

"Wait!" said Ryder. "That's not your bone!" But the girl was moving quickly toward the stand of trees that separated the cottage from the rest of the farm. "It doesn't belong to you!"

At that moment, Ryder caught a glimpse of the prayer hill, just visible over the tops of the trees.

"Oh, Aata's blood," he cursed under his breath.

Dawn was breaking. Silhouetted against the pink sky were three black shapes. Tents. Witch tents—without a doubt. The girl in white wasn't the only one to have come in answer to his mother's call.

Ryder went back to the cottage and found Mabis standing in the middle of the room, wearing her reds. Her crimson sleeves were pushed up to the elbows, and the ankles of her pants were wet. In one hand, stalks of uprooted maiden's woe dripped water onto the dirt floor.

"I can't believe you made me throw my bone into the fire," she cried.

"What? Made you?"

"Did you see the tents? I should have known they'd come."

A thick perfume entered Ryder's nose. The black

trumpets smelled spicy and pleasant, but underneath that first fresh scent there was another, more subtle aroma—the hint of something too sweet, like rotting fruit.

"The witches will want me to cast for them, I'm sure of it," Mabis continued, her voice strained and nervous. "But how can I throw the bones without my anchor?"

"Where did you get that maiden's woe?" Ryder demanded. There were at least four open flowers in his mother's hand and one or two buds. "They can't have grown so quickly. I've been pulling them up!"

"I told you, Ryder," she said. "It was my own will that kept me away." The black trumpets scattered water as she gestured at him. "You don't think there would be something left in the ashes, do you? Something of my bone? You could get it for me."

"Oh . . ." Ryder's mind raced. He should tell his mother about the white witch. But . . . they'd all be better off without that bone, wouldn't they? Without her continuing to believe the unbelievable? "I've just come from the fire. Your bone is gone."

Mabis narrowed her eyes at him. He'd always found it difficult to keep secrets from his mother, but this time he met her gaze. After all, it was the truth.

"What's that on your mouth?"

Ryder wiped his lips with his fingers. It was ash from where the girl had touched him. "Uh . . ."

Just then there was a loud knock at the cottage door, and both of them jumped. The door opened, but it was not a witch.

"Dassen!" said Mabis. The village tavern keeper filled the doorway. He was all huge shoulders and red face and red hands rough from work. His eyes were shrewd, though. To Ryder, they seemed to take in everything, in spite of the dim morning light, including the bunch of maiden's woe in Mabis's hand.

"They want you to come," he said to her. "And only you."

CHAPTER 4
BARBIZA

Falpian wasn't alone. Strange girls were sleeping in his bed. On either side of him were bodies, sleeping bodies, their outlines distinct underneath the down quilts. He froze, eyes wide in the dark.

"Hello," he whispered. "Is someone there?"

A narrow thread of light was visible between the curtains. He sat up silently, letting his eyes adjust. It wasn't a dream. He could smell these girls, he could hear them breathing. With his heart thumping in his ears, Falpian slowly reached out a hand and grabbed the end of a soft white coverlet. He yanked it back. . . .

Nothing. There was nothing there. The lump beside him was just a lump—and the others, too. Falpian patted down the covers with his hands, even put his head under the bed. What had made him think they were female? he wondered. But they had been. He could almost see their faces—an older one and a younger one. Their odd names. *Sweetlamb.*

Something huge and pale materialized from a shadowy corner, and Falpian yelped. A monstrous animal gave a leap, knocking him back onto the bed. It pinned him down, shaggy face looming over him. Falpian tried to move, but the thing was at least twice his weight. Long, oversize canines curved saberlike from its upper jaw. It barked, releasing a string of drool into Falpian's face.

"Yes, yes," Falpian grunted. "I love you, too."

Moments later he was stumbling into the kitchen and opening the heavy door to the outside. His dog, Bodread the Slayer, bounded out, tail wagging. Bo was happy at Stonehouse, Falpian thought—going wild, hunting for his own breakfast. He'd been the runt of the litter once, and he was still small for a dreadhound, though that was a bit hard to believe sometimes. When Falpian was a little boy, he'd begged Bron and his father not to drown the scrawny puppy, which was how he'd gotten a dreadhound in the first place. They were supposed to be magician's dogs—but by the time anyone realized that Falpian would never be a magician, he and Bo were inseparable.

The great gray beast looked back at him, then out toward the red mountains, as if he wanted Falpian to join him, as if there was something out there he wanted his master to be happy about too.

"You go on, Bo. Catch me a rabbit."

He shut the door again and sat down, rubbing his eyes. In front of him on the table, the bronze scroll container lay open at one end, but the rolled parchment that had been inside was still unread. It sat next to the holder, its red wax seal unbroken.

"Kar's eyes," he cursed softly. At least his dreams and his dog had distracted him for a while.

Written hastily in black ink above the scroll's seal was the message: *Not to be opened for fifty days. Until then, sing your brother's prayers and make yourself useful.*

Fifty days. Was his father serious? It was enough to give anyone bad dreams, enough to drive anyone mad. To have some great purpose, some important mission, and then to be forbidden to know what it was? It was nonsense, it was unfair, it was some cruel form of torture!

For the hundredth time, Falpian picked up the scroll and ran his finger over the red seal, willing the wax to crack. Whatever was written on that parchment was the thing he had to do to make his father look him in the eye again. It was the thing he had to do to make things between them go back to the way they'd been before—he just knew it!

"'Make yourself useful,'" Falpian muttered. "What does that even mean?"

When he was a boy, Falpian had assumed his father's

love was something permanent, something he didn't have to earn. He and his twin brother Farien were special. They would be a singer pair someday; their harmonies would make a magic unheard of since the old times.

As years went by, his mother's jewels disappeared one by one, sold to pay the tutors and the singing masters. Falpian's little sisters learned to mend the holes in their silks so that stitches didn't show. But every sacrifice would be rewarded a hundredfold when the great Falpian and Farien came into their magic. That was the thing, though: They never did.

Falpian stared at the scroll, half wishing it would burst into flames so he wouldn't have to think about it anymore. He imagined long lines of Caraxus family ancestors, all sitting up at Kar's great feast, lips curling as they looked down on him, the food of the God turning bitter in their mouths. His father had worn that same look when he spoke to Falpian last, as if he tasted something foul. His manner toward his sons had changed abruptly about a year before Farien's death. The tutors and the singing masters were dismissed, and everything about Falpian and his brother was suddenly wrong—their taste in books, their lack of skill with weapons, the way Falpian spoiled his dog. Magicians-to-be were allowed such caprices. Ordinary young men were not.

Without thinking, Falpian squeezed the scroll and

watched as the wax seal began to separate from the parchment, revealing a pink stain underneath. If he squeezed a little harder . . .

No. Quickly he stuffed the scroll back into its bronze container. He stood up and strode into his small, book-lined study, opening the bottom drawer of an ornate desk with dragon legs. For a moment he hesitated, but the words on the cylinder—*duty, honor, sacrifice*—were like a chastisement. He shoved the container into the drawer and slammed it shut. His father was a man to be obeyed, even if he was all the way on the other side of the Bitterlands.

Later that morning Falpian stood at the edge of the plateau, clutching his coat around him. In the mud, the dog's footprints, big as dinner plates, led down to the wild green gorge. The Witchlands were so close, just over that mountain with the crooked spire. All his life Falpian had been told that someday the Baen people would take back what the Witchlanders had stolen during the war. Now that time was almost here, and he just wanted his father to believe he could be a part of it.

It was a sign of his father's arrogance that he assumed both his sons would be able to sing. Magic was a rare gift, carefully kept alive in the bloodlines of a few families. But then, the Caraxus family had magicians going back a thousand years—Falpian *should* be able to sing. He had studied so hard—the names of the keys and what magic they produced, how to awaken a humming stone in the heat of battle. . . . And what a lot of useless information that was, he thought bitterly, for someone who would never use it.

But at least I have a mission, he told himself. *At least I have the scroll.* He knew he should be more thankful. The fact that he had a part to play at all was a great gift. Surely he could wait fifty days for it. And until then, he'd find other things to keep him busy.

According to Bron, there was an echo site not far off the gorge path. It should be tested. It wouldn't take long, but when he was done he'd find another task, and another—for fifty days or a hundred days or a thousand days if that's what his father wanted.

As Falpian started down the steep path, shreds of his dreams came back to him—a Witchlander woman with wild eyes and a mouth stained black, an old horse with a yellow mane, the sound of bones clattering on a dirt floor. He was sure he had seen his own dear sisters too, but they were strange and far away, talking to strangers, walking on water like the witches were supposed to have done during the war.

"Dreams mean nothing," he said aloud, trying to convince himself, trying to say what his father would. "Just . . . sing your brother's prayers and make yourself useful!"

*   *   *

"Tell us about the dreadhounds, Dassen," Skyla said. "And their long saber teeth."

"Ah, dreadhounds. Never turn your back on one. They like to attack from behind." The tavern keeper made two long teeth with his fingers.

"No," said Pima, covering her eyes. "That's too scary."

Skyla gave a sigh. "All right. Tell us about how you were in Barbiza and saw the Baen ships."

Skyla had laid out a feast for breakfast: honeycakes cooked over the fire and drizzled with fresh cream, bread with both butter and cheese, and a pot of the preserved sourberries, slippery in syrup. It wasn't often they had guests.

The tavern keeper smiled, and his eyes gleamed as he spoke, but every once in a while he would look to Ryder and a shadow would pass his face; Ryder could see he had something to talk to him about, something he wouldn't say in front of the girls. Ryder wished they could have a moment alone.

Pima and Skyla didn't seem to notice. They leaned forward over their wooden plates, enthralled by Dassen's stories of the war. Why they were so interested in things that happened twenty years ago, Ryder couldn't imagine. Not now. Not when at that very moment Mabis was up on the prayer hill doing who-knew-what in those black tents.

"I was just a boy, really," Dassen said. "Younger than

Ryder here. I was working at my uncle's tavern in Barbiza when the Baen ships pulled into the harbor. Oh, they were uncanny, those ships. Their hulls were covered with strange writing, and they seemed to sail with no wind. Their masts were so tall they left scuff marks on the sky."

"Ohhh," Pima said, her eyes round.

"We didn't know then that they were part of an attack, that there were other ships pulling into Tandrass at the same time. We trusted the Baen, you see. We traded with the Bitterlands back then, and some of the blackhairs even lived among us." He shook his finger at the girls, as if to bring home a lesson. "We let down our guard."

"Did you see the black magicians?" Skyla asked. "The singers?"

He shook his head. "Not many of those, thank Aata. Heard them twice, though, during the war: once in Barbiza, once at the Battle of the Dunes." He gave an exaggerated shudder. "Hope never to hear them again. They call it singing, but it sounds like . . . metal scraping stone."

Pima crammed a whole honeycake into her mouth and licked her fingers.

"What did the witches say, Dassen?" Ryder interrupted, unable to refrain any longer. He'd finished his breakfast and was standing at the open door, looking up at the prayer hill. "Were the witches annoyed by my mother's firecall?"

The girls both turned to frown at Ryder.

"Didn't ask," Dassen said. "I was at the coven to deliver my tithe and traveled back down with them is all. Witch business is above my head, I'm happy to say. I'll leave that to your mother."

Ryder nodded.

"Now let me tell you about the time I saved your father's life," Dassen said as the two girls clapped their hands.

Ryder had known Dassen for as long as he could remember. He and Fa had fought side by side during the war, had saved each other's lives a dozen times if their accounts were to be believed. When Ryder was small, he'd often begged to visit Dassen at the tavern. His father would lift him up to see the Baenkiller, the sword the tavern keeper displayed over the bar. Ryder had loved to count the notches carved along the hilt—one for every blackhair killed.

Ryder turned away from the door and helped Skyla clear the plates. When they were done, Dassen took his humming stone—a trophy from the war—out of his pocket and let Pima and Skyla pass it back and forth between them. Ryder had seen it a hundred times; it was just a broken piece of rock, but the girls oohed and aahed at the strange Baen designs etched over the surface.

"Brew us some of that sweet tea, Ryder, like your father used to make." Dassen settled himself into his chair and brushed the crumbs out of his bushy blond beard, but he gave Ryder a knowing glance. Ryder complied, breaking off some of the dried herbs that hung in bunches from the ceiling and tossing them into the kettle on the hob.

"Friend of mine got this off the body of a real black magician," Dassen told the girls. "Why, if this stone were whole and the singer working it had the gift, he could use it to move an object with his voice, stop your heart with a curse . . . anything."

Ryder rolled his eyes and couldn't help but smile. Dassen had some wild stories about black magicians, in spite of the fact that he'd never actually seen one. As he was dipping a ladle into the tea, the tavern keeper sidled up to him.

"Mabis do that often?" he asked softly.

"What?"

Dassen looked over his shoulder. Pima was trying to work the piece of humming stone. She held it in both hands and was blowing on it furiously, her pale eyebrows knitted.

"I saw the maiden's woe."

Ryder tensed. He didn't want Dassen telling his tavern patrons about *that*. They wouldn't understand. "She's careful," he insisted. "It helps with the prophecy."

"So I've heard, but she had so many flowers. More than a quarter of one can be deadly. You've never seen her take more than that, have you?"

Ryder felt his stomach flip. "No, of course not."

"What are you two talking about over there?" Skyla asked.

"Terrible thing," Dassen said, turning around with a grin. "This boy's beard's gone missing!"

Ryder frowned, touching his bare face. He tried to laugh along with the joke, but Dassen's words rang in his ears. A quarter of a flower—that must be wrong. Ryder had seen Mabis take five flowers in a night and still be fine the next day.

"It's working!" Pima yelled. "Listen!"

They all turned their attention to the stone. Sure enough, a muffled whine seemed to be vibrating from its core, making the breakfast plates rattle faintly on the table.

"By the twins," Dassen said.

Pima got up and started dancing around the room. "I'm a wicked blackhair!" she sang, delighted. "I'm a wicked blackhair! I'll stop your heart with a curse."

Dassen, Skyla, and Ryder all leaned in toward the stone, their mouths open in surprise. After a few moments the whine of the stone got softer and softer, like the buzz of a dying insect, until finally they could hear it no longer.

Pima frowned. "Is that all it does?"

Before Dassen could answer, the door to the cottage swung open. Mabis stood in front of them, holding her bone bowl in both arms. There was an obvious black ring around the inside of her lips, and the look on her face was crazed and triumphant.

"I've seen it all," she said. She was trying to get through

the door, but the bowl was too big to fit. Finally she thought of tilting it, and she made it into the room, but not without spilling her set of bones and sending them skittering over the floor.

"No matter," she said, laughing. She carefully set down the bowl, then lurched up again. "We're to go back to the tents at sunset." Mabis was suddenly solemn. "Oh, it was so clear." She stood swaying back and forth, holding herself as if she were cold.

"I didn't need the anchor bone at all," she murmured, almost to herself. "I should have remembered what my father used to say: The magic is in the witch, not in her bones."

Dassen stood up, clearly shocked by what he saw. "Mabis, what have you done?"

She seemed not to hear. "Every once in a while it's as if my mind turns a corner, and then I can see forever. I love that feeling. Even though I'm seeing terrible things, I could stay in that feeling forever." She tottered backward, grabbing onto the wall for support. "I'll rest now," she said. "Wake me up at sunset. We're all to go at sunset." And with that, Mabis staggered toward the sleeping chamber.

Ryder drew a deep breath. Mabis said she had done a casting without the anchor bone—but if she didn't think she needed it anymore, what would keep her from taking the flower now?

*   *   *

Falpian had never liked singing. He'd always felt, wherever he was, that his father's ear was cocked toward him, judging him, expecting magic that wasn't there. It had made his stomach twist, made his tongue clumsy in his mouth.

Now he stared down into the deep gorge. He had left the safety of the path and was standing on a small, slanted ledge about a third of the way down from Stonehouse. Below him, the tops of trees tossed. He kicked a pebble off the ledge and watched it bounce off the jagged rocks— down, down, until it finally hit the ground. Was a person really supposed to sing here? He took a breath and tried a note, but his reedy voice was quickly torn away by the gusting wind. Other ways of making himself useful sprang into his mind, safer ways.

From somewhere in the gorge, a fearsome howl echoed, and a flock of green birds rose up chattering from the trees. Bo was hunting again. Well, at least one of them could find their voice.

Falpian checked his feet, but he already knew they were in the right spot. The stone ledge was clearly marked with two footprints inlaid in green and gold mosaic. The mountains were full of these ancient platforms—or so he was told—places where the echo was just right, where a trained magician could harmonize with the voice that came back to him, and sometimes form a low kind of magic. But Falpian didn't need magic to test the site. He just had to sing, in any key, and listen, checking that time and erosion hadn't diminished the echo. It was a simple task, but, he realized, a critical one. If there really was another war coming, an echo site along the border would take on strategic importance. A lone magician singing here could stop the hearts of many Witchlander soldiers marching through the gorge—if he was good enough, and if the echo was true.

Falpian tried the simple keys first—the key of velvet antlers, the key of cloud shadows—but his voice couldn't seem to make the tones. He took another breath and started again in the key that had been running through his mind since he got up—the key of rocking waves. He started soft and slow, making up the song as he went, but soon his voice grew louder and more confident. Song filled the gorge, melody twisting on melody. The music he was creating surprised him, as if it wasn't completely his own. The hairs rose on his arms and on the back of his neck, and his vision seemed clearer: the mountain a deeper red, the gorge a more fertile green.

The echo that reverberated through the air reminded him of Farien's voice, and as he sang, Falpian felt a sting of grief for his brother. He imagined him sitting up at Kar's great feast, listening for his prayers, wondering why his death wasn't being properly mourned. It must be wrong, Falpian decided, to use his brother's mourning season to conceal some unknown mission. Guilt made his throat close.

As the echoes died away, Falpian began to notice the cold again, the wind that gusted through his clothes. He should go back to Stonehouse, get a better coat. Clearly the echo site was fine and his task was done. But Falpian didn't want to leave.

Yes, this is what it should have been like, he thought as he began to sing again. He and Farien had never been able to make their voices mesh the way they were supposed to, the way everyone—everyone!—expected them to. But these harmonies were rich and complex, charged with strange energy.

Falpian gasped, and the song stopped abruptly. For a moment he'd felt that someone else was singing with him—not an echo, but an actual person. It made no sense, he told himself, and yet, at the back of his mind, he was aware of someone, someone just out of sight and earshot. A presence.

"Hello?" he said aloud. "Is someone there?" He felt foolish, but the words were familiar somehow, as if he'd been saying them in a dream. Of course no one answered. Falpian shook himself and sang again.

The world swelled with color, blinding and bright. *This must be magic,* he realized with a shiver, *or something like it.* Below him, the birds in the trees grew restless, agitated by his song. They rose up in front of him in a great spiral, a dazzle of motion. He could see everything so clearly now, as if a veil that had been in front of his eyes all his life had finally been lifted. He shifted his song slightly, and one of the birds stopped in midair. Had he done that? The bird hovered right before his eyes, flapping uselessly, making no headway, as if flying against a strong wind. He *was* doing it! Falpian marveled at its green iridescence, and he laughed, making his laughter part of his song. No wonder he had frustrated his tutors; this was so easy! For the first time he understood what he had always been taught: The world was made of music. All the things that seemed solid—the trees, the birds, his own body—were really just vibrations in the great God Kar's endless song.

Now all the birds had stopped, even their wings motionless. Falpian's voice held them up. He could hear their little hearts whirring inside them, and he knew he could stop them, too. He could stop all those little hearts and make the birds rain down like stones into the gorge.

He let them go. The birds, frightened, darted away, back to the trees. The world dimmed. Falpian steadied himself on the rocks, breathing heavily, listening to the memory of voices still humming in the gorge. A feather landed on the platform, and Falpian edged forward to pick it up, careful of the sheer drop. It was drab and grayish now, though moments before it had glittered like an emerald.

His legs folded underneath him, and he sat down on the cold stones, trying to make sense of what had happened. Was that what it was like to have magic? The idea filled him with more guilt. After all he and Farien had suffered, after all those years of trying and trying, it couldn't be this easy. It was too natural, like breathing, like something anyone could do.

Farien had been like a ghost the year before he died, thin and sad, hardly speaking to anyone. Full of shame. Had it been for nothing? Were they just late bloomers as their mother had tried to tell them? Or . . . could this magic have come from Farien somehow, a parting gift from a dead twin? Could Farien be the presence he had felt?

The wind pulled at his clothes, but Falpian didn't fear the height anymore. Wherever this magic came from, it made him fearless, unassailable, and he liked the feeling. He ran the feather over his cheek, thinking back to the fragile hearts of the birds, how easy they would have been to stop. A human heart was no different. He had been worried about the part he would be asked to play in the coming war, but now he knew: If the message in the scroll asked him to kill, he could do it easily.

CHAPTER 5

THE RIGHT HAND OF AATA

A pair of blue wings hummed across the path, and Ryder caught his breath. It was just a jewelfly, but for a moment the insect seemed to glitter like its name, leaving a trail of iridescent light.

"What's wrong?" asked Mabis.

"Nothing," said Ryder. "Nothing." But all day this had been happening. He'd always sung in the fields, but today the song had seemed to have a life of its own—and a few times he'd actually thought there was someone singing with him. He would lift his head from his work, straining to hear a voice that was just out of earshot—and when he turned back to the hicca, the berries would seem to glow on their stalks, and the bickerbirds and redrumps would be so bright in the sky that they almost hurt his eyes. He couldn't explain it.

Mabis slipped her arm through his. She had slept all

afternoon, and the maiden's woe had almost entirely worn off. Only someone who knew her as well as Ryder did could see that there were still some residual effects: the twisting of the hands, the brightness in her eyes. It was time for their audience with the witches, but Ryder found himself walking slowly, dreading what they would say.

Behind them, Pima squealed with laughter, riding Dassen like a horse. The tavern keeper bucked and pawed, weaving in and out between the trees.

"Why is he still here?" Ryder muttered. He could understand Dassen staying for breakfast, but why wait all day for the meeting with the witches? Surely there were things to do in the tavern.

"Because I asked him," said Mabis. "I need him."

That explained it then, but Ryder didn't know what use he could be. As far as Ryder was concerned, Dassen had already seen too much. He would be sure to spread the news that Mabis was eating maiden's woe to every one of their neighbors. Tell something to Dassen and everyone knew; the tavern was the hub of village gossip.

Ryder and his mother left the stand of trees, the light of the setting sun at their backs. In front of them was the prayer hill with the red mountain rising up behind it. The color seemed to burn his eyes. Ryder blinked and took a step back. Suddenly he was sure he could see every blade of grass on the hill, every zanthia tree on the mountain.

"Are you sure you're all right? You have the strangest look on your face."

"You must hear that," he said.

"Hear what?"

"Someone is singing. Someone is singing up in the mountains."

When Ryder looked back to his mother, her brown face pierced his heart. She was so beautiful. He could read the worry lines around her eyes the way a witch could read a casting. Everything she'd done, he realized—the fire-call, the bones, the maiden's woe—she'd done for love. Goddess, how brave she was. She'd die for him without a moment's hesitation. Mabis grabbed his arm, and the colors of the world dimmed, like a cloud going over the sun. The moment was gone.

"Shh," she said, looking behind her at Dassen and Pima. "Don't let the witches see."

"See what?"

"Are you having dreams?" Her voice was low.

Of course, his dream. The song he'd just heard was the one from his dream, the song of the sea that had lifted him up, then let him fall like a betrayal. Ryder nodded, taken aback.

"About what? Quickly now!"

"Girls. Two little girls who look exactly alike."

"Twins," Mabis said. The worry lines on her forehead

relaxed. "That's all right, then. A dream about Aata and Aayse can't be bad." Ryder didn't mention that these twins had black hair and black eyes—definitely not the prophets.

Mabis licked her fingers and smoothed down her hair, tilting her head toward the black tents. "Just keep quiet about voices and singing," she said. "The witches don't need to know all our business."

A man in reds stood at the entrance flap to one of the tents, his hand shielding his face from the slanting light of sunset. When he saw them, he waved. As the party drew closer, Ryder could see that his beard was twisted into four spiky braids that stuck out like fingers from his chin.

"Kef!" Ryder called. He left his mother's side and hurried forward. Not many years before, Kef had lived in the village, the son of the dyer and his wife.

Ryder bowed low and awkwardly made the hand gestures of the traditional witches' greeting. Kef snorted. His teeth were badly crooked, but that didn't change the sincerity of the smile.

"Ryder," he said. "If you prayed more often, you'd be more graceful." He clasped Ryder by the forearm. "No need to bow to friends."

Ryder was glad that Kef still thought of him as a friend. He'd never felt the two years' difference in their age before, but now . . . This witch in reds with his impressive beard was so different from the boy he had once known. More than once, when Ryder's family had come to town to trade, he and Kef had climbed up onto Dassen's roof with armfuls of honeyplums stolen from the orchard, and spent the day laughing and throwing pits at unsuspecting passersby. It was something Ryder never would have done on his own, but Kef always had a knack for finding hidden mischief in a person and drawing it out. It had been a shock to everyone when he joined the coven after his parents' deaths.

Kef held the tent flap open for them, nodding politely to all, but as Ryder ducked through, he caught a look of concern or maybe even pity on his friend's face. It made him think that Kef would have had more to say had they been alone.

Inside, it was hot and dim. The tent was made of thick black felt and decorated around the seams with curling red embroidery. In one corner an oil lamp sputtered, giving off a smell of burning goat's fat. An older woman stood near the lamp with her arms crossed. Mabis acknowledged the witch with the barest incline of her head, while Dassen mumbled a few words of greeting. Pima turned shy and hid behind Ryder, wrapping her arms around his waist. Soon after, Skyla hurried in.

"Where have you been?" Ryder hissed. She had disappeared that afternoon, leaving a half-filled sack of hicca in the fields.

Skyla looked at him with frown marks between her eyes. There it was again—that same look of pity and concern that had been on Kef's face a moment earlier. Before Ryder could ask her what it meant, Skyla nodded toward the tent flap, and, in a flutter of white sleeves, the girl from the fire pit entered.

Seeing her in the light of day, it was clear to Ryder that she must have a touch of Baen blood. It wasn't unusual, especially in the towns along the border, but it must have been embarrassing for a witch to have a blackhair among her ancestors, and maybe more than one, by the look of her. Her face was not as light as milk—like the girls in his dream—but there was a paleness to her brown complexion. Ryder had known few people in his life who did not have blond hair and coppery skin, the color of weak tea in a white cup. He had seen brown eyes before, but none like ripe hicca berries, so rich and dark. Her hair was dark too, a honey blond, almost brown, and it was so long that her braid brushed the backs of her knees. He'd always heard that the Baen were ugly, but she was beautiful in spite of her Baen blood. Or maybe even because of it.

"That's the mark of Aayse," Mabis whispered without turning her head. Ryder looked at his mother blankly. "On her neck. It means she is one of Aata's Hands—that she has taken a vow of silence."

Ryder had noticed the mark but had taken it for a

birthmark; now he saw that it was a circle of red paint. A vow of silence. *That* was why she hadn't spoken. He felt a flush of embarrassment. He had thought her too haughty to speak to a villager.

The witch in white gave no clue that she recognized him. Gracefully she lifted her arms and bowed low with two twists of her pale hands. The meeting had begun. In unison, the people in the room returned this silent greeting. Ryder was even clumsier now than he'd been when bowing to Kef. He caught the girl's eye as he stood up, but she quickly looked away, putting her hand automatically to a pouch at her waist. It came to Ryder in a flash that his mother's bone must be there.

When the greeting was finished, all but the older woman followed the girl's lead and sat down on the ground. Pima scrambled into Ryder's lap.

The older witch gestured to the girl in white. "This woman is the Right Hand of Aata," she said, confirming what his mother had told him. "She has joined us only recently, but already she has become our greatest bone-shaker. It is our honor that she has left the Dunes coven where she was born and has chosen to study with us."

Dunes coven. Ryder knew of it. It was near Tandrass and the sea—she had seen the ocean, this girl.

"Aata's Right Hand will not speak to you, and you must not address her directly," the older witch continued.

Already Ryder didn't like this woman. Her eyes were small and pitiless, and her lips were a tight, angry line. "My name is Visser. I am one of the six coven elders, and I am authorized by them and by Sodan, our coven leader, to make any decisions in the matter Mabis has brought before us."

As she spoke, Visser edged in front of the girl in white. Was she protecting the young witch, Ryder wondered, or making it clear that she was in charge? She did not introduce Kef, but he sat cross-legged by the tent flap, giving her his full attention.

Visser went on. "I hope you are feeling better now, Mabis."

Mabis seemed taken aback by the question. "I'm fine, thank you."

"All day Aata's Right Hand has thrown the bones and considered your words." Something in the woman's icy tone told Ryder what she was about to say. "You will be happy to know, I'm sure, that she saw absolutely nothing."

The tent fell silent. It was just what Ryder had wanted them to say, and yet he hated to see the hurt astonishment on his mother's face.

"You should have left your bones in the coven, Mabis," Visser said, "where a true witch could have used them."

"Visser!" Kef said in surprise. The older witch gave him a withering look, and he lowered his eyes.

"It's all right," said Mabis. The shocked dismay she had shown just moments before was gone, replaced by a frosty calm. "I remember Visser well. Even as a child, she could curdle cream with that tongue of hers." So they knew each other. Visser had given no indication of that. But of course they would have; Mabis had grown up in the coven.

Visser's anger flared. "I remember you, too, Mabis. I remember that much was made of your talents, but even then you had no discipline for prayer, no true heart for the teachings of Aata."

"Prayer seemed irrelevant during the war."

"Blasphemy!"

"Enough!" It was Dassen. Ryder was surprised by his vehemence. "Mabis, hush. This is a holy woman."

"Holy woman," Mabis muttered. "If you knew what I know, Dassen . . ."

"And you," he said, turning to Visser. "Have you forgotten who her sister was? We would have lost the war if it hadn't been for Lilla Red Bird."

Visser seemed momentarily flustered at the mention of the name. Ryder had never met his aunt, but he'd heard the stories. Lilla's prophecies had been crucial during the war, or so it was said, and she hadn't been content to hang back with her bones while others did the fighting, either. She'd insisted on leading attacks herself, and even after the war was over, she and others like her had hunted down blackhairs until every one of them was scoured from the Witchlands.

"Lilla Red Bird was a great witch," Visser said finally. "But having a famous boneshaker for a sister is no guarantee of talent."

Dassen frowned. "I mean no disrespect to you and to Aata's Right Hand, but if Mabis says there are Baen coming, surely we should all err on the side of caution. We villagers can take up arms, prepare—"

"Baen?" said Visser, raising her eyebrows in mock surprise. "Mabis has told us nothing about the Baen." She looked from one person to another, and a smirk appeared on her lips. "Mabis, you should share your prophecy with these good people."

Ryder looked to his mother, but for some reason she hesitated.

"Visser, please." Kef spoke softly from the corner.

The older woman ignored him and pressed on. "Tell them."

Mabis drew herself up haughtily. "A walking grave. It comes up out of the ground. It swallows whole farms."

Ryder started. This was new. Hadn't the prophecy been something about an assassin? An assassin in the mountains?

"What do you mean?" said Dassen. "Is it an earthslide, a ground shaking?"

Mabis stood up and began pacing the inside of the tent like a caged animal. "Oh, I know it sounds ridiculous—don't you think I know? But my visions are so clear."

"Tell them," said Visser again.

Ryder's mother turned to the group, her eyes fierce. "A monster," she said. "A monster that comes up out of the ground." She stared into space now as if she could see her vision in front of her. "Death himself is coming to the village."

Ryder's face went hot. A monster? She had called witches down from the mountain for this? She had neglected her children and ignored the farm for this? Pima turned around in his lap and gave him a searching look. "Don't worry," he whispered. "It's not real."

"I know it sounds strange," Mabis began. She looked from one face to another. "Skyla, Ryder, you believe me. . . ." Skyla frowned and looked at her knees; Ryder didn't meet her eye.

Finally Kef leaned forward. "You've been told that your prophecy was false," he said gently. "Be glad of it! What you saw was a horrid vision. Be glad it is only . . . sickness that makes you see these things."

Ryder expected anger from his mother, but when she answered there was only surprise and disappointment in her voice. "Sickness? After all I went through during the war . . . this is what the young think of me in the coven, that I'm sick?" Mabis let out an exasperated breath. "Things are worse there than I thought."

"I believe you." It was the tavern keeper who spoke. Ryder stared at him. Was he serious?

"I know you do, Dass," Mabis answered.

Ryder looked from one to the other in surprise. He'd always thought of Dassen as Fa's friend, but now he sensed that they had something of their own, some deep connection he didn't know anything about. Maybe this was why his mother had wanted Dassen here: because she knew he would believe her, no matter what. With a stab of guilt it occurred to Ryder that maybe he should have been that person. But how could he be? He had believed all his life that prophecies were fake. Hadn't Mabis herself drummed it into his head since childhood?

"Will you do something for me?" Mabis said softly. It suddenly felt to Ryder that he was eavesdropping on a private conversation, that his mother and the tavern keeper had forgotten that there were other people in the tent.

"Anything," Dassen said. "You know that."

"Tell the villagers that when the time comes, they must stand in the river."

"What's this?" Visser interrupted. "The river?"

Mabis raised her voice and looked around the tent. "I have told Dassen and I tell you all: When the time comes, running water will offer some protection."

"Oh, Mabis," said Visser, shaking her head. "You embarrass yourself."

Dassen ignored her. "I will tell them in the village. I will make sure everyone knows."

Visser looked like she might have said more, but the girl in white stood up and put a hand on her arm. "Yes, I quite agree," Visser said, as if the girl had spoken. "We're finished here."

Aata's Right Hand nodded and made a hasty bow to them all, again eyeing Ryder nervously as she stood up. *She's eager to leave,* Ryder thought as he bowed back. *She's afraid that any moment I'll accuse her of stealing my mother's bone.* But Ryder didn't say a word as the two women filed out of the tent. He and the white witch were co-conspirators now.

He tried to take Mabis by the arm, but she shrugged away his help. Kef stood up but remained by the exit. As Mabis passed to leave, he reached out and gently touched her on the shoulder. "I wouldn't want you to go without knowing that there are many in the coven who remember you, who would be happy to take you back." His voice was as kind as Visser's had been harsh.

"Take me back?" Mabis laughed ruefully. "After what you've just seen?"

"Don't you think you should be with the brothers and sisters of the coven? Especially now?" Ryder didn't understand the sadness in his crooked smile.

"There is nothing in the mountains for me."

Kef shook his head. "Not even Aata and Aayse? How can you presume to throw the bones when you have no faith? Did you even pray this morning before you came to us?"

Mabis hesitated, then shrugged. She hadn't. They all knew that.

"You cannot be a boneshaker while looking down your nose at our beliefs," Kef went on. "You're either a witch or you're not."

"Why are you here, Kef?" Mabis said abruptly. "You're not an elder. You're not a boneshaker."

"No . . ." Kef seemed to hesitate. Ryder hadn't thought to wonder why such a new member of the coven would be sent to answer a firecall. To carry the gear and light the fires?

"It's not really me you want to lure to the coven, is it?" Mabis said.

"I don't know what you mean."

"Don't you? All this concern about my health, my faith." Mabis put a hand on Kef's wrist and pulled him close. "Tell old Sodan that my health is fine. And as for my faith, ask him why I lost it. Ask Visser. They know. See if either of them will dare to tell you."

With that she took Ryder's arm and swept out of the tent.

Instead of going into the cottage, Ryder lingered outside under the silvernut trees, looking down on the valley. The sun had set, but there was still light in the sky. His mother and sisters had gone inside. Far below on the path, Ryder could just make out Dassen's little brown horse. Dassen had been invited to stay the night but had insisted that he'd already left his establishment too long in the hands of hired girls. At this time of the year the tavern would be busy. Farmers from far and wide would be bringing their hicca to the village mill to be roasted and ground, and they would need a place to eat and drink. Dassen would probably tell them all to be sure to stand in the river when the monsters came. Ryder's cheeks went warm at the idea.

It's all over, he tried to tell himself. *Things will go back to normal now.* But dread lay coiled at the pit of his stomach. He had the feeling that the future was stealing up behind him, about to tap his shoulder with a cold finger, about to break the spell of this perfect twilit night.

Again and again, the image of the white witch floated to his mind—the strange girl lit up by the moon, the dying embers of the fire. Guilt, he told himself. Guilt over letting her take his mother's bone. But it wasn't just that. It was as if the girl were a puzzle that his mind was trying to solve.

The singing he had heard earlier in the day was gone, but the world still seemed to shimmer. Strange as the day had been, he didn't want it to end, didn't want the time to pass. It seemed to Ryder that his whole life was leaving him somehow, slipping over the horizon with the setting sun. He wanted to reach out and call it back.

"How did she know?" he said out loud. "If there is no magic, if boneshaking is a fake, how did that girl know the bone was in the fire? What told her to look there?"

He searched for a logical explanation, but his mind kept sliding back to the illogical ones, in spite of himself.

What if everything he believed was wrong?

CHAPTER 6

MAIDEN'S WOE

"Kef needs to talk to you."

Skyla had come up beside him, trouble on her face. She had a rough pack slung over her shoulder.

"What's that?"

"Just talk to Kef. He's in the planting hills."

Skyla smiled weakly at him, but Ryder wasn't in the mood for games. That pack was the one they took when they went away somewhere—when they spent the night in the village or took the tithe to the coven. Ryder yanked it from her shoulder and tore it open.

"Stop it!" Skyla said. Girls' underclothes and a few other items spilled out onto the dirt at their feet.

"Where do you think you're going?" Ryder demanded. He picked up a scrap of blue cloth and shook it in her direction. "Is this Pima's dress?"

Skyla bent down and gathered the fallen things,

bundling them tightly into her arms. "The witches have invited Pima and me to stay in the coven for a while."

Ryder almost laughed. "Mabis would never agree to that."

"I just asked her, and she said yes. It's an honor."

Ryder frowned in disbelief. Mabis would *never* let them go to the coven. But the look in his sister's eyes said the opposite. Why would Mabis allow it? "Is this what you were doing this afternoon? Begging for an invitation? Well, I'm sorry, Skyla. This is no time for a pleasure trip."

"It's not . . . ," Skyla began. "No, you don't understand—"

Ryder didn't let her finish. "It's all over, Sky. You were there. Mabis saw nothing. The witches can take our tithe up with them, we'll get the rest of the crops in, and we'll have just enough for the winter. We can finally go back to the way things were—you're not going to ruin it by shirking out of the last of the harvesting."

He expected an angry retort, but Skyla only lowered her voice and said almost gently, "Do you really think everything can go back to the way it was?"

"Of course."

His sister's eyes were filling with tears. "You don't understand. I didn't either until they explained it to me."

Skyla hardly ever cried, and now it was twice in two days. The last time was in the hicca fields when she'd asked Ryder what he thought she wanted. A realization came over him. Maybe now he knew.

"You want to be a witch," he said, even more certain as he spoke the words. "You want to stay in the coven for good. Study there."

"No! I mean—well, yes . . . But it's not about that."

It was so obvious now—Skyla always had been a romantic when it came to the witches—but he was surprised she could be so selfish. "You can't, Skyla. We can't always get what we want."

"Oh!" she said, fully bursting into tears now. "Just talk to Kef!" And with that she ran toward the prayer hill, clutching her belongings to her chest.

Yes, he'd talk to Kef.

In the dying light, Ryder could see Kef's dark silhouette at the top of the largest planting hill. He was waiting for him, pacing and looking down on the valley.

"You can't have them!" Ryder shouted, climbing toward him through the rows. Most of the hicca was stripped now, and the bare stalks stood up like spines from the soft earth.

Kef held up his palms in a gesture of truce and called down to him. "We need to talk."

"You can't have my sisters," Ryder said, breaking into a run. He reached the top quickly and stood panting in front of the broken pole where the lucky man once stood. His mother's words came back to him. *It's not really me you want to lure to the coven, is it?* Mabis had known. Mabis had known what Kef was up to. But how could she just let this happen?

Kef must have seen the hard look on Ryder's face, because he backed away, his hands still raised. Ryder pressed forward. "They're needed on the farm. Do you think that just because you're witches you can take whatever you want?"

"Ryder . . ."

"I'm no fool. I know you'd love to have the nieces of Lilla Red Bird in your grip. But you can't just come here and break up our family!"

Kef took a step forward, reaching out a tentative hand to touch Ryder's shoulder. "Skyla came to *us*. And sending Pima was your mother's idea." The false calm in Kef's voice was maddening—he sounded like he was trying to soothe a horse with its leg caught in a fence. Ryder pushed his hand away.

"I don't believe you. Mabis had it right. You're here to lure them to the coven."

"No, not them. You. It's you the witches want."

Ryder struggled to take in what Kef had said. "The witches want . . . what?"

"Sodan sent me along to speak to you because we're friends. Ryder, you can't really be surprised."

It was almost laughable. "Oh, I'm surprised."

"I know your feelings about witches, but—don't refuse too quickly. Life can't be easy on this farm. It wasn't easy when . . . when your father was alive. But in the coven, you'd have everything you need. And Mabis might decide to come too if you were going. It would be the best thing for her."

"My mother would starve before she went back there! And I'd join her."

Kef gazed at him, unperturbed. "You can't put off your destiny forever."

"My what?"

Kef paused, shaking his head. "She never told you, did she?"

"Told me what?"

Kef scowled at the ground. "She should have," he muttered. Then he lifted his chin. "Sodan says that before you were born, your mother's sister threw the bones and made a prophecy about you."

Ryder narrowed his eyes. "My mother's sister? Lilla Red Bird?"

Kef nodded. "She said you would have the gift, that you could be a great boneshaker. Like her. Like your grandfather."

Now Ryder really did laugh. At Kef, and at himself, for almost falling into such an obvious trap. "Oh, Kef, what have they done to you? Don't you remember? You and I used to sit up on Dassen's roof and talk about what nonsense all that was."

Kef's voice stayed calm and kind. "I remember. You used to tell me you were meant for something more than farming. And you *are* meant for something more. You'll find it in the coven, Ryder. I did."

Ryder's laughter died on his lips. "Listen to me. You might actually believe what you're saying, but I've lived with a boneshaker all my life. I know how it's done. The secret to making some horse's ass believe a prophecy is to be flattering. 'Oh, you have a great destiny. Oh, you're so different from everybody else.' How many poor young men and women have been tricked into coven life with that foolishness? I wonder. Is that how they got you, Kef?"

A look of anger flashed across Kef's face, breaking through his calm serenity. "Coven life means something to some people, Ryder. It means something to me."

"Well it doesn't mean a thing to me, so you can just pack up your tents and go. My sisters are staying."

Kef took a deep breath as if to recover his composure. "You don't understand. There are reasons why Skyla and Pima should come with us, *must* come with us." Ryder felt himself flush with anger. "Even your mother sees it's for the best."

"You don't seem to be hearing me, Kef." Ryder drew himself up to his full height.

"We're having a peaceful conversation. I see no reason to change that."

"Are we?" Ryder stepped forward, his hands tightening into fists. When they were boys, Kef's few extra years had given him the advantage, but now Ryder was both the taller and the heavier of the two.

Kef stepped back again in alarm. "She's sick!" he said abruptly. "She's worse than you know."

Ryder froze. The words made no sense to him at first, but they seemed to strike him in the chest like an arrow. His hands fell to his sides.

"I'm sorry," Kef said. "I practiced what I was going to say and . . . that wasn't it."

"You mean Mabis," said Ryder, shaking his head. "She's fine."

"The others think differently, and . . . and I do too. My parents were dyers, Ryder. They taught me about plants like maiden's woe and darkroot. They're dangerous. I think your mother's in trouble."

"Mabis knows what she's doing."

Kef pulled nervously at his braided beard. "Don't you think there might be a reason she's letting your sisters go to the coven—the coven she hates? She wants to spare them. She knows what's coming."

"No!"

"I'm sorry, Ryder. I've done this very badly, I know."

Again he tried to put a hand on Ryder's shoulder, but Ryder turned away with a hiss, hating the pity in his friend's eyes.

"You're wrong," Ryder insisted.

For a while, the two of them stood in tense silence. The dry hicca stalks made a shushing sound in the breeze. In the valley, small points of orange light began to appear—villagers celebrating the end of the harvest with great bonfires.

"You might not remember this," Kef said softly. "But when we were small, a stranger followed the river to the village." He hesitated, searching for words. "This man, he'd gotten a taste for maiden's woe in the summer when it was thick and plentiful, and by the time the chilling came, he couldn't live without it. My parents took him in at first, but he got so violent they couldn't let him stay." Kef turned to Ryder now with emotion in his voice. "I remember him, Ryder. I remember him begging for maiden's woe like he was begging for his life. Eventually the miller took him in, but—"

Ryder interrupted. "I know what you're trying to say, but Mabis isn't like him. She's strong."

Kef shook his head. "It's no use lying to you. Your mother will resist the flowers for a time, three days at most. Then she will give in to her craving and eat as many as she can—I saw it today when she came to throw for us. This can go on and on, but when the chilling comes and the river freezes, there won't be any flowers left. There will be nothing to feed her hunger, and after a few days it will become unbearable." This time, Ryder didn't shake off the hand Kef set on his shoulder. "I'm not saying she'll die of it. I honestly don't know how many die and how many live, but she will become a person your sisters shouldn't see."

Ryder's thoughts blurred into one another. "But . . . I just have to keep her away from them," he said weakly. "I just have to find where she's getting them and pull them all up!"

"Even if you could, it wouldn't help her now." Kef's words were hard, final.

Ryder struggled to speak, struggled to find the argument that would refute what Kef was telling him. It couldn't be true. He could fix this. If he could just find out where she was getting the flowers . . . Ryder gulped for air. He felt like the hand of the Goddess had just come down and swept him to the ground.

"That man," he said. "What happened to him?"

Kef hesitated.

"Tell me!" Ryder demanded, his voice breaking.

"He died at the miller's, so I was told, begging for the black trumpets with his last breath. No one ever learned his name."

A loud wailing sound rose up from the direction of the cottage, and both of them turned. It was Pima's voice, sounding the way Ryder felt. Someone had told her she was leaving home, he guessed, and she didn't like the idea any better than he did. He tried to imagine what it would be like not to wake up to her sharp little knees climbing all over him.

Up on the prayer hill, one of the black tents sagged, then came gracefully down. The witches were getting ready to leave.

"You're not going tonight, are you?" Ryder asked, a ripping feeling in his chest. He thought he'd at least have one more night with Skyla and Pima.

Kef nodded. "Visser and Aata's Right Hand are eager to get back to the mountain. You can send word to the coven if—" He stopped and corrected himself. "You can send word to the coven when your mother is herself again, and we will send your sisters back."

Ryder shook his head dully. Skyla wouldn't want to come back. And why should she? His own dreams were dead and buried under sixtyweights of earth—why should he do the same to hers? "You should go," Ryder said, his voice ragged.

"What will you—?"

"Just go now. Please, Kef," he said.

Kef nodded and withdrew.

Ryder looked down into the valley, the lights from the bonfires blurring in front of his eyes. A year ago the whole family, including Fa, had celebrated the harvest in the village. Ryder remembered going to a dance in someone's hay barn. He'd hated it. The only person he had danced with was Pima. Toward the end of the evening, he had found a quiet place to watch without being seen, a place where no one would come up to him and say, "Look how tall he is," or "Where's your beard?" or "Have you met Farmer Someone's daughter?" Ryder had watched his mother and father dance that night. They held hands, swinging each other around the floor, Mabis's hair flying around them in a circle. It was only a year ago, but his mother had looked so young and pretty then.

"Stupid woman," Ryder whispered to the night. "Stupid, stupid woman. Why did you even start?"

And then Ryder bent down low into the hicca stalks and cried silently into the earth.

CHAPTER 7

A SPOT UPRIVER

"Long ago there lived two sisters," said Mabis. "Twins. They were alike in every way except that one, Aayse, could not speak." She sat in bed, staring intently at the space where Ryder was standing, but she didn't seem to see him.

"I brought you some tea."

Mabis smiled and made a wide gesture with her arms, as if she had an audience for her story, as if invisible children were sitting on the dirt floor of the sleeping room. "Not being able to speak taught Aayse about the great silences."

"Mabis." Ryder sat down on the edge of the bed. He needed to get her to eat; she was getting thinner by the day.

His mother blinked her eyes. "You never call me Maba anymore."

It was true. Ryder had invented the name when he was little—a cross between Mabis and Ma—but at some point both he and Skyla had stopped using it, though he couldn't have said when.

His mother took the cup and inhaled the steam. "Mallon leaves, nice and sweet." But she held the tea in her lap and didn't drink. Ryder saw that the inner parts of her lips were black.

"Oh, Mabis, not again."

His mother looked at him blankly. She no longer used telling the future as an excuse for taking the flower. More often than not, she offered no excuse at all.

Ryder still couldn't guess where she got the maiden's woe. It appeared from nowhere. When he checked the riverbank it was always empty, and Mabis could slip away like a shadow when his back was turned, with only an occasional wet footprint or damp sleeve to prove she'd been gone.

"What happened to your will?" he asked softly.

Her eyes drifted back to him. "It lasted as long as I needed it."

"You know that every time you take the flower it makes it worse. It will just be harder for you when the chilling comes."

His mother settled back against the wooden bed frame, the tea forgotten. "Don't scold."

Ryder smelled the maiden's woe on her breath. Sometimes he thought the sickly sweet aroma was seeping out of her pores. He knew from her lips that she must have eaten the flower that morning, but it didn't seem to affect her as it used to. Often her lips would be black but her eyes would be lucid and clear; other times she would rave like a madwoman.

"I've been thinking about your father," Mabis said. "It's been such a quiet year without his stories."

"I know." Ryder had never liked hearing Fa tell "The Life of Aata and Aayse," the story Mabis had been reciting. It reminded Ryder of the gulf between them: Fa believed it and Ryder didn't. Now he found he missed hearing all his father's tales, even that one. "If I made you some honey-cakes, would you eat them?"

"He knew the Goddess and her prophets better than any of those coven witches—for all their talk."

"I could open a pot of sourberries."

"Fish," she said. "I'd eat a fish."

"It's the wrong time of year."

Mabis shrugged. She put her tea aside and brought her knees up to her chest, brown feet showing below her patched nightdress. "Fish or nothing." She smiled, and her voice took on a singsong tone again:

"We live between the two great silences: the silence that existed before the world began, and the silence that waits for us at the end of all things. The prophet Aayse understood these silences. They are where all magic comes from. They are the fabric the Goddess used to make the world."

Mabis paused, then frowned. "I can almost believe it," she said. "But not quite. Once I did." She hugged her knees tighter. "I used to believe in Aata and Aayse. I used to believe that the Goddess made me and made the world and would gather me into her arms when I died. I just can't anymore."

"Why would you even want to?"

Mabis looked up, surprised by the question, and her voice cracked with emotion when she spoke. "Because I want to see your father again."

Ryder felt a lump in his throat, as if he'd swallowed a stone. As he watched, his mother's face twisted, and her eyes grew shiny with tears.

"Don't," he said. "Don't think about it." A tear rolled down her cheek. Ryder sat frozen beside her, not knowing what to say, uncomfortable in the silence.

"Oh, Ryder, what have I done? Your father broke his youth trying to plow this land. I might as well have fed him poison with a spoon."

"Stop," he said softly, putting a hand over hers. "Please stop. That wasn't your fault. He loved it here. He loved this farm."

Tears continued to roll down her cheeks. "He always said the soil was too rocky here for hicca, but . . . I couldn't live in the valley. I thought I was giving up the coven, but I only half gave it up. I kept my bones. I lived between the witches and the village, halfway up the mountain and halfway down. . . ."

She wiped her messy face with the sleeve of her night-dress and smiled sheepishly, as if part of her knew that she wasn't the kind of person who suddenly burst into tears. A feeling of helplessness welled up inside Ryder, and he struggled to push it back down. He should be on a ship right now, he thought, exploring distant countries, not watch-ing his mother fall apart, not watching her get thinner and thinner with nothing to be done. Ryder had gained nothing by staying home and giving up his dreams, nothing at all.

"Mabis, why did you leave the coven?" he asked. He put the cup of tea back into her hand as if it held some cure for her sorrow.

"I lost my faith. I've told you that."

"But why?"

"Oh . . ." Mabis twisted the wooden cup, sloshing tea onto her nightdress. "I saw something. Something I wasn't supposed to see. Something . . . I was going to say horrible, but it wasn't really. Something I couldn't understand. There are secrets in the coven, Ryder. Secrets valley people could never guess. Secrets even many of the witches don't know." She sighed. "I wish I could talk to my sister. When I made the firecall, I was sure that Lilla would come."

Ryder put his hand over hers to stop the tea from spilling. "Mabis, you know that Lilla Red Bird is dead."

His mother nodded. "Dead and buried." He was relieved by the finality of her words. It was one thing to want to see her husband again, another to forget that someone had been dead for twenty years. "Still, I hoped she would come. I so wanted to talk to her. There are things I need to ask."

Ryder looked away. He was so tired. How much more of Mabis's ravings could he put up with? "I'll make the honeycakes now."

"No. Not honeycakes. Too sweet."

"Bread, then."

"No," said Mabis firmly. "Fish."

"You don't even like fish. And my nets aren't mended. You'd eat some bread—I know you would." He rose to go.

As he was pushing aside the red curtain, Mabis called him back. "What is it like to have a Baen in your head?"

Ryder stopped short. "What?" It was such a strange thing for her to say, and yet . . . for some reason he couldn't brush the words aside as more of his mother's ramblings.

"You hear him in your dreams, don't you?" she asked, as if the idea both fascinated and repelled her. "Is he telling you to murder people? Is he telling you to worship his disgusting gods?"

"Who?" Ryder's mind spun.

"Your friend," said Mabis. "The stranger in the mountains.

The Baen in the mountains." A Baen in the mountains. In Ryder's mind something slipped into place, something fit together like a key turning in a lock. *Hello? Is someone there?* "Those people killed your grandfather, you know. At Barbiza. Just because he wore red." She said it like an accusation, as if he could somehow be responsible for something that had happened before he was born.

"I thought it was monsters you believed in now," Ryder said carefully. "You haven't talked about assassins in the mountains since before the witches came."

Mabis drew herself up haughtily. "One prophecy doesn't cancel out another. I foresee many things: assassins, dreadhounds . . ." Her voice grew graver as she spoke. "Monsters. Bonfires burning black." She squeezed her eyes shut. "But I don't need any gift of prophecy to see that Baen. He's burrowed into your head like a needleworm."

A great shiver coursed through him. The possibility that a Baen might be in his head, giving him nightmares, made him feel like he needed to bathe in the river.

"I don't think the blackhairs can help doing it," she went on. "It used to happen every once in a while when the two races lived together—someone would start having dreams, usually a young witch or someone like you, someone born to magic."

"Born to . . . ?"

"He is my punishment, this Baen. My punishment for robbing you of what you are. It's funny. I worked so hard to make sure the witches didn't get you. But magic found you just the same—just not the magic I was worried about." She pulled the threadbare blanket around her shoulders.

Ryder shook himself, as if he could shake off the strange inkling that some of what she was telling him might be true.

"No. There is no Baen in my head. And I'm not 'born to magic,' of all things." But he couldn't help remembering what Kef had said, that Lilla Red Bird had made a prophecy about him once.

"Oh, there's not much time!" she said, sounding suddenly desperate. She got out of bed with the blanket still wrapped around her and began to pace the tiny room. "There's not much time to make you understand. Somehow I always knew I'd lose Skyla—but you I tried to keep. It's rare, the gift of magic. The witches hide how rare it really is, but you have it, just like my sister did."

"I don't believe you!" Ryder cried out. "It's the maiden's woe that's making you say these things. . . ."

"Ryder, Ryder. Please try to understand! Part of the reason I wanted to keep you from magic is because I saw what it did to my sister. Lilla saw too much, and the war, it shattered her. No one talks about that when they tell stories about Lilla Red Bird, the great warrior witch; no one talks about what she had to become. I just wanted to keep you safe."

"I can't listen to you anymore—there are things to be done."

"Ryder, please," she began. She reached out a hand as if to catch his sleeve, but then she stopped herself and sat back down on the bed. "Yes." The troubled look on his mother's face abruptly disappeared, and she smiled warmly up at him with stained teeth. "Things to do. Like catching my fish."

Ryder made a fist in frustration, struggling to keep his voice calm. "I told you. My nets aren't mended—"

"That's too bad," Mabis interrupted with a sigh. She settled herself back onto the bed and leaned against the headboard. "Because I know a secret way to get upriver. And upriver is where the fish are lazy and easy to catch."

Ryder froze. Upriver. Where the maiden's woe came from.

"I'll tell you all about it," she went on. "But in return, you have to promise to catch me a nice, plump fish."

Ryder tried to keep his face placid, but he could feel the smile curling at the corner of his lips. "I guess you win," he said. "Fish it is."

A sandbar. It was so simple. A sandbar split the river down its center. It was covered with water, of course—that was why Ryder and Skyla had never noticed it before—but once he knew it was there, Ryder could see the ripples parting around it, could see that the water wasn't so dark where it was. He had only to wade into the river at a shallow point, then follow the length of the sandbar upstream. Places that would have taken half a day to reach by land—by hacking a path out of thick underbrush or climbing over slippery rocks—Ryder could get to in almost no time at all. He saw parts of the riverbank he had never seen before.

Maiden's woe was everywhere. Every time he saw some, he had to leave the bar and wade to the bank, and the river was bitterly cold. Still, Ryder plunged his hands into the icy water with relish. The plants needed water, and it was satisfying to see how quickly they began to shrivel in the sun after he'd pulled them up and tossed them out onto the shore. He tried to push aside the feeling that it was too late, that his mother had taken so many of the flowers that keeping her away from them now might even hasten her death. She was Mabis. Her will—and his—would keep her alive. For the rest of the morning, he attacked the black trumpets like a soldier killing his enemies.

It was when the sun was high in the sky that he began to hear it. A sound. An evil sound—and it seemed to be coming from just up ahead. *Metal scraping stone*—where had he heard that phrase before? In a flash it came to him: It was how Dassen had described the singing of the Baen right before the attack on Barbiza. Some Baen magician must have crossed the border! Cursing, Ryder took off along the sandbar at full speed, his waterlogged shoes slapping the water as he ran.

Abruptly the song stopped.

Hush-sh-sh. Hush-sh-sh. There was another sound in his ears now. It was like a great forest of dry leaves rattling in the wind. A waterfall, he thought; it must be huge. But turning a bend in the river, he found that the falls were smaller and farther away than he had imagined. A thin stream of water tumbled over a rocky wall and into a green lake thick with maiden's woe. The rock wall hugged the edge of the water and amplified the sound of the falls. *Hush-sh-sh. Hush-sh-sh.*

"I know you're here, Baen!" Ryder shouted. His voice echoed with the sound of the water. He waded to shore as quickly as he could, then ran around the sandy edge of the lake toward the waterfall.

No one. There was no one. If a Baen had been here, he must have melted into the rocks. Ryder turned a circle where he stood, spray from the waterfall wetting his face. He was alone. And yet he had the oddest feeling that someone had just been there, disturbing this peaceful place.

There was a small rocky outcropping in the center of the lake, with a bridge of haphazardly placed stones leading out to it. Thinking it might be the best way to see the whole panorama of the shore, he ran back and hopped from stone to stone toward the slippery little island. When he got there, he looked up and down the sandy bank of the lake, but there was nothing to see.

The music must have been in his mind. His mother was right: There was a Baen in his head.

A fisherwing screamed its call and Ryder jumped, startled. The screech had sounded in his ear, but, stepping back and looking up, he could see the bird on a high ledge above the waterfall—a trick of the echoing rock walls.

Suddenly he cried out in astonishment. Two huge pairs of eyes stared out at him from either side of the falls. It was a mosaic: the faces of two women set in multicolored stones. Before, it had been obscured by the water and by jutting rocks, but from this one spot on his little island, Ryder could see it perfectly.

One woman was like him, blond and blue-eyed, while the other, like the girl in white, clearly had Baen blood. Ryder knew they were witches, though, both of them. They both wore the mark of Aayse on their throats: two red slashes depicted in crimson stone, the symbol for the vow of silence. This lake must be some holy place, Ryder thought. He must have gone so far upriver that he was now at the base of witch territory.

At his feet he saw the glimmer of colored tiles. Two footprints marked the rock, inlaid in green and gold. Ryder placed his feet on the marks, and the falls grew louder; they made his whole body vibrate. As he listened, it seemed to him that the lake was not as murky as it had been a moment before—he could clearly see the roots of the maiden's woe reaching down into the mud. The two women looked down at Ryder so serenely. They were beautiful in their opposition: dark and light, like morning and evening, like two sides of a coin. Yes, this was a holy place.

No Baen would dare make magic here.

"Stay out of my head, you blackhair!" Ryder yelled to the sky. The echoes of his voice swirled around him like music.

CHAPTER 8

THE CHILLING

Ryder's soaked woolen leggings clung to him, and his leather shoes had begun to fall apart, but he felt oddly pleased. He'd found the source of his mother's flower. And he'd caught her a fish. It was still twitching in his net when he came up over the prayer hill, but the moment he looked down on the family's land, he dropped the net and ran.

The stand of trees was still there, and most of the barn, but the cottage . . . The cottage looked as if it had been blown apart by a great wind. Ryder hurtled down the hill. When he got to the clearing, he stood, his breath in shallow gasps, struggling to take in what he saw. Only the door frame was left standing, and the table Ryder's father had made, still covered with dirty breakfast plates. The rest of the cottage lay in piles of rubble and toppled walls. Pots and pans were strewn over the ground, and shelves and furniture lay splintered as if dropped from a great height.

"Mabis!"

Ryder cast his eyes through the debris but saw no sign of her. He stepped into the rubble, pushing aside stones and lifting up bits of broken furniture. A corner of blue fabric poked up from underneath the stones of the toppled fireplace—his mother's shawl. Heart thumping in his ears, he kneeled to uncover it, trying to remember if Mabis had it on that morning—but it was just the shawl. Mabis wasn't there.

"Hello!" he called again, desperation in his voice. From around the barn came a chilling moan.

"Maba!" he cried, and ran toward the sound. It wasn't his mother.

Yellowhead's eyes rolled, and pink foam streamed from his lips. He lay on the ground in a pool of blood, both back legs broken. When Ryder came close, Yellowhead strained in terror to get up, screaming again. Ryder had never known a horse could make such a human sound. The tortured pain of it sent a wave of nausea through his body.

"Whoa, boy. It's me, boy. It's me." Ryder dropped to the ground and lay beside the horse, his arm around his neck. Yellowhead blinked his eyes and stopped straining.

"Goddess, Goddess, Goddess," Ryder whispered to himself. "I don't want to have to kill him. Don't make me have to kill my horse."

Just then a great shudder radiated through the horse's body, and Yellowhead was still. It took Ryder a moment to realize that the first prayer he had ever made had been abruptly answered.

"Aata's ghost, don't just sit there, you fool!" Ryder looked up to see Dassen standing red faced before him. He was holding his sword, the Baenkiller, over his head.

"We can't afford a new horse," said Ryder weakly. He saw that his hands were covered with Yellowhead's blood, and he quickly wiped them on his shirt, leaving red streaks. Dassen was looking over his shoulder.

"Quick, boy. Come with me. There are more behind me."

"But my mother!"

"She'll be safe. She knew it was coming, remember?"

They ran, Dassen gripping him by the wrist, pulling him along. A few times he stopped to circle back as if to confuse their tracks, as if something were following them.

"Where are we going?" Ryder demanded, but Dassen didn't answer.

Suddenly there it was, right in front of them: a thing that couldn't exist, a monster straight out of his mother's twisted nightmares. A *walking grave*.

It was a man—at least, it had the rough, ungainly form of a man—but it seemed to be made of packed brown earth. It swayed back and forth in front of them, as if it didn't so much see them as sense their vibrations. A wide mouth hole opened and shut, opened and shut, in the middle of its face, but other than that it had no features—not even eyes. Dassen motioned for Ryder to stay still and lifted his sword, but just as the blade came singing through the air, the creature leaned out of its path. It grabbed the sharp tip of the weapon and pulled Dassen to his knees.

"Go! Ryder, go!" shouted Dassen.

Ryder turned and started to run, but another creature was staggering toward them. Ryder couldn't fathom how it could be real, how it could move. It looked like something a child would build out of the river mud and leave to crumble in the sun. He felt his stomach shrink, and he backed up into Dassen.

"I told you to get out of here," the tavern keeper barked. He was on his feet now, swinging his sword with lightning speed at the first creature.

"There's another one," said Ryder. "We're trapped!"

"Take this!" Dassen thrust the Baenkiller into his hands.

Ryder knew he should object, but the second creature was almost upon him. Without thinking, he attacked, stabbing at it with all his strength. The sword made a dull, muffled sound as it entered the creature's body, exactly as if Ryder had plunged it into the ground. He yanked the weapon back, only to find it had made no mark. Fear gripped him. He raised the sword again, but the thing gave a swoop of its arm and the Baenkiller was ripped from Ryder's hand. The next thing he knew his skull was hitting a tree with a thudding crack. Pain shot through him. He struggled to stay conscious, but everything around him was doubled and spinning.

Dassen rushed to stand between Ryder and the creatures, fighting them both now with only his bare fists. One of them landed a powerful blow to his jaw, sending him to the ground, but the tavern keeper was up in moments, pressing on, his fists a blur. A piece of one of the creatures flew off and landed on the ground right beside Ryder. Dazed, he picked it up, crumbling it to nothing between his fingers. Dirt. It was just dirt. How could these things exist?

Ryder thought of running—Dassen had told him to, after all—but what chance would the tavern keeper have on his own? Slowly Ryder stood up. The sword glinted on the ground just beyond the fight. Without taking his eyes from Dassen and the creatures, Ryder slipped around them and picked up the weapon. He was close enough to smell the creatures now, but there was nothing strange about them; they smelled like tilled soil. He crept up behind one of them and positioned himself for a mighty strike. He swung the sword as hard as he could. In a spray of brown clumps, the creature's head left its body!

Ryder felt joy surge through him—but the feeling didn't last long. A stone at his feet whizzed toward the creature, then a clump of earth. Ryder ducked and shielded his head as sticks and bits of debris came flying toward the creature from all directions. It was as if there was some powerful magnet at its core that pulled matter to it when it needed to reform itself. In moments it was whole again. Now both creatures turned and lurched toward him. He swung the sword wildly, stumbling back.

"Don't take my ear off, boy!" Dassen shouted.

Again the tavern keeper was pushing himself between Ryder and the creatures, punching with fists that seemed to be made of iron. One of the creature's arms broke off and came sliding to the ground, but that hardly seemed to slow it down. Ryder could see how formidable Dassen must have been during the war, but he could also see that the older man was losing. The more he fought, the more the creatures grew new limbs from the earth and debris at their feet.

All at once, the two creatures encircled Dassen, seemed to merge around him. Ryder could hear his screams, but he could barely see Dassen now—the creatures were trying to suffocate him.

Ryder lifted the sword again and started hacking at the earth surrounding Dassen's body. The tavern keeper's arms were still visible, and Ryder could see his face—it was twisted with fear and pain.

"Grab my hand!" Ryder shouted, but Dassen didn't seem to hear. Ryder managed to grab one of his arms. As hard as he could, he pulled, and pulled again.

"Just go, you fool!" Dassen moaned. "Just leave me!" but Ryder strained with all his strength.

Finally Dassen came loose, and Ryder fell back hard, the heavy man on top of him. They both stumbled to their feet, but Dassen winced when he tried to put weight on his right leg. In front of them, the ground was a churning mass of earthen arms, flailing out in search of their lost victim.

"Can you make it to the village?" Ryder said, quickly picking up the sword again.

"We don't have to," Dassen answered. He put his arm around Ryder for support. "Just get me to the river!"

Another creature came to the edge of the river as Dassen and Ryder stood in the shallows. It didn't exactly look at them, as it had no eyes, but it seemed to know they were there. It stood on the bank, swaying back and forth as if it could smell them. It didn't come into the water, though, and after a while it lumbered away. *Stand in the river*, Mabis had said. And she'd been right.

She'd been right about everything.

"The fish!" Ryder said, a realization washing over him. "My mother sent me upriver to get a fish. She did it to get me away—to save me. She knew this was going to happen!"

Dassen nodded, not the least surprised, and Ryder remembered how Mabis had trusted him to believe her when no one else did. Ryder promised himself he would be like Dassen from now on. He would never doubt his mother again.

Time passed. The two men stood shivering in water up to their thighs, not knowing if it was safe to leave. Pain warped Dassen's face. He had limped badly getting here and now leaned heavily on Ryder's shoulder.

"I can't see the mill," Ryder said. His voice was hollow. The valley was lit by shafts of late afternoon sunlight, though darkness seemed to be coming with surprising speed. He should be able to see the mill and the little houses along the road where the blacksmith lived with his wife and sons. He told himself that he was wrong, that he couldn't really have seen those things from this vantage point. He must be too far away.

"They'll be in the river," Dassen assured him. "I did what your mother said. I told every single one of them— more than once."

He had, too; Ryder didn't doubt it. The villagers would have thought he'd gone mad—but they wouldn't think so now.

"I've got to get you back to town," said Ryder. Dassen's shivering was growing worse, and his face was ashen under his beard. "We'll follow the river. It will keep us safe."

"Not for long. Look at the sky."

Ryder looked up. Behind him, fingers of dark purple stretched toward them from over the mountain. The chilling. "Aata's blood, why today?"

"We should thank the Goddess it wasn't yesterday," Dassen said.

"How long have we got?"

The tavern keeper shook his head. "Could be anytime. I think you should go—make your way down to the valley. Don't worry about me."

"I won't leave you!"

"I'll follow as quickly as I can. Go, boy. I'd do the same in your place."

"Really, Dass? You'd leave me injured in the river with the chilling coming? I don't believe that for a moment." A thought occurred to him. "Just what are you doing so far from the valley? Are you going to tell me you just went for a walk? You're here because you came to help me and my mother, to see if we were safe—don't tell me you'd leave." Dassen looked away. "Now put your weight on my shoulder. We've got to get out of the water—now. Just pray those things are gone."

Dassen clambered painfully up onto the bank. "I see them!" he cried. At first Ryder thought he was talking about the monsters—but there was joy in Dassen's voice. "There are people in the water! Look! Down by the bridge!"

It was true. As Ryder squinted through the trees, he could just make out a tight group of villagers standing in the river. They *had* listened. Maybe his mother was down there with them. Ryder was sure she would have saved herself. After all, she'd sent him to the safety of the river at the right time. She'd known.

"Here it comes!" Dassen warned, looking up at the sky.

Ryder had a moment to stumble out of the water and prepare himself. Then, like a heavy weight pressing down from above, the cold came. Ryder heard a hissing sound, like an intake of breath, as the water on his clothing froze stiff. He gasped, and Dassen let out a bellow of pain. Cold. Frigid cold.

"Hurry up!" said Dassen. "Keep moving." His words were clouds in the air now, and his beard was white with ice. Above them the clouds, like purple fingers, seemed to reach out to grip the valley. Winter had arrived.

"The river will be frozen by tomorrow," said Ryder. "What will we do about the creatures then?"

"We'll fight. And we'll pray to the Goddess. What else can we do? We don't even know what these things are or what magic made them."

What magic. Out of the blue, Ryder remembered the singing he'd heard in his mind, and he remembered the conversation he'd had with his mother that morning. Something even colder than the chilling snaked its way around his heart and tightened its grip.

"Yes we do know, Dassen," he said. "My mother told me. She said there was a Baen in the mountains. He must have made these things."

Dassen's face hardened. Then he looked at Ryder and smiled grimly. "Well, we Witchlanders know how to kill a Baen, don't we?"

CHAPTER 9

THE COVEN

Pima's hair was damp with sweat, and her brow was creased. Even in her sleep, she looked troubled. Ryder knelt next to the small bed, feeling awkward in his borrowed clothes.

He didn't want to be here. Being inside in this too-warm witch's hut made him feel singled out, favored. He should be with the other villagers, standing on the outskirts of the coven in the bitter cold, warming his hands over the bonfires and waiting for word from the coven elders. All the way up the mountain, the villagers had talked of blood. There had been deaths in the valley—few because of Mabis's warning—but enough to give them all a taste for revenge. Soon, Ryder hoped, the witches would add to their number, and in the morning they would all swarm across the border like a tide.

Pima murmured in her sleep, and her eyes flickered open. "I thought you were gone."

"Not yet," he said.

"Are you going to kill a Baen?"

Ryder was taken aback. He and Skyla had decided not to tell her where he was going. "What makes you say that?"

"You've got the Baenkiller."

Ryder's hand went to the sword poking up over his left shoulder. Dassen had done him a great honor by lending it to him. His knee had been too bad for him to come, but Ryder had seen the bitter regret in his eyes when the party of villagers left to go up the mountain.

Pima didn't seem interested in an answer to her question. Tears were seeping out of the corners of her eyes.

"Don't," Ryder said softly.

"Why didn't Maba come too?" Pima asked. "I want her to come here."

"I told you, she has things to do. Special things. She'll be back. . . ." He let his words trail off. His mother's body had not been found, though there had been a thorough search for her. Ryder believed she must have lived, must have saved herself, but when he talked about her, the questions started to float up to the surface of his mind. Questions like, Could she really survive in this cold? or, If she's alive, why doesn't she just show herself? "We have to be brave," he said.

The witch Yulla poked her head into the room, and Ryder looked up, hoping the coven elders had finally finished their endless deliberations. Somewhere in one of their secret mountain caves, witches were throwing the bones and discussing the attack. But Yulla only smiled and offered him another cup of tea.

"No, thank you," he said, more sharply than he meant.

As much as he wanted to, Ryder couldn't find fault with Yulla, the distant cousin who had taken in Pima and Skyla. She was round and patient, always smiling. Her own husband and young children had died years ago of the scabbing disease. Sometimes Ryder thought she looked at Pima almost hungrily. *My sister's already got a mother,* he wanted to snap—but he knew he should be glad Skyla and Pima were so well cared for, and he kept his lips set tight. Yulla bobbed her head shyly, leaving them alone again.

"When you come back, we'll go to sea," Pima said, her eyes closing again.

"All right," he whispered. "When I get back." He stroked her forehead, trying to smooth away the worry lines. "You'll be my little cabin girl."

Next to the bed, a wooden chest spilled over with toys, enough for a rich man's child. Ryder had never given much thought to the way witches lived, but he found himself appalled by how much wood Yulla used on her fires, by how many useless little objects she had lying about, by the idea of a child with a bed of her own. He wanted to scoop

Pima up in his arms and take her home. But they didn't have a home anymore.

Pima had fallen back to sleep, but Ryder didn't want to rejoin Skyla and Yulla in the other room, didn't want to make conversation. Like Pima, he couldn't get Mabis out of his mind. She must have known the girls would be safe up here, just as she had known to send him to the river at the right time. *If it weren't for Mabis, Pima might be dead right now,* Ryder thought. The guilt he felt for not believing in her completely, the way Dassen did, wormed at his heart.

"I'll bring you that Baen's head," he whispered to the sleeping girl. "I'll put the Baenkiller right through his eyes." As if that could make up for anything.

"Ryder!" Skyla poked her head through the door. "Kef's here. The witches are back."

Finally.

The coven was built into the side of the mountain. Tiered stone steps curved past little round huts, winding around mountain trees with roots like claws, disappearing into the darkness at the top of the settlement. Night had fallen, but high torches lined the steps, making pools of light.

Ryder had never been to this part of the coven before. Like most villagers, he had always left his tithe in the clearing below the huts and had never been asked to come any farther. Dassen used to boast that of all the covens in the

Witchlands, this one was the oldest, the most holy. Ryder had always doubted it, but now he saw the weather-worn pictographs carved into the stone torch holders, the deep depressions eroded into the stone steps, and he wondered if it might be true, after all.

Witches were arriving home from somewhere higher up toward the mountain's crooked spire. They walked together in groups of two and three as they came down the steps, swinging their glims—round glass lanterns that they carried on chains. Ryder had never seen glass lanterns before. They seemed miraculous, like fire wrapped in water, and he could see them glowing like firebugs all the way up the mountain.

He was surprised to see how many of the witches had darker hair or a hint of Baen features. He'd thought that the girl in white was something out of the ordinary, but there was more mixed blood here than in the village, though he couldn't think why. The witches murmured softly to one another, but conversations stopped when they saw Ryder, and without meeting his gaze they slipped into the round huts or disappeared along dirt paths that branched off from the coven steps. They seemed too calm, too subdued for people readying themselves for war. Kef steered him in the other direction, down the steps and toward the flat stretch of land beyond the last coven torch, the place where the villagers had set up camp.

"Do the witches want to attack tonight?" Ryder asked Kef. He could see the villagers moving in the dark ahead, putting out cooking fires and packing up their rough tents. It was probably a good idea; there was a smell of snow in the air.

"Visser has told the villagers to go home," Kef said. "That the danger is over."

"What!" Ryder stopped short.

"The monsters are gone. They're dead now—if you can call it dead—at least that's what you villagers have told us."

It was true enough. By the time Ryder and Dassen had gotten back to the village, the creatures had already begun to slow. Perhaps it was the cold, or perhaps their lifespan was shorter than a jewelfly's, but by dawn the next morning, the earth men were stiff and still, and the bravest of the villagers were pushing them over, stomping their bodies back into the ground.

Ryder thought for a moment. "No," he said finally. "This is a mistake. The Baen can make more of those creatures whenever he wants. The danger is *not* over. We'd be fools to think so!"

"I'm sorry, Ryder, I'm just telling you what Aata's Right Hand saw in her bones. If there is a Baen over the border, he has every right to be there. We have no reason to believe he is responsible for this magic."

"No reason! What about my mother's prophecies?"

A pair of witches stared at Ryder as they passed, and Kef pulled him off the steps, leading him to a space between two of the witch huts. He lowered his voice. "Think, Ryder. Think what a serious thing it would be to cross the border. We don't want another war."

"It's already a war, and the blackhairs have begun it! Help me convince them, Kef. Please. Help me convince the witches not to do this."

"I can't."

Ryder turned away in frustration. Inside one of the huts, he could see a man bending over a hearth, distorted by the warps and bubbles of a glass window. These witches were too comfortable, he thought, with their warm fires and their glass windows, untouched by the destruction the creatures had wreaked in the village.

"You're quite a lackey, aren't you?" Ryder hissed. "Go tell Ryder we're stealing his sisters. Go tell Ryder he should go back to the village. No wonder they took you into the coven. Do you empty their chamber pots, too?"

Kef's face hardened under his braided beard. "If they asked me to, I would. It is an honor to live here." Ryder rolled his eyes. "Don't be angry. We were friends once, Ryder. And we should be now. Now, more than ever, after what we've lost."

Kef was fingering the blue bead at his neck, still visible above the open collar of his coat. Ryder remembered it as something Kef's mother used to wear. She'd been a pretty woman with arms blue to the elbow from dying cloth, who fed stray dogs and always kept her house tidy. How Kef's father had adored her. And what a terrible death she'd had to suffer. All at once Ryder regretted his harsh words.

"Kef," he said gently, "just because the witches took you in doesn't mean you have to do everything they say. Where's the boy who dressed the village lucky man to look like the blacksmith's wife? Where's the boy—"

"Don't!" Kef said with a harshness Ryder didn't understand. "I hate to even think of those days, Ryder. I'm not that person."

Kef's vehemence surprised Ryder, and hurt him a little too. Ryder had grown up too far from the village to make many friends. He and Kef hadn't had the chance to see each other very often, but Ryder remembered every occasion: a few islands of frivolous pleasure in a life that was otherwise a sea of hard work.

"Harmless fun, Kef," he said.

"No. Not harmless. Listen, Ryder, the witches aren't just here to throw the bones and guard the border. They're here to guide us. They must be obeyed."

"Without question?"

"Yes! You might not like Visser or Aata's Right Hand or even Sodan, but when they make a decision, their words are the voice of the Goddess. And trust me, the Goddess does not look kindly on those who think her words are open to interpretation."

Ryder was about to argue, but he had the feeling there was nothing he could say to change his friend's mind. Kef was right: He wasn't the boy Ryder had known anymore.

Skyla rounded the corner, her breath in clouds. She wore an elegant red coat that Yulla had given her. *Even the clothes people wear here are extravagant,* Ryder thought. A villager had loaned him the coat he was wearing; it was made from an old blanket.

"What's happening?" she asked, panting. "Why are the villagers leaving?"

"They're not," Ryder said firmly.

He left them both and ran.

In the frozen meadow, men and women were saddling their pack animals and rolling up their gear. Ryder caught one of his neighbors by the sleeve. It was Raiken, who owned the farm nearest Ryder's. Raiken had six children and another on the way, but because of Mabis's warning the whole family had made it to the river in time.

"What can we do, Ryder?" Raiken said. Beside him, a gray mare shook her mane in the dark, blowing white breath out of her nose. "Our hands are tied. The witches won't agree to let us cross the border."

"Let us? They can't stop us!"

"I know what you're feeling," said the farmer. He scratched the back of his head and looked away, embarrassed. "I don't like it any more than you. Tarkin was my best friend." Tarkin the miller and his wife had been killed by the mud creatures, leaving their only son an orphan. "We all want vengeance. But witches . . . They have their reasons, and it's not for us to question them." He sounded just like Kef.

"Why not? Why shouldn't we question them?"

Ryder looked around in frustration, regretting that Dassen hadn't come—he would have changed their minds. Without waiting for an answer, he leapt onto a low wooden platform. It was empty now, but earlier in the season it would have been piled high with bags of hicca and hicca flour—tithes kept off the ground until they could be stored.

"Good villagers!" Ryder cried. "Think of your homes! Am I the only one who wants revenge for what this Baen has done?"

There were a few scattered cheers from the crowd, and most of the villagers stopped what they were doing to listen, holding up torches and lamps. Skyla and Kef were watching Ryder from the base of the platform, but they didn't try to stop him.

"Hear me!" he called. "Think of the ruin those creatures made of our village. Now look at this beautiful coven in front of you, every hut standing, not a window broken.

Why should we let these pampered witches tell us how to protect ourselves?"

Villagers began to gather around him now, their faces golden in the torchlight. They were people Ryder had known all his life, farmers mostly, simple people who believed the teachings of Aata and Aayse—but surely a few of them would be willing to defy the witches. Surely he wasn't the only one who doubted their power, who wondered what they really did to deserve their tithes.

"Harkiss," Ryder said, pointing to the village blacksmith. "You lost family in the attack. Don't you want revenge?" Harkiss stood with his arms crossed, his face unreadable, but at his side his two tall sons nodded gravely. "You always said you wanted to fight the Baen. This is your chance!"

"The witches tell us that the danger to our village is over," Raiken said.

"Yes, that's what they say, but how can we believe them when they failed to predict the first attack? I say this Baen can send another pack of creatures over the mountain whenever he wants!"

"He's right!" said someone. Old Mag pushed her way to the front of the crowd. She was wearing a too-small leather jerkin and a leather helmet over her gray hair. "Are we truly going to wait for this Baen to kill us in our beds? Are we just going to lie down and let their monsters bury us?"

Ryder smiled. Old Mag had fought during the war, and she looked full ready to do it again, in spite of having grandchildren Ryder's age.

By now some of the witches had noticed what was going on, but they held back in tight groups at the edge of the meadow. From the platform, Ryder could see a small red litter carried by four bearers moving down the mountain path, but it stopped near the other witches, in a pool of light formed by the last torch on the coven steps. Ryder was too far away to see the face of the person who sat hunched on top, but he guessed it must be Sodan, the leader of the coven. Sodan never deigned to come down to the valley—few villagers had ever seen him. If Ryder had caught this man's attention, maybe he was doing something right. He raised his voice, hoping that old Sodan could hear his every word.

"I say we cross the border now, take this Baen magician by surprise, and slit his throat! Now, who is with me?"

"Stop this, boy," said a sharp voice from the crowd. "Stop this now!" It was Visser, the witch who had come down the mountain with Kef and Aata's Right Hand in answer to his mother's firecall. She pushed her way through the villagers and glared up at him from the base of the platform. "We witches don't have to explain ourselves!" She beckoned Ryder toward her, and as he bent down, she grabbed him by the ear, lowering her voice so that only he could understand. "Aata's Right Hand has seen things in her casting. Things you would not want revealed."

"Reveal what you want," Ryder said, pushing her hand away. He stood up and yelled hoarsely at the crowd. "I say again, who is with me? Whatever happens, I will be crossing the border tonight!"

The cheers were louder now, and their meaning was unmistakable: A good portion of the villagers were on his side.

"You asked for this," murmured Visser. The gray-haired witch clambered up onto the platform. "Good people!" she cried. "The creatures you have told us about did not come from over the mountain. We witches would have seen them pass."

"That doesn't mean anything," Ryder answered, just as loud. "That Baen could have been singing on one side of the mountain and the creatures could have formed on the other."

"Unlikely. From the reports you yourselves have given us, it seems that these creatures appeared somewhere between the coven and the village. It is logical to assume that this was where they were formed."

Between the village and the coven. In other words, from somewhere near Ryder's farm. "What are you saying?" Ryder hissed.

The villagers looked from one to the other, confused. "Is the Baen among us, then?" said Old Mag, looking around as if he could be hiding in the crowd. "Did he cross to our side of the border?"

"It was not our intention to reveal all we have seen," said Visser. "But Ryder has forced our hand. We believe that our poor sister Mabis, driven mad with maiden's woe, was experimenting with strange magics. It was she who made the creatures."

"What!" Ryder felt heat rise to his cheeks; he could scarcely believe what he'd heard. He stared hard at Visser, expecting to see the guilt of her lie written on her face, but if she felt any shame, she hid it well.

"Perhaps the grief over her husband's death . . . ," she began.

"Don't believe her!" Ryder shouted to the crowd. "You've known my mother all your lives. Tell this witch you don't believe Mabis could have done such a thing!"

"But Mabis predicted the attack," someone said from the crowd. "She made the firecall and sent the tavern keeper with a warning." It was Kef, looking as surprised by Visser's pronouncement as Ryder himself. Obviously, not all the witches had been privy to the explanation that Mabis made the creatures. Visser glared at the young witch, and he looked to the ground, frowning.

"It is easy to predict what you plan to do yourself," said Visser.

"No!" said Ryder. "It doesn't make sense."

"Listen to me!" Visser shouted to the crowd. "The Right Hand of Aata has thrown the bones. These things are not to be disputed."

"I dispute them!" Ryder said. "Aata's Right Hand has no skill! If she did, she would have seen the monsters!"

"What do you know of such things?" Visser spat.

"Surely she's not the only boneshaker in the world. Send messengers to other covens. Have them throw the bones. My mother is innocent!"

A look crossed Visser's face then, a look of almost panic, but she quickly recovered herself. "Other covens agree with our predictions," she said sharply. "There is no danger from the Baen."

Ryder frowned at that, wondering if Visser was telling the truth, wondering why no one from any other coven had predicted the attack and tried to warn them. Were all the boneshakers in the Witchlands as incompetent as Aata's Right Hand? Had no one but his mother seen the danger?

"Please!" Ryder called out to the crowd. "Raiken, my mother saved your family with her warning. You said so yourself as we came up the mountain."

Ryder's neighbor stood twisting his gloves in his hands, embarrassed by the eyes of the villagers that were suddenly all upon him. "It's true that Mabis takes the maiden's woe," he said finally. "This summer I saw her in the river pulling it up. My wife saw her too."

"No!" Ryder bellowed. "She only did that to help her prophecy. She saved you! My mother saved you all—you'd be dead if it weren't for her!"

Visser grabbed him by the arm. "I'm sorry," she said. "We would have held this information back. But we cannot start another war by killing this Baen."

Ryder shook himself free. "You witches," he sneered. "You sit up here, doing no work, eating our food, and for what?"

"But are we out of danger?" Raiken asked Visser, his eyes avoiding Ryder. "Couldn't Mabis create more of those hideous things?"

"She didn't make them!" Ryder yelled, shaking with anger.

"We feel there is little chance of that," Visser said. "She is almost certainly dead—I'm sorry, Ryder. If her own creatures didn't kill her, the craving for maiden's woe surely has by now."

Ryder looked to Sodan's litter, wondering if he was behind all this, but the coven leader sat hunched and unmoving. Only the slight puff of his breath proved he was more than a pile of blankets. A little higher up on the coven steps, Ryder caught a glimpse of white. It was a young woman. He recognized her long braid and graceful stance—Aata's Right Hand.

"You!" he roared, forgetting everything else as blind

fury swept over him. He leapt from the platform into the crowd.

"Ryder, don't!" he heard Skyla shout.

"Stop him," Visser cried, but the villagers parted as he ran.

His boots thumped on the frozen ground, and in moments he had reached the edge of the meadow. Torchlight dazzled him. He passed the litter without a glance and dodged through the startled group of witches who had been watching him from a distance. A woman in red came out of one of the huts and cried out as he flew by. Aata's Right Hand stood above him on a platform of the tiered steps, her lips parted in surprise, a glim in her hand.

"What have you been saying about my mother?" Ryder shouted up to her.

The girl stepped back in alarm. She wore a white coat that went down past her knees, and her long braid was slung forward in front of her. Ryder ran toward her, taking two steps at a time, but just as he reached the platform, someone grabbed his shoulder and yanked him back. Kef—he always could run fast. They struggled briefly. Then Ryder hit Kef in the chest with the flat of his hand, and Kef stumbled backward into the crowd of people who were swarming up the steps after him.

Aata's Right Hand stared at the scene with horror in her eyes—and something else, too. For a moment Ryder thought he saw the guilt and shame he had expected to find in Visser. Two more men grabbed him and held him back by the arms—Harkiss the blacksmith and one of his boys.

"You're a liar!" Ryder said to the girl, trying to pull free. "I can see it in your eyes."

She gave a small gasp and the glim dropped from her hands, smashing on stone. Then she turned and bolted, a flash of white.

"Coward! Thief! Come answer for what you've done!"

Ryder tried to break away and run after her, but many hands pulled him back. The next thing he knew, he was lying on the cold platform, surrounded by angry, shouting faces. He struggled, but after a while he realized it was useless, and he stopped, panting at the dark sky. The hilt of the Baenkiller jabbed painfully into his back.

"Let me talk to him!" Skyla pushed her way to Ryder's side. "Let him up, please! He's just upset!"

"I'm not upset." He sat up. "Where is that girl?"

"Ryder, shut up," Skyla hissed, her voice sharp. Then, to the others: "Let me talk to him in private. Please. He's had bad news. Surely you can understand that."

"You don't believe it," Ryder said, still quivering with anger. "Tell me you don't."

"Of course not," said Skyla. "It doesn't make sense." She had led him in between the huts to a large wooden building without walls—a shrine, Ryder guessed. Its sloped roof was held up by tall, thin pillars. Here, witches could perform their prayers in open air and still be protected from the weather.

They climbed a few rough steps and walked out onto a bare floor. Ryder couldn't see much at first; they had only one glim that Skyla carried on a chain. Wooden planks creaked under their feet. To Ryder, it seemed like cheating to kneel down and greet the earth on a raised floor, but then, he was no expert on praying.

Skyla crossed to a low railing, hanging the glim on a hook as she leaned out over the valley. Ryder came up beside his sister, but there was little to see. It was a moonless night, and the stars were snuffed out by thick winter clouds. In the valley, all was dark. Only a few lamps and torches were visible, below them and to the left, snaking their way down the mountain path: The villagers were leaving, going home.

Ryder turned away and sank down onto the plank floor, trying to quiet a cold rage that threatened to choke him. He pulled the Baenkiller from his back and checked for damage—it seemed unharmed.

Skyla stared down at him, light from the glim reflected in her eyes. If anything could melt the shell of ice inside him it was probably those knowing eyes, like his father looking at him from beyond the grave. Ryder kept his attention on the sword, polishing a dull spot with the end of his coat sleeve.

"I know what you're thinking," she said.

He glanced up. She probably did, and anyway, there was no use hiding his intentions. "I'll need food. And a good knife."

"You'll die." Skyla folded her legs and settled down in front of him, putting a gloved hand on his knee. "You'll die if you go after that Baen alone."

"I suppose."

"I heard her prophecies too. Mabis didn't say anything about a Baen."

"Yes, she did—the assassin, don't you remember?"

Skyla furrowed her brow, considering. "But the witches—they won't let you go."

"Who will tell them?" Skyla didn't answer, and Ryder tried to read her face. Would she give him away?

"The witches say the danger is over," she went on. "Maybe they got that part right." Ryder shook his head. "Fine then, think of Pima. She's lost so much. First Fa, then Mabis. If she loses you, too . . ."

"Mabis isn't dead," he snapped. "Don't say that. There was no body. And Dassen . . . Dassen is still organizing searches. . . ." He looked away. He shouldn't speak about

Mabis out loud. It made something inside him threaten to break, like a dam holding back water. "You and Pima should go back down to the village as soon as you can. Dassen will take you in. I don't want you staying here—with these people."

There was a pause.

"No," Skyla said.

"No what?"

"Just no. I'm not leaving the coven." A spark of anger flared in her voice. "I'm not going to spend my life washing cups at Dassen's just because you've decided to die some stupid death."

"You'd let Pima live with people who say Mabis tried to murder a whole village?"

Skyla's pale eyes flashed. "This place is good for her—you'd see that if you thought of anyone besides yourself. She'll have friends her own age, and she's learning things, and there's plenty of food here."

"She's miserable!"

"She'd be miserable anywhere. She misses her mother." Skyla stood up and paced the floor, hugging herself against the cold. "Pima could do a lot worse than grow up a witch, Ryder. What else can she become? A farmer's wife? The witches were wrong about Mabis, I can see that. But not all witchcraft is wrong."

Ryder sheathed the Baenkiller and stood up. "Until

Mabis gets back, I am the head of this family," he said, softly but firmly.

"No!" she said, her voice just as firm. "If you want to be the head of this family, you have to be here."

Ryder gritted his teeth. It was too simple to believe that he took after his mother and that Skyla took after Fa. At that moment his sister was all Mabis—stubborn, hard as iron. Ryder had that vein of iron in himself, too, and recognized it when he saw it.

"You just want to be a witch yourself," he grumbled. "You don't care about Pima."

The hard look on her face turned to pity, and she tried to take his arm. "I wish I could explain it to you, Ryder. I wish I could make you understand."

"I understand. You want to see the future and have everybody bow at you."

She sighed and turned away, and he could see that she was biting back more harsh words. She leaned out over the railing. After a while, he came to join her, both of them looking out into the frigid blackness.

"Oh, look!" she cried. As they watched, the chilling clouds parted, revealing a patch of brilliant sky. They both stared—stars were a rare sight in winter. Ryder knew he should be moved. "Yulla says that when the Goddess made the world she threw the stars into the sky like a casting, and that the witches of old could read a person's destiny in the stars the same way they read the bones."

"Any star tries to tell me my destiny, I will wrench it from the sky."

Skyla laughed at that. "Of course you will." She slipped her arm through his and put her head on his shoulder. Below them on the mountain, the branches of bare trees clicked together in the frozen wind.

"You'll need tinder and flint, I guess," she said after a while, "and a better pair of gloves. I know of a storage shed not far from here. There is no guard."

He nodded. "Thank you."

"If there really is a black magician out there, he'll stop your heart with a curse and feed your body to his dread-hound."

"Sounds like a story of Dassen's." But after all Ryder had seen, Dassen's stories didn't seem so far-fetched anymore. *Never mind*, he thought. The Baenkiller could stop hearts too.

"You look different in the starlight," Skyla murmured, looking up at him. "Your face is hard as stone."

"Not the stars' fault," Ryder said. "They're gone." He pointed at the blank sky, but his sister's eyes didn't leave his face.

"Ryder—"

"Let's go," he interrupted, tired of talk. In his mind he was already over the border, tracking the Baen, making him pay.

PART TWO

When you sing the winter keys, do not forget:
They are also singing you.

—Baen saying

CHAPTER 10

HAUNTED

Don't go to sleep.

Falpian sat cross-legged on the rug, trying to keep his eyes open. A fire crackled in the grate. The wind rattled the glass in the small, square windows. Outside there was nothing but blackness and snow, hurrying down, hurrying down. His shoulders drooped, and his tired mind drifted from one thought to another. He was thinking about being buried in snow. How soft it would be. Like a down coverlet. At home he used to watch the snow from his window; it fell into the sea and disappeared. Here was different. It had been coming down all day and into the night. Great drifts were inching up the sides of the house, erasing him.

Falpian sighed. He should be sinking into real down coverlets right now. He should be letting sleep cover him in drifts. The humming stone sat on the floor in front of him. It seemed to stare at Falpian like a malevolent gray eye. He stared back. The stone was average-looking. Only a few lines of writing scratched over its surface distinguished it from an ordinary river rock. After a while, Falpian's vision began to blur, and the object became part of the intricate pattern of the rug, like a gray island in an ocean of curling embroidered waves. *Don't go to sleep!*

In one corner of the room, Bo snorted but didn't wake up. He lay with his legs splayed open and his belly showing. Lucky dog. Falpian rolled his head in a circle, listening to his neck crack. He shook out his shoulders. Might as well begin. Praying was a last resort; he'd tried everything else.

Falpian leaned forward and blew a long, even breath over the humming stone. Nothing. He tried again. This time he felt it awaken. As yet, the stone made no sound that he could hear, but in his corner, Bo opened one eye.

Hesitantly Falpian tested his voice. A note. Then another. As he sang, the stone on the floor began to release its own distinctive humming—*thrum, thrum, thrum*—so far, so good. The dog was fully awake now. He crouched low to the floor and looked up at Falpian with round, intelligent eyes. The humming of the stone grew louder. On the mantel, a set of little iron figurines twisted back and forth with the vibrations. Still good. Falpian didn't know why he was so scared—he'd done this a hundred times— but something had happened to him in the four days since the chilling, something he couldn't understand. Not even singing could quell the rising panic in his heart. Sometimes he even thought it made it worse.

Falpian's voice merged with the sound of the stone, getting stronger and more confident, one note winding around another. He was ready now. In a booming voice, he began the low, sad notes of the prayer for the dead.

The song struck him, as it always did, as too beautiful. It had no words, only sounds. They should have been harsh and ugly, full of grief. But they weren't. It was painful the way the prayer made his heart lift. Here at Stonehouse, Falpian had learned to love singing as never before, and the guilty joy of it made his voice ring in the night like a sad and beautiful bell.

My brother, he thought as he sang. *I feel your angry spirit. I have been selfish, reveling in my newfound magic when I should have been in mourning. I have not sung you half as many prayers as you deserve. I know that you must be the presence I've been feeling on this mountain. I know that you must be sending me these dreams. But please, what has happened to make them so full of malice? I will go mad of them. Please . . .*

A wall of feeling struck Falpian in the chest. Hatred. Pure hatred. For a moment he was somewhere else entirely, not Stonehouse, but some dark, cold place. He looked around, terrified, but all he saw was blackness. He reached out a hand and felt snow. Falpian stopped singing, and the vision abruptly faded. On the floor, the humming stone was still vibrating.

This was wrong, all wrong. The song of the stone should have begun to fade as soon as Falpian closed his mouth, but instead it grew louder and louder, rising in pitch until it reached a deafening whine. Falpian put his hands over his ears. Bo was running around and around the room, his huge gray body knocking over chairs, making the candles teeter on the tables. Falpian could see the dog's jaws opening and shutting, but his bark was swallowed up by the piercing shriek of the stone.

There was a loud bang from one of the windowpanes, and the humming finally stopped. Falpian sat wide-eyed in the abrupt silence. He rubbed at his arms, still cold from the brief vision he had experienced. What had happened? He'd studied the principles of magic nearly all his life, but had never heard of a humming stone doing that—not with only one singer. He poked at it tentatively. The stone was hot to the touch, and there was a small burned spot on the rug. He got up and examined the window by the door. A diagonal crack split the thick, bumpy glass. Had the sound of the stone done that?

In the bedroom, Falpian caught a glimpse of himself in the mirror: dark circles under his eyes, black hair greasy and wild. He looked haunted. He climbed into bed with his clothes on and pulled the covers around him. Bo started to bark again. Falpian could see him through the archway of the bedroom door. His paws were up on the sill of the cracked window. Bark, bark, bark, as if there were something out there in the blackness. The dog looked back at him wistfully; clever as he was, he couldn't work the latch to the outside door with those big paws.

"Go to sleep, Bo."

Falpian pulled the covers over his head. Let the dreams come; he didn't care. Being awake was getting to be as bad as dreaming.

Squinting into the morning, Falpian pulled shut the door of the stone cottage. The cold air bit his face, and his white breath was torn away by the gusting wind—but at least the blizzard of the night before had finally stopped. Chilling clouds tinged the world lavender, even the snowdrifts. Falpian missed the sky already—he missed blue—and winter had only just begun.

Bo bounded away from him, oblivious to the cold. A dreadhound was made for snow: long, shaggy coat for warmth, big snowshoe paws. He found his favorite tree and lifted one leg. Too late, Falpian remembered the chamber pot still sitting under his bed. He'd never realized how many little annoying tasks servants had been doing for him all his life. He'd empty it later.

It was the dog's fault he was up so early. Falpian had

slept, actually slept—two hours at least. Bliss. He could have gone on and on for days. The dreams hadn't come. Nothing had come except a numbing white sleep. But Bo—stupid dog—had dragged all his covers off, had breathed doggy breath into his face, slobbered doggy slobber.

"Come on back now. It's too cold. You can hunt later." Maybe Falpian would be able to get back to sleep, back to that numb white place. Bo looked at him with knowing eyes but didn't come. He rubbed one of his long saber teeth against a sapling; he was a lazy dog, but he always kept his teeth sharp.

"I know you understand me, bad thing."

Bo wasn't listening now. His pointed ears were swiveling back and forth as if he had caught some impossibly dim sound. He took a long sniff of the air. Then, without warning, he took off, kicking up sprays of snow with his powerful hind legs.

"Bo!"

As Falpian followed through the powdery drifts, he thought of the night before, of that wall of overpowering hatred he had felt when he tried to pray. Humming stones didn't do that, not on their own. There was definitely some sort of angry presence in these mountains.

"There was nothing I could have done to save you," he pleaded to the cold air. But if Falpian's brother was listening, he made no sign.

The dog was digging at the back of the house. He'd paw at a drift for a little while, sniff, look around, then dig at another—like he was looking for something. From the corner of his eye, Falpian caught the gleam of something metal and stopped short. A sword. A sword was leaning against a tree.

For a long time Falpian didn't move. Dreams were one thing, but this was something real. Solid. Could it have been there all along? he wondered. Could it have lain so close to the house all this time without his noticing? That seemed impossible. He turned a circle where he stood, but could see no footprints other than his own and the dog's. They were alone.

With new energy Falpian pushed forward through the drifts. He picked up the sword and brushed off the snow. It was a beautiful thing, worthy of his father's collection. Falpian pulled it from its leather scabbard and admired the blade—Witchlander make, without a doubt. He was about to slip it back into its sheath when, from out of the snow, something grabbed his boot.

"Kar's breath!"

The sword and scabbard flew out of Falpian's grasp as he launched himself backward into a snowdrift. Panicked, he floundered after the weapon, then turned back to the tree, expecting to see some witch warrior rise up, poised for attack. Nothing. Panting, he edged toward the area where the thing had touched him. It was still there, low to the ground, poking out of the snow—a gloved hand. He nudged it with the sharp tip of the sword. It was limp.

Keeping the weapon in readiness to strike, Falpian dug around the hand. There was a little cave under the snow, a little cave with branches for flooring. Inside, a large person was curled up in a ball. When he saw a shock of blond hair, Falpian jumped back again, pointing the sword. A Witchlander! The man wasn't conscious, though, and his lips had an alarming blue tint. Grabbing Falpian's leg must have taken his last bit of strength, a gesture to save his life, not an attack. He had dug himself a shelter—Falpian had read of this in survival texts. In the storm he must not have realized that he was only steps away from the house.

"That's quite a nose you've got, Bodread," Falpian said gravely. The dog sat a few footfalls away, gazing at him with unruffled curiosity. Falpian knew he should probably just turn around and walk back into the cottage. Either that or use the sword to end the stranger quick. Bo gave a whistling whine, stared at Falpian with liquid eyes.

"I know, I know, but we can't be soft. He could be a witch."

He wasn't wearing reds, though. And Falpian couldn't help but be reminded of another limp form, of a body washed up on the beach—hair matted, lips blue. The sudden vividness of the memory made him wince. Hadn't he wished a thousand times he could have done something to save his brother?

"All right, but just remember this was your idea," he told the dog.

He propped the sword up against the tree, then grabbed the stranger under the armpits and heaved. He was heavy. Probably pure muscle.

Both of the man's boots came off as Falpian struggled toward the house. The cold air was painful in his lungs, and by the time he reached his door, he was covered in icy sweat. Bo followed a few steps behind, wagging his tail like a flag.

Falpian pulled the heavy body through the kitchen, snagging the round carpet with the stranger's feet and dragging it along with them.

"Build up a fire," he ordered, forgetting for a moment that there was no servant to hear. When he got to the bedroom, he laid the stranger down on the floor and quickly threw some logs on top of the glowing embers. He unbuttoned the man's coat and lifted his arms from the sleeves. Then, grunting with the effort, he half pushed, half rolled him onto the bed.

Falpian didn't like what he had to do next, but he knew damp clothes could be deadly. He pinched the man's socks off one by one, keeping them at arm's length as he set them to dry on the bedroom fire screen. He decided to leave the shirt, but he had no choice about the leggings—they were soaked. Gingerly he undid the stranger's belt and pulled his leggings off at the ankles. Luckily he was wearing woolens underneath—and Falpian decided he wasn't *touching* those.

Bo jumped up and pressed his long body right up against the Witchlander's.

"Stop that, Bo," Falpian said. "Get down."

The dog stared at Falpian but didn't move. Nose to tail, he was even longer than the stranger. Falpian snapped his fingers and motioned to the floor, but Bo only blinked.

"Fine. Sleep with a Witchlander. Don't blame me if he gives you fleas."

He covered both man and dog with blankets and went outside to retrieve the boots and sword. When he came back to the bedroom, the stranger was already shivering. Shivering was good; it meant his body was warming up. But it also meant that Falpian didn't have long to decide what to do. He sat down at the edge of the bed to stare at the person he had found.

He was a Witchlander, all right, not some mixed-blood peasant or a Baen man tanned by the sun. Falpian had seen a few before. There were Witchlander sailors who sometimes traded illegally in the port cities, and a friend of his mother's had Witchlander servants from before the war. He'd never been so close to one, though.

Tentatively he reached out to touch the stranger's hair. It was so blond. Almost white, like an old man's. His eyes must be blue as sky, Falpian thought, but he didn't quite have the courage to open them up and look.

It's always best to assume the witches know every move we make, and every move we're going to make. Bron's words rang in Falpian's mind.

True, the stranger wasn't wearing reds, but the witches might have sent him, or he might be in disguise. It was a stupid thing Falpian had done, saving a Witchlander. After all, it wasn't just Bo and himself he was putting in jeopardy. It was the mission. It was whatever was in the scroll. This wasn't really his brother washed up on the shore. But then again . . .

"Bo, he's got no beard!"

The stranger was so big and broad that Falpian had assumed him to be a full-grown man. Now he wasn't sure. Witchlanders never shaved—everyone knew that—but the stranger's face was as smooth as a girl's. Relief swept over him. He'd done the right thing. The witches wouldn't send a boy, would they?

"Maybe he's just some farmer's son or goatherd lost in the snow. Maybe . . ."

The stranger opened his eyes, and Falpian jumped

from the bed with a cry. He'd been right. His eyes were blue. They were daggers made of sky.

For a long moment, Falpian stood frozen. As clear as a word in a book, he could read the hatred in the Witchlander's frigid gaze. It terrified him. Then the stranger's eyes fluttered. His head sank back against the pillow, and he was unconscious again. Falpian realized he'd been holding his breath.

"We're fools, Bo," he said coldly. "A goatherd or a farmer's boy wouldn't bring a sword."

All his doubts about what to do with the stranger had flown away.

CHAPTER 11

THE CROUCHING SPIDER

He was in a field of swaying golden plants with round berries growing close along the stem. He slid his hand down the stalks so that the berries came loose. One stalk, then another. He'd done this many times before. Falpian wasn't alone in this dream. Somewhere in the rows, a young man was singing in a deep, throaty baritone.

Falpian followed the voice down a hill, and as he went the soil under his feet grew sandy and white. The tall plants disappeared. *This is my dream now,* Falpian said to himself. The singing man was gone, but he still heard the echoes of the voice inside his head. In front of him was the ocean.

Falpian went to the very edge and let the waves lick over his bare toes. He knew this place. He came to the sea often in his dreams, to the place where his brother had drowned. "Hello?" he said. "Is someone there?" He never knew quite who he hoped would answer. Farien? Or some-one else that he'd been looking for?

Falpian waited. It was a perfect summer day: the sky infinite and blue, the water clear like glass. Then, a ripple, a shape. There was something out there. Something small and white was bobbing on the surface of the water. A bottle. A wave brought it to rest at his feet.

Falpian uncorked it and unrolled the note inside. It said, *I'm going to kill you.*

Falpian's eyes snapped open. It was late afternoon, and the room was growing dim. The chair he'd been dozing in was hard, and his back was sore.

"You're awake," he said. The young man in the bed didn't move, but somehow Falpian knew he was right. The time had come. He went over in his mind all the things he'd learned about conducting an interrogation. Falpian had never understood why his tutors made him memorize such things. Now he knew. They kept you from having to think too hard about what you were doing; they made it easier to do unpleasant things.

One: Secure the prisoner.

He stood up to check the Witchlander's restraints. While his captive slept, Falpian had placed an iron collar around his neck and attached it to a thick chain—it was Bo's collar and leash, but Falpian never made him wear it.

He had replaced the fastening pin of the collar with a tiny padlock from his jewel casket, and the chain he had secured around the slats of the headboard. He'd tied the prisoner's hands and feet as well, but those restraints were hidden by the blanket. Falpian wondered now if the blanket was a mistake, a kindness his father would have scorned.

Bo lifted his head as Falpian approached. He rolled over, showing his belly, and Falpian rubbed it with a sigh. Dreadhounds were a special breed. They were supposed to know things, have an almost human wisdom—or so it was said—and yet Bo had hardly left the stranger's side. He seemed to have no idea that the prisoner was an enemy, that he posed any kind of threat. Falpian adored his dog, but he was starting to agree with his father's assessment: Bodread the Slayer was a lapdog in a dreadhound's body.

"I know you're awake," Falpian said quietly. "I'm going to leave the room to let out my dog. When I come back, we will talk. Your chain is just long enough to reach the chamber pot, so if you want a moment of privacy, this is your only chance. As I'm sure you know by now, I've tied your hands and feet, but I think you'll manage."

There was no answer, no movement from the prisoner. Falpian snapped his fingers, and this time Bo obeyed, thumping to the floor with his tail wagging.

When Falpian returned, he carried a silver tray on which stood a cut-glass goblet and a glass decanter. The stranger was still in the bed, still exactly where he had been before. The chamber pot on the floor was empty, but all around it there were large, round blotches darkening the embroidered rug. The prisoner had pissed on the floor.

"The manners of Witchlanders are just as charming as I've always heard," Falpian said archly.

The prisoner turned and glared at him, the pretense of sleeping over. "Really?" He touched his collar with tied hands. "Because I find Baen hospitality a bit disappointing."

Falpian had to keep himself from stepping back. The hatred in the stranger's blue-eyed stare seemed to mingle with his dreams.

"That's necessary. I don't know who you are or why you're here. Explain yourself." The prisoner turned to the wall.

Falpian set down the tray on a small table out of reach of the prisoner's chain. He poured himself some water from the glass decanter and sat down. He wished the stranger would turn over and look at him; he'd deliberately chosen a glass that would catch the light.

Two: Develop a persuasive argument.

"You must be thirsty, after your ordeal. I've read that when someone is lost in the snow, the need for water can be just as dangerous as cold."

There was a pause. "Are you offering me a drink, or are you just talking?"

Falpian hesitated. "I don't mean to be cruel, but it would be foolish to give nourishment to someone who might be here to do me harm. If you tell me who you are and explain your reasons for crossing the border—"

The prisoner gave a short laugh. "Yes, yes, I understand now," he interrupted. "Thank you, but I'm not thirsty."

Falpian drank the water quickly and poured himself a second goblet full, holding the decanter high so the prisoner could hear the sound of the liquid splashing against the glass. "If your intentions were honorable, you would not hesitate to tell me what they were."

The stranger wriggled to a sitting position. "You can pour that water over your head for all the good it will do. Maybe I just don't want to explain myself to a blackhair who takes me prisoner for no reason."

Again, Falpian had to fight to hide his fear. How uncanny-looking Witchlanders were, with hair and eyebrows paler than their face. And were they all that big?

"You carry a sword," Falpian said. He made his voice clipped and efficient and told himself that his fear didn't show. "Surely you can see my position. I could have let you die out there in the snow, but I didn't. I may be a blackhair, but I saved your life."

The stranger shrugged. "I'm just a poor trader from Tandrass, if you must know. I was traveling to the villages along the border and became lost in the storm. As for the sword, I always carry it." He glared again. "Never know who you'll meet on the road."

Falpian allowed himself a faint smile. Carefully he set down his glass and leaned forward. "Liar," he said. "You're no trader. You are a hicca farmer. And this is the farthest you've ever been from home."

The stranger's mouth dropped open.

Three: Know the prisoner.

It was the hands that had given him away. Falpian had been careful to examine the prisoner's roughly made clothes, the little pouch filled with tinder and flint and a few strips of dried meat—but when he'd seen the calluses he'd known: Only years in the hicca fields could make someone's hands so rough. The part about being far from home was a guess, but a logical guess, and one that had paid off.

"Now, Witchlander," Falpian said softly. "Stop wasting my time. What is your name and why are you here?"

The prisoner must have been afraid all along, but for the first time Falpian saw it, saw it in the ashy tinge to his brown skin, saw it in the tight line of his mouth. Fear. Between them the air seemed to vibrate.

Suddenly something thudded against the bedroom window, and Falpian jumped in his chair. His hand knocked the water goblet, and it fell to the rug with a crash.

"Nervous, Baen?" the stranger asked.

It was Bo. He was standing on his hind legs, looking in at them through the tiny bedroom window, dog breath fogging up the square of glass.

Four: Control the setting.

Falpian had considered tacking blankets to the windows. He knew how important it was not to allow unexpected interruptions to distract the interrogation. Now he cursed himself for not doing it. The advantage he had gained by exposing the stranger's lie seemed to melt away.

Without speaking, he let Bo in. Covered in snow, the dog bounded into the bedroom.

"Bodread . . . ," Falpian whispered in frustration as Bo shook snow in every direction and began sniffing the wet spot on the rug. Before Falpian could stop him, the dog had lifted his back leg. "Bo, don't!" The dog made a small addition to the urine on the carpet.

Laughter burst from the prisoner. "Might as well join us, Baen," he said, nodding to the floor. "You must need to relieve yourself after all that water you drank."

Falpian felt his cheeks go red. The young man's laughter was forced, but that was no consolation. Falpian had definitely lost control of the setting. In fact, he had lost control of the interrogation. Quickly he gathered up the rug, roughly yanking one end that was caught under a leg of the bed.

"Perhaps it's time to take a little break," he said through clenched teeth. "You might find my dog amusing, but don't forget he is a dreadhound. At a word from me he'll tear out your throat." Falpian noted with satisfaction that his captive seemed to believe him: Though he tried to hide his fear, the stranger was eyeing the dog nervously.

"Bodread the Slayer," Falpian commanded. "Stay. If he moves, kill."

Bo, hearing his name, thumped his tail on the floor.

Falpian slammed shut the door of the bedroom and threw the soiled rug into a corner. As much as he would have liked to blame Bo, he knew the failure of his first interrogation was entirely his own fault.

Five: Be ready to harm and to kill if necessary.

The prisoner must have known that Falpian wasn't prepared, must have been able to sense it somehow. Of course, not every Baen interrogation had to involve torture and death, but Falpian had been taught that every interrogator must be prepared to take these steps. If he wasn't, the interrogation was likely to fail.

Quickly he bent through the little door of the kitchen pantry. Rows of tightly packed foodstuffs rose to the ceiling—bottles of marsh beer corked tight, preserved jellies covered in wax to keep them from spoiling. Falpian reached above the jars of pickled fruits to the high shelf where he had hidden the stranger's sword. Maybe seeing it would convince the prisoner he was serious. Maybe Falpian would only have to make a few cuts.

He swallowed and took the sword from its leather sheath. But how can a man prepare himself to do such things? Falpian's tutors hadn't said a word about that. Where did this revulsion come from? he wondered. This deep feeling that harming his prisoner would be wrong? When he was singing in the gorge, when he had held the lives of the birds in his hands, killing had seemed such an easy thing.

For the first time, Falpian thought he could understand the depths of his father's disappointment. It wasn't really about the magic. Falpian was like poor Bo, a lapdog at heart. For so long he'd felt that if he could only have the gift of magic, this feeling of being a failure would fall away from him like a shed skin. But Falpian had magic now. He could sing. And yet he was still himself. His father, if he were here, would still be wearing that look on his face as if he'd eaten something sour. There was a weakness inside of Falpian, a wretched kindness he must have gotten from his mother. He saw it now through his father's eyes, and self-loathing coursed through his veins. If he had known where in his body this weakness lay, he would have driven the sword right through.

Falpian looked down at the weapon in his hand and noticed the notches on the hilt. The Witchlander had taken lives, he realized. He would always have the upper hand until Falpian was as ready to kill as he was.

Be ready to harm and to kill if necessary. Be ready . . .

Falpian left the pantry. With the sword shaking in his hands, he kicked open the bedroom door.

The stranger was not in the bed.

The headboard where the chain was attached had been broken in one snap like a stick of kindling. But the prisoner couldn't have left the house: The glass in the bedroom window was undamaged, and the door in the kitchen was the only way out. The stranger had to be in the study.

"Useless, stupid dog!" Falpian hissed to Bo. "Can't you even bark?" Bo cocked his enormous head.

From where Falpian stood he could see both doors into the study—the one from the kitchen and the one from the bedroom. "I hope you will remember that I saved your life," Falpian called. He cursed himself for hesitating in the pantry while the prisoner made his escape. "I only did what anyone in my place would do."

He took a deep breath and charged through the bedroom, throwing open the study door with a bang. It, too, was empty. On the floor were some shards of glass and coils of rope. The prisoner had used the broken pieces of the water goblet to cut his bonds. Clever. Quick.

Falpian made the circle again: kitchen, bedroom, study, kitchen. Bo followed as if it were a game. Though he had been gone only moments, when Falpian re-entered the kitchen, the door to the outside was wide open and the stranger's boots weren't in their place by the fire. How on earth?

"Curses of Kar," said Falpian. He stood in the door frame in his stocking feet and waved the sword at empty air. The storm had started up again. A ledge of new snow came up to his knees, and the prints Bo had made earlier were already gone.

Footprints. There were no footprints! If the stranger had gone out, where were his? Falpian quickly pushed shut the door and leaned his back against it. Oh Kar above, he must be a witch, a real red-wearing, throat-cutting witch—everyone knew they could appear and disappear at will, tell the future, walk on water.

A thorough search convinced Falpian that he was truly alone and that the open door was not just a ruse. He checked and rechecked: under the bed, behind the doors, in the pantry. He looked out each window, but all around the cottage, the snow was fresh and untouched.

He sat down at the kitchen table and pulled his knees up to his chest, a feeling of cold dread chilling his blood. Falpian might not know where the stranger was, but the stranger certainly knew where he was. In front of him on the table, the notches on the sword hilt seemed to mesmerize him: one, two, three, four, five. . . . How could such a young man have killed so many?

Quickly he got up and returned the sword to its hiding place. It was too heavy for him to use effectively if it came to a fight, and besides, Falpian had a better weapon than that. His own weapon. A Baen weapon.

With the humming stone in his hand, he sat down cross-legged in front of the kitchen fire and tried to steady his mind. Outside, the fir tree groaned in the wind. Above him, a board in the roof made a creaking sound. Then again: *rieeeeek*. Falpian smiled. What a fool he had been—a disappearing witch indeed.

Falpian awakened his stone. It came alive with the first breath, as if impatient for magic. In a corner of the room, Bo lifted his head.

When Falpian was about twelve years old, he and Farien had been called into their father's study. Gently, and with great formality, their father had taken a stone out of a velvet pouch and laid it on the desk in front of them— a gift. A loaded gift.

The Witchlander was on the roof, of course. Falpian could see him now with the vision singing gave him. He was squatting by the chimney, wearing just his shirt and his woolens, the long chain still hanging from his neck. How patient he was. The snow collected on the top of his head and on his arms. Only his eyelids opening and shutting showed that he was alive. And his heart—that was moving too.

Humming stones were costly items, and yet their father must have hoped that Falpian and his brother wouldn't have it for long. A talented singer pair would be too powerful; their harmonies would crack a stone with the strength of their merged voices. But through the years, the stone remained pristine.

Falpian sang louder, and louder still. His voice felt limber and strong. How proud his father would be if he could reach out with his voice and stop the stranger's heart. Beside him Bo whimpered and cried, pulling at Falpian's clothes with his teeth, but Falpian was too focused to be distracted. *I could do it,* he thought. *I could kill this Witchlander.* The simple harmonies he could make with the stone weren't as powerful as those at the echo site, but they were powerful enough. His father would tell him that he *should* do it.

And then a curtain was drawn back. Sitting on the floor, Falpian felt his eyes grow wide, but he wasn't seeing what was in front of him; he wasn't even seeing the young man on the roof. Disconnected images flew at him like tangled dreams: a laughing girl, a woman with black lips, a horse struggling in a pool of its own blood. Falpian closed his eyes, squeezed them shut, but the pictures still came. Emotions hit him in the chest like a blow. Grief. Such raw, angry grief. And something else hit him too: the shock of recognition. *I know this anger,* he thought. *I know this grief. I know you.*

Then, in an instant, the images, the feelings, were gone. When Falpian turned his mind back to the roof, the stranger seemed small and alone, not a muscle-bound witch, but something delicate and short-lived, like a crouching spider.

Falpian stopped singing and opened his eyes. He got up and pulled at the door, ignoring as best he could the blast of cold air. Gingerly he stepped out into the snow in his stocking feet, hearing the door close behind him.

"Come down," he called. "It's too cold." The stranger could see him but didn't move. "I'm sorry. I used the chain because I was afraid of you. Perhaps I should be. But I'm not a killer, and I don't want to harm you."

Without hesitation, the stranger stood up and, in one fluid motion, threw himself off the roof, straight at Falpian.

CHAPTER 12

ASSASSIN'S HEART

The Witchlander had him down in the snow and was yelling into his face, something loud and guttural, full of fury.

Falpian flailed and twisted, almost slipping out between the stranger's legs before being rammed down hard again. The stranger straddled him, pinning his arms. His face was red from exertion, and he weighed as much as a bull.

Falpian continued to struggle, kicking up sprays of snow. When one arm became free he clawed at his attacker's eyes, but the stranger quickly pinned his arms again. He was still yelling something, but somehow fear had taken away Falpian's ability to understand words.

From inside the house, Falpian heard the sound of frantic barking. Bo! Hope warmed him for a moment. But no, even a dreadhound couldn't get through that heavy door.

Falpian's breath hurt in his lungs—he could barely

move. The stranger's face hardened to a look of cold determination, and he leaned down, pressing the length of icy chain against Falpian's throat. Falpian struggled again with renewed energy. He couldn't believe that there was nothing he could do. *I'm not a killer, and I don't want to harm you.* What a stupid thing to say. Why not tell the Witchlander all his weaknesses?

Finally Falpian stopped struggling, exhausted. The world quieted. The snow fell. He began to shiver, but with cold or fear he didn't know. This person would take his life. Falpian would never see his mother again. He would never again collect rattle shells with his sisters, or weave them little boats out of the eelgrass.

"Please," he said again, not caring about the icy tears at the corner of his eyes. "I'll give you anything you want."

"Did you make them?" the stranger demanded hoarsely. He was panting, and Falpian could see a vein pulsing in his neck.

"What?"

"Did you make those things? Tell me, or I will kill you right now."

Falpian didn't know what to say. "Things?" He could hardly hear his own voice.

"The gigantic things!" The Witchlander was almost shouting now. "That come from nothing . . . that come up out of the ground!"

Falpian racked his brain, desperate to say the thing that would keep him alive. "Trees?"

It was definitely the wrong answer. The stranger's face flushed with anger, and the chain tightened against Falpian's neck.

"I'm very sorry," Falpian croaked, "but I don't know what you're talking about."

To his surprise, the Witchlander didn't kill him, but sat back on Falpian's waist, something that might have been grief contorting his features. Falpian brought his hands to his throat. For a brief moment it looked as if the stranger would start to sob, but it was only a moment, and Falpian could have been wrong.

"I know you don't," the stranger said grimly. "I don't know how I know it, but I do."

Abruptly the stranger stood up, and Falpian was left to stare at the snowflakes swirling down from a bruise-colored sky. He took a deep, racking breath. His feet were soaking wet, and there was snow all the way up the back of his shirt. When he sat up, he felt the pull of a strained muscle in his shoulder.

"You'd better have a key for this collar," the stranger told him, heading for the door.

When they went inside, Bodread the Slayer was waiting for them. He sat rigid in the middle of the floor, growling, black lips curled. The stranger gave a shout and backed up against the door frame.

"Bo," Falpian cried. "What's wrong?"

The dog glared at him, saber teeth gleaming, and in that moment Falpian saw a real dreadhound in front of him: brutal and deadly. The saber teeth were impressive, but Falpian knew the other teeth could do as much damage: rows of sharp white incisors, big molars at the back for crushing bone.

Bo gave Falpian and the stranger two angry barks—one each—then turned and went to the fireplace, where he promptly flopped himself down and stretched out in front of the grate.

Falpian couldn't be sure, but it felt for all the world like he'd been scolded.

"Bodread really is quite harmless," he said nervously, only half believing it himself. He couldn't help but notice the deep claw marks that raked the wood all around the door latch.

"Key!" the Witchlander demanded, holding out the chain that was still hanging from the collar at his neck.

Falpian didn't think he could refuse. He retrieved the key and, with shaking hands, fit it into the lock at the stranger's throat. When the collar was finally off, the Witchlander hurled the entire thing—chain, padlock, and all—out into the snow.

Falpian wasn't sure what to do next. Was he the prisoner now? he wondered. But the stranger made no move to restrain him, only stood awkwardly at one side of the room, rubbing his neck where the collar had been.

After a moment, he turned to Falpian. "Why are you here?" he asked sharply.

"Why are *you*?" Falpian countered. "You're the one on the wrong side of the border."

He didn't expect an answer, but after a long silence the Witchlander shot him a stricken look. "There's a Baen in my head." His voice shook, and his strange eyes were red rimmed. "It's you . . . isn't it?"

Oh, Falpian thought. *Of course.* All that talk about trees coming up out of the ground. The stranger was a madman.

"Sit down," he said gently. "You must be hungry."

But the Witchlander had spied the barrel of snowmelt Falpian kept by the fire. He quickly crossed the room and sank down in front of it, drinking deeply. Falpian felt a twinge of guilt. All the things he'd done to this man—and he was just a poor lunatic.

"I'm sorry," he murmured.

After a pause, the stranger turned and looked at him, wiping his mouth with the back of his hand. "For what?"

"For . . . tying you up, for not giving you any water."

"Seems logical to me. I did come to kill you."

Falpian's guts turned to ice. The Witchlander stood up,

but still he made no move against Falpian. Instead he went to one of the windows by the kitchen table and squinted out, as if the trees themselves might be watching.

"There are no other Baen in the area? Just you?" His voice grew suddenly harsh. "I'll know if you're lying."

Falpian kept his voice light. "No Baen but me."

The Witchlander frowned and sat down in front of the fire, taking care to leave plenty of room between himself and Bo. He seemed too big for the chair—all knees and hands and elbows. Falpian wondered again how old he was and decided that in spite of their difference in size, they were probably the same age. Poor fellow must have wandered away from his keepers. Or perhaps Witchlanders didn't care for their sick—just sent them out into the snow to die.

Falpian went to stir the cauldron on the hob and was surprised to see that the fish stew he'd set to warm before the interrogation was only a little burned. It seemed like an age ago. He ladled white glops of it into two wooden bowls and handed one to his guest.

"My name's Falpian."

The stranger took the bowl eagerly with shaking hands. "Is it?"

Falpian sat down with his own portion. Bo turned onto his back and lazily pawed the air as if he had never been that other dog, that menacing dreadhound with the flashing teeth. Falpian rubbed his belly with his foot. The stranger eyed them both warily, and Falpian could see he was trying to hide his fear, trying to act as if sitting by the fire with a dreadhound was nothing to him. Something about this bravado made Falpian almost like him.

"What is this?" the Witchlander asked, turning the stew over with his spoon.

"A Baen dish. Salted fish cooked in fish eggs." The stranger grimaced, but he took a bite. "It's not usually so coagulated."

The Witchlander seemed to shudder as he swallowed, but he managed to eat the whole bowl and even helped himself to more. After that, they sat in silence, taking turns feeding logs to the fire. Darkness fell, and the wind howled around the house. *What am I going to do with him?* Falpian wondered. Being mad didn't make the Witchlander less dangerous. In fact, it probably made him more so. Falpian was well aware that the stranger's mood could turn at any moment—and then Falpian would be at his mercy. What if he wanted to stay all winter?

"Are you sure you don't want to tell me your name?" he asked. "Or anything about yourself?"

The Witchlander turned those piercing eyes on him again. "There's an assassin in these mountains," he said. "I have to stop him."

Falpian nodded and looked to the floor. It seemed

prudent to agree with everything he said. "Did the Baen in your head tell you that?"

"I thought it was you. But then . . . I heard your thoughts when you were singing."

"Heard my thoughts?" Falpian repeated. Maybe it was a mistake to ask the stranger so many questions. He stood up and started to collect the dirty bowls. "That's . . . interesting." He was reaching for a spoon when the Witchlander grabbed him by the wrist.

"Don't believe me?" he hissed.

The pulled muscle in Falpian's shoulder twinged, and the grip on his wrist was painful, but he made himself look into the Witchlander's eyes. He'd been avoiding them, he realized, they were so bright and strange, but now he looked deep. He saw no madness there. Only sorrow and pain.

"I heard your thoughts," the stranger said again. "And you don't have an assassin's heart."

The truth of the statement hit Falpian like a slap. He could almost imagine his father nodding in agreement.

"Well." He yanked his hand away. "How lucky for you." The stranger stood up abruptly and Falpian flinched, almost dropping the bowls.

"I'll stay the night and leave at dawn," the Witchlander said. He stepped over Bo to get to the bedroom door.

"All right," Falpian answered. He was in no position to argue.

"And my name's Ryder."

"Nice to—" The door slammed.

Falpian let out a hiss of annoyance. "By all means, take my bed," he muttered.

CHAPTER 13

DREADHOUNDS

Outside Falpian's cottage, Ryder stood in the dawn light, his arms reaching up to the sky. *I greet the sun, I am the sun,* he thought—the first words of Aata's prayer, words that were never spoken aloud.

The last time Ryder had seen his mother, she was praying. She was standing in the clearing, her feet bare, her arms outstretched, when Ryder came out of the barn with his mended fishing nets. He couldn't get the picture out of his mind; she hadn't prayed since he was a little boy.

Ryder tried to set thoughts of his mother aside and concentrate. The chilling clouds were low and dark, threatening more snow, and the great white mountain seemed to hunch under their weight. It was the same mountain Ryder had known all his life, but it looked so foreign and strange now, with its crooked spire reversed.

He bent backward, holding the position for as long

as he could. He didn't know much about praying, but he knew you were supposed to be silent inside and out, empty of thought, a vessel for the Goddess. He came up slowly, put his palms up to the sky, and lifted one bent leg behind him, keeping his eyes fixed on the mountain for balance. *I greet the air, I am the air.*

You should be resting.

On such a beautiful morning? Mabis had said. *Aata performed her prayers until the last day of her life.* His mother's hair had been a tangled mass, her skin yellowish and pale, but she'd smiled, and her eyes seemed clear and bright again. She was happy. *Go get my fish, Ryder—a big one.*

Ryder came out of the sun position and shook out his arms, then kneeled down with his hands in the snow, pressing his forehead to the ground. *I greet the earth, I am the earth.*

He had stopped on the river path to watch his mother pray. She was still as flexible as she had always been, bending backward in the sun position until her golden hair nearly brushed the ground. He'd marveled at the joy prayer seemed to bring her, at how beautiful she still was.

An old legend from his childhood had come back to him at that moment—a legend about Aata. It was said that at the end of her life, the great witch had disappeared during her morning prayers. While greeting the sun, she had made the gestures so perfectly, so silently, that she became sunlight itself and was never seen again. As a child, Ryder had been frightened of that story. Once, in the days before Pima, before Skyla, before he could reach the latch on the door to the cottage, he had believed in such things. He hated to watch his mother pray because of that legend, always afraid that she might vanish like that herself one day, always afraid that her edges would turn bright before his eyes and she would disappear in a flash of gold.

Ryder shivered on his hands and knees, tears melting pockmarks into the snow. *I should have stayed there watching her forever,* he thought. *I should have known somehow that I'd never see her again.* He wiped fiercely at his eyes. He had thought that praying might tell him what to do, but it only seemed to strip him bare, leave him shaking like a sapling in the winter wind.

A great, smelly wetness slimed across his face, and Ryder recoiled in disgust. The dog. The beast of a dog was licking him with that obscene tongue. Ryder backed away on his knees, rubbing his face with the sleeve of his coat. The creature sat in the snow in front of him, its head cocked to one side.

If Ryder had been asked to design the ugliest thing he could imagine, he could not have come up with anything better than the face of Bodread the Slayer. It was both terrifying and silly, like a child's picture of a monster— black lips, huge girlish eyes mostly covered by scraggly gray hair, and those teeth, those enormous unlikely teeth that curved down from his upper jaw. If the Goddess did exist, what could she have been thinking when she created such a thing?

The dog came toward him again with its enormous tongue, a long strand of drool leaking from the corner of his mouth.

"Oh no, no, no. Thank you, I'm feeling much better." Ryder laughed and quickly stood up. He reached out a hand to pat the dog's head, but then he drew it back, remembering the snarling creature he'd seen the day before. This was a dreadhound, after all. When the Baen magicians attacked Barbiza and Tandrass in their black ships, the dreadhounds were the first to come ashore, tearing out the throats of everyone in their path. For all Ryder knew, a dreadhound might have killed his own grandfather. He started to turn away, but then remembered Dassen's advice—never turn your back on a dreadhound—and walked backward toward the Baen's cottage.

The Witchlander slammed the door and glared at Falpian. "I want some answers."

Those eyes again. Ryder's gaze made Falpian want to shield his face; it was too early to be stared at by eyes so bright. "Answers to what?"

"You had a dream last night. Don't try to deny it."

Ryder sat down across from Falpian at the table.

Was this more madness? Why would Falpian deny his dreams? He hadn't slept well on the study couch, but he had slept. And there *had* been dreams: confused, meaningless dreams. "How did you know? Did I call out in my sleep?"

"You can't control them, can you?"

"What?"

"Your dreams."

"Control my dreams?" Falpian laughed nervously. "I'd bash my head in with a candlestick if I thought it would help." He sat back in his chair and tried to act friendly, casual. After all, Ryder had said he was leaving that morning. Falpian just had to keep him calm for a little while longer. "Can you people control your dreams?"

Ryder scowled but didn't answer. Outside, Bo galloped up to the window and peered in at them, his ugly face warped and distorted by the glass. He barked plaintively. When Falpian and Ryder made no move to come out, he went away again, nose to the ground.

Falpian got up slowly, muscles aching from yesterday's fight. "Eat before you go. I'm heating up the fish-egg stew."

Ryder was still glaring at him, his brown face hard, but when Falpian looked more closely, he saw how tired he looked, and sad. An unexpected twinge of pity went through him. Ryder's coat looked like an old blanket lined with fur that someone had sewn arms onto—in fact, that was probably what it was. And he was about to go out in the snow in that, to who knew where.

Falpian sighed and went to the fire, slopping stew into two bowls. If he let this poor lunatic leave, wouldn't it be the same as killing him? But then, Ryder was just a Witchlander, after all.

"Here," he said, putting one bowl in front of Ryder and the other at his own place.

Ryder's lips curled at the sight of the stew, but he dutifully began to eat. "Why are you living here in the middle of nowhere?" he asked, his mouth full.

Falpian frowned, spreading his napkin on his lap. "This *is* Baen land."

"But where are your people?" Ryder pointed his dirty spoon like a weapon, making Falpian flinch. "What's the purpose of this place? Are you a spy?"

Falpian felt annoyance prickling at him. He took a while to answer, pretending to be savoring the first taste of his breakfast, which in fact was a bit too burned and chewy to really enjoy. "There's no reason I should tell you my business." Immediately he regretted his words. What was he doing? Only madmen got into arguments with other madmen.

"I told you mine," Ryder said.

"When?"

"I'm looking for an assassin. A witch predicted he would be here."

Falpian froze. *Oh Kar above*, he thought. "You didn't mention witches before."

Ryder shrugged, but Falpian was struggling to hide his fear. Maybe it wasn't madness that had sent Ryder over the border. Maybe the witches knew something. After all, Falpian *could* be an assassin. If the message in the scroll said to kill somebody, he would do it—or try, anyway. Whether he had an assassin's heart or not.

Falpian dabbed his face with his napkin and tried to make his voice indifferent. "This witch didn't say anything more than that?"

Ryder hesitated, and Falpian watched the hard look on his face turn to confusion. "I don't know," Ryder said finally. "I don't know anything. I thought the Baen in my head and the assassin were the same person, but . . . the prophecy was so confused!" He lowered his voice to a whisper. "He's evil, I know that. He can make monsters. They're made of mud. They come from nothing!"

Falpian stifled a nervous laugh. Just when he was starting to think Ryder was sane! Monsters? Made of mud? It sounded like a tale of the gormy man come to life.

Ryder didn't miss his disbelief. "Don't change the subject," he snapped. "We're talking about you, not me." The Witchlander leaned forward, his chair creaking.

"You're telling me what you're doing here, Baen."

Falpian shrank back a little, both alarmed and annoyed by the note of threat in Ryder's tone. He knew it was wrong to use Farien's death to hide his mission, but he didn't think he had much choice. Besides, it was *a* reason he was here—just not the only reason.

"I am in mourning, if you must know," he said. "That's what Stonehouse is for. I'm supposed to spend a hundred days here. Meditating and praying and such . . ." He paused, but further explanation seemed necessary. "My twin brother Farien died this summer."

He expected the usual display of sympathy, but Ryder only turned back to his stew, grunting into his bowl. "Well, that must be nice."

"Pardon me?"

"It must be nice to have the whole world stop for you just because someone in your family died—we don't all get that, you know."

Falpian slammed his hand on the table, making the wooden bowls jump. "You wouldn't understand. He wasn't just my brother; he was my talat-sa. It's a very . . . it's a very complicated relationship that you couldn't begin to understand. We shared our dreams. . . ."

Ryder's eyes narrowed to slits of blue light. He carefully put down his spoon. "What exactly do you mean, shared your dreams?"

But Falpian was in no mood to say anything more. "It's private," he snipped.

Ryder leaned forward again, but before he could speak, a long, low howling came from somewhere outside. Falpian had heard his dog's hunting howl many times, the mournful wail he gave right before he took off after prey, but this was different somehow—angrier and less musical. Something about it sent cold fear up Falpian's spine. Both he and Ryder leapt from their chairs.

Sleet blew into Falpian's face like pinpricks. "Bo! Bo!" He ran around the side of the house, snow filling up his unlaced boots. "Come here, Bo!"

Ryder came up behind Falpian, and the two stopped and looked around, trying to work out from which direction the howl had come. Falpian clutched his coat closed around the neck, half blinded by the sleet. *Please, Kar,* he thought, *don't let anything happen to my dog.*

"There!" said Ryder. He grabbed Falpian's elbow and pointed.

Across the plateau, just before the sheer drop that marked the edge of the gorge, two dreadhounds were slung low, circling each other. Bo was by far the smaller, a puny gray blotch against the white snow.

"Someone's brought a dog," said Falpian, curious but relieved. Whoever it was must be Baen.

"The assassin," Ryder said darkly.

"No! Kar's sake! It's probably just a messenger from my father." At that moment the two dogs launched themselves at each other, snarling wildly. "Bo!" This was madness. Bo couldn't fight. "Hello!" Falpian shouted to the master he knew must be somewhere near. "Please! Call off your dog!"

The two animals were a blur of teeth and tails and blowing snow. A high-pitched yelp sounded—Bo had been bitten!

"Bodread!" Falpian staggered forward.

"Where are you going?" Ryder grabbed his arm. "Without a weapon they'll both tear you apart!"

Falpian nodded—a weapon. He raced back into the house and stumbled to the pantry, boots slipping on floorboards. He grabbed Ryder's sword from where he'd hidden it. A jar of pickled fruit fell off the shelf with a crash, but Falpian left it where it was.

Harrooooo! Bo's shrieking howl seemed to quiver through the house. The sound was so full of fear and pain that Falpian let out a cry. He flew back out through the door, almost crashing into Ryder.

"Go back! Go back inside!" the Witchlander shouted. "That thing's killed your dog and it's coming for us!"

"What!"

Ryder pulled at his coat, but Falpian staggered forward, clutching the sword to his chest. A huge, pale shape was galloping toward him out of the whirling sleet. Falpian wiped at his eyes.

At the edge of the plateau, something gray lay motionless.

"Oh," Falpian groaned.

He ran toward the attacking dreadhound, fumbling with the scabbard of the sword as he went. He raised the weapon over his head. The strange dog was almost upon him, its mouth open, its massive curved fangs ready to strike.

Then the creature gave a yelp. It faltered. Something was on its back.

"Kar's eyes!" Falpian shouted. He stopped, and Ryder was beside him in moments. Bo was on the dreadhound's back, gripping the larger animal with powerful claws.

"Never turn your back on a dreadhound," Ryder murmured, wonder in his voice.

With one swift movement of his head, Bo sank his long saber teeth into the other dog's throat. This was what the saber teeth were made for, Falpian knew, their one purpose—the jugular vein. Blood spurted from the wound, a surprise of red in the white landscape. Falpian put his hand over his mouth and stepped back. The dying dreadhound fell to its knees, trying frantically to shrug Bodread off. Quickly Bo yanked his teeth through the dog's neck, tearing the throat wide open. The dog collapsed heavily into the snow and was still.

Bo stood over his kill, muzzle dripping blood. He lifted his head and stared at Ryder and Falpian. For one brief moment, Falpian thought he would attack, but then Bo threw back his head and gave a howl of fearsome joy. *That's not my Bo*, Falpian thought. *That's not my lapdog.*

Somewhere near, another dreadhound answered Bo's howl. Then another. Ryder gripped Falpian by the arm.

"I hear them," Falpian said. He turned a circle where he stood, but could see nothing. "Two more dreadhounds. Maybe three." He thrust the sword into Ryder's hands. "Here. Take this."

"Where are you going?" Ryder called, but Falpian had already taken off at a run toward the path that led to the gorge. "You coward!" Ryder shouted. "I can't fight them on my own!"

CHAPTER 14

ASSASSIN'S KEY

Falpian skidded down the steep slope. The sleet was harder now, heavy drops that froze as they hit the ground. About a third of the way down the path, he stopped. He couldn't see Ryder, but he could hear Bo barking and snarling from up above. As quickly as he could, he climbed out toward the echo spot, hugging the icy rocks and shivering.

"Kar above," he hissed, half prayer, half curse. The ledge was slick with ice. With wobbling knees, he placed his boots onto the tiled footprints. He chose a winter key, one he could sing his fear into: the key of slivered glass. There was no time for hesitation. He took the deepest breath he could. And as soon as he began to sing, the world cracked open.

Winter keys were more dissonant, more deadly; Falpian had never sung them well. Now he was shocked by the cold strength of his own voice, shocked by the stark and stunning world his voice revealed. He made up the melody as he went, and the more he sang, the more clearly he could see the world. Below him, the trees were brittle with ice and glimmered like jewels. Sleet fell around him as if it were made of light.

Falpian turned his mind to Bo and Ryder on the ledge above, two small creatures in a sea of snow. He saw the dead dog at their feet. He saw Ryder's fear. He saw Bo's bloodstained saber teeth. He saw the other dreadhounds slinking around Ryder and Bo in ever-tightening circles. Falpian's brain was full, his brain was going to split, crack his skull. Sleet fell around him like stars; sleet hit his body like shards of glass. *I'll die of this*, he thought, but still he sang.

Falpian could hear so many hearts pounding in his ears—his, the dog's, Ryder's. Someone else's, too, someone near, someone hiding. One of the dogs lifted her head. They were all female, but this one was the lead, smarter than the others. She sensed the danger. Breaking off the attack on Ryder, she came bounding over the plateau toward Falpian and the echo site.

Falpian lifted his face to the cold sleet, reaching out his arms. He could feel the dreadhound's warm body racing toward him. Farther away, the two other dogs lifted their heads, understanding too late that invisible fingers gripped their hearts. Ryder and Bo shrank back, diminished in

Falpian's mind. Now all Falpian could see was his prey. *Who doesn't have an assassin's heart?* he thought. He closed his fists, and with a shudder of joy, he snuffed out three lives.

The music stopped, and Falpian found himself sitting on the stone ledge, gasping, the cold air like knives in his lungs. He wanted to laugh. Why did people shrink away from winter, he wondered, safe in their blankets, hiding by their fires? If they knew how beautiful winter really was, they would walk out naked into the snow, walk and walk, until their frozen hearts split open with joy.

He sat for a while, gripping the rocks, waiting for his vision to return. It took him a while to realize that the world had always been this dim, muddy gray, that his vision now was exactly as it had been before.

"Ryder?" he called. It was strange not to be able to see over the lip of the plateau, to be limited by his eyes. "Bo?" The enemy dogs were dead, Falpian was sure of that, but the master, the heartbeat he had detected when he sang . . . It was a common battle strategy for a man to send his dogs in first, then strike when chaos was at its highest; the master was still near.

Falpian inched back to the path, feeling like a blind man. He was afraid now. What had happened to him on the ledge was already beginning to seem unreal, like something he had read about, or seen from far away.

The body of the attacking dreadhound had slid partway down the path. Falpian approached her warily. Dead eyes stared at nothing. Her body was twisted in an unnatural position, pink belly exposed. *I know this dog,* Falpian thought. Surprised, he stepped forward.

Kneeling in the snow, he took hold of one of the dog's saber teeth, turning her head to the side. There was a dark patch on one of her ears, a small blotch like black ink.

"Kildread," he whispered. This was one of his father's dogs. She and Bo had shared a sire. Revulsion overcame him as he remembered the joy he'd felt at killing her. What was she doing here?

At that moment, he heard the clang of swords. Falpian clambered farther up the path until he could see over the edge. On the brink of the plateau, Ryder was fighting someone. It was Bron, his friend Bron.

This was all some terrible mistake. With expert swordsmanship the older man was driving Ryder closer and closer to the drop. Ryder was going to be killed.

"No! Please stop! Bron, stop!" Falpian heard the desperation in his own voice, and yet he hardly understood it. Why should he care so much if the Witchlander died?

Ryder glanced down, distracted by Falpian's words. Bron took the advantage and raised his sword, aiming a powerful blow at Ryder's skull.

"Watch out!" Falpian cried.

Just in time, Ryder ducked, and Bron's sword swung through vacant air. The Baen man lurched forward as the force of the empty blow upset his balance. He teetered on the edge.

"Ryder, help him!" Falpian shouted.

It was too late. Bron pitched forward over the brink, falling like tossed stone. Desperately, his arms flailed, grasping at nothing. Falpian turned his face away, but he heard the sickening thud as Bron hit the ground below.

The sleet was slower now, and Falpian's hair and clothes were stiff with ice. There was hardly any blood. Bron's legs didn't seem broken. Still Falpian knew, though he couldn't have said how, that the kennel master was near death.

"Bron," he said, voice breaking as he knelt in the crusted snow.

Pain twisted the man's scarred face. He struggled to lift his head, but after a moment it fell back again. "Strange. I thought I heard your father's voice."

"Shh. Don't try to talk."

"Assassin's magic. He was always best at winter keys."

"It was . . . It was only me." Bron didn't seem to hear, and Falpian didn't repeat himself. It felt like lying; the person on the ledge seemed like someone else.

Bron tried to lift himself again, wincing terribly with the effort. "The dogs. Where are my girls?"

"They're fine," Falpian lied, his voice shaking. "They're right here." He laid his hand over Bron's. "Don't try to move. I need to find a way to get you to the cottage."

"No. It's too late," Bron said. To Falpian's surprise, he seemed to smile at this, and his black eyes were full of warmth. "I'm glad I failed. I thank Kar I failed. It wasn't right."

"Failed?"

"I swear, I didn't know." He took a great, rattling breath. "I didn't know when I left you what I'd be asked to do."

Falpian sat back on his knees, clutching his coat around him. Nearby, the trees in the gorge swayed stiffly, their frozen branches clicking together in the wind.

"You tried to kill me," Falpian murmured. "You sent the dreadhounds to attack. You sent them to . . ." He shook his head. But why? Was it because Ryder was in the house? Did Bron think he was a traitor, conspiring with the enemy?

"Bron," Falpian said. "You're my friend. How could you think . . . ?"

Bron murmured something too soft to hear, and Falpian leaned forward. "The war is close, Falpian." He drew another ragged breath. "Men are being trained; black ships are being built in secret—you should know this now." Falpian glanced around, afraid Ryder might be near, but the Witchlander had stayed up on the plateau. Bron raised his voice, clutching at Falpian's coat. "It's time for the Baen people to take back what they have lost!" A fit of coughing interrupted his words. Falpian imagined he could see his friend's life draining into the snow.

"Please!" he begged. "Don't talk." Blood was seeping from the corner of Bron's mouth—Falpian had to get him to shelter. "I'll be right back. That man at the cottage—he'll help me get you up there."

"Don't go!" Bron clutched at him again. "I need to explain. I want you to understand." He lay back. "So many are afraid. The Witchlanders nearly killed us all in the last war. Too many of the lords want to cower in the Bitterlands, making do with what we have. We need to attack, Falpian, like we did at Barbiza and Tandrass. And we need every Baen man behind us. Your father knows that."

"But I don't understand," Falpian said. "What does this have to do with anything? What does it have to do with—with me?"

"A boy of high birth, a young man praying for his dead brother, someone innocent, with his whole life ahead . . . It was thought that if the witches attacked such a man in cold blood, the Baen people would throw support behind the war." Bron paused and lay panting for a moment. Then he looked Falpian full in the face. "I was sent to kill you. And make it seem as if the witches had done it."

"Oh," Falpian said. He knew he should feel something,

but no emotion came. He heard the words, but they were wrong somehow. *It's all a mistake,* he thought. *My father would never allow it.*

"I begged your father to send someone else . . . but I was the only one he trusted."

"My *father?* He sent you?"

Bron must have seen the stunned look on Falpian's face. "Caraxus loves you. Do not doubt that if I had succeeded, he would have mourned his sacrifice for the rest of his life."

"*His* sacrifice," Falpian repeated. He thought back to how distant his father had been with him, how cold. Falpian had taken this for disappointment. Had it been guilt as well? How long had his father been planning this? How long had he felt that Falpian was worth more to him dead than alive?

"How—how could he do this to my mother?" Falpian asked softly. "Even if he didn't care for me. She's already lost one son." But Bron wasn't listening.

"I hear them. My girls." Bron hoisted himself up on his elbow with a groan.

"Don't get up."

"Beautiful sound, don't you think? Dreadhounds baying for their kennel master." His scarred face broke into a smile.

Falpian frowned and looked about, ears alert for any

sound, but there was nothing, only the crack of ice in the branches. When he turned again, Bron was dead.

Falpian threw open the door of the cottage. Bo, wet and bedraggled, thumped his tail against the floor as his master passed, but Falpian didn't stop. He went straight to the desk in the study and pulled out the bronze container. For a moment, he held it tightly in his hands.

"Please," he prayed. "Tell me it was all a lie. I know I have a mission here. I know I'm supposed to do something important."

The words engraved over the scroll holder seemed to move and twist as they caught the light. *Duty, honor, sacrifice.* Falpian pulled the scroll out and broke the wax seal. Slowly he unrolled the parchment.

It was blank.

He turned it over, stared at it back and front. His father had written nothing. Falpian had no mission here. None at all. He felt his body shake as rage coursed through him.

"Why?" he demanded coldly, as if his father could somehow answer. "Why give me a scroll at all?"

The pretense of a mission seemed so cruel—Bron could have killed him just as easily without it. Was it just to keep him on the mountain? Did his father think that without a mission, Falpian might come home early with his tail between his legs, ruining the plan? Did he think Falpian such a craven wretch that he might shirk the duties of his mourning season?

"You know nothing about me!" Falpian shouted, hating the tears that were stinging his eyes. He picked up the metal scroll holder and hurled it across the room. It hit the window with a bang, leaving a star-shaped crack in the glass.

"Is he dead?"

Falpian wheeled around, breathing heavily.

"The assassin, is he dead?" Ryder stood in the doorway wearing Falpian's nightshirt and a pair of his leggings.

"Assassin?" Did Ryder think Bron was the one the witches told him about? Briefly Falpian wondered if there might be some truth in that. But no, Bron couldn't have anything to do with Ryder's confused notions of evil men and creatures made of mud. "Yes . . . he's dead," Falpian said carefully.

"Well, stop talking to yourself and help me. I have to hurry." Ryder turned abruptly.

"Who told you you could wear my clothes?" Falpian demanded, following Ryder into the kitchen.

"No time to dry my own."

Ryder disappeared into the pantry and came out again almost immediately, carrying armfuls of white packets tied with string. It was lump—survival food made of dried meat and berries held together with lard. He stuffed the packets into his pack.

"You're certainly in a hurry all of a sudden," Falpian observed. Ryder turned and gave him such a look of anger and pain that Falpian took a step back. "What's wrong?"

"What's wrong? What's *wrong?*" Ryder's eyes were wild, and there was a desperation in his voice that Falpian hadn't heard before. Falpian's own anger and pain were so fresh, it was disconcerting to see them on someone else's face. "Are you blind?" Ryder gestured to the window.

Falpian went to the door and pulled it open, staring out at the frozen plateau. In front of him, the bodies of the dreadhounds lay like mounds of dirty snow. Beyond them was the crooked mountain, and beyond that, rising up like a pillar, was a line of smoke. Bloodred smoke.

Black for war, green to gather, red when the coven is under attack, Falpian thought.

"But it can't be an attack," he said. "It's too soon."

Ryder grabbed him by the shoulder and spun him around. "What do you mean 'too soon'?"

Falpian stammered as the Witchlander's blue eyes bored into him. "I don't mean anything. I—"

He'd forgotten how much hatred could be communicated by that stare. Falpian's eyes fell to the velvet pouch on the windowsill, but Ryder was too quick. He grabbed the humming stone and stuffed it into the pack with the other supplies. Then he took the rope from the table and came toward Falpian again.

"Don't," Falpian said, shrinking back. "What are you going to do?"

Ryder grabbed him by the collar. "Change your clothes," he said, pushing him toward the bedroom. "Change anything wet, and do it quick. You're coming with me."

CHAPTER 15

THE BEST JOKES

A glaze of ice covered the trees, making them sparkle in the weak winter light. The sleet had stopped, and all was white and silent in the gorge. Falpian trudged through the crusted snow, his hands tied in front of him. Whenever he tried to stop and catch his breath, Ryder pushed him roughly from behind or whacked him with the flat end of his sword.

"Bo!" Falpian shouted. "Attack! Kill him! I know there's a real dreadhound in you somewhere!"

It was no use. Bo just stared at Falpian and cocked his head, then bounded off down the path, leaving wide stretches of untouched snow between his footprints. Up ahead, he turned a corner and disappeared.

"Stupid dog!" Falpian yelled. "I should have let them drown you!"

He walked on in brooding silence, listening to the

snow crunch under his feet. Around him, the glittering silence of the trees was too beautiful. It seemed to sap his anger, and Falpian needed his anger. Without it, his heart felt brittle and cold, heavy with ice like the branches. He wished he could keep his mind from drifting back to Bron's dying words; he wished he could erase what he knew from his mind; but the thought of his father's betrayal raked over him again and again.

"Where are you taking me?" he asked dully.

"Coven. Witches will find out what you know."

Witches. Falpian lifted his eyes to the mountain. Lilla the Blood-Smeared. They cut off the hands of their victims and used them for prophecy bones. He knew what would happen to him up there.

"If the coven's been attacked, maybe all the witches are dead," he said hopefully.

A sudden blow to the head jolted him, and Falpian stumbled to one knee; Ryder had cuffed him from behind. "If there are no witches left, who's tending the fire? Who made the smoke? Answer me that, Baen."

Falpian turned and glared. Obviously he'd hit a nerve with his captor. "Fine, fine. Clearly there are enough witches left to boil me for dinner." He stood up, brushing snow from his knees with tied hands.

"Don't be so dramatic," Ryder said, pushing him on again. "If it's true—as you've been insisting—that you don't know anything about the attack, then you have nothing to fear. I've never been one to defend witches, but they wouldn't kill someone without cause."

Falpian turned around. "They killed people without cause all the time during the war!"

"I told you to keep moving!"

Falpian turned and tramped on, scowling. Up ahead, a high branch cracked under its own weight, and he watched it fall, raining diamonds.

"It was different during the war," Ryder added gruffly. "You attacked us. Barbiza. Tandrass. The black ships. We were defending ourselves."

Falpian snorted. "What about all of Kar's priests you executed without trial? What danger did they pose? And what about all the Baen farmers and merchants who lived in the Witchlands before the war? You sent them all over the border to the Bitterlands, and those who wouldn't go you killed."

"That never happened."

Falpian was shocked by Ryder's arrogant sureness. "What? My mother was a Witchlander back then—her people were innocent farmers! Half of them died during the war, or lost their homes at the very least."

"If they looked like you, they weren't Witchlanders. They were Baen. They belonged in the Bitterlands, and those farms weren't their homes."

The statement struck Falpian somewhere deep. He turned again, his voice shaking with quiet anger. "If a family has lived in the same house for generations, worked the land, paid their tithes, how is it not their home?"

Ryder shook his head. "I know there were Baen living in the Witchlands before the war, but they were all in league with the black magicians from the Bitterlands. When the fighting started, what were we supposed to do? Just let them stay on *our* land, plotting behind *our* backs?"

"My mother's family had nothing to do with the black magicians!" Falpian's voice echoed through the trees. "Some of my aunts and uncles even worshipped the Goddess." He could see that Ryder was surprised by that, and pressed his advantage. "You people used the war to steal every piece of land you could. What do you think you're walking on? Twenty years ago this path was covered with innocent Baen men and women leaving the Witchlands with everything they had on their backs. And did you people ever stop to wonder if the land could feed them all? Kar's sake, why do you think it's called the Bitterlands?"

Ryder looked him up and down with a smirk. "You seem well fed to me."

"I'm one of the lucky ones. There are always beggars at our gates."

"Oh, what a tragedy, you have to look at poor people,"

said Ryder. "Besides, the attacks on Barbiza and Tandrass justified everything else."

Falpian felt the blood rush to his cheeks. A picture of his mother came back to him: a woman in blue looking out at the ocean, fingering her remembrance beads. Such a long string—one bead for every relative Falpian would never meet. Even as a child, he had always known somehow that his mother's heart was somewhere else. It was in the land of stories, the homeland that he had never seen: the Witchlands.

"You are taking me to my death," Falpian said coldly. "If you know anything about witches, you know it's true. At least have the courage to admit it." At that Falpian turned on his heel and hurried on, depriving Ryder of the satisfaction of pushing him.

That was better. Anger was better than the dull feeling of loss that threatened to swallow him. He was so angry that he almost turned again in his tracks, resolved to fight Ryder for the humming stone in his pack—but common sense got the better of him. How could he fight with his hands tied? He'd never win. Besides, Ryder was bigger, stronger, meaner . . .

. . . but was he faster?

Up ahead the path curved to skirt a ditch filled with snow-covered brambles. Falpian glanced back. Ryder had sheathed the Witchlander sword, and Falpian could do a lot in the few moments it would take to pull it out again. Maybe, if he was fast enough, he could get back to the echo site with enough breath in his lungs to sing. But he and Ryder were more than halfway through the gorge now, and every step was taking them farther and farther away from the only place where Falpian had a chance. He had to act now.

As they passed the curve, Falpian turned and butted Ryder as hard as he could toward the ditch. Ryder lost his footing and staggered back. Without waiting to see him fall, Falpian bolted.

At full tilt he raced back toward the echo site, but almost immediately he could hear Ryder behind him. He left the path and took off through the trees, leaping over low bushes turned to crystal by the storm. Ryder followed, so close that Falpian could hear his labored breath. They skidded down a small gully and out onto a frozen creek. Falpian slipped and tottered, unable to keep his balance. Ryder caught up with him now, his sword unsheathed. Falpian fell to his knees. He squeezed his eyes shut, feeling Ryder grab him by the hair.

"My sisters are in the coven, and the coven has been attacked," said Ryder, his voice hoarse in Falpian's ear. "Can you understand that? I need to get home." Falpian gasped as Ryder pressed the cold blade to his throat. "I swear, Falpian, if you slow me down I will leave your blood in this gorge. Do you doubt me?"

"No," Falpian said through clenched teeth. "I don't doubt you." Ryder pulled him to his feet.

Ryder's sisters. Witches! Falpian hadn't known that. As they made their way back to the path, Falpian thought of children playing with bones, learning blasphemies for nursery rhymes, and he thanked the God his own sisters were far away.

At the base of the mountain, they took a short rest. Falpian sat on a log, eyes tracing the path that twined dramatically upward through the trees. Maybe he'd drop dead of exhaustion before he even got to the coven.

"Your mother's people," Ryder began. He handed Falpian a bit of the lump.

Falpian brought it greedily to his mouth. "What about them?" he mumbled.

"I was thinking. You said your mother's people came from the Witchlands." Ryder chewed a chunk of lump. "But you must have learned to sing from somewhere."

Falpian kept eating, his voice nonchalant. "My father lied about his age and crewed one of the black ships that attacked Tandrass when he was sixteen." He knew he shouldn't antagonize Ryder, but after feeling a blade at his throat, he couldn't resist. He looked up at him and smirked. "Kill anyone you know?"

Bo caught them a rabbit—a big one, white and fluffy in its chilling coat. From the blood on the dog's jaw, it was obvious he'd kept another for himself. Falpian had always made a mess of skinning rabbits, but Ryder laid it on a rock and paunched it with cold expertise, then made a few decisive cuts and peeled its skin off like a jacket. It was still warm, and the purple flesh steamed in the cold air. Falpian gaped, both revolted and impressed.

They were a little less than halfway up the mountain, and the view of the gorge was dizzying and gray. Falpian was bone tired. His lips were chapped, and his face was burned by the wind. They'd stopped their climb in the middle of the afternoon, and Falpian had thought it was because Ryder could see how tired he was. Now he understood it was because everything took so much time: building the shelter, gathering wood and kindling, melting the snowpack so they had a good place to build a fire. All through the afternoon, Ryder kept frowning up at the mountaintop, and Falpian could see that it nearly killed him to stop, could see that what he really wanted to do was carry on all through the night toward his sisters—even if he died trying.

Ryder skewered the purple mass of rabbit on a long stick and handed it to Falpian. "Here. Can you at least roast this?"

Falpian grasped the stick clumsily. His hands were still tied, and he was barely able to move his fingers from the cold. "Where are you going?"

Ryder was already walking away toward a stand of bare

zanthias. "More wood," he grunted. "And don't get any ideas. There's nowhere to run."

Falpian leaned the stick over the crackling fire, enjoying the warmth that was beginning to thaw the front half of his body. Beside him, Bo looked up lovingly, his gray tail sweeping the snow back and forth.

"I don't suppose you want to chew these ropes so I can get free," Falpian said. Bo's tail swept harder, sending a spray of snow hissing into the fire. "I didn't think so."

The rabbit was just starting to drip fat, giving off a mouthwatering scent, when Falpian was hit with the revelation of Ryder's mistake. The pack. Ryder's leather pack was sitting right there in the snow. And the humming stone was inside it.

Carefully he set down the half-cooked rabbit, eyes darting toward the stand of trees. His fingers were still numb and clumsy, but it wasn't hard to pull the pack open, even with his hands tied. There it was, the humming stone.

He kneeled down and blew a hurried breath. Nothing—the stone made no sound. Nervously he looked behind him, trying to ignore Bo's big, staring eyes. He regretted what he had to do. But he'd already determined that Ryder was stronger and faster, and there was no way to put him to sleep for a while, or transport him far away—this wasn't a nursery tale where magic did exactly what you wanted. His only option was to stop Ryder's heart. Falpian blew another breath across the face of the stone, and this time he heard a low rumble. Bo was growling at him.

"Stop that," Falpian hissed, but when he held up the stone to try again, the dog's growling turned to a snarl. "This has gone far enough. You're a dreadhound. My dreadhound. The witches will kill you, too. We've got to get away. We've got to get back to Stonehouse and . . ." Falpian hesitated. "And then . . ." He lowered his hands. What exactly were they going to do after that?

He glanced again toward the trees, but Ryder was still nowhere to be seen. The zanthias were bare now, but Falpian remembered how they had turned the mountains scarlet, how he had wished on one of their feathery pods on his first day at Stonehouse. *Don't let me disappoint my father again. I'd rather die than disappoint him again.* When he thought of returning home, Falpian could only imagine disappointment on his father's face. A realization swept over him.

"Oh," he said aloud. "I was wrong."

He should have seen it before. Just because the scroll was blank didn't mean there was no mission. His father hadn't given him a blank scroll out of cruelty—or to make sure Falpian stayed on the mountain. It was a gift. His father had given it to him so Falpian would know, in the last days of his life, that he would play a part in the coming war. His father *would* be proud of him. All he had to do was die.

His mission was to die.

When Ryder returned, Falpian and Bo were just where he'd left them. Falpian stared into the fire. He didn't look up as Ryder took the stone from the white ground and quietly slipped it back into the pack.

"Will you make sure the witches do not bury me?" Falpian said, his voice strangely calm. "My people believe that a man cannot reach the afterlife unless his body is burned and his smoke rises up to Kar."

"It won't come to that," Ryder said. But Falpian heard the doubt in his voice.

The cold. Falpian hadn't known how deeply it could get inside you. How it could own you. He and Ryder lay back to back in the dark of the snow shelter, their packs for pillows, evergreen branches for bedding. Outside the wind howled for their blood. Falpian's hands were tied behind him now, a precaution he couldn't really blame Ryder for, but one that made it impossible to get comfortable.

"Didn't you almost freeze to death the last time you made a snow shelter?" he said, his teeth chattering.

"I wasn't careful," Ryder said curtly. "I didn't stop soon enough, and I let my boots get damp. We'll be fine."

Ryder was obsessed with damp clothes. He'd insisted that he and Falpian dry theirs in front of the fire before they went to sleep, but Falpian wasn't sure that toasting his socks on sticks was really going to help him now.

"I almost wish I was in the coven," he muttered. "Boiling in the witches' cooking pot." A short burst of laughter escaped him. It wasn't the least bit funny, but he couldn't help it.

The mission was on course, he tried to tell himself firmly. His father wanted him to die, and he was going to do it. His father wanted to make it look as if Falpian had been killed by witches, and now he really was going to be killed by witches. Missions weren't supposed to be easy, after all.

He laughed again, mirthlessly, shivering at the same time.

In the dark, Falpian heard Bo give a great yawn. Ryder had made him an evergreen bed too. It wasn't necessary—a dreadhound could bury himself in snow with only his nostrils showing and survive the coldest weather—but Ryder probably didn't know that. Falpian had to admit it was kind of him. He tried to push aside the idea that there were things he liked about Ryder, in spite of his ignorance. Someone who lived so close to the border would be quick to die when the war came.

"You might not believe this, but I'm sorry," Ryder said.

"What?" Falpian wasn't sure he'd heard right.

"This morning when we were talking about the war, about your people—I probably said things I shouldn't have."

"Oh." He didn't want Ryder to apologize; it only made him more human than he already was, even harder to view as an enemy.

"The truth is, I never thought much about the Baen. My father told a lot of stories about the war, but they never changed. You'd ask him a question, and instead of answering he'd just start in again on one of the stories you'd heard a hundred times before. After a while you just stop asking. My mother wouldn't talk about it at all, but . . . I think there were things about the war she wasn't proud of."

Ryder had a father too, and a mother. Falpian told himself he didn't want to know, but he wriggled around to face Ryder, curious in spite of himself. "Was she a witch like Skyla and Pima?"

"How did you know my sister's names?"

"You told me this afternoon—when you said they lived in the coven.'"

"I did?" Ryder asked sharply. "I don't remember. . . ."

"How else would I know them?"

Ryder didn't answer.

"It's different with us," Falpian told him. "My people don't allow women to practice magic. They're too . . . delicate."

Ryder made a sound that was almost a laugh. "How can you stop them?"

"Oh, they just know they shouldn't, I suppose. My

mother wouldn't dream of doing anything so unladylike. In the old days there used to be terrible punishments for women who tried to sing—tongues cut out and things like that."

"That's horrible!"

"Yes. I suppose." It seemed like ancient history, not something that could ever happen to anyone he knew.

"Listen," said Ryder. "There's something I want to ask you. This morning at Stonehouse, you were talking about your brother."

"My brother?" Falpian said.

"You said something about dreaming someone's dreams. You used a word."

He hesitated. "Talat-sa?"

"Yes, tally-sa. Tell me about tally-sa."

Why that of all things? It was as if Ryder wanted to find all his tender spots. But it wasn't a secret, after all. At home, when a black magician came to seek his father's counsel, the conversation would inevitably turn to their talat-sa, how powerful they would be if only they could find him. When Falpian was younger, these men would look at him with awe or envy and tell him how lucky he was. How pleasant a Witchlander's life must be, not to even know the word.

"My people believe that everyone in the world has a talat-sa, a twin in spirit. In the Bitterlands, men go on long quests to find theirs, and usually never do. My father never found his."

"And you say your brother was yours?"

"Yes," Falpian said. "It's different when you have a true twin. When my brother and I were born, there was great rejoicing in my family. Farien and I would never have to look for each other. We'd grow up dreaming the same dreams, finishing each other's sentences—that sort of thing. We were supposed to make the leaves fall from the trees with the sound of our voices and know when the other was in trouble from a long way away. . . ." His voice trailed off. Of course, none of these things had happened with his brother. When Farien drowned, Falpian was reading in his bedchamber. If only he had looked out the window, he might have seen his boat. But he didn't look. There was no warning in his head. He never knew his talat-sa was in trouble.

In the dark Bo gave a whistling whine, as if he understood the conversation. He had failed too that day. Dreadhounds were supposed to be special dogs, attuned to their master and their master's talat-sa, but while Farien drowned, Bo had slept peacefully at the foot of Falpian's bed.

"Is that the only reason two people would dream the same dreams?" Ryder asked. "If they are . . . twins in spirit?"

Falpian wondered why Ryder was so interested. "Yes," he said. "For a while I thought my brother was sending me visions even after his death." Falpian shifted position on his evergreen bed. He wasn't so sure about that now. He'd been assuming that his strange dreams came from Farien, that their connection had finally been made but too late, and that the dreams were some sort of twisted vision of the afterlife. Now he wondered if he had imagined it all.

Beside him, Falpian could feel Ryder's body shaking. It took a moment to realize that he was laughing.

"What is it? What's so funny?"

Ryder's laugh was audible now, a snorting chortle that was clearly trying to stop. Falpian found himself laughing too.

"Twins in spirit," Ryder managed to say.

Falpian laughed harder, though he didn't get the joke. He tried to stop, but something inside him had broken, spilling out high-pitched cackles. "What's so funny about twins in spirit?"

"Nothing," Ryder said. "Nothing. I'm sorry. I just . . . I just had a funny idea about a Baen and a Witchlander. . . ."

Falpian took a deep breath, tried to calm himself. "That wouldn't be possible," he said seriously. "It would be like a Baen having a talat-sa who was a . . ." Another peal of laughter spilled out. "A goat."

"Yes, I suppose it would."

Falpian turned away from Ryder then, realizing that in another moment, his laughter could turn to sobs.

*　　*　　*

In his dream, there was laughter too. Falpian was standing on the marble floor of a magnificent dining hall. In front of him was a long table, every seat filled with well-dressed men and boys. It was the feast of Kar, he realized in wonder, the afterlife, the place where the righteous went when they died. Falpian craned his neck, trying to see the head of the table. It was said the great God Kar sat there, singing the world into being, but he didn't hear anything, and in either direction, all he could see were more diners, more table, stretching to infinity. Maybe he didn't want to meet a God with a thousand eyes and tongues, anyway.

He followed the sound of laughter past the feasting and carousing. There were no women, but that didn't surprise him. Women had no souls and couldn't reach the feast of Kar.

He found his brother holding a big joint of meat. It was Farien who was laughing—laughing and laughing with bits of food coming out of his mouth. The men around him were laughing too. Some pointed at Falpian.

"Am I some joke?" he asked. He recognized some of the diners from the portrait gallery back home. His Caraxus family ancestors. "I'm going to die for all of you—for the Baen people—what more do you want?"

They laughed harder. And someone bleated like a goat. Beside Farien there was an empty chair, but Falpian didn't want to sit in it.

"You're such a muttonhead," Farien said, tears streaming out of his eyes. "Even your dog gets it."

Muttonhead. Falpian had forgotten that one. Seeing Farien reminded him of how annoying his brother used to be sometimes.

Then, to Falpian's horror, a piece of Farien's face came off—though he kept on laughing. There was a hole in his cheek now, something brown showing through. Someone pulled at Falpian's sleeve, but he couldn't take his eyes away. Pieces of his brother's face were flaking off, coming away like mosaic tiles. His brother was disappearing, being replaced by someone else.

Someone pulled his sleeve again, and this time he looked. Standing beside him were his own two sisters, their eyes like black stones.

"You're not supposed to be here," he said.

They smiled at him and cupped their hands to tell a secret. Falpian bent toward them. "It is the great God Kar who plays the best jokes," they whispered.

CHAPTER 16

THE GODDESS HAS STAINED YOUR EYES

Ryder knew things about Falpian. Pictures came into his mind as he climbed. A house. A stable. A courtyard shaded by an old blisterberry tree. A woman in blue silk throwing petals into the ocean—Falpian's mother performing some ritual for her dead son.

Not long after they'd started out, it came to Ryder that the wind sweeping toward them from the mountain's summit was whistling in the key of torn clouds. What in Aata's name did that mean? All his life Ryder had wanted to explore, to see sights that were foreign and strange; now they were coming to his mind unbidden, more vivid than his own memories. He and Falpian had some sort of connection, that was certain, but Ryder didn't want it. Skyla and Pima were in trouble; that was all that mattered. He didn't want a talat-sa.

"We'll have to hurry if we want to make the coven

today," he said. A scarf was wound around most of Falpian's face, and yet Ryder could see dread in the Baen's dark eyes. "Just tell the witches what you know, and I will escort you back to the border myself." The words were swallowed up by the frigid wind. "They don't really put people in cooking pots, you know!"

When the path got too steep for Falpian to climb without stumbling, Ryder untied his hands and cut him a staff. The Baen didn't run away, only looked at him woefully, as if resigned to his fate. Ryder almost wished he *would* run. They trekked up the mountain, hardly stopping to rest, as the dim glow of the sun arced purple over their heads. Ryder tied evergreen branches to their boots for snowshoes. They ate lump from their pockets and melted snow in their mouths for water. As they neared the top of the mountain, Ryder noticed that the zanthia trees had become squat and stunted, bent backward by an ever-present wind into gnarled poses, like witches bending to the sun.

It was midafternoon when they reached the border. The path didn't go all the way to the summit, but came to rest at a flat place on the shoulder of the mountain. At their feet a plain black stone pushed its way out of the snow, only its rounded top showing.

"Is this it?" Falpian asked. "Just this stone? I expected the border to be—I don't know—more dramatic somehow."

"Just this," Ryder said quietly. He looked down on the

bare trees and the drab snow-covered valley, and his heart swelled. Home. His family. For two days he had kept up a fierce pace, but now that he was so close he found himself hesitating, dreading what he might find. Bo, sensing his mood, leaned his great head against Ryder's thigh.

"Firecall's gone out," Falpian said, pulling the scarf from his face as he came up beside him. Ryder nodded. He had been searching for any sign of the red smoke, but saw none. "I hope your sisters are all right." Ryder eyed Falpian suspiciously, but the Baen seemed to have meant what he said. "It's . . . odd, I almost feel like I know them, like I'd recognize them if I saw them. . . ." Falpian shook his head as if to shake off the thought and looked out to the valley again. "They say the prophet Aayse is buried somewhere in these mountains."

Ryder was taken aback. "How would you know about her?"

Falpian gave him an arch look. "I have been educated." He began to recite in a soft singsong voice: "'When the great witch died, the skies were dark for days. Her sister Aata tore her hair and wept. She begged the Goddess to send her sister back across the river of sorrow, back into the land of the living. For nine days she stayed in Aayse's tomb, neither eating nor sleeping.'"

Ryder gaped. It was from "The Life of Aata and Aayse," the story his mother had been telling on the last day he saw her. How very strange to be here now, listening to it on the lips of a Baen.

"'And then the Goddess came,'" Ryder murmured. "'She spoke to Aata in a language without words, comforting her, teaching her the magic that lies in silence, the magic her sister had tried to show her. When Aata left her sister's tomb, she had been changed.'"

"My mother liked to read me that passage," Falpian said, then added with a hint of bitterness, "Grief is her hobby. She's made a study of it."

Ryder thought again of the dark-haired woman casting petals into the sea. She'd already lost one son. "Is it true what you've been saying?" he asked curtly. "Do you really know nothing about an attack on the coven?"

Falpian peered at him. His lips looked painfully chapped, and patches of windburn stood out against his pale cheeks. "Ryder," he said gently, "you know my people couldn't have done it. Look at this path! No army has come this way."

Ryder shook his head. "But I told you, it wasn't an army. If it's the same thing that attacked my village, it was—they were—things. Men made of earth and sticks and nothing else. You can't kill them!"

"Listen to yourself! You don't really believe in the gormy man, do you?"

Ryder grabbed Falpian by the coat. "You know what it was? You know what they're called?"

"No!" Falpian cried. He took hold of Ryder's arm, but it was more a gesture of reassurance than defense. "Of course not! That's just a story. Something you tell children. You know, 'Wash your face or the gormy man will get you.' It's not real."

Ryder let go. "The ones I saw were real enough."

"If the Baen had magic like that, don't you think we would have used it against you during the war?"

Ryder frowned at him for a moment, then cursed. Part of him wished he could doubt Falpian, but he knew the Baen was telling the truth the same way he knew all those other things about him, things he'd never been told, but that were in his head like his own thoughts. Falpian really didn't know—not about the attack on the village or on the coven.

"I'm letting you go," Ryder said abruptly. Falpian stared, but Ryder avoided his gaze. "Don't ask why. I hardly know myself." He took off his pack and pulled out some crumbled bits of lump, stuffing handfuls into the velvet pockets of Falpian's coat. "Here, take this. I won't need it now. You can sleep in the shelter tonight."

"I—I don't understand."

"I'm letting you go. Are you really going to argue?"

"But . . ."

Ryder didn't want to explain. Said aloud, the words would sound ridiculous—brothers in spirit. The last thing he wanted was a brother. More family just meant more people to worry about, more people to protect. More people to grieve for when they died.

"My mother sent me to you. She gave a prophecy that there was an assassin on the mountain and that he must not succeed. I thought it was you at first, but then . . . it seemed like you were the one I was supposed to save *from* an assassin. I don't understand it. I never believed in prophecies or magic, but I told myself I'd never doubt my mother again. For some reason you're supposed to be alive." With that he shouldered his pack and started down the path toward the coven.

"There's more to it," Falpian said in a quiet voice behind him. "I know there is."

Ryder turned. Falpian was staring down at him, his dark eyes puzzled. Bo stood next to him, making his high whistling whine, looking back and forth between the two young men.

"What is it you're not telling me?"

Ryder frowned, shrugging. "In the past two days, there have been so many times when you could have killed me," he finally said. "How can I take you to the witches now? You're right. They'd slaughter you in a moment. I can see who you are in a way . . . in a way they never could."

This was as close as Ryder wanted to come to admitting

that there really was a bond between them, that there was something to this talat-sa business. Without waiting for a reply, he turned on his heel and started down the path, walking as quickly as he could.

There was a small boulder at the edge of the plateau just big enough for Falpian to sit and think. Part of him was happy, elated with relief, but this was an illogical feeling. His duty was still clear: Bron hadn't killed him, Ryder hadn't killed him, the witches hadn't killed him—but that didn't mean he was really free. Now there was no one left but Falpian to do what had to be done.

This would be even better for his father's plans. There would be a body now. There would be a funeral pyre on the beach. The nobles would come and murmur, *Shame, shame. So young, and in mourning, too. We cannot let it stand. Haven't the Witchlanders taken enough? Now they steal our very children from us.* His father would wear blue for mourning, and he would fix his face with grief.

Yes, Falpian's duty was clear. He must go back to Stonehouse and finish the mission. He must make Bron's death and his own look like an attack by the witches. He must start a war. But instead he sat motionless on the boulder.

Ryder had disappeared into the trees, leaving heavy footprints. Bo seemed eager to follow; he stood whimpering at the top of the path, throwing Falpian pathetic glances.

"Go ahead!" Falpian snapped. "Go ahead and join your new master if you're so in love with him!"

Bo stared at him, then settled into the snow with a sigh, his chin on his paws. Falpian was relieved by this response; he didn't really want to be left alone.

He slid down off his stone perch and paced back and forth, trying to make sense of what he'd learned. The coven had been attacked, that much was clear. But by what? The idea that Ryder was mad had been gradually falling away as Falpian got to know him, but there was no believing in the gormy man. Was there?

And yet . . . what if it *was* real? He could almost see the creature lurching up out of the dirt to punish the wicked, just like in the old stories. The Baen didn't have such magic, did they? If they did, surely Falpian would have heard a whisper of it. And even if he hadn't, how could Baen magicians work such spells right under the witches' noses without getting caught?

Bo made a bored little moan, but Falpian ignored him. If it wasn't a Baen who made whatever had attacked the coven, he reasoned, it must have been a Witchlander— but why would they harm their own people? Could the witches be experimenting with new magics? Maybe they had discovered some powerful new weapon they couldn't yet control.

Falpian stopped short in the snow. The very idea made him want to go straight home and tell his father. *This* was the reason he couldn't die: His father had to be told that his forces couldn't attack now, not when the enemy might have some potent new magic.

But a moment later he was frowning and shaking his head. What could he possibly tell his father? That Baen soldiers might be in danger from monsters out of a nursery tale? His father would think the whole story was just a weak excuse for Falpian's not completing his mission. And maybe he'd be right. Falpian had no idea what Ryder had really seen—bandits in some sort of costume, perhaps. That was certainly more likely than a throng of gormy men.

Falpian stamped his feet to beat away the cold, and as he did, his eye fell on the border marker. Only the rounded top was poking out of the snow, but it was enough for him to see Witchlander pictographs written on the stone. *Stop, Baen,* they said.

How arrogant, Falpian thought, for the Witchlanders to write a message to the Baen in pictographs. But of course it was practical, too. The Baen alphabet was becoming rare, even in the Bitterlands. Soon it would be an artifact, like the Baen language itself, taught only to scholars and magicians. Everyone spoke Witchlander now. He brushed the snow from the black stone and read the words.

Stop, Baen.

Set no foot farther.

The Goddess has stained your eyes that we may

know your darkness.

Good men and women will shudder at the sight of

you and take up arms.

Stay in your bitter lands and beg forgiveness,

or Baen will be no more.

A chill ran through him. *Baen will be no more.* The Witchlanders were just waiting for another attack, weren't they? They'd use it as an excuse to exterminate every Baen they saw, and they wouldn't stop at the border this time. It was what the Witchlanders really wanted, a world without the Baen.

Just then an idea occurred to Falpian that made him smile, made him feel a little warmer in spite of the frigid chill. This time his people must be sure their attack succeeded. He didn't like the idea of war, but if it was coming, the Baen must win. And Falpian could help with that.

Rumors of the gormy men were not enough, but if Falpian could find out more, confirm their existence and find out who made them, or root out some other piece of intelligence that would help his people when the fighting came, it would justify his staying alive. Since the last war, no Baen had set foot in the Witchlands. No one knew what had changed, how strong the enemy was. His people needed a spy. His father needed a spy.

Falpian stared down into the gray trees, and his heart quaked. He thought he could almost feel the witches' presence, strange and malevolent beyond the bare treetops. But for the first time since he'd unrolled the blank scroll, he could imagine coming home alive and having his father welcome him. He wouldn't have to go far across the border, he told himself. He'd see what he could learn observing the coven from the trees, and if he was caught, he'd ask for Ryder. Ryder trusted him. He'd let Falpian go, hadn't he? Falpian could use that.

"Father," he said aloud, "I'm going to prove to you that I'm worth more alive than dead."

It was a ludicrous plan, probably. But behind him, Falpian could see only death, and ahead of him there was at least a chance. Somewhere over the border was an offering he could lay at his father's feet, some gift of information that would wipe the look of disappointment off his father's face for good. And Falpian was going to find it. Besides, it seemed right to be doing something foolish and brave, as foolish and brave as lying about his age and crewing a black ship at the age of sixteen.

Bo barked and gleefully thumped his tail; he seemed

to understand that he and Falpian would be crossing the border.

"I don't know what you're so happy about," Falpian said. "We'll probably die."

Without giving himself a chance to change his mind, he took a deep breath, raised his chin, and stepped forward. Then, following Ryder's footprints in the snow, Falpian Caraxus and Bodread the Slayer crossed the invisible line in the path, the first Baen and his dreadhound to enter the Witchlands in twenty years.

PART THREE

Cursed are those who believe in a Goddess, who cannot see that a world created by a woman would be a backward place, that rivers would run uphill, animals would rule over humans, the sun would give off darkness instead of light.

But worse still is the Baen woman who tries to sing. Remove her from the company of other women. Cut out her voice, and fill her mouth with mud.

Make her silent.

—The Magician's Enchiridion

CHAPTER 17

TALAT-SA

Ryder came out of the trees below the coven and broke into a run. It was as he'd feared. The witches' settlement had been destroyed.

"Skyla!" he called. "Pima!"

He ran past a great black circle in the clearing where he'd tried to convince the villagers to cross the border. The firecall must have burned there, but now it was almost cold, with only a few coals glowing in its center.

"Is anyone here?" he called. He stopped, winded, at the foot of the stone steps.

Only one hut was still standing, the nearest to the clearing, but it was listing badly, and its door swayed open and shut in the wind. Beyond it, on either side of the steps, piles of splintered wood marked where the other huts had been. Ryder tried to remember which one had belonged to his cousin Yulla.

He made himself climb the snow-covered steps, steeling himself for what he might find. The once high torches lay across his path like fallen trees. Remnants of witch lives were strewn everywhere: baskets, cooking pots, broken chairs—even a few goats wandered forlornly through the rubble. It was just like in the village. It was just like . . . Ryder felt suddenly dizzy, thinking of the day he'd found his cottage destroyed. His ears rang. Yellowhead. His horrid rolling eyes. His screams. Why had he left Skyla and Pima here? How could he have left them unprotected? He took a deep breath, trying to calm his rising panic.

Behind him something clattered. Ryder stiffened. It was a familiar sound, but it took him a moment to place it. When he finally did, he turned and skidded back down the steps to the only surviving hut: Someone was throwing bones.

Inside, a woman sat alone in the darkness. She was staring so intently at her casting that she didn't seem to notice him. One of the smaller bones had rolled to the doorway, and Ryder squinted at it in disbelief. It looked like his mother's anchor bone.

"Mabis?" Ryder whispered to the shadows. His voice quivered with hope.

The woman stood up and moved around the casting to greet him. It was Aata's Right Hand, the girl in white, her cheeks stained with old tears.

"Are my sisters alive?" Ryder asked sharply.

She nodded.

"Both? Both alive and unharmed?"

She nodded again.

Ryder turned abruptly, knees weak with relief. He walked away, not caring where he was going, the air cold in his lungs.

When he reached a small, snow-covered garden at the back of the hut, he finally stopped and took another deep breath. They were alive. They were all right. A movement in the snow startled him, but it was only a flock of bicker-birds, hardly visible against the white ground. A great basket of seeds lay overturned, and the little birds hopped about, jostling one another for the biggest portion of an unexpected winter feast. As he stepped forward, they lifted into the air and swirled around him, whistling and chattering as if it were spring. Ryder's heart lifted with them. He still had a family. *Thank you, Aata. Thank you, Aayse.*

The girl in white was watching him, but ducked inside when Ryder looked her way. He followed her back into the hut, leaving the door ajar. The floor was badly slanted, and the furniture lay in a tangled pile at the near side of the room. The stone fireplace was cold.

"Have they gone to the village?" he asked. "My sisters and the others?"

Aata's Right Hand shook her head, pulling a thin shawl around her shoulders. Her quilted tunic and loose pants were streaked with dirt. Ryder moved toward her, avoiding the bones, his boots tracking snow.

"The caves, then?"

She nodded.

"Why aren't you with them? Have they banished you?" He looked at her shrewdly. "Or are you ashamed to show your face after that false prophecy you gave?"

The girl's expression hardened. She bent to her knees to collect the bones strewn over the slanted floor.

"Why don't you speak?" In the dim light, Ryder could see that the red mark signifying her vow of silence was now just a dark smear at her throat. "After all you've done, why should the Goddess care if you break your vow or keep it?"

She ignored him, but he could see his words stung. Awkwardly she drew together the heap of bones. They were smaller and newer than Mabis's set—deer and goat mostly, the partial jaw of a rabbit with some of the teeth still attached. She raised them over her head, then dashed them to the floor as if she wished they might break. Ryder suppressed a cry, stepping back against the wall as bones slid toward him. They rolled and skittered to the low part of the room, making a wide casting. She bent to peer at them, then gave Ryder a searching look and pointed to the floor.

"What?" he said.

She pointed again.

"Are you asking me if I can read your bones?"

She nodded as he stepped toward her.

"Can't you?"

The girl tried to look away, but Ryder grabbed her roughly by the shoulder. "Can you read them or not?" Aata's Right Hand stared up at him with fear in her eyes. "It's so convenient that you can't speak, isn't it?" he hissed. "You have so much to answer for."

She pulled away, then grabbed a lump of charred wood from the hearth. Hurriedly, she began to draw some symbols on the curved wall.

"Don't bother," Ryder said. The girl continued to write. "I said don't bother. I can't read—not enough to understand, anyway."

She stopped and glared at him, then shook her head and threw the coal back into the hearth.

"I asked a yes or no question. Can you read the bones?"

After a slight hesitation, the girl shook her head.

"Could you ever read them?"

She shook her head again.

Ryder felt a cold anger sweep over him. "Why?" he demanded. "Why for Aata's sake did you ever say you could? Are you insane?" Tears were coming to her eyes now. She pointed to the writing on the wall as if the lines and circles there could somehow justify her actions.

"Speak!" Ryder shouted. "It's because of you. It's because of you that the witches ignored my mother's warnings. She might be . . . She might . . ." He couldn't say the word "dead." Wouldn't say it. He pushed past her. "I'm wasting my time. I'm going up to the caves to speak to Sodan and the other elders."

Outside, Ryder stared up at the mountain's crooked peak. It couldn't be far, not compared to all the climbing he had already done, but he was so tired.

"Wait," said a voice.

Ryder wheeled around, startled.

Aata's Right Hand pulled her shawl tighter. "Did you kill the Baen?" Her voice was hoarse and breathy.

A moment before, Ryder had scorned her for not speaking; now he felt a stab of pity. "Your vow."

"After all I've done, why should the Goddess care if I break my vow or keep it?"

Ryder winced, hearing the cruelty in his own words. In the light of day, he saw how defeated she looked. There were dark circles under her eyes, and her cheeks looked sunken.

"The Baen was innocent," Ryder said. "He didn't make the creatures."

Her brow furrowed. "Who else could it have been?"

"So you don't think it was my mother anymore?"

She paused, and in that moment, Ryder saw what she must be thinking—that Mabis couldn't be responsible for the second attack because she must be dead.

"A witch did this," he told her before she could give voice to her thoughts. "Someone who understands magic. Maybe you, for all I know."

The girl's brown eyes widened. She gestured to the ruin around her. "How could I do this? And why? Why would any witch destroy her own coven?"

He gave a short laugh. "Why does a witch do anything? Why does a witch pretend to throw the bones when she can't—ruining lives, leaving chaos in her wake—?"

"Stop! I know what I have done. Do you think I don't? Three witches died in this attack. And one was an elder!"

She looked to the ground, and Ryder saw a tear fall into the snow. Pity washed through him again, but he tried not to show it. It was *her* fault. It was all her fault. It was only her beauty that made him feel sympathy for her, and her beauty was a trap—dangerous as a Baen song.

When she spoke again, her voice, so long unused, began to crack painfully. "A year ago, I foretold a few events—small things, really, but Sodan and the elders were very excited. They gave me the title of Aata's Right Hand. They said I had the gift." She cleared her throat, lifting her eyes to Ryder's. "My mother had it, but she died when I was born. My father said I had it too, that the gift was in my blood." She paused. "Ryder, I tell you now what I have never told anyone. Those prophecies—I never made them. They were thrown by someone else."

"By the red!" Ryder swore.

"There is another witch in the coven—one who isn't allowed to throw the bones. She told me some prophecies and said I could pretend they were my own." Her face twisted with grief. "When I say it out loud I hear how horrible it is. Even at the time, I knew it was stupid. But it all started so innocently. This woman kept telling me that I really did have the gift and that soon I'd be able to make prophecies of my own. I have wanted to be a boneshaker since I was a little girl. I performed Aata's prayer every morning; I took the vow of silence. I didn't see any harm in pretending. I thought it was only a matter of time before I became the witch everyone thought I was."

Ryder's voice was hard. "And when you came to my cottage, why did you say my mother's prophecies were false?"

The witch pursed her lips, hesitating. "When we saw your mother's firecall, I consulted this witch. She . . . she didn't say anything about monsters! She only said I would find the bone in the fire and with it I would finally be able to read for myself."

"So you only came down the mountain to steal my mother's bone," he said. "And you never stopped to think she could be giving a true warning?"

She shook her head. "Ryder, she seemed so . . . I'm sorry, but it all seemed so unbelievable. I couldn't . . . And Visser was so sure she had gone wild on maiden's woe. . . . Oh Goddess, I'm so stupid. Sodan is always saying that the magic is in the witch, not in her bones. I should have listened!"

"The witch was wrong, then. You got the anchor bone and still couldn't read?"

"I . . . I'm not sure." She crossed her arms against the cold. "I've stared at those bones so long I think they've driven me mad. I spent my life studying the teachings of Aata and Aayse, memorizing the patterns and relationships of bones, waiting for visions of the future that never come. I left my father in the Dunes so I could study here. I left my family. And it was all for nothing!"

Ryder had forgotten that she came from Dunes coven. It must have been lonely for her here, not being able to speak to anyone. She'd always be a stranger. "There aren't any boneshakers in Dunes who can teach you?"

She shrugged and dried her eyes with the corner of her shawl. "There aren't any boneshakers anywhere. I went to all the covens. Sodan convinced me to study here because he taught your grandfather and Lilla Red Bird—but he doesn't have the gift himself."

Ryder felt his stomach drop. No boneshakers? No boneshakers at all? He remembered he had once asked Visser why she didn't send messengers to other covens to confirm his mother's prophecies. Now he remembered the look on her face, as if she wanted to stop him talking at all costs. But he couldn't blame Visser for wanting to keep *this* secret. The covens were blind. If there weren't any bone-shakers, the Witchlands were completely unprotected.

Suddenly the girl stiffened, her gaze fixed somewhere over his left shoulder. "Goddess, help us," she breathed. "Don't move. There's something behind you. There, in the trees!"

Ryder turned and at first saw nothing. Then, from out of the forest at the high end of the coven, a gray blur came hurtling. Bodread the Slayer. The dog stopped, lifted his great head, and howled—a chilling sound. Aata's Right Hand grabbed his arm.

"I know this dog," said Ryder. "He's not . . ." He was about to say *dangerous*, but the word caught in his throat. Ryder searched the trees for Falpian. Had the Baen crossed the border? Could he be that foolish?

Bo lifted his head again, and it came to Ryder that he couldn't be howling at the two of them. With a sickening foreknowledge of what he would see, he turned around. A huge white figure was slouching toward them from the clearing.

"The gormy man," Ryder said softly. The term Falpian had used seemed appropriate—a creature from a child's nightmare. It was like the mud creatures that had attacked his village—a huge, rough shape, at least a man and a half high—but it was different now.

"It's made of snow!"

Bo galloped toward them down the steps, leaping over debris and fallen torches as if he might take flight. Aata's Right Hand cried out as he hurtled by, but the dreadhound was fixed on the creature and didn't even slow his pace. Without hesitation, he hurled himself at the gormy man, raking his saber teeth over its blank face.

"The caves," Ryder said. "Where are they?" The girl released her grip and ran inside the hut. "Where are you going?" he yelled. A moment later she came out again, and Ryder saw she was pushing his mother's bone into a pouch at her waist.

"Follow me!" she said.

They took off up steps, tripping over the wreckage of fallen huts as they went. At the top of the set the steps ended, but Aata's Right Hand continued running, quick as a deer, toward the trees.

"Come on!" she yelled.

Ryder had trouble keeping up with her. The incline was steep, and Aata's Right Hand was so light and graceful that she ran on top of the crusted snow, while his heavy steps broke through. He pressed on, but running uphill was like running in water, and after all the climbing he'd done with Falpian, he was on the brink of exhaustion. Behind him, cracking branches told him that the creature was following—Bo hadn't been able to slow it down for long.

Breathless, Ryder stopped, the entrance to the caves just visible through the trees. Ahead of him, Aata's Right Hand was a smear of white against the snow.

"Keep running!" she called back to him. "It's right behind us!"

Ryder knew they shouldn't lead that thing to the caves, but he was too tired to shout a warning, and the white witch tore on. *At least she'll make it,* he thought. But what protection would the caves give her if the creature followed? Ryder pulled the Baenkiller from its sheath. It seemed small and flimsy, a child's toy. Fear and exhaustion weighed on his shoulders. He couldn't win a fight now—if he ever could, against that thing.

Then the gormy man was upon him, barreling straight through the brush and snapping young trees at the base. For a moment Ryder was paralyzed by its sheer size—taller than any man. The creature threw back its white head, opening its round mouth hole. Ryder would have thought it was howling with the delight of capture, except that it didn't make a sound. Feebly he swung the sword, but the creature pulled back, easily avoiding the blow.

Bo must have been following right behind, because now he hurtled out of the trees and threw himself onto the creature's back, gripping its body with his claws and plunging his saber teeth into its neck—but the creature had no arteries to sever, no jugular vein. Ryder heard a snap as the gormy man threw Bo to the ground. The dog gave a painful yelp—one of his saber teeth lay broken in the snow.

Ryder rushed forward with the sword, but the gormy man felled him to his knees with one swipe of its arm. If only Falpian were here with his humming stone. But then Ryder remembered: He was the one with the stone—he'd forgotten to give it back when they parted at the border.

A flash of white shot past—Aata's Right Hand. She had doubled back and was coming at the creature with a thick branch, using it as a battering ram. Incredibly, the snow creature lost its balance for a moment, dropping to one knee.

Ryder cast the Baenkiller aside and fumbled with his pack. It was probably a mistake—all his knowledge of humming stones came from Dassen's stories—but he knew he'd never kill the creature with a sword. He blew on the stone as he'd seen his sisters do with Dassen's stone, but nothing happened.

"Wake up!" he croaked. He shook it up and down frantically.

The gormy man had regained its balance and was driving Aata's Right Hand backward, though she was still swinging her branch like a wild creature. Bo had joined the fight again and was snapping and snarling at the creature's legs. Aata's Right Hand fell to the ground, but now

Ryder stepped forward, holding the stone in front of him. Knowing it was his last chance, he blew a long, even breath. This time the stone came to life with a low thrumming. *That's right*, he thought, *I've done this a thousand times.* He didn't stop to wonder when. In moments, music was rolling out of his mouth like honey.

Aata's Right Hand turned to him, and Ryder caught the look of shock on her face. Singing, he stepped toward the creature. He knew this song, knew it like an old friend, but his tongue was slow and thick; it didn't make the sounds he wanted.

The creature backed away at the sound of his voice, disappearing into the trees. The witch stared at him in amazement, then darted away, a white blur.

It was too easy. The creature was unharmed and probably hadn't gone far. Ryder knew he should stop singing and bolt for the caves, but now that he'd started, he couldn't make his tongue stop moving. Everything had become bright and blinding—the snow, the trees, the stones, the purple clouds. It was as if a skin had been peeled off his eyes and he was seeing the world for the first time in all its frightening beauty. He didn't want to see it. He hadn't asked for this. Skyla wanted magic, not him. There was too much to know. The snowflakes falling languidly around him all had names. Why couldn't he stop singing, for Aata's sake?

At the edge of his consciousness, Ryder began to hear another voice, a voice he knew almost as well as his own. He was drawn toward it, seemed to float. Falpian. Falpian was coming up from the coven path.

Now this was magic. Ryder could feel that their two voices together dwarfed the magic of the humming stone. Falpian was the same person Ryder remembered, but he was someone else, too, someone stronger and darker, someone Ryder knew from a thousand dreams.

Bo howled ecstatically, bounding around the two young men in great circles. The black branches of the trees shivered, and snow-covered stones lifted off the ground to hover in the air. All Falpian's thoughts, all his secrets were coming toward Ryder in a rush—too many to understand at once. He tried to hold them back. Again he tried to stop singing, but couldn't.

With a loud crack the humming stone broke in two, sending a spasm of pain through his arm. It made no difference to the song, but Falpian's jaw dropped, and he stared at Ryder with a look of joyful recognition on his face.

"No, no," Ryder tried to say. "I know what you're thinking, but I'm not your tally-whatever." The words came out like music.

Falpian grabbed his arm. The gormy man—no, now two gormy men—were coming fast. Falpian's song changed, and the two creatures froze in their tracks. He was controlling them, or trying to. In fact, he was doing some incredibly complicated things with his voice, and somehow Ryder could predict every one of them, meeting Falpian's tenor with a deeper harmony of his own.

They were simple things, these creatures—Ryder saw that now. They drew on whatever matter was at hand to give themselves form—before it had been mud, now snow. At their core, though, they were just a dark, hateful spell. But whose hate was it? Whose spell? The things in front of him thought nothing, wanted nothing, except to destroy.

Falpian was trying to kill them, trying to squeeze their hearts, but it wouldn't work; the creatures had no hearts, only snow and hate. Ryder closed his eyes, focusing only on the song. Somehow he could still perceive the world around him, even without his eyes. He saw the seeds sleeping under the earth. He saw the cells of his own body humming with life. He saw the gormy men in front of him, frozen, and yet writhing with dark energy.

Stir a wind, Falpian, he thought.

Ryder, is it you? Are you really my talat-sa?

Stir a wind. They have no hearts. We have to blow them apart.

Falpian seemed to understand. *Wind. I'll use a winter key.*

Ryder opened his eyes. He had no idea what a winter key was, but all at once their song shifted as if it had a life of its own. The tips of the trees bent toward them, and a wind began to grow. It swirled around and around the horrid things, pulling at their snow limbs, blowing away their twisted branches.

The creatures resisted, tried to pull the snow back to themselves, but Falpian's voice was strong now, full of buried rage, rage as hard as needles. The key of slivered glass. Now Falpian held nothing back. Emotions, too many to understand at once, swept through Ryder's mind: Falpian's father, the pain of betrayal that was like a wound that wouldn't heal. Ryder and Falpian unwound the creatures like scarves, smaller and smaller, until they were nothing but that frigid core of hate. Still they sang.

Falpian had found a well of new strength, but it was dark and full of anger. It frightened Ryder. It reminded him of the hate he sensed inside the gormy men. For the first time Ryder understood just how powerful Falpian could be, how dangerous. But Falpian's anger made their voices strong, and Ryder had no choice but to try to sing with him as best he could. Their voices blasted what was left of the creatures into shards, spreading them thinner and thinner on the wind until the spell inside them flew apart—and the gormy men were gone.

Ryder dropped to the ground and put his hands to his ears. He didn't want to hear anymore, he didn't want to know anymore, but he couldn't stop singing—and Falpian couldn't stop either, couldn't stop until Ryder did.

Falpian pulled him toward the mouth of the cave, and

Ryder caught a glimpse of Kef standing near the entrance, staring at him in amazement. Aata's Right Hand was screaming something, but Ryder couldn't hear her over the sound of his own voice. It hurt, it hurt his brains, this music. *I'm just a farmer*, he wanted to yell. He'd been a fool to want something more, something bigger than his own small life. This was too big.

All at once, Ryder became aware of a rumbling, a deep quivering in the air, as if the mountain itself wanted to join their song. Falpian grabbed him by the arm and pointed up toward the mountain's crooked spire. He and Aata's Right Hand tried to pull him into the cave, but Ryder resisted. Bo didn't think they should go in there either. He was pulling frantically at Ryder's coat with his teeth. *He must be afraid of the mountain*, Ryder thought. *The mountain is going to sing.* There was a word for this, he knew, but he couldn't think what it was. There were other witches at the entrance now, some beckoning, some pointing up and screaming silently, their voices overwhelmed by the song. It was a trio now— Ryder, Falpian, and a rumbling bass note that seemed to shake the world. One witch grabbed Aata's Right Hand and pulled her deeper into the cave.

At the same time, Falpian bent down and gathered up a great wad of snow. He grabbed hold of Ryder's hair and shoved the snowball into his mouth. Abruptly, their singing stopped. Ryder fell back, choking. Thank Aata. He could hear himself cough, could hear the screams of the witches, but mostly what he heard was the roar of a . . . He looked up and saw that a great wall of snow was careening down from the top of the mountain. Snowslide. That was the word he'd been looking for.

"Run!" Falpian yelled.

CHAPTER 18

IN THE CHAMBER OF
AATA AND AAYSE

Falpian lay with his cheek pressed against a cool stone floor. His hands and feet were tied. *I found my talat-sa.* A feeling of joy swelled inside him, despite the pain of his bonds. Ryder was the presence he'd been feeling all this time; Ryder was the reason his magic had finally crystallized. Ryder was his twin in spirit.

Falpian didn't even mind that his talat-sa was an unbeliever. The great God Kar plays the best jokes; he understood that now. Even deep inside these witches' caves, he could hear the echoes of the God's laughter.

"I don't know what you have to smile at."

Falpian sat up abruptly, feeling dazed. Next to him was a witch, a male witch in reds. Falpian had a vague memory of more witches, frightened witches—a hundred frigid blue eyes piercing through him—the fear that they would tear him limb from limb right there. Someone had taken him to this quiet chamber, pushed him through winding tunnels, tied him up with rough hands. Falpian had the strangest feeling that he knew the witch who had spoken, but of course that was impossible. An impressive braided beard stuck out like fingers from the man's chin, but he probably wasn't many years older than Falpian himself.

"The snowslide," Falpian said. "Was anyone hurt?" The witch scowled but didn't answer. Falpian had seen Ryder inside the caves, he was sure of that, but . . . "My dog! Do you know if my dog is all right?"

He tried to recall what had happened to Bo, but his memory was fuzzy and blurred. He and Ryder had run one way into the caves, and Bo had gone the other—but whether the dog had made it out, or been crushed under that wall of rock and snow, Falpian couldn't say, and the bearded witch didn't seem to want to tell him. Bo must have made it, Falpian decided. He was a smart dog.

"What are you going to do to me?" he asked. The witch was nervously fingering a blue bead at his neck, a gesture that seemed familiar. Falpian found a name that was on the tip of his tongue. "I know you. You're Kef!"

The witch gaped. "I was told not to let you speak."

Falpian barely heard him. He was distracted by the thought that he'd actually known this man's name. He knew it because when he sang with Ryder, they'd shared things. Faces, knowledge, secrets. In fact, he realized, they'd been sharing thoughts for a long time, mostly in their dreams. How could it have taken him so long to figure it out? Even Ryder had known. Even his dog had known. Amazed, he tried to search his mind for other useful bits of information, but it was all a tangled mass of images. He did seem to know some farming techniques he hadn't before.

"Hicca," he said with a laugh. "Ryder gets the knowledge of the finest tutors and librarians and I get hicca."

"I asked you not to speak," the witch warned.

"But I'm a friend of Ryder's!"

"Do I have to find a gag?" There was more fear in his tone than anger, but still it alarmed Falpian, made him suddenly notice the damp cold. "You are to stay here and be silent until the witches are ready to interrogate you."

Falpian swallowed. Hopefully, wherever Ryder was, he was pleading for Falpian's life—but then, Ryder must know now that Falpian was a spy, must have learned it when they sang. And Ryder would know other things too—his father, the coming war. He'd know everything. Ryder wouldn't be pleading for Falpian's life; he'd be arguing for his execution.

Falpian drew his knees to his chest, wishing Bo were there to keep him warm. The leather straps that bound his hands were uncomfortably tight, and his fingers were numb. The knowledge that he had found his talat-sa kept colliding with the fact that they were enemies, that soon their people would be at war with each other. The great God Kar might play the best jokes, but this was a cruel one, very cruel. He sank back against the cave wall, and the sense of joy that finding his talat-sa had given him drained away like water.

"Ryder told you my name?" Kef asked. It wasn't exactly true, but Falpian nodded. "If you really are his friend and mean this coven no harm, the witches will learn it in their bones. They will learn all. You will have nothing to fear." Falpian didn't find the thought consoling.

For a while he sat with his captor in silence, examining the chamber where he had been taken. It was long and narrow, with entrances on either end. Oil lamps sputtered in nooks, giving off the smell of roasted goat. Mosaic friezes in reds, turquoises, and gold decorated the walls. To Falpian's right were two large heads, the tiled portraits of two blond women. One face was perfect—red lips and cheeks and glittering eyes formed from a hundred different shades of blue tile—but the other was cruelly damaged. Dug-out hollows in the rock formed the eyes, and the yellow hair was crudely painted on.

"Aata and Aayse," Falpian said, then remembered he wasn't supposed to speak. "Sorry."

"You know of our prophets?" the witch asked sharply.

Falpian hesitated, but Kef seemed to want him to answer. "Yes. The silent sisters. The founders of witchcraft."

The man nodded and then, like Falpian, leaned back against the wall of the cave, looking up at the two heads. "There must have been a flood once, to cause such damage. Or spiders. No one can repair it now—the technique is lost." There were craftsmen in the Bitterlands who could do such work, but Falpian knew better than to mention it.

They fell silent again. Falpian wiggled his fingers, trying to get the blood moving in his hands, but it only made them hurt. The smell of the lamps reminded him how hungry he was. There was still some lump in his pockets, but with tied hands he couldn't reach it, and he thought it unwise to ask for help. Kef kept looking toward the nearer entrance, the one that led back to the main cavern, and Falpian could see he must be waiting for someone. He wondered who. His interrogator?

"I don't know why she had me bring you here," Kef muttered, more to himself than to Falpian. He glanced again at the heads of Aata and Aayse. "This is a holy place."

Again his fingers went to a small bead at his neck, and Falpian squinted at it in surprise. This was the last place in the world he would expect to see Baen writing, and yet there it was, scratched deep into the bead—a word in ancient Baen.

"*Yarma!*" Falpian said, smiling with relief. The word meant "friend."

"Shh!" Kef hissed, as if Aata and Aayse were listening.

He seemed to understand the writing on the bead, but Falpian wondered if he was aware of its deeper meaning.

"Where did you get that?"

"I wear it to remember my parents," the witch said curtly. "It belonged to my mother."

During the war there were Witchlanders who were friendly to the Baen, who would give them food as they were trying to make their way to the Bitterlands or even hide them if their lives were in danger. These friends of the Baen would wear the word on their clothes or paint it on their houses in plain sight. The Baen alphabet was so different from pictographs that most Witchlanders would mistake it for decoration or random scratchings.

"Your parents were good people," Falpian said. He couldn't believe his luck. Maybe this witch would help him escape. Maybe crossing the border hadn't been so foolish after all. But Kef's face had soured.

"My parents helped the enemy during wartime. They defied witch law. I wear this to remember that they are *not* who I want to be."

"Oh," Falpian said, the hope of a moment before guttering out like a candle. "But it's not wartime now. I'm not your enemy now."

"If the witches tell me you are an enemy, you are an enemy. If they tell me you are a friend, then you are a friend."

Falpian sat back against the wall with a small sigh, and Aata and Aayse stared serenely down at him, as if his fate had been decided long ago. It wasn't like Kef to be so obedient, Falpian thought, then remembered that they had never met. More and more of Ryder's thoughts and memories were unpacking in his mind, jostling with his own thoughts, making room, changing him. He had memories of Kef as a sly, sweet, mischievous person, completely different from the pinched and nervous man he saw in front of him. Laughter. A high place. The taste of honeyplums.

"You're right," Kef said, relenting from his harsh tone. "We're not enemies now."

Falpian's words thrown back at him made him wince with guilt. In point of fact, he *was* an enemy. He was a spy. He was helping to start a war. These strange feelings that told him Kef was a friend were a lie.

"I saw you," Kef continued. "I was standing by the entrance to the caves, and I saw you and Ryder destroy those creatures. You were singing, and the snow was coming off their bodies in long strands. It was incredible!"

Falpian's memory of singing with Ryder was hazy and distorted, like the memory of a dream. They had destroyed the creatures, hadn't they? He had used a winter key.

"You saved every witch who was in those caves. I saw it with my own eyes. I've known Ryder a long time, and he's not one to trust the Baen—neither am I, for that matter—but if you're here to help us destroy those things, I'll make an exception."

Kef meant to be reassuring, but Falpian only felt more guilt, pricking like needles. The witch smiled now for the first time, showing crooked teeth, but Falpian couldn't bring himself to smile back.

The sound of footsteps made them both start. At first Falpian thought the time had come for his interrogation, but the person who entered came from the far end of the chamber, opposite the entrance Kef had been glancing toward. In the dim light, Falpian could see it was a woman, a small ageless witch with short cropped hair. She ignored the two young men and stood with her arms outstretched in front of a small shrine. Falpian could just make out the color of her tunic: Her witch's costume was not red, but black.

"Who is that?" he asked in a low voice.

"Hush! A holy woman come to pray. She will pay us no heed."

It seemed to Falpian that her small, birdlike eyes gave him a darting glance, but it was hard to tell. A moment later she was leaning backward into what he knew was the witches' sun position. She was so flexible. Falpian couldn't imagine how she held the position for so long, how she stayed so still.

"We call her Aata's Left Hand," Kef whispered softly.

"She is the keeper of the catacombs. She comes out of the tunnels at dawn and dusk to pray for the dead."

Falpian guessed it was dusk, but there was no way to be sure. He wondered how the witch knew when it was time to pray. "It's true then, that you keep the bodies of your dead in caves?"

The man nodded. "All the witches who have ever lived on this mountain since the time of Aata and Aayse."

"And that poor woman lives down there? With the corpses?"

He nodded again. "The catacombs are forbidden to everyone but her." As Falpian watched, Aata's Left Hand shifted her position again. "Sometimes, when there is a death, helpers will bring in the body, but they must wear blindfolds. The black witch is a very holy person. She has given up her life, her family, even her name to watch over the dead. She has given up worldly concerns."

Falpian looked at the praying woman again, seeing her differently now. Again she seemed to be glancing toward them, but if she wondered who Falpian was, she didn't let it interrupt her prayers. Falpian had always thought of witches as soldiers and murderers, but they were worshippers, too. Or loyal young men like Kef, who liked the taste of honeyplums.

If my father attacks this coven, he thought, this reverent witch will die. Kef will die. Ryder . . .

He tried to tell himself that the woman's prayer was an abomination. She was praying to a Goddess, after all, and how could anyone believe in a female God? And yet her prayer was strangely moving. She was as graceful as the black herons that fed by the seashore back home.

"I never knew Aata's prayer was so beautiful," Falpian whispered. At the other end of the chamber, the black witch made a final bow to her shrine and slipped out.

"I've always thought so," Kef agreed. He smiled again, that crooked smile that Falpian somehow found so familiar. This time Falpian smiled back.

"Kef! You were told not to let him speak. Their voice is their weapon."

Another witch had slipped in unnoticed from the nearer entrance, an older woman in reds with a severe face and a thick gray braid. Her voice was low, but there was no mistaking the venom in her words.

"Visser, forgive me," Kef said. "Is it time? Shall I take him to be interrogated?"

Instead of answering, the witch jerked her head. Kef jumped up and hurried to her, and for a while they whispered under the spitting lamps. As Falpian watched, the young witch's eyes widened in horror. A sinking feeling crept over Falpian. The older witch handed Kef a long dagger.

"No!" Falpian cried.

He tried to get away, using his feet to propel himself backward across the cave floor. Kef caught up with him in a moment and cut the leather cords around his ankles.

"Get up," he said.

"Please!" Falpian said. "Don't kill me! I'm Ryder's friend, remember?" He tried to get to his feet, but his legs had gone to sleep, and he fell back to his knees. Kef grabbed him roughly by the coat, but Falpian saw the doubt in his eyes. "You saw us destroy those creatures!"

With his hand still on Falpian's collar, Kef looked to the older witch, his face a dull gray. "Does he have to . . . ? Do I have to . . . ?"

"The witches have spoken," Visser said firmly. "*He* made the creatures that attacked our coven."

"They are sure? Before they said it was Mabis."

"Aata's Right Hand made a casting. It is certain."

"She's lying!" Falpian shouted, trying to twist from Kef's grasp. "Aata's Right Hand can't read the bones! No one can. The covens are blind." He stopped struggling and blinked in the dim light of the cavern as the weight of his own words fell over him. Blind?

Visser ran toward him, her face a mask of rage. She slapped him hard across the face. "You see why we do not let them speak," she said. "Their words are poison."

"Yes," Kef said, the doubt gone from his voice. "I see." He hauled Falpian up by the collar and yanked him so roughly toward the other end of the chamber that a silver button flew off Falpian's coat.

"Wait!" Falpian said over his shoulder. "Where are we going? Didn't you just tell me the catacombs were forbidden?"

"Just do as you are told," said Visser, looking behind her as if to be sure no one was following.

Falpian turned and clutched at Kef's reds with his bound hands. "Please! *Yarma!*"

"Do not use that word!" Kef hissed as he pushed Falpian into the dark tunnel. "I am no friend to you."

CHAPTER 19

YARMA

"Hello! Is anyone there?"

Ryder felt his way in darkness across a rough stone floor. His wrists and ankles were bound tight. He didn't know where he was, but he sensed a high ceiling above him, and the air smelled rich with roasted hicca and dried fruits. It made his stomach growl, but this was no time to think of food.

On the other side of the chamber was a thin yellow bar of light, like the light under a door, and Ryder was inching towards it. It *was* a door, he discovered—wooden and very heavy. He pulled himself to stand and ran his fingers over it, but he felt no handle or knob, only rusted metal hinges.

"Hello!" he called again. His fists made a dull thump against the wood. "Let me out!"

There was no answer. Ryder leaned back against the door and slumped to the ground. His head ached. Falpian's

entire life had stampeded over him while they were singing, and now Ryder's brains were crammed full of unwanted
thoughts, frightening thoughts. He turned and, still sitting
on the stone floor, banged the door hard with his tied feet.
"Let! Me! Out!"

A sound. A thud. On the other side of the door, a bolt
was drawn. Light filled the chamber, and Ryder winced.

"Get back!" said a man's voice, one he didn't recognize.
Ryder shielded his eyes with his fists. "I said get back! Back
away from the door." The man, whoever it was, was afraid
of him; Ryder could hear it in his voice.

Ryder crawled toward the center of the room, then
turned again to see who was speaking. Two figures stood
in an arch of light, a man and a woman, both with glims.

"You're sure you want to do this?" the man said. "Their
voices drive you mad, they say. Even one of them can be
dangerous."

"Aata's blood," the smaller figure said. "He's my brother.
If he hasn't driven me mad yet, I suppose he never will."

"Skyla?" Ryder said, squinting into the light.

"It's up to you, I suppose," the man said. "Though I
don't know why the elders would allow it. If I hear you
scream, I'll do what I can." The man shut the door again,
fearful and quick, as if he were throwing her to a pack of
dreadhounds. The girl raised her glim.

"It is you," Ryder said, smiling. "Oh, thank the Goddess!"

He held out his hands to her. "Here. Undo these ropes and let me look at you."

"Stay where you are," she said, edging away. "I want to be sure you are really my brother."

"Who else would I be?" He laughed. "Now quick, and do as you're told."

"You sound like him."

"Why in Aata's name did they tie *me* up? Where's Falpian?"

"Is that his name?"

Ryder paused. He heard the fear darkening his sister's voice, remembered the looks of horror on the witches' faces when he and Falpian sang. He tried to imagine what they must think of the Baen, and as his mind swung around to their point of view, he was struck by the gravity of Falpian's situation.

"They're going to kill him, aren't they?"

"He's as good as dead now. They say he's the one who made the creatures."

"What!" Ryder cried. "Skyla, that's not true! He didn't!"

His sister knelt down on the floor and sat her little glim between them, its light flickering deep inside the glass. Ryder thought she looked older somehow, but maybe it was just the way the glim lit up her face. Tentatively she reached out and put her cool fingers over his hands.

"How do you know?" she asked. "Sodan and the elders

say that this has happened before. In the old days, when our people used to live together, sometimes a blackhair would try to infect a man with strange dreams, addle his mind. They say the Baen has done this to you." Her large, pensive eyes peered into his. "Maybe you only think he's innocent because that's what he's made you believe."

Ryder pulled his hands away and shook his head. "It doesn't work like that. It's . . ." He struggled to find words, but what could he tell her? He sighed and looked around, as if an explanation might be in the air, and for the first time, he noticed his surroundings.

"Aata's vow!" he couldn't help saying.

The chamber must have been used for winter stores. Rows and rows of shelves rose up around him, disappearing into the darkness of a high ceiling. Each shelf was filled with wooden crates or large rounds of cheese or seemingly endless jars of preserved fruits. Opposite the door, bulging sacks were piled on flats, one on top of the other against the wall—hicca, he guessed, or hicca flour.

"One of our storage chambers," Skyla said. He noticed the word "our," noticed the casual gesture of her hand as she waved it over the shelves.

"Maybe you are clever to be a witch." Ryder thought of all the tithes his family had paid over the years—probably enough to fill this room—and of all the witches getting fat as ticks on his labor. A sliver of anger pulled through him as he remembered how the witches couldn't throw the bones anymore, remembered how it was all for nothing. "Goddess take me if I ever pay another tithe." When he turned back to Skyla, he found that she was laughing. "What?"

"It really is you, isn't it?" she said, and she threw her arms around his neck, almost knocking over the glim in her exuberance.

"Of course it is." He couldn't hug her back with tied hands, but he leaned toward her, drinking in the scent of her hair. "Foolish girl."

A moment later Skyla pulled back, and he saw her wipe her eyes with the sleeve of her reds. "Your stink is making my eyes water."

He smiled and didn't dispute the reason for her tears. "I climbed a mountain in these clothes. How's Pima? Is she all right? Are you?"

Skyla nodded. "It was horrible when the monsters attacked, but Yulla kept her head. She carried Pima on her back all the way to the catacombs."

"I'm sorry, Skyla," he said, guilt overwhelming him. "I should have been with you."

"I don't understand. I don't understand what's happening. If your mind hasn't been addled then . . . what? You left to kill a Baen and came back a singer."

"I'm not a singer," he said sharply. "Don't say that."

"The coven is in chaos," Skyla went on. "No one knows what to do, and everyone is fighting. Aata's Right Hand has broken her vow and confessed to Sodan that none of her prophecies were real, that they were made by someone else! Some want her banished from the coven, but of course she can't leave now. The snowslide has trapped us all in the caves, but no one wants to start digging out until we know for sure there won't be another attack. Most of the witches wanted to kill the Baen immediately, and a few of them wanted to kill you, too. But Aata's Right Hand told everyone who would listen that you saved her, that you and the Baen destroyed two creatures with your voices." She took his hands again. "Tell me, is that true?"

"Yes!" Ryder said. "And she wasn't the only one who saw it! Weren't there others at the cave entrance?"

He was sure he had seen Kef there at least, but Skyla shook her head. "Everything was so confused. Most saw only that you sang and the snowslide came. Aata's Right Hand isn't from this coven—she's an outsider. And hardly anyone wants to believe her now, not after she pretended to be a boneshaker. Some of the witches actually hiss at her when she opens her mouth, and the ones who've taken the vow themselves put their hands over their ears."

"I need to speak to the elders," Ryder said. "To the whole coven. They can't kill Falpian."

"You don't understand," Skyla said. "Sodan did listen.

Aata's Right Hand convinced him to at least hear your friend's story. But when they went to get the Baen for interrogation, he was gone, along with Kef and Visser."

"Gone?" said Ryder. "Where could they go?"

"Down here, there are many places where he might have been taken. Another storeroom like this one, maybe." She hesitated. "But Ryder, Visser was among the witches who did not want to listen to the Baen—who wanted to kill him outright before he could do any more damage. I don't . . . I don't think there's much hope for him."

"No!" The words fell like stones into Ryder's heart. "Skyla, you've got to untie me! Falpian might be a Baen, but he deserves more than a knife in the dark for something he didn't do."

Skyla bit her lip. "Would you really mourn for him if he died?"

"I . . . would," he admitted.

She stared at him uncomprehending. "Is he a traitor to his people, then? Is he on our side?"

Now Ryder was the one to hesitate. He knew why Falpian had crossed the border; he'd seen the thoughts of war in his mind. "No," he said. "He is not on our side. But Skyla, are we only allowed to care about people who are on our side?"

Skyla leaned back, frowning. She must have heard the emotion in his voice. For a while they were both silent.

"I won't try to tell you that he's not dangerous, because he is," Ryder went on. "Sodan *should* question him. I hope he does. Falpian is a black magician. He knows things, things that are happening in the Bitterlands, things that scare me. But when I needed help destroying those creatures, he didn't stop to wonder if he should. He just did it. He has a better heart than he gives himself credit for. Besides . . ." He moved a little closer to her. "I believe our mother sent me over the border to save him, to keep him from being assassinated. She must have done it for a reason. Maybe the witches are right and he's addled my head—you can't see the world from somebody else's point of view and not be changed—but as far as I know, I'm still thinking with my own brains, and my brains are telling me that we shouldn't let him die."

His sister considered his words. "I always thought your head was made of rock," she said finally. "The poor Baen would need a chisel to addle it. Give me your hands." From the sash of her reds she pulled a small knife sheathed in leather—she'd come prepared, he realized. Ryder held out his wrists.

"And there's something else," he said. "If there is even a chance that Falpian and I can destroy the creatures, why would Visser want to get rid of him so quickly?"

"You mean . . ." She paused. "You mean you think she might have made them?" She didn't seem as surprised by the idea as he would have thought.

"If not Falpian, it *must* have been a witch—no one in the village has this kind of magic."

"Aata's Right Hand told me that's what you'd say."

"She did?"

There was a sharp bump, and the door swung open. Ryder started, guilty as a criminal, but Skyla didn't even look up. It was the white witch.

"Here." She tossed a bundle of clothes at Ryder's feet—reds. "Put these on."

"The guard?" Skyla asked.

"I told him he was wanted by the elders, but my lie will be discovered quickly."

"I don't understand," said Ryder. "Are we going to find Falpian?"

"Aata's Right Hand has another idea," his sister said. "And I think you should listen to it."

The tunnels were narrow and dark. They hadn't seen any bodies, not yet, but the dank, musty smell reminded Falpian of a time back home when he'd found a dead rat in one of the attics.

The covens are blind, Falpian thought as he walked. *The witches can't read their bones.* It wasn't a secret that would save him, or even do him any good, but he couldn't help but marvel at the sheer size of it.

"Where are you taking me?" he said over his shoulder

to his captors. Kef grunted by way of answer and gave him a push between the shoulder blades. Falpian stumbled forward into the semidarkness.

When they came to a fork in the tunnel, Visser took the right-hand path, giving instructions to Kef before they parted. "You know where to meet me," she said quietly. "Finish the task as quickly as you can. There is much to be done."

Falpian stole a glimpse at Kef and saw that his eyes were sick with dread; they both knew the "task" she was referring to. Visser's glim receded as she hurried off down the passage. Falpian remembered what Kef had said about these tunnels being forbidden, and thought Visser knew her way quite well for someone who wasn't supposed to ever come here.

"Where are you taking me?" he asked Kef again.

Kef raised his glim, steering Falpian by the scruff of the neck. "The preparation chambers. You will have the honor of lying beside dead witches—that is, until the spring comes and the ground is soft enough to bury you."

"Bury me!" The thought frightened him even more than dying. He didn't want to spend his afterlife as a wandering spirit on the wrong side of the border.

If only he could escape with this secret, this enormous, unexpected secret that had fallen into his lap, that he'd stolen from the mind of his own talat-sa. Wasn't this what he'd crossed the border for? Falpian had called himself a spy, but he'd never expected to find out something this big. The covens blind! Even the most peaceful of the Baen nobles would have to agree: It was the perfect time to attack.

This was the gift he could lay at his father's feet, the gift that would prove that he was worth more alive than dead. But of course, his father would never receive this gift now. Kar's sense of humor was getting darker and darker.

"That witch was lying and you know it, Kef," Falpian said. "I didn't make those things. You saw Ryder and me destroy two of them with your own eyes—why would I destroy my own monsters?"

"I don't know," Kef said. "I don't have to know."

"You're just going to do what you're told."

"That's right."

They walked on, and the rough stone walls seemed to close in on them. At times Falpian had to hunch to squeeze through the passageways, scraping his shoulders as he went. They passed dark alcoves leading off to other tunnels, but Kef kept them on the main path. The air grew thin and stale. *I could run,* Falpian told himself, but without a lamp he couldn't get far.

Behind them, something rattled, like a foot slipping on stones. Kef turned and raised his glim, keeping a hand on Falpian's collar. The two stood silent, but there was only blackness behind them. "Visser?" Kef called, his voice belying his nerves.

"It's probably just your guilty conscience," Falpian snipped, hiding his own fears. Kef narrowed his eyes and pushed Falpian on. "If your parents were here now, they'd tell you to think for yourself. *They* did. *They* knew that not all Baen were evil, no matter what some witches claimed."

"My parents aren't here now."

"But if they were—"

"My parents were punished for what they did during the war—punished for helping the Baen!"

Ahead Falpian could dimly see a widening in the tunnel, could just make out the outline of a door. It must be the preparation chamber, he thought—the place where Kef would kill him.

"Punished how?" he asked, turning around, trying to slow their pace.

"The Goddess took them. That's all I'll say."

But Falpian knew more, remembered more. Disparate images from Ryder's memory coalesced in his mind. "The scabbing disease," he said, his voice growing gentler.

Kef's face darkened. "Ryder certainly has told you a lot about me."

The scabs. A bad way to go by any reckoning. And worse to watch. "Kar's sake," Falpian said softly. "I'm sorry.

But plagues . . . They kill the good and bad alike, you know. There's no explanation—"

"No," said Kef firmly. "No. Only children and the old die of the scabs. There had to be a reason why two healthy people were taken. They were the only ones in my village to die of the disease that year—the only ones! And I knew why. I knew the secret they were keeping."

Kar's eyes, thought Falpian. How could he argue with that logic? How could he argue with just a few steps left? "You can't kill me because of your parents! What have I got to do with them?"

"I begged to join the coven so that I could atone for what they'd done," Kef said, his voice raw. "I told the witches I'd do anything. And killing you is what they've asked of me. I'm . . . sorry."

Another noise behind them made Kef wheel around, his light upraised. Again nothing. This was Falpian's only chance. He took a deep breath and balled his hands into tight fists. When Kef turned back, Falpian swung his hands upward as hard as he could. His fists connected with Kef's jaw, and he heard a click as teeth snapped against teeth. Frantically, he grabbed for the knife at Kef's belt, but he missed as Kef stumbled back. The glim smashed against the ground, spraying hot fat.

"Where are you?" Kef said to the dark. Falpian pressed his body against the wall of the tunnel, trying to quiet the beating of his heart. At any moment, Kef's knife would find his flesh.

There was a loud, cracking thump, and Falpian heard Kef cry out in pain. Something fell heavily to the ground. Falpian stayed frozen, listening, but all was quiet. It was probably a trick. Kef was probably trying to wait him out, trying to get Falpian to make the first sound. Someone grabbed his arm, and Falpian screamed.

"Follow me," said a voice, a woman's voice.

"Who are you?" Falpian cried.

"Quickly. He's unconscious now but could wake at any time. I used a stone. Poor boy—but I'll go back to him when you are safe."

"What? Who?" Falpian saw nothing in front of him but pitch blackness. "Who are you?" he managed to sputter.

"*Yarma,*" said the voice. "Friend."

CHAPTER 20

THE BLACK WITCH

It was pitch-dark, but the mysterious woman seemed to know where she was going. "Stay here," she said. A cool hand guided Falpian to the corner of a stone table. He gripped it tightly. She'd cut his bonds, and his hands were still tingling back to life.

"Where are you going?" His voice sounded high and quavery and he didn't care. He wasn't convinced this person was a friend—maybe she just wanted all the Baen-killing for herself—but without her he was trapped in a mountain full of dead witches.

"I'll be back soon." The woman's voice was gravelly but pleasant, like the singing of a rusty door.

After the cramped tunnels, Falpian felt dwarfed by the blackness all around him. This must have been the place Kef had called the preparation chamber, whatever that meant. Falpian couldn't guess its dimensions, but something about the way his voice carried gave him the feeling of space and high ceilings.

"Hello?" he called. There was a slight echo in the room, but other than that he got no answer. He ran his hands over the cool stone of the table and touched what he thought was a large crate or box sitting on top. He moved his hands up the wooden sides. There was no lid, but inside the box was some sort of sand. He pinched a bit of it and touched his fingers to his tongue. Salt.

From far across the room, a light appeared. Then another. The two lights bobbed toward him. "That's better," said the voice. "I do hate the dark."

As the lights came closer, Falpian began to distinguish rows of rough wooden shelves around him, each one filled with bottles and jars. Dried plants hung upside down from nails driven into the cave walls. He could see where he was now, could see that the stone table was very large, and that the box he had touched was one of three, about as long as men. There was something in the nearest box that he hadn't noticed before.

"Kar's thousand eyes!" he yelled, jumping back.

A woman holding two glims hurried forward. Falpian pointed in horror at a mound sticking up out of the salt. Fingers.

"One of the witches who died in the attack," she said calmly. "This is where I will prepare their bodies."

Falpian gagged and wiped his tongue on the sleeve of his coat—he'd actually tasted the salt around those corpses! The witch tilted her head, bemused. It was the woman in black he had seen praying in the chamber of Aata and Aayse. She was older than her flexible body had led him to believe. Now Falpian saw the deep lines around her mouth and eyes, saw that her short-cropped hair had paled to white. Her eyes were sharp, though, he noticed, bright and curious.

"I'm sorry," he murmured. "I meant no . . . disrespect." She looked him up and down. "Please, don't be alarmed. My name is Falpian." He remembered that you were supposed to bow to witches, so he quickly bent over, stooping so low that he could see the tile work on the dusty floor. "I know you probably haven't seen a Baen in a long time. . . ."

"I thought you would be older."

Her words didn't register. "I'm not here to harm you."

"You've come too early."

He stood up. "Honestly, I—what?"

The witch stared at him with her bright bird's eyes. "Come along." She turned and began to walk quickly toward the other end of the chamber. "There is an exit," she said over her shoulder. "But I'm afraid it is a long way down, and you will have to climb back up the mountain on the Witchlander side. It will be dangerous, but it's the only way. We must get you back across the border."

"Wait!" Falpian stood where he was. "I—"

"Young man!" The witch raised her two glims. "You must go home. Now. Don't you know what we did to people like you during the war?"

Falpian's mouth went dry. He knew. He hurried toward her, not wanting to be left in the dark. "But I have a friend. He's here in the caves. I need to speak with him."

"You have no friends in the covens," she said sharply. "No friends but me. You must go forward." She was right, of course. It was foolish to want to see Ryder again—what made him even think of it? He'd only be caught by the witches, and he had a mission to complete.

"Why would you call yourself my friend?"

The woman stared at him in the light of the glims. Her eyes were still bright, but something in the depths of them made the hairs on the back of his neck stand up. He'd thought her eyes were birdlike; now he remembered what strange little creatures birds really were. Then she laughed a jovial laugh that made Falpian wonder why, a moment before, he had been afraid of her.

"Follow me," she said, and she turned without answering the question. "I can't go with you. But I will show you the way!"

Ryder let out a deep breath when he got to the chamber. He'd made it through the main cavern without being noticed, though all the while he'd felt as if the Goddess were shining a light on him from above, angry at his wearing reds. Aata's Right Hand had said they would call too much attention to themselves if they all went together, so Ryder was alone, waiting in the dim quiet for the two girls to join him.

From the walls, blue-stone eyes stared at him placidly. Ryder took a large lamp from the wall and held it up to better see the portraits of two women. One of the faces was especially fine; the light glittered on blond hair made of hundreds of gold and yellow tiles. But the second portrait was damaged, with only a few of its original stones remaining.

"The twin prophets," he murmured. He drew a finger across the yellow hair in the damaged portrait, then examined the yellow stain on his finger.

His sister came out of the tunnel and slipped in beside him. "What is it?" She must have seen these portraits before, but to Ryder they were new and strange.

"I've seen something like this somewhere else," he said, thinking of the day the monsters came when he saw the two faces at the waterfall: one Witchlander, one Baen. Ryder bent down and picked something off the floor—a shard of jet-black stone with a curved edge—and a wild idea flashed through his mind. He tried to fit it into the empty eye socket of the damaged portrait, but it was hard to tell exactly where it belonged.

"What's wrong?"

"Nothing." He had no time to think about Aata and Aayse, and the history of ancient witches wasn't any of his business anyway. Aata's Right Hand entered the tunnel, and Ryder let the shard drop from his fingers.

"What exactly are we doing here?" he asked her sharply. "I should speak to Sodan. Does he have people searching for Falpian? Does he know it might be a witch who made the creatures?"

"Sodan is a good leader," the white witch said, "but old age makes him too careful. He won't allow us to do what must be done." She spoke in a harsh whisper, and Ryder realized she must have lost her voice from all the talking she had done—arguing for his life, and Falpian's. She reached into a pouch at her waist and held something out to him. "Please, take this."

He frowned when he saw what it was. "My mother's bone? Aata's sake, what good is that? I can't throw."

"Yes, but someone can. I told you that another witch made my prophecies, one who wasn't allowed to throw the bones. You can ask her to make another casting and tell us who made the creatures."

Ryder held out little hope that this would work. "Well, where is she then? Is she meeting us here?"

Skyla and Aata's Right Hand shared a glance.

"There is only one witch who would be forbidden to

throw," Skyla said. "The Left Hand of Aata. The black witch. We have to go down into the catacombs and find her."

He thought about this for a moment. "No. Absolutely not. What we should be doing is looking for Falpian—he and I are the only weapon against the creatures. Besides, I'm not leaving Pima up here when for all we know there could be another attack."

"You can't help Pima if Sodan just has you tied up again!"

He shook his head. "Think, Skyla. Whoever Aata's Left Hand is, she's no better at boneshaking than Aata's Right. Neither one predicted the attacks, did they? And if this black witch is the one who said that Mabis made the creatures, then I have nothing to say to her."

"But she didn't!" Aata's Right Hand interrupted, her voice cracking. "That was my fault." She sighed and put her hand to her throat. Ryder glared coldly and waited for her to go on, but she hesitated, seeming not to want to, and Ryder saw that it was more than the pain of speaking that made her falter.

She lowered her eyes. "When the monsters made the first attack on the village, I knew I'd made a terrible mistake," she said. "I had your mother's bone by then and I tried to make a casting—but I couldn't see anything. I could never see anything! I came here to this chamber, where

I'd met the black witch before—but she said the bone was mine now and that she couldn't throw again. I went to the elders with the intention of confessing everything—all my lies. But then . . . they asked me to cast for them, and I decided I would try it one more time."

She looked up at him now, and her eyelashes glistened with caught tears. "I was right here in this chamber. I threw the bones, and I looked at the pattern on the floor as I've done a thousand times. . . . They say that if a witch can hold the pattern of bones in her mind and truly understand them, then the bones will disappear before her eyes and a vision will come. A vision of the future. I looked. And then, suddenly . . ."

Her gaze slipped away from Ryder's face, and he could see that she was looking somewhere behind him, looking to the slanted floor of the cave, as if the bone casting was right there in front of her. Ryder felt a chill go through him, reminded of Mabis and how she'd stare at nothing.

"I saw a place. A waterfall. A green lake thick with maiden's woe. I thought it was somewhere near, but I didn't recognize it." She squeezed her eyes shut as if to squeeze out the memory. "It wasn't a vision, I know that now. I must have made it up—but I swear I didn't realize it at the time. I wanted to see one so badly. And it seemed so real."

Ryder glanced at the portrait of Aata and Aayse. He knew the place. He'd heard someone singing there the day the monsters came. Perhaps the vision was a true one. "You . . . you saw my mother there?"

Aata's Right Hand shook her head. "I wrote out . . . the things I saw for the elders, and they discussed it for a long time. Then they told me that the maiden's woe was a reference to your mother, and that there was a lake like this very near your cottage."

"That's it? That's all the evidence you needed to decide she was guilty?"

"I trusted them!" she said. "I wanted to believe that what I saw was real. And it seemed to make sense!"

Ryder let out a hiss. "Come on, Skyla. I'd rather try my luck with the elders. I don't see why we should believe anything she has to say."

"Wait!" The white witch ran to block his exit, holding out her hands. "Don't you understand?" she pleaded. "I believed you. I defended you. You said a witch must have made the creatures, and I agree. I'm sorry about your friend, but he must be dead by now. This is our only hope."

"He's not dead," Ryder insisted. "I'd—I think I'd feel it if he were."

"He's in the tunnels," said Skyla firmly.

Ryder turned. His sister was bent over something at the other end of the narrow chamber. From the stone floor she picked up a small, shiny object. Ryder stepped toward her. It was a button. A silver button from Falpian's fine coat.

"They must have come this way," Skyla said.

"That settles it, then," said the white witch. She grabbed Ryder's hand and pressed the black bone into his palm. "If your friend is in the tunnels, perhaps the Left Hand of Aata has seen him. Ask her. And ask her to make a casting one more time. She will be in the preparation chambers. I have never been there, but it shouldn't be far. If anyone can get her to throw the bones again, it's the two of you."

"Us?" said Ryder. "Why us?" He looked to Skyla.

"Because she's our mother's sister," Skyla said. "She's our aunt—the great boneshaker, Lilla Red Bird."

CHAPTER 21

A CASTING OF BONES

"Hurry up!" he said, though Skyla was already close at his heels. They were descending a narrow passageway leading down, down into the mountain. Ryder held a clay lamp on a chain that he'd taken off a wall in the chamber of Aata and Aayse. It was a large, unwieldy thing, and every time its hot fat spilled over the lip and onto the stone floor, he cursed.

"This witch is dead; no, she's not dead. That witch can throw the bones; no, she can't throw the bones—there are too many lies and secrets in this place."

"I agree," muttered Skyla.

He stopped short and turned around. The lamp swung on its chain, making eerie shadows on the tunnel walls. "You don't have to come, you know. These catacombs are forbidden. Aren't you breaking your own witch rules to be down here?"

"Ryder, shush!" She pointed. "There's something ahead." More softly she added, "Do you think I'd let you come down here alone?"

Ryder turned again in the narrow tunnel. Farther on, the path diverged, and from the left-hand passage a faint yellow glow was coming toward them.

"Who's there?" a voice called. Ryder felt Skyla squeeze his arm as a figure in black emerged from the passage.

"By the twins!" said Ryder. The woman in front of them had his mother's face. In fact, she could have been an older version of Mabis, except that she was smaller and thinner, and her cropped hair was almost white. And the eyes—they were different too. They were sharper, and without the wry humor that always glinted in his mother's. The woman cocked her head to one side as she looked at them, a strange birdlike pose. Was that how she got her name? Ryder wondered. Was it really Lilla Red Bird?

All at once Mabis's words came back to him from the day the monsters came. *When I made the firecall, I was sure that Lilla would come.* She had known, then, that Lilla was alive, living deep in the mountain's heart. How she must have missed her sister all those years. A sudden longing to see his mother again surged through him.

Skyla poked him in the ribs and whispered in his ear. "Give the greeting."

Quickly he thrust the lamp into his sister's hands and

bowed low. "We are looking for the Left Hand of Aata," he said to the floor.

"These are forbidden places," the witch snapped.

Ryder rose from his bow. "You are Lilla Red Bird, aren't you?" he asked hesitantly, knowing already that it must be true.

"Do not call me that! Lilla Red Bird is dead. Her name must never be spoken."

That rule certainly hadn't been followed, Ryder thought. The name Lilla Red Bird was spoken everywhere. She was the great hero of the war. He wondered if this woman even knew how famous she was—how many stories were told about her in Dassen's tavern or by parents trying to get their children off to sleep.

"We . . . ," he began. "We are Mabis's children."

If he'd been expecting a happy family reunion, he didn't get it. The black witch looked him up and down, and her face seemed to grow darker, though her words were kind enough.

"Ryder. Named for my father. You have joined the coven, then." He realized that she assumed from his reds that he was a witch, but before he could correct her, she went on. "I threw the bones that predicted your birth. My little sister thought she was sick from eating blister-berries."

So she really had thrown a casting about him once.

Had she also really predicted that he would grow up to be a boneshaker, as Kef had claimed?

"The anchor bone," Skyla hissed, poking Ryder in the ribs again. He took it from the pouch at his waist and held it out to the black witch.

"The coven is in trouble," he said. "The whole village. Will you help us? Will you make a casting?"

"My bone." She stared at the little knob of charred black vertebra, and for a moment the look on her face was almost greedy. Then her eyes narrowed. "Why don't *you* use it? Why don't you make a prophecy?"

Ryder had the feeling he was being tested somehow. "I can't," he stammered.

"Can't?"

"I know—I mean—I was told that you made a prophecy that I would be a boneshaker." Beside him, he heard Skyla stifle a little gasp. "But I'm not," he added quickly, glancing at his sister. "She was wrong."

Lilla drew herself up haughtily, as if Ryder's suggestion that she had made a false prophecy had wounded her pride. "I did not say that you would be a boneshaker. I said that you would have the gift. A boneshaker must pray to the Goddess. She must learn the words of the prophets. She must memorize the relationships between the bones and study the ancient castings. Did you do these things, Ryder?"

He shook his head. "No. Mabis . . . She didn't teach me anything about the bones. I don't even know their names."

The Left Hand of Aata let out a long breath. "As I thought, then. A wasted gift." The words were hard, but she seemed almost relieved. Perhaps she liked being the only boneshaker.

Ryder thrust the bone into Lilla's hands before she could object. "Please. Make a casting. You are the only one who can help us."

"No," she said. "I mustn't." She tried to hand him back the bone. "I gave it up to become the Left Hand of Aata."

He shook his head, refusing to take it. "But we know you threw before, for Aata's Right Hand."

"Child, we witches believe that the keeper of the dead must give up everything. She must become dead herself. When I agreed to become the black witch, I agreed to give up my name, my family, my old life . . . and my old life had everything to do with this bone! You must not ask me."

"Please, Aunt," said Skyla. "The coven is in just as much danger now as it was during the war. One more casting might save lives!"

"I told you I cannot!" Her voice was sharp, angry. She thrust the bone roughly into Ryder's hands, and for a moment he saw a steely determination in Lilla Red Bird that frightened him. It was a glimpse of the warrior she must have been once. Ryder was glad she'd been on their side during the war.

"Perhaps you could help in another way," he said nervously. He was beginning to wonder if mentioning Falpian was a good idea. His aunt didn't want anyone in the caves; what would she do when she found there was a Baen disturbing her sanctuary? "There is . . . a person in the catacombs. A young man."

"He is not to be harmed," she said icily.

Ryder and Skyla shared a glance. "You've seen him, then," said Ryder. "I must bring him to the other witches."

"I told you, he is not to be harmed!"

"I don't want to harm him; I want to help him."

Lilla's eyes narrowed. "What is Falpian to you?"

"He's . . . my friend," Ryder said, amazed that they were talking about the same person. "What is he to you?"

Lilla studied him as if he were a particularly complex casting she was trying to read. She didn't answer Ryder's question, but he reasoned she must have seen something in the prophecies she made for the white witch, something that made her believe Falpian was important. What was it about that Baen? In her confused way, Mabis had also believed there was something special about him—if not, why would she tell Ryder to cross the border to stop his assassin?

It made him uneasy to think that their future might

be in Falpian's hands. Ryder had a connection to the blackhair—he couldn't deny that—but after sharing his mind, he knew Falpian wasn't on the side of the Witchlanders. How could he be?

"He said he had a friend in the coven," Lilla murmured. "But I didn't see how it could be true."

"Seems there's a lot that your castings didn't tell you," Skyla said archly. Ryder shot her a glare and shook his head— Lilla wasn't the kind of person he wanted to antagonize—but his sister went on. "You said it yourself, Ryder. She couldn't even predict the attack on the village."

Lilla's small eyes flashed with anger. "The future is a vast land, Niece. When a witch throws, the little grain of it that comes to her is not always the one she asks for."

Skyla shrugged. "It's obvious your skills have been exaggerated."

Lilla's face turned to stone, but Skyla didn't back down. Their glances crossed like blades.

"Don't," Ryder whispered softly. What was she doing?

"I am the last great boneshaker of the covens," Lilla hissed.

"That is what they say," Skyla agreed. "And I can see that the best way to keep your reputation would be to never throw."

"Are you trying to bait me, girl?"

It was just what Skyla was doing, Ryder realized. She

was betting that if Lilla shared her sister's looks, she might also share her flaws, and Mabis had always had a little vanity mixed in with that iron will of hers.

Ryder held up the bone, remembering the greedy look he had seen in Lilla's eyes. His mother had worn that look too, and now he understood that it hadn't been just the maiden's woe she coveted.

"Mabis once described to me what it was like to see the future," he said. "She told me that every once in a while her mind would turn a corner and then she could see forever. She loved that feeling. Even when she was seeing terrible things, she loved it." He held the bone out a little closer to her. "It must be so difficult for you. There is so much more of the future to know."

Lilla grabbed the bone from his hand. "Insufferable. The both of you. Just like your mother." But a smile flashed across her face, revealing yellowed teeth. It was the first sign that their aunt might actually be happy to see them. She turned on her heel without another word and started down the right-hand path.

"Where are you going?" Ryder called. "Are you going to cast for us?"

"A witch needs more than one bone to make a prophecy, Nephew," she answered without looking back.

He and Skyla followed the bobbing light of her glim down dark passageways and branching tunnels that Lilla navigated without hesitation. The air was close and heavy, with an unpleasant smell of decay. Ryder kept glancing behind him, wondering if trailing after this gruff, unyielding witch was the right thing to do. He was worried about Falpian, and he was worried that he shouldn't have abandoned Pima up above with the other witches when there was a chance of another attack.

They turned a curve, and Skyla caught her breath. A body—the first they had seen—lay in a hollow cut out of the rock. It was wrapped in bandages. They didn't stop, but Ryder caught a glimpse of a mask on which a realistic face was painted—a young man's face with eyes closed.

As they continued, there were many bodies, each nestled in a small, carved-out hollow. Ryder peered at them as he passed, keeping his hand in front of his nose. Once he saw a mouse sitting on the pointed slipper of a well-dressed corpse. It was bigger than a cottage mouse, with huge eyes and a long, forked tail. It scurried away quickly, but after that Ryder thought he could hear rustling up ahead every time Lilla turned a corner.

Finally the black witch stopped in front of one of the smaller hollows. The man inside looked no different from many of the other corpses they had passed. Around him were things he must have used in life: a string of blue beads, some rotting fabric that may have once been a cloak, a knife with a horn handle. The wrappings on his face were thin and translucent, molded to the bones underneath. Painted blue eyes peered out of sunken sockets, and Ryder could see teeth underneath the painted lips.

"Hello," Lilla said softly.

She kneeled down, setting her glim on the uneven stone floor. Without any hesitation or disgust, she ran her fingers gently down the body's bandage-wrapped arm. A caress, Ryder thought, finding it hard to watch. Then, to his shock and horror, she grasped the man's wrist in both hands and twisted. There was no snap, just a dry, tearing sound. Skyla gave a little scream.

"What in the name of the Goddess are you doing?" Ryder shouted.

"I'm doing what you asked," Lilla said calmly. She turned on her knees and held out the lump of bandages. Skyla shrank away, but Lilla didn't seem to notice. She put the bundle on the tunnel floor and pulled apart the decaying wrappings to reveal a withered gray hand. One of the fingers had broken off, and she quickly pulled off two more and began rubbing them between her palms. The burial preparation and the dryness of the caves had completely desiccated the body. Soon Lilla had made a little pile on the floor: eight yellowed bones. To these she added the black one.

"Nine bones. Enough for a casting," she said. Carefully she replaced the rest of the hand by the corpse's side.

"Aata's vow," said Skyla. She was pressed up against the opposite wall of the tunnel now, her face the color of ashes.

"Oh, I know my father wouldn't mind," said Lilla casually.

"Your father!"

"My father, your grandfather."

"I'm going to be sick," Skyla said.

Lilla took her glim and held it up, peering into Skyla's face. "You are the one who asked for a casting, my girl. Do you want it or not?"

"She's gone mad," Skyla said to Ryder. "This is wrong. I know it's wrong. Let's take our mother's bone and leave right now."

Ryder looked from one to the other, hesitating. Was Lilla mad? He remembered what Mabis had told him, that the war had done things to Lilla, that seeing the future had done things to her. Was it wrong to make her cast again? His poor aunt. Why was she even here, languishing among the corpses? Surely there were others who could be the black witch.

But when he looked at her face, his pity dissolved. Calm. Hard. Sure. Mabis's face, and yet, not. No, they couldn't assume she was mad. People had thought Mabis was mad, and look where not listening to her had gotten them.

"Let's hear what she has to say, Skyla," he said finally.

Lilla Red Bird cocked her head at him and gave a slight smile. She gestured to the black bone. "Do you know what this is, Mabis's children?"

Skyla glanced at it, then looked back to her feet. "My mother's bone," she murmured. "What of it?"

"You know the story of Aata's set?"

Skyla was silent.

"You are both witches now," Lilla said. "Surely you have been taught the story." Ryder felt himself blush at being called a witch. He reminded himself that Lilla didn't know everything, even if she was a great boneshaker.

"Aayse made the first prophecy bones for her sister so that she could read the future," Skyla said. "But when Aayse died and Aata had her vision of the Goddess, she realized she didn't need them anymore. She gave one bone to each of her loyal followers."

Lilla held up the charred black knob. "And those were handed down, witch to witch."

Ryder stared at the bone, skeptical, but seeing it in a new light all the same.

"Is it true?" said Skyla, looking at Lilla now. "Do we really have one of Aata's bones? Are we descended from one of the original followers of Aata and Aayse?"

"Irrelevant. It is a witch's belief that matters. Your mother made true prophecies with this bone because it meant something to her, because Aata and Aayse meant something to her—as much as she might have tried to deny it. And my father's bones mean something to me."

Skyla crossed her arms, and Ryder could see that she was considering what she had heard. Gingerly she skirted around the bones on the floor and peered into the low hollow at the man inside, her nose slightly wrinkled. "That is our grandfather, then."

"It is," Lilla said. "He went to Barbiza to trade for the coven—and this is how they sent him back to me." She looked into her father's face as if she saw the man and not a dead body. "I was so angry. I've often wondered if the war would have been different if he had lived. If I would have been different."

"Is that . . . ?" Skyla said. "Ryder, look!"

Ryder followed Skyla's gaze and saw, at the man's feet, a wooden bowl like the kind some witches used to hold their prophecy bones. Inside it lay a gray stone.

"A humming stone," Ryder said.

Lilla nodded. "Our Fa was interested in the old magics—from any culture."

Ryder saw the tears coming to her eyes and didn't know how to react. He had to keep reminding himself that this small woman with her strange cropped hair and her bad teeth was *her*. Lilla Red Bird. Her prophecies alone would have ensured her fame, but she'd been a fighter, too, a great warrior. Dassen liked to say that if it weren't for

Lilla, they'd all be worshiping Kar. Ryder never had much respect for witches, but this woman was different. She had seen things, knew things.

"I think she must know what she's doing, Skyla," he said. "I think we have to trust her."

His sister nodded, and Lilla smiled her yellow smile. She turned to the bones. Ryder thought she would begin her casting right away, but instead she held a small bone up in front of her, turning it in her fingers to see it from all angles.

"I name you conflict, the soldier," she murmured finally, and set it down onto the stone floor.

Skyla leaned forward, fascinated now; Mabis had never done this before a casting. Without hurrying, Lilla examined each bone and gave it a name: the ghost, the shadow man, the eye that sees, and the eye that doesn't see. They were the same names Mabis used when talking about her bones. Ryder remembered hearing that his grandfather had named her set long ago, the same grandfather that lay before him now.

"And you," said Lilla, holding up the black bone. "My anchor. The heart of the casting." None of it meant anything to Ryder—anchor, ghost, shadow man—but he felt a strange pang of jealousy when Lilla held up the black bone and called it hers.

The naming finished, she gathered up the bones in

her cupped hands and abruptly tossed them out without a word. Ryder and Skyla held their breath.

Lilla didn't move around her casting, as Mabis would have done; she only stared, slack jawed and silent as the time slid by. How did she even tell them apart? Ryder wondered. They were mostly knobby finger bones. And why did his mother's bones have markings when Lilla needed none on hers? His own ignorance annoyed him.

After a while, Lilla's eyes grew round and wide, and it came to Ryder that she wasn't looking at the bones, not really, but at some vision, some door to the future that he and Skyla couldn't see and had no inkling of. He wondered what it was like. *Mabis should have taught me this*, he thought bitterly. Lilla's hard words filtered through his mind. *A wasted gift.*

Suddenly there was a sharp intake of breath. Lilla leaned in closer to the casting, her hands tightening into fists. "Visser!" she said. She looked up at him, and her eyes flashed with anger. "How did I not see it?"

Visser? Ryder had never liked the woman, but by Aata, why would she destroy the coven, the village?

"Visser made the creatures?" said Skyla. "But how?"

Lilla cast her eyes about, ignoring the question. There was a horn-handled knife at her father's side, and she reached for it, pulling it out of a leather scabbard. "She must be stopped. Even now she plans some great desecration."

"More creatures," Ryder said. "We must warn Sodan and the others."

"No!" said Lilla. "You have no time. The bones tell me she is in the catacombs already, making her way to the lower chambers. I will warn the others. You must find her—find her quickly." She thrust the knife into his hands. "I will tell you the quickest way down—the two of you can travel faster than I can. I will leave Visser to you, Ryder. If your ancestors mean anything to you, you will put this knife between her ribs. She must not be allowed to do what she plans."

CHAPTER 22

THIEVES

First there was a staircase that twisted downward and downward, hewn out of solid rock. It seemed to have no end, seemed to Falpian to bore right into the center of the earth. Only occasionally did it open out into some level of the caves, and he was never sure what he would see. Once it was a wall of bodies, reaching up to the ceiling, each corpse resting in a carved-out hollow. The mice in the hollows had no fear of him, only lifted their heads at his glim, a hundred black eyes sparkling, then went back to their work. A chest cavity must make a perfect nest.

At other times his light would reflect on glimmering stone tiles, and Falpian would emerge from the narrow stairwell to gaze at ancient chambers with high ceilings and twisted pillars.

"Hello!" he called in one such place, his voice high

and small. He got no answer, of course, and didn't know what he would have done if he had. He continued on.

A persistent, nagging voice at the back of his mind kept telling him to turn around. What if the gormy men should come back? Ryder couldn't fight them on his own, not without Falpian's help. He had to keep reminding himself that he was a spy for the other side, for Kar's sake. He was exactly where he was supposed to be: on his way home. He'd found the information he'd crossed the border for: The coven was blind and vulnerable, ripe for attack. His mission was almost complete.

I'm sorry, Ryder. Falpian tried to link minds with his talat-sa, tried to say good-bye to him across the distance of the cave tunnels. They should be able to do it, with practice anyway. But Falpian didn't feel an inkling of Ryder's mind, and maybe it was just as well. His talat-sa would hate him now.

Still the staircase wound on and on. The lump in Falpian's pockets was almost finished, and he was dizzy with thirst. He began to wonder if she had lied, this black witch, and had only sent him on this path because the thought of Falpian wandering in the dark forever had amused her. Perhaps she was following him right now the way she'd followed Kef, hiding somewhere in the blackness, a stone in her hand.

Abruptly the staircase came to an end, and Falpian

found himself in a high chamber with five tunnels leading away from it, all going farther down. The black witch had described this place, had told him to take the middle path, and yet, Falpian hesitated. The air was fresh here, cold and sharp in his nose. He lifted his lamp. Somewhere, high above the reach of its beams, there was probably an opening to the outside—if it wasn't the middle of the night, he might have even been able to see sunlight—but the opening, if it even existed, was unreachable.

Reluctantly he left the fresh air of the chamber and walked on, but he had gone only a few steps down the tunnel when he noticed something on the stone floor. A brooch. A woman's jeweled brooch was walking slowly across the floor, the golden pin sticking out like a tail. He bent over. Underneath the brooch was a dark red spider, about the size of a honeyplum. Its legs were hairy and banded with fine black lines.

"Hello, little thief," Falpian said. He'd always liked spiders and thought that thief spiders were particularly beautiful, with their velvety bodies and glassy red eyes. Of course, back home his mother was vigilant against them. Thief spiders loved anything shiny. Many a nobleman had discharged his servants for stealing, only to find, years later, a nest of thief spiders under his floorboards, hiding generations of lost treasures.

The spider waved two of its hairy legs at Falpian in complaint.

"Oh, I'm sorry," he said, and he set the brooch to the ground. "You're quite right. It's yours." The spider ran to the brooch and squatted on it.

Falpian would have liked to touch the little thief, but he knew they had a nasty bite. He turned to leave and was surprised when the creature followed, leaving its shiny possession.

"Some other spider's going to get that," he warned, but now the red eyes were fixed on something else. Falpian moved his pretty witch glim to the right, and the spider went to the right. He moved his glim to the left, and the spider went to the left.

"Well, I'm sorry, but you can't have that," he said. He stamped his foot and the spider scurried away.

Up ahead there were more. The little thieves darted along the walls or scuttled between his feet, but they were fast and disappeared if he tried to crush them. They came out of nooks in the rock to stare, their red eyes following the glim as it passed.

The tunnel was getting narrower now, and the spiders were getting thicker. Every time Falpian glimpsed a movement out of the corner of his eye he jumped, startled.

They eat insects, he told himself, *pretty, shiny insects—not people, not me.* But as he walked, a story Farien once told him surfaced to his mind. Something about a lost boy. Falpian had always thought his brother made it up to scare him; now he wasn't sure. After a frantic search, a missing child was found in an abandoned barn not far from his home. He was alive, but bloated with swelling bites, covering his face with his hands. Thief spiders nesting in the barn had been attracted to the glimmer in his eyes. When the boy's hands were pulled away, there were nothing but bloody holes where his eyes had been.

Something fell from the ceiling onto Falpian's shoulder, and he gave a yelp, brushing it off. He started to jog down the tunnel, but the floor was uneven and he tripped repeatedly. When he came to a fork in the path, he stopped; he couldn't remember which way the black witch had told him to go. He looked back and was alarmed to see a great mass of spiders following along behind, coming toward him across the floor. He stamped his feet on the ground and yelled, and they seemed to hesitate, but only for a moment. He turned and ran, choosing the right-hand fork at random.

"It's just a glim!" he cried. "I need it!"

The walls seemed to be alive with them now. They rained down on his shoulders and on his neck. He felt a sharp, painful bite on his back, then another. He tried to brush them off, but they were under his clothes, wriggling down his spine.

He came to a great, long crevice that opened up in the wall like a black scar. It got wider as it went along, and Falpian caught a glimpse of the glimmering hoard inside. It was the nest. Coins, jewels, bits of metal and broken glass—all were of equal value to the little thieves. Anything shining or sparkling they took for themselves and brought back to the dark—beads, bits of mosaic tile they had loosened from the wall—he even thought he saw a gold ring with a bony finger still inside, but he was going too fast to be sure. Falpian didn't stop, didn't slow down, and from the mouth of the nest, spiders poured.

"You can't hurt me!" Falpian shrieked. But he didn't believe it. They could kill him with enough bites, stab out his shiny eyeballs.

Suddenly he was in an open cave, slipping on a stony floor. A rank smell hit his nose, but he didn't stop. At his feet was a small, greenish pool. Water. Falpian hesitated for just an instant, his glim reflecting like a glass moon. Then he splashed in and turned around, betting spiders couldn't swim.

They could.

Or rather they could walk on the surface of the water as witches of old were said to do, gliding gracefully, held up by nothing. Falpian cursed. He splashed at the spiders and they drowned, capsized, but there were more, many more, coming at him from every side. His little patch of water was getting smaller and smaller, overrun by red bodies.

"Take it!" Falpian cried. And he swung the glim on its chain. It sailed in an arc over the water and crashed on the stone floor of the cave, splattering fat and glass. Darkness. He squatted down in the water with his hands over his head, fearing the spiders would still attack. He squeezed his eyes tight, afraid they might see a glimmer. All was silent. The water was frigid, and the spiders didn't come.

He opened his eyes, but it was no different from closing them. Darkness was all around.

Ryder?

Still there was no answer in Falpian's mind. There was nothing in his mind, nothing but darkness and a tight knot of fear.

Ryder? Can you hear me?

CHAPTER 23

ALL THE NIGHTMARES

Somewhere above him, water trickled over rock. There was a frigid dampness to the caves now; it sank into Ryder's bones, made his teeth chatter. They must be near the river. Moisture seeped into the tunnels and covered the bandaged bodies with splotches of green and black mold. The burial hollows were older and more elaborate here, with intricate carvings showing remnants of bright paint, but everything seemed to be rotting away.

Behind him, Ryder could hear Skyla breathing heavily. She was trotting to keep up, but he couldn't slow down, not with Visser planning another attack. It was frustrating how many twists and turns there were, how many forks and branches they had to navigate, all leading downward and downward. Were they a quarter of the way down the mountain by now? he wondered. Halfway? It was impossible to tell. Lilla had given them clear directions, which

Ryder had carefully written on his arm in charcoal—a cross for right, a circle for left. Every time they came to a fork in the path, he licked his thumb and rubbed away a mark so they wouldn't get confused.

"I used to think the Left Hand of Aata was lucky," Skyla said. They had reached a place where the tunnels narrowed dramatically, and Ryder had to slow his steps and hunch forward like an old man. "I thought it would be so still and quiet, like Aata when she was in her sister's tomb, listening to the whisperings of the Goddess. But I don't feel the Goddess here. Do you?"

In the narrowing space, the smell of mouse urine was almost overpowering. "Not really."

"I hate it here."

Ryder glanced behind him and saw how haggard Skyla looked. Her face was smeared with dust. "I know you're tired, but these tunnels can't go on forever."

"No, I mean, I hate it *here*. I hate this coven. I don't know why I came." Her voice shook. They'd been walking half the night, and it was clear her nerves were fraying with exhaustion. "There's something wrong with this whole place."

Ryder turned a tight corner. "Don't look," he warned.

They had come upon another burial hollow. The face of the person inside had been chewed down to the bone, and on its chest was a knot of writhing baby mice, still blind and hairless. Ryder pulled his reds up over his nose.

"Oh Goddess!" Skyla shouted. She wrapped her arms around his waist, and he felt her face pressing into his back. "This is what I mean! Poor Lilla is stuck down here and for what? She can't keep the catacombs all by herself. I don't understand what Sodan is thinking."

They hurried past as quickly as they could. Mercifully, the passage soon opened up again, and after a while they came to a crossroads. The air was a little sweeter here, though Ryder still had a horrible feeling at the back of his throat, like he might start to retch at any moment.

"You were right, Ryder, you were absolutely right." Skyla was red faced and livid, as if seeing the nest of baby mice had been the last drop of water before a dam broke. "Why do we give the witches our tithes? Why is it hardly anyone can throw the bones anymore? Did you see how many empty huts there were before the monsters came? The coven is smaller than it was. Less than it was, somehow. But no one will tell me why."

Ryder was staring at his arm, trying to figure out if the mark he'd made was a straight line, which would mean taking the middle passage, or a cross, which would mean they should take the right-hand path.

"You know I never understood why you wanted to join the coven," he said, somewhat impatiently. "What did you think it would be like?"

He decided that they should go straight on, and he

turned back to tell her so, but when he lifted the lamp he saw that she was holding her breath, trying not to cry.

"You'll think it's so stupid," she said.

Ryder cursed inwardly, but he set down the lamp on a flat part of the floor and put his arms around her. He should have sent her with Lilla to be with the rest of the coven, but it was too late to think of that now.

Skyla buried her face in the shoulder of his reds and let out a sob. "I thought the people here would be like Fa. He knew. He knew there was some kind of magic running through the world's veins. He could feel it." She stood back and wiped her eyes. "He made me feel it too. He taught me that the whole world was a holy place. That's why he loved our old farm, loved the dirt under his feet. Everything was magic to him."

"We have to hurry, Sky," he said gently, not knowing what else to say. He picked up the lamp. It felt lighter than when they'd started out, and it sputtered a little—there was only about a thumb of oil left in the bottom. Skyla took a deep breath and nodded.

As they descended, there were more bodies, more hollows. Many of the dead had bowls at their feet. Usually they contained nothing or perhaps a few prophecy bones, but occasionally Ryder noticed one like his grandfather's, containing a humming stone. Notions that had been forming in his mind in the chamber of Aata and Aayse began to take shape. Without slowing down, he touched some of the carvings that swirled over the stone arch of one of the hollows.

"It's so unfair," Skyla muttered. "Of all people to be touched by magic, I can't believe it was you."

Ryder held out his hand to help her over a pit in the sloping stone floor. "Is that what I am?"

"If Lilla Red Bird said it, it must be true. Besides, all magic is one magic—that's what the teachings of Aata tell us. If you can sing, you can learn to throw the bones too. But by the Goddess, Ryder, if you become a great bone-shaker, I am just going to have to hang myself from a high tree! How can you hear the whisperings of the Goddess—you!"

Ryder didn't know whether to laugh or be annoyed. "Listen," he said, "I'm going to tell you a secret." He stopped in front of a particularly beautiful hollow, so big it was almost a small room. The man inside lay on what looked like a stone bed, with four short pillars twisting up from each corner.

"That feeling you describe, the feeling that the world is somehow a holy place—of course I feel it. I'm not saying that I believe it's the Goddess whispering at me or the great God Kar singing me a lullaby, but yes, I feel it and I always have." He wiped his sister's tearstained face with the corner of his sleeve. "I think you like to see me as some sort of big, bossy oaf with all the sensitivity of a boulder in the middle of the road, but of course, of course, the world is crackling with miracles. Do you think I'm blind? I just don't like to talk about it as much as you do."

"Oh," she said sheepishly.

He laughed at how surprised she looked. "I'm not offended. I've been doing a very good imitation of a boulder in the middle of the road. I don't know why. To please her, I guess." He knew he didn't have to say which "her" he meant.

"I talked about going to sea, but it wasn't really the sea I wanted. I wanted that vast, important thing that I guess we both felt was out there. It's just . . . now that I've caught a glimpse of it . . ." He thought back to how it felt to sing with Falpian and winced at the idea of ever singing again. "Aata's breath, if the Goddess really has given me a gift, do you think I can ask her to take it back?" He laughed at himself. "There, you know my deep, dark secrets. Do you want to know one more?"

She raised an eyebrow at him. "Of course."

"I suppose it's not so much a secret as a question, one you might ask old Sodan when you see him next." He gestured to the alcove in front of them. "Why is there Baen writing all over these catacombs?"

Skyla looked around blankly, then back at him. "Where?"

"Right here. Everywhere." He pointed to the curling script that snaked around the pillars in the hollow and wove in and out between the decorations on its arch. "Haven't you noticed? It's on almost every other alcove now."

Skyla looked closer. "That's not writing. It's just some kind of . . . decoration." She traced her finger along the curls and dots carved over the arch. "It *is* intricate. Are you saying . . . ?"

"Baen," he said. "It's the same as on the humming stones."

"Why would a witch have Baen writing on his tomb?"

"Maybe this isn't a witch," he said. "Or maybe this is a different kind of witch."

"But they're just squiggles. What is it a picture of?"

"Their writing isn't a picture of a thing. It's a picture of the sounds you make when you say the name of the thing." He frowned. He knew what he'd just said was correct—it was one of those strange flecks of information that kept floating through his mind, little gifts from Falpian—but it didn't make any sense at all. How could you make a picture of a sound?

"I know what Mabis would have said about that," said Skyla. "Even their writing is wrong."

Ryder looked more closely at the bandaged body in the hollow, but the paint that had depicted its face was blackened and worn, too much so to discern the race of the dead person. Was he a Baen? Skyla was looking too, probably wondering the same thing.

"Do you remember when we were children," she said, "and we used to put on that Baen helmet that Fa brought from the war? I was terrified by that thing. It was like . . . all the nightmares of childhood."

Ryder nodded as he peered into the dead face. "I expect the Baen have nightmares of us."

Ryder?

"We'd better go," Skyla said.

Ryder held up his hand. "Shh. Do you hear that?" For a moment he could have sworn he'd heard Falpian's voice calling out to him.

"Yes," Skyla said. "I hear it."

But she was referring to something else. From up ahead there came the faint banging sound of stone on stone. The voice Ryder thought he'd heard was driven out of his mind.

CHAPTER 24

THE TOMB

Ryder, Falpian said to himself. *Ryder, come back!*

For a moment it had worked—he was almost sure of it. Falpian stood shaking in the frigid water, afraid to move, trying to remember what his father had said about linking minds with his talat-sa.

He couldn't see a thing, and his boots were soaked through. Around him in the blackness there were scuttlings. Rustlings. Some Falpian attributed to spiders dragging away shards of glim—but there were other noises. And smells, too, foul smells, like the droppings of an unknown animal. Something made a sound right by his ear—the beating of small wings. He heard a little splash at his feet and stifled a cry. He was going to die here in the dark if couldn't find Ryder's mind.

Once, back home, his father had grown impatient with the tutors and singing masters and had tried to teach

Falpian and Farien himself. Falpian remembered sitting in a chair with his eyes blindfolded. Somewhere in the house his brother was hiding.

"Stretch your mind," said his father. "Call to him."

Scents from the kitchen wafted up the stairs. Cook was making fish stuffed with apples for dinner, Farien's favorite. Was he down there? Falpian tried to do as his father told him and stretch his mind through the rooms of their old stronghold by the sea. His mother would be upstairs with her ladies; his sisters were playing in the garden.

"He's in the servant's closet on the second floor," Falpian said, pulling off the blindfold. Farien always used to hide there when they were boys.

His brother cursed. Farien had been in front of him all along, but Falpian hadn't been able to feel it. Their father turned away, red faced.

"You try," Falpian said to his brother. "I'll hide now."

"It's no use."

"Our magic will come. Mother says—"

"We're useless. We're worse than useless." The look in Farien's eyes was wretched.

"Father, tell him that's not true."

But their father said nothing. Falpian saw his brother flinch when their father slammed the door, leaving them alone.

"It wasn't our fault," Falpian called to the dark.

"Our fault," the chamber echoed back to him.

"You should have loved us just the same."

"Same. Same . . ."

"I hate you!"

"Hate you! Hate you . . ."

Falpian brought a hand to his lips. He was shocked by his own words, but letting them out gave him a strange feeling of relief.

Farien had grown so thin and sad near the end, like a shadow. He spent more and more time in his sailboat, going farther and farther out to sea. How Falpian wished he could speak to him one more time. And now his father would make him lose another brother, his talat-sa, before he even had a chance to know him.

Why? Why did Falpian tie himself in a knot for a father who couldn't love him?

"I'm not Farien!" he shouted. "I'm not going to waste away, pining for a kind word!" The echoes of his voice swirled around him.

The echoes. Of course!

The echoes weren't good enough for this to be an echo site, but perhaps they were good enough to let him see a little, with the sight that singing gave him. In the darkness, a glimmer of hope sparked.

Falpian tried a note, tried to harmonize with the sounds that came back to him, but the echo lasted only a moment—not long enough. He took a tentative step to his right and tried to sing again.

He had never done anything like this before, but it wasn't unheard of. An echo site like the one at Stonehouse wasn't made, after all; it was found. Magicians of old had painstakingly sung into gullies and mountain passes, listening to echoes and planting flags at promising places. He just had to be patient and do what they did, he told himself, and he took another step.

This time when he sang, he caught a glimpse of something, the ghost of an image in his mind. Fruit. The ceiling of the cave was hung with quivering fruit. Falpian was so surprised that he stopped singing, and his vision was snuffed out. He sang again.

No, not fruit. Stormbats. They hung upside down from the ceiling like bunches of grapes, keeping warm by pressing close. Gracefully they swooped down all around him, catching thief spiders or picking the dead ones out of the water. This was the splashing he had heard. Stormbats were a good sign. Stormbats needed openings to the outside.

Falpian's voice grew louder, bolder. He had a stitch in his side, and every time he took a breath, however small, his vision dimmed. But he was grinning as he sang. Could *he* do this? Could his father find an unmarked echo site?

I don't need your approval, he thought. *I'm a black magician in my own right now.*

Opposite the tunnel he had entered, he could see three passages. Two led down to twisting paths. The other . . .

Falpian struggled to visualize it, though his lungs hurt like fire. The right-hand tunnel led down . . . There! A storm-bat swooped through—a straggler, flying home to the colony. That must be the way.

Falpian's knees buckled, and he struggled for air. He stumbled out of the pool, slipping and sliding on the wet floor of the cave. He fell, but he quickly got up again, waving his hands in front of him until he reached the rock wall.

He felt along the wall for the right-hand tunnel and staggered down it, hoping what he had seen was more than some trick of his mind. The path dipped down and made a turn.

Ahead, something made his eyes sting, something bright. It was—Kar's eyes, he hadn't imagined it—it was daylight! Falpian rushed forward. There was light ahead, and it wasn't a lamp, or a torch. It was morning.

Falpian emerged into a large chamber. He breathed deeply. Air. Clean, cold air filled his lungs. Shafts of natural light fell from the ceiling. He blinked again and again, dazzled. Light filtered in from a little round hole in a lower corner of the chamber—an exit! Falpian lurched toward it.

After a few steps he stopped short. Ryder. His talat-sa. "I feel you now," he said aloud, laughing to himself with relief. "I must have been trying too hard before."

The passage he had just come from was on the far

right, but there were many other openings and stairways leading off into dark tunnels. Ryder was somewhere close. Falpian took a tentative step forward. One arch was bigger and more ornate than the others. Falpian closed his eyes and immediately felt drawn to it. There. Like a needle to a lodestone. His talat-sa.

"There you are," he breathed.

"There who is?" said a voice from a shadowed corner.

Falpian's eyes snapped open. He wasn't alone.

"Stop what you're doing," said Ryder. "Stop right now."

Visser stood caught in the middle of a high chamber, holding a large rock over her head. She lowered her arms, staring at Ryder and Skyla with a mixture of shock and guilt. A stone sarcophagus dominated the room, and Visser had been about to smash something carved on top of it, something Ryder couldn't make out.

"You shouldn't be here," she spat. Her gray braid had come undone, and her face glistened with sweat in spite of the chill.

Ryder stepped into the room and immediately felt the awe it was meant to inspire. A low stone lamp illuminated walls covered with intricate carvings and half-faded murals. Writing, both Baen and Witchlander, spread over everything like black vines, including the floor and ceiling. The sarcophagus stood at the center of the room, surrounded by four mosaic pillars studded with green and blue glass. Between the pillars, garlands of long-dead flowers gathered dust. It seemed to Ryder to be a reverent place. A sacred place. Whatever Visser was doing, it was wrong.

Ryder handed Skyla his lamp and pulled Lilla's knife from the sash of his reds. "We know you made the monsters," he said. "Come with us. We're taking you up to the elders."

Visser snorted. "You don't know what you're talking about."

"Innocent people have died!" Ryder's voice shook as he said the words, in spite of himself. "In Aata's name, why did you do it? To show your power?"

"No!"

"Why, then?"

"Don't be a fool!" she cried. "It was that blackhair—it must have been. He's tricked you." Visser dropped the stone she was holding to the floor. She walked right up to Ryder's blade. "You wave that knife around, young man, but do you even know how to use it?"

Ryder held his ground, brandishing the weapon, but she was right to call his bluff. Angry as he was, he still wasn't sure he could do what Lilla had asked and put the knife between her ribs.

"Don't let her scare you, Ryder," Skyla said urgently. "Remember what she's done."

Skyla swung the lamp awkwardly on its chain, threatening Visser with it as if it were a weapon. Ryder moved forward too, steeled by his sister's words. Visser held up her hands and backed away, but Ryder and Skyla pressed forward until they had her trapped in one corner of the room.

"*You* should understand," Visser said to Skyla. There was a note of pleading in her voice. "The witches are *your* people now. They're trapped by the snowslide. I need to lead them through the forbidden tunnels and down to the lower exit. If they dig their way out, more of those things might be waiting for them."

"That doesn't explain why you're *here*," Skyla said sharply.

"Yes," said Ryder. "What does leading the witches through the tunnels have to do with destroying this place? Just what is that?" He nodded to the sarcophagus. Visser pressed her lips tight.

He kept his eyes locked on the witch and edged over to the sarcophagus, dead blossoms turning to dust under his feet. On top, the life-size figure of a woman had been carved from different pieces of colored stone: white for her bare forearms, red for her witch's costume. Visser had done cruel damage—the face was almost gone—but it was obvious what she was trying to hide. She hadn't yet destroyed the eyes. They were open, staring up at the ceiling, irises as black as Falpian's. And the hair was another clue. Black stone curls cascaded down the side of the sarcophagus.

"She's Baen," Ryder said. "You did this because she's Baen."

He touched the rough place where the nose had been, and anger coursed through him. The sculpture must have been so beautiful. There were fine veins on the hands, and the fingers seemed about to twitch with life.

Disparate images and thoughts that had been floating around inside his head now slid into place like the pieces of a puzzle. "Oh Goddess," he breathed. It wasn't just wrong, what Visser was doing, it was . . . blasphemy. "Visser, how could you do it?"

"It was necessary!" Visser said, desperation in her voice now. "It's still necessary. Leading my people through the tunnels might be the only way to save them. But by the red, they can't see this."

Skyla gave Ryder a questioning glance. "I don't understand," she said. "All right, the woman buried here is Baen, or has Baen blood, but we've seen others like her in the catacombs. Why is this one so important?"

"Tell her, Visser," Ryder said firmly.

She shook her head. "No! No one must ever find out! There are secrets in these caves that should stay hidden forever!"

Ryder didn't agree, and for him it wasn't a secret anymore.

"Think, Sky," he said. "We've heard Fa tell this story a hundred times. 'When she died, the women hung her tomb with flowers.'" Ryder reached up to touch the crumbling flower garlands that hung between the pillars. "'Aata stayed by her sister's side, neither eating nor sleeping, for nine days and nine nights. And then the Goddess came.'"

"Aayse?" said Skyla with awe in her voice. "The tomb of Aayse?" She hurried to the sarcophagus and held the lamp over the ruined face. Hesitantly she ran her fingers over the damaged lips. Ryder wasn't sure how his sister would react, but then a smile lit up her face, and she looked at him across the carved body with shining eyes.

"This is incredible!" She lifted the lamp to the mosaic friezes along the wall, gazing around the chamber again as if seeing it for the first time. "Was Aata a Baen as well?" She addressed her question to Visser, but it was Ryder who answered, excited to have someone with whom to share the thoughts that had been circling in his mind.

"I don't think so. Remember the mural in the chamber at the top of the mountain? One woman blond with blue eyes, the other part destroyed?"

"But Aata and Aayse were twins."

"Twins in spirit," he said, thinking of Falpian's description. He hesitated for a moment. "Aata and Aayse were talat-sa."

Skyla's face showed her confusion: She didn't know the word. Ryder struggled to explain. "They were a singer pair like . . . like Falpian and me."

"The prophets were nothing like you and that Baen!" Visser snapped.

But Ryder hardly heard. He was remembering a conversation he'd had with Falpian on the mountain. "The Baen don't allow women to use magic," he went on, words tumbling out excitedly. "And Falpian told me they used to have cruel punishments for women who tried to sing. What if one of those punishments was cutting the vocal cords?" He ran his fingers gently over the figure's throat and was amazed to find exactly what he was looking for: a raised slash carved over the voice box. A thrill rippled through him.

Aata and the witches who came after her took a vow to be silent, but silence had been forced on this woman.

"It makes perfect sense!" he said. "Aata was like us, and Aayse was Baen. But Aayse was mute, so they couldn't sing together. They had to invent a whole new kind of magic. Witch magic. A silent magic."

He stopped speaking as the enormity of what he was suggesting began to dawn on him. How brave Aata and Aayse must have been. As brave as Mabis. For the first time he felt proud to be descended from their followers.

"Imagine if that were all true," said Skyla, the lamplight

illuminating her bright eyes. "The story is probably written on these walls. A person could spend her life studying this place, translating these writings."

"No, no, *no*!" cried Visser. "No one is going to translate this heresy. We have to destroy it before anyone else finds out about it. Don't you see? The other witches can't see Baen writing in a sacred tomb. They can't see—whoever this is." She gestured to the sarcophagus. "It would destroy the coven!"

"It's Aayse," Ryder insisted.

Visser's eyes were wild. "I'll never believe that."

"I think you do already. And besides, what *you* believe isn't important. Not after what you've done."

"I swear by the prophets, I've done nothing!"

Ryder hissed at the hypocrisy of Visser swearing by Aata and Aayse. "Lilla Red Bird told us you made the creatures; she saw it in a bone casting."

Visser gasped, speechless.

"Actually," Skyla began hesitantly, "Lilla didn't exactly say that Visser made the creatures."

"What?" Ryder gave his sister a look. "Of course she did."

"Think," Skyla said. "She told us that Visser planned 'a great desecration.' Lilla could have been talking about destroying this tomb."

Ryder looked from Skyla to Visser and back again. He didn't know what to think now. "Oh, for Aata's sake," he finally said. "We'll just have to take her back up to Sodan and the elders. They'll decide." He raised his knife again and glared at Visser. "And I won't allow you to make another mark on this chamber."

"Why should you care?" Visser said haughtily. "You're no witch. This place has nothing to do with you."

To his surprise it was Skyla who defended him. "How can you be so arrogant as to think this place is only for witches?" she demanded. "The most devout man I ever knew was my father. He may not have had a drop of magic in him, but he prayed to the Goddess every day. And there are fifty more like him in the village. This place is theirs! It belongs to them and to my brother as much as it does to you. Do you think that because we wear red we have some right to destroy it?"

"Do you think your father wanted to know this?" Visser's sharp voice echoed in the high ceiling of the chamber. "That everything he ever believed in was a lie? I'm doing it for him. And for the witches, too. You have seen how small our coven has grown. The young leave us to go to the cities. No one can throw the bones anymore. No one has faith. This tomb would only cause confusion and doubt."

Skyla trembled with restrained fury. "Maybe we witches can't throw the bones anymore because we've forgotten where we come from. You don't give your own people enough credit, Visser."

"It's not just me," Visser insisted. "Keeping our secrets, keeping the catacombs forbidden—it is a decision that Sodan and the elders have made. We didn't make it on a whim."

"Do the elders know what you're doing now? Do they know you are destroying this place? Did Sodan make *this* decision?"

Visser frowned, and Ryder could see that she had acted on her own, but there was no guilt on her face. "I know!" she shouted, pointing to Skyla with a jabbing finger. "I know what knowledge of this place would do among the youth of our coven."

"I *am* the youth of our coven!" Skyla shouted back. "It is unbelievable that you can't imagine that we might be inspired by this knowledge. You are robbing us. You are turning our history to rubble."

"Foolish girl. Why do you think your mother lost her faith? Learning the truth didn't *inspire* her."

Skyla was struck silent. Their mother, thought Ryder. Of course. She must have seen this place, or found out about it somehow. After fighting in the war, how could anyone accept that one of the prophets was a Baen? Skyla faltered, seemed confused. Dust motes floated in the air, lit golden by the lamps.

"Promise me," Visser said to Skyla, her voice gentler now. "Promise me you'll forget this place and never speak of it again."

Skyla squared her shoulders, and in her eyes Ryder could clearly see the vein of iron that ran through his family, the stubbornness that had probably been exasperating other witches since the time of Aayse herself. "You'll have to cut my throat to keep me quiet, Visser."

CHAPTER 25

THE MANY EYES OF KAR

"Hello," Falpian said. "I didn't expect to see you here." The black witch emerged from the shadows. "Is Kef all right?"

"Kef?" The woman's black costume seemed to pull the shade along with her as she stepped into the center of the chamber.

Falpian stood where he was, still dazed and blinking in the morning light that filtered through the ceiling of the cave. "Yes. The man. With the beard. You hit him on the head with a rock."

The witch frowned and cocked her head in that quizzical way that Falpian had seen before. "Strange that you would ask after the health of someone who tried to kill you."

That was true enough, and Falpian shrugged, not knowing how to answer. Something about the way the witch looked at him was making him nervous. Her eyes—

he remembered now that he didn't like them. There was something wrong in their depths.

"I thought you had come too soon, but perhaps it is time," the witch said, a little coldly. "The present catches up to the future with alarming speed—I had forgotten that. Still, I expected you would be halfway up the mountain by now."

"Spiders," Falpian whispered, not knowing exactly why his mouth went dry.

"Ah. It is the glass they want, not the light. Did you cover your glim with a cloth?"

He shook his head, and she gave him a smile an indulgent parent would give a child. He looked away uneasily.

The beauty all around him seemed incongruous with the irrational fear that seemed to have taken hold of his body. The murals on the chamber walls were so bright—almost too bright. As his eyes adjusted, Falpian saw that these were the most impressive he had seen yet. Ancient kings held court; battles raged; great masted ships sailed on blue-tiled seas. A whole history must have been depicted on these walls.

"Beautiful," he said, gesturing vaguely.

"All for you." She turned a circle where she stood, her arms open wide. "It's all for you."

Falpian's logical mind was saying, *This is just a kindly woman—a little odd, perhaps, but she has been good to you.* At the same time, a deeper, more animal part of him was whispering, *Run, run, run.*

"For me? What do you mean?" he asked, his voice too high.

"Let me show you something."

She gripped his arm and pulled him over to a wall near the large stone arch. The tiled pictures there were smaller and less impressive than some of the others, but still, Falpian cried out in amazement. Gormy men. About a dozen of the creatures, depicted in muddy brown stone, stood stiffly on top of a glittering green hill. Below them, in the foreground, an army retreated in horror. Horses galloped away riderless, rolling their eyes. Men and women trampled one another, desperate to get away, looks of dread frozen on their tiny faces.

"Can you read it?" she asked.

At first Falpian didn't know what she meant, but then he saw the Baen writing. It coiled over and around the picture, but with letters so stylized he could hardly recognize them. He looked again at the other murals. There was Baen writing there, too, but it seemed to be hopelessly mixed up with the images and with Witchlander pictographs.

"Music," he said finally. "They are the notes of a spell."

She nodded, running her fingers lovingly over the tiles. "All for one voice."

He looked again, surprised that a witch had the knowledge to discern this. She was right. The writing seemed to be the score for an echo site. Falpian wondered where it was; the magic would probably only work in that one place.

"You read Baen?"

"My father was very interested in your culture. Before the war, he would seek out Baen scholars, have long debates and discussions. He taught me to read. And even to sing a little."

The next question seemed obvious, but Falpian had trouble forcing it out of his mouth. When he did, it sounded ridiculously casual. "You . . . made the creatures, then?"

"I made them for you."

"Stop saying that!" Falpian said. "You don't know me. I didn't ask you to kill anyone."

"This place is a gift! It will save Baen lives when the war comes."

Her words made Falpian pause. The war? How did she know?

"I saw the future," she answered, though he hadn't voiced the question aloud. "A stupid little witch asked me for a prophecy, and I threw the bones for the first time in twenty years."

Falpian was curious now, in spite of the voice that told him to flee. "What exactly did the bones show you?"

She smiled, showing bad teeth. "Men in armor. Firecalls along the border, all burning black. You."

"Me?"

She nodded. "I am old. I don't need to make a casting to know my death looms. My bones told me that someone strong was coming, someone with both the skill to sing and the rage to kill. Someone who would finish my work for me if I couldn't finish it myself."

Her work? "It's not—I'm not—" Words stuck in his throat. Did she really think he was going to sing up the gormy men for her? "I'm not going to help you!"

The witch's face contorted with sudden anger. "Have you no family in the Bitterlands? No one you love? When the war comes, do you think the Witchlanders will let them live?" Falpian shrank back, but he remembered the words on the border stone. *Baen will be no more.* "Another war will give Witchlanders an excuse to drive you into the sea. You must win now or die."

"Maybe this war should never start, then!"

She threw up her hands in frustration. "Foolish boy! The war never really ended. If a man dies of starvation in the Bitterlands, isn't it the Witchlanders' fault? Isn't he a casualty of war?"

"But *you're* a Witchlander. You're a witch!"

"I have my reasons for choosing the Baen side."

Falpian shook his head. "I need a better answer than that."

For a moment her hard blue eyes seemed to plead with

him. "To atone," she finally said. "I did terrible things to your people during the war, terrible things, but this chamber . . ." She lifted her hands to the mosaics on the walls. "I can give your people this gift to make up for what I've done. Don't you see? This place *must* be in Baen hands now that war is coming. It's too precious!"

Falpian stood back, looking again at the high-ceilinged walls. An alarming thought occurred to him. Did she mean that every piece of writing in this chamber was a spell? All that coiling black lettering that wove under and over the richly colored scenes, was it *all* music? Making the gormy men might be the least of the magic depicted here. She was right. His people would gain a great advantage if they possessed this chamber.

"This is a treasure trove," he murmured.

"No. It is an armory. And I can take it for the Baen people with your help."

No, Falpian thought. *No, no.* "Please. You have the wrong person." There was desperation in his voice now. "I don't want to hurt people. I'm not like you. I—I don't have an assassin's heart."

The witch's face softened into something like pity. "Do you think anyone is born a killer? Do you think I was? Trust me, I know what I'm asking. An assassin's first murder is himself. He kills the man he was." Falpian gave a little start, thinking of his father. Had *he* killed the man he was?

"I'm saving lives," she went on. "Baen lives. Another war is inevitable. But if it's decisive, if it's brutal and quick, then every Baen in the Bitterlands will still be alive at the end of it. Don't you want that?"

Falpian swallowed, thinking of his mother and sisters. "Yes," he said. "I want that."

The black witch smiled at him again, but Falpian felt heavy and sick. Why had he ever wanted to sing at all? Why hadn't anyone explained to him that when Kar gives you a gift, he will inevitably expect you to use it? His father must have known that when he ran away to war. He must have been just like Falpian once. For the first time in his life, Falpian felt pity for his father. But this wasn't about him. This was about who Falpian was. And he was a Baen. A black magician. There was no changing what side Falpian was on. There never had been.

"You killed Kef, didn't you?" he asked. "You went back and finished him after I left."

"Yes. He would have done you harm."

Falpian nodded, seeing the cold logic of it. "And now you're going to sing again, attack the coven one more time."

"By the time the chilling ends, there will be no one here but ghosts."

"Oh," Falpian breathed, thinking of Skyla and Pima, thinking of his talat-sa.

I could stop her now, he said to himself. *I could overpower her, hit her with a rock like she did to poor Kef.* But he didn't move. Falpian dropped his eyes to the floor and again felt Ryder's presence somewhere in the tunnels, somewhere close. Now he wished he couldn't feel him so clearly, wished he didn't see his side of things so well. Ryder was his brother, just as much as Farien had been—his people believed that about talat-sa, and he believed it too. But when his options were to either fail his brother or to fail his people, the choice seemed clear.

"I'm sorry," he whispered, knowing that wherever he was, Ryder could hear him.

Ryder heard the singing from the tomb of Aayse and took off at a run. He followed the sound, the horrible sound— like pure anger turned to music. Skyla and Visser followed close at his heels. He didn't stop at the high mosaic-filled chamber, though he caught a glimpse of brilliant reds and greens as he rushed toward the small opening in the rock from which the unnerving song seemed to flow.

Even before Ryder had fully squeezed through to the outside, he knew what he would find: the lake, the lake that Aata's Right Hand had seen in her vision. He'd heard someone sing there before, the day the gormy men made their first attack. It was the same singing he heard now.

For a moment, everything went white as he blinked and squinted in the brightness of the late-morning sun. He shaded his eyes with his hand, the cold air freezing the hairs on the inside of his nose. A few steps to his left, the cascade of the waterfall was still and frozen. Ahead, standing on the small rock island in the middle of the frozen lake, was a figure dressed in black. Lilla. Lilla Red Bird.

It was hard to believe that the low, scraping rumble echoing off the stone cliffs was actually coming out of her mouth. It was a horrific sound—like madness and anger and sorrow—but Ryder could almost understand it.

A winter key.

An assassin's key!

"Falpian!" he cried.

The Baen was staring across the ice at Lilla, black hair stark against the snow. He turned and gave Ryder a tortured look. Ryder started out toward the witch, but Falpian caught him by the arm.

"Go back!"

"What?"

"Hide," said Falpian. "Go back into the caves. I'll make sure she doesn't hurt you."

"How can you . . . ?"

"She'll stop your heart. She could do it in a moment. She could do it right now if she wanted—that island she's standing on is an echo site!"

Behind Lilla, whorls of snow were twisting, braiding themselves upward into white columns. "But she's making the gormy men!" Ryder cried.

Lilla lifted her arms as if dancing to her own tuneless music. There were movements to this spell, as if the magic of Baen singing had been somehow meshed with a witch prayer.

Skyla emerged from the hole on her hands and knees. "What's happening?" she cried, holding her hands to her ears.

Visser followed, taking in the scene with wide, staring eyes. "Lilla!" she called. "What in Aata's name are you doing?" But the witch on the ice didn't hear.

"I've got to stop her!" Ryder shouted to them. "I've got to try." He shook off Falpian's tight grip.

"Come to see my work?" boomed a voice. Lilla's voice. The music had abruptly ended, and the witch's too-loud words echoed over the rock walls. Skyla grabbed Ryder's hand and pointed, but he already saw: Ten or twelve fully formed creatures stood around Lilla's island like a silent army.

I'm sorry, I'm sorry, I'm sorry. Ryder could hear the words echoing inside his own skull—Falpian was feeling guilty for not having stopped Lilla before she started singing.

It's all right, he tried to think back to him. *It's not your fault.* Falpian's pale face seemed to grow even paler.

341

"I'm a little annoyed with you, Nephew," Lilla said. Something about the calmness of her words made a chill run down Ryder's back. She didn't move from her rocky platform, but her voice carried in the crisp air. "Didn't I tell you to put a knife in Visser's ribs? Didn't I put a knife into your hands? I wanted her dead. The tomb of Aayse is precious." Behind her one of the creatures stirred slightly, as if shrugging off an itch.

Visser's mouth gaped open. "What have you done?" she hissed at Falpian.

"What has *he* done? Are you blind?" said Ryder.

"He's done something to her," she said. "Lilla is a witch. Why would she want to kill me? Why would she want to harm her own people?"

"She's gone mad," said Ryder. "You can't blame Falpian for that!"

"Lilla!" Visser called over the ice. "I don't understand any of this. I heard you make the creatures with my own ears, and yet I can't believe it. You say you want me dead for what I've done, but isn't what you have done so much worse? Your own coven, your own relatives, people in the village who honor your memory. Why? What could you have against them? They are innocent."

"Innocent?" Lilla's sharp voice cut through the air.

Ryder stepped forward.

"Stay here!" Skyla hissed, trying to pull at his clothes,

but he wrenched himself loose, picked his way over the hump of ice formed by the waterfall, and climbed out onto the frozen lake.

"Stop, Nephew," Lilla warned when he was about half a dozen steps from the island. "Don't come any nearer. I need only to sing a few more notes, and my children will tear you apart."

Ryder froze. Now, in the light of day, he could see how frail the black witch was, how sickly. Her tunic was frayed almost to rags, and the wind whipped around her small, bony frame. If he had not seen it himself, he wouldn't have believed that such a fragile-looking person could have made the dark and powerful spell he had just heard. But of course, she had it too, the family trait—that stubborn, iron will. Well then, they'd just have to see who had more of it.

"I wonder," he called. "How did the great Lilla Red Bird come to this?"

"That name is forbidden!" Lilla snapped.

"It is a proud name. Lilla Red Bird was a hero of the war."

"Lilla Red Bird was a murderer of children. Baen children. Did you know that?"

Ryder felt his stomach drop. He glanced nervously at the still creatures behind her on the ice, huge and rough and inhuman. The knife Lilla had given him was concealed in the sash of his reds, but he was afraid to use it, afraid that if he tried, she would sing the last notes of her spell and bring the gormy men to life. The only thing he could think of doing was to keep her talking.

"The Baen struck first, at Barbiza," he said. It was the reasoning he'd heard all his life, though he didn't believe anymore that it justified everything his people had done in the name of revenge—stealing land, driving all the Baen into the Bitterlands, killing innocent people. How much of that had Lilla been responsible for?

Lilla pointed past the frozen waterfall to where the others were standing. "Your friend knows the truth," she said. Her voice changed, became warmer. "Falpian! Come here."

Falpian looked around as if hoping she was pointing at someone else, but Visser grabbed his arm and shoved him out onto the lake. He avoided Ryder's eye as he half walked, half slid across the ice.

"Tell my nephew who I am," Lilla said when Falpian had reached Ryder's side.

The Baen shielded his eyes as he stared up at the witch perched on her rocky island. "I heard them call you Lilla, but you can't be—" His voice faltered. "You can't be the Lilla my people speak of."

The black witch looked almost proud. "Of all the names hated by the Baen, of all the witches most reviled for their part in the war, I am the worst, aren't I?"

Dread and disbelief contorted Falpian's features. "But . . . you were killed long ago," he said.

"Tell him what you call me!" Lilla drew herself up and glared down at Falpian with pale, mad eyes.

"I think—I think you must be Lilla the Blood-Smeared," Falpian said, quaking. "Butcher of the war."

At the sound of the name, the monsters began swaying, throwing back their heads in silent roars. Ryder held his breath, waiting for the creatures to attack, but the moment didn't come.

"I hated the Baen when my father died," Lilla said. "I wanted to kill you all." She crossed her arms against the cold, taking no notice of the creatures behind her. "But at the end of the war, something happened. My little sister and I were walking the sandbars. They had been useful during the fighting—quick escapes, bloody ambushes. We had seen the mural." Lilla raised her eyes. Ryder didn't turn around, but he well remembered the two striking faces that adorned the rock. "We saw that it was a Baen woman and a Witchlander, but it didn't mean anything to us at the time—not until we found the entrance. We knew that the caves were forbidden, but we thought, after the war, that we were entitled somehow. Perhaps we were.

"That little opening in the rocks changed everything. We found the tomb of Aayse. Mabis lost her faith the moment she saw it, but I . . . How could I turn my back on Aata and Aayse? They were my life."

"You began to think about the Baen and what you had done to them," Ryder said.

Lilla nodded. "My father would have hated the things I did to avenge his death. You see now why I begged to become the keeper of the catacombs. I wanted to murder that name, Lilla Red Bird. I wanted to murder what she had done."

Lilla looked to Falpian now, as if pleading for forgiveness. "We were so terrified of you—even before Barbiza. Your magic was so much more powerful than our own. We won the war because our numbers were greater, our numbers and our cruelty. That is the only reason. But now the pendulum is swinging back. We will make it right, you and I."

"Make it right!" Ryder said with disgust. "I think you just like to kill people."

Lilla glared. "I am balancing the scales."

"And what about Mabis? Did you think about her when you were 'balancing the scales'? Did you consider the life of your own sister?"

"Mabis was the only one who could have stopped me," Lilla said coldly. "Who else? You? With your wasted gift? She was my one enemy. But I made sure the greedy little Aata's Right Hand would take her bone away and leave her helpless."

"Goddess!" Ryder said hoarsely, angry at the tears pricking at his eyes. "Why didn't you just kill yourself—it would have been better than what you've done!"

"Even if I died, others would carry on my work. My creatures are made of hate and anger, and there's always plenty of that." Her eyes fell on Falpian. "Would you like to sing the last commands?"

Falpian threw a look at Ryder. "No, not now," he begged. "Please."

Lilla held her hand out to him and smiled. "Come. Sing the notes that will wipe this mountain clean. Come take your revenge."

She seemed to trust Falpian, Ryder realized. Maybe this was their chance. *Get her to leave the echo site,* he thought. *Once she's off, I'll make sure she doesn't get back on.* He hoped Falpian had heard.

The Baen stepped forward, and Ryder watched as he climbed onto the island. Ryder tried not to smile as Lilla stepped aside to let Falpian take her place. Carefully Falpian set his feet on the mosaic footprints. *I'm sorry,* came his thoughts. His face had gone bone-white, full of grief.

Ryder felt the breath go out of him. "Falpian?" he said aloud.

"I'm so sorry."

"What are you doing?" He stepped forward. "No! You're important! My mother's prophecy . . ."

The Baen's voice was ragged with emotion. "Don't you understand? It was never Bron. It was me. *I* am the assassin your mother warned you about." He screwed his eyes shut in agony. "It was always me."

The truth of Falpian's words hit Ryder like a sledgehammer. *Aata's breath, I'm such a fool,* he cursed himself. *Mabis risked everything to warn me—she ate poison. And I didn't listen.*

Furiously he rushed forward, reaching the island in a few short strides. But Lilla was ready. She threw herself in front of Falpian. Ryder grabbed her around the waist and tried to pull her aside. Slipping on the ice, they both fell down hard. Ryder scrambled back up, but Lilla grabbed his leg and pulled him down again, leaping on him like an animal, scratching desperately at his face with her fingernails.

"Hurry!" she yelled to Falpian. "Sing!"

To Ryder's horror, Falpian opened his mouth and sang.

And the rocks and the cliffs sang with him, sang with voices Falpian could hardly believe were his own. He'd be famous for this among the Baen, he thought dully. His father would put garlands around his shoulders and open his arms wide. Once the image would have filled him joy; now all he felt was disgust. A bitter rage welled up inside him—rage at the stupidity of Baen and Witchlander alike, rage at everything that had turned him into the ally of Lilla the Blood-Smeared.

The creatures behind stood like vacant husks, awaiting their commands. It would take only a moment for him to send them on their way. And yet, he hesitated. Time slowed. Falpian could hear his own heartbeats, but there were vast stretches of silence between them. Snowflakes hung suspended in the air. He closed his eyes, but he could still see the little corner of the world where he stood as if from a great height—Lilla and Ryder, Visser and Skyla, all tiny and frozen below him. There was something about this crow's-eye view that made Falpian feel safe. He knew that if he wanted, he could withdraw and withdraw, higher and higher, until the whole world was just a tiny speck in one of the many eyes of Kar.

Can't get away that easily.

Hello? Is someone there?

Somewhere, he knew, he was still standing at the echo site. Somewhere his body was still singing. It was cold and tired and full of anger. But here, here all was warm and still. The voice had come from behind him and high above, a man's voice. Someone familiar and kind.

Bron?

Open your eyes. This time it was a woman's voice—his mother's and his sisters' and the old cook's who'd fed him sweets when he was little.

Darling, if you give them hints, they'll never learn. Not Bron. Someone else. Someone . . .

I like this one. The woman again.

He doesn't even believe in you.

Oh, you can't take their notions personally. He thinks you have tongues of fire and a thousand eyes.

Sometimes I do.

Kar? Falpian asked. *Is that you? Am I dead?*

A peal of laughter rang out, beautiful as music. Women's laughter. But women weren't supposed to be at the feast of Kar. *Open your eyes.*

If he opened his eyes, the world would start again. He'd be back at the echo site. He was there now, really; he'd never left. All this was happening in no time at all, in the still, small space between two notes of his song. It occurred to him that maybe the witches weren't so mad to study silence after all.

Kar, can't I stay here? Falpian asked. *I don't want to do this.*

Open your eyes, the woman said again, more firmly this time.

His shoulders shook with held sobs. *But it won't do any good. I'm a Baen and Ryder's a Witchlander. We'll always be on opposite sides.*

There was a rustling behind him, and Falpian felt a shiver of warm breath on the back of his neck. The woman's voice was a quiet murmur in his ear, like clear water bubbling over stones:

There are no sides.

Falpian opened his eyes and the world came back, blinding and cacophonous. He was on the echo site, and the sound of his own voice was painful in his ears. In front of him the faces of two women stared at him from either side of the frozen waterfall—one Witchlander, one Baen. It took him a moment to realize that they weren't real, that he was looking at a mosaic set in stone.

Falpian didn't know who they could be, but their serenity was mesmerizing. They were so beautiful in their opposition—like two sides of a coin. They were . . . balance. And they made it very clear to him that the retribution Lilla wanted wasn't balance.

His song changed, drained of anger. Falpian made his choice. He was no assassin.

The world was moving again now. Ryder and Lilla still struggled on the ice. The gormy men. Falpian thought quickly. He wasn't sure he could destroy them by himself, but he could make them destroy one another. He felt their blank faces turning toward him as he sang the command.

Ooomph! Something cracked him on the temple and sent him flying onto the rocks. He sat up, dazed, clutching his head. Visser, holding a thick log, stood over him.

"Visser, stop!" he cried, his ears ringing with the blow.

He glanced over to Ryder for help, but he had Lilla by the wrists and was dragging her away toward the entrance to the caves. Falpian got to his knees and scrambled over the rocks in the opposite direction, his eye on Visser all the while. He made it out onto the ice, letting out a strangled cry as he slid into one of the motionless gormy men. Visser raised the weapon again.

"Don't!" he yelled. He shielded his head with his hands as the blow came down hard onto his right arm. He yelped in pain and got onto all fours, fighting to get up, but he slipped again and again on the ice. Visser raised the log for a third time.

Then there was another cracking sound and Visser went down hard. Her forehead smacked the ice. A girl stood behind her holding a stone. It was Skyla.

"Oh Goddess," she said, her voice raw, "did I kill her?" Her eyes darted fearfully to the silent white creatures all around her, but still they didn't move.

Falpian crept toward Visser. There was blood on the ice. "I don't know," he said gravely, looking up at Skyla.

"Tell me my brother was right about you," Skyla demanded. She looked at the stone in her hand and threw it away in disgust. "Tell me I did the right thing and that you're not here to kill us all!"

Falpian opened his mouth to answer, and a sudden pain exploded through his body. For a moment his vision turned to specks and all he knew was pain—hot, searing pain that seemed to be melting the bones in his left thigh. He realized he was screaming.

"What's wrong?" Skyla cried in alarm. "What's wrong with you?"

Falpian looked down at his legs, expecting to see blood. But there was nothing. Nothing at all. This was Ryder's pain.

He gave an anguished cry and pointed. Behind Skyla, Lilla was climbing back up onto the island. And farther away near the frozen waterfall, Ryder's crumpled form lay motionless on the ice.

CHAPTER 26

THE GORMY MAN

"She got my knife," Ryder mumbled. A new song of Lilla's was screeching in his ears.

"He's alive!" said Skyla, breathless.

Ryder was on his back, looking up at the bare branches of trees, at a stained and blotchy sky that seemed to churn dizzily and grow darker as he watched. From his right leg, waves of pain radiated, horrible pain—so bad it seemed to blend with Lilla's song.

With difficulty, he lifted his head. They were in the trees at the side of the lake. Someone must have dragged him here, but he couldn't remember it. Skyla and Falpian knelt on either side of him. Visser sat nearby, her knees to her chest, holding a handful of snow to her head. Through the trunks of the trees, he could see Lilla singing, but she was alone.

"Where are the gormy men?"

"Gone," said Skyla. "Lilla made them scatter a few moments ago. Some went up the mountain, some down."

Pima. "Oh Goddess, we've got to stop them! Lilla knows the witches are in the caves, and the snowslide won't stop those things. She's sent them to attack!" Ryder tried to get up, but the pain in his leg overwhelmed him. "I just need a moment," he gasped. "She stabbed me. A dagger."

"No need to tell us about it," said Falpian. "It's still there."

Ryder raised himself up on his elbows. The hilt of the dagger protruded from his thigh. Around his leg, blood seeped into the snow in a widening blossom.

"Aata's breath," he said. "All right. Give me a stick or something to bite, and then pull it out quick."

"I don't think we can," Skyla told him, peering closely at his leg. "It's too deep—you'd bleed too much. We're just going to have to wrap it up and get you down to the village." She began to unwind the sash of her reds.

"No!" Ryder argued. "We've got to fight or there won't be a village to go to." A crack of thunder split the air, making him start. "What in Aata . . . ?" There were no thunderstorms in winter.

He looked up at the sky again and saw that the chilling clouds were thick and bloodstained—a deep red turning to black. They seemed to be gathering right over Lilla's head.

"What is she doing?"

Falpian stared at Lilla in alarm. "There were a lot of spells written in the caves—who knows what she can do?"

Crying out, Ryder struggled to his feet. "Give me a sword, a stick, anything—she's got to be stopped."

"Hold still!" Skyla ordered. She bent over Ryder's leg and began to tie up his wound with the sash of her reds, leaving the knife protruding from his thigh.

"Think, Ryder," Falpian said, taking hold of his arm to keep him from falling. "Back at Stonehouse, I could have stopped your heart with just a humming stone—she could kill you a hundred ways before you get to that island. We've got to sing."

Ryder shook his head. "I can't. I don't know how we even did it the first time. It was some kind of . . . accident."

"Why do you deny it?" Falpian was shouting now, his face close up to Ryder's. "You're a singer. Do you know how rare this is?"

"I said, hold still!" Skyla yelled. She yanked the two ends of her makeshift bandage into a knot and stood up. Both Ryder and Falpian winced in pain.

"I don't want to be a singer!" Ryder snapped. "And I don't want to be your brother under the skin or whatever it is. I didn't ask for this."

"Do you think I asked to have some Witchlander oaf for my talat-sa?" Falpian said. He gripped his own thigh in the same place where Ryder was wounded.

"The nephew of Lilla the Blood-Smeared, of all people? I could have *killed* you just now! I betrayed my people when I didn't."

"That reminds me," Ryder said. He swung his fist at Falpian, but the blow only glanced off the Baen's jaw.

"Arhh!" Falpian clutched his face. "What was that for? I said I *didn't* betray you!"

"I know how close you came."

"Are the two of you out of your minds?" Skyla shrieked, coming between them.

"Just give me a sword and I'll run her through," Ryder insisted. "I'll die out there. I'll get my spine snapped by one of her monsters. I don't care! Just give me a sword!"

Falpian lowered his voice, and his face softened. "A sword is not the weapon the God has given you."

"The Goddess," Skyla corrected. "But he's right." She reached for her brother's cheek. "Ryder, Lilla thinks your gift was wasted because you never learned to throw the bones. She should know better—she's seen the tomb of Aayse—but she doesn't. She's not expecting you to be able to sing, and she's certainly not expecting Falpian to join you. It's the only weapon we've got. But we're running out of time!"

Ryder looked to the churning red-black sky and suddenly felt afraid. Even if he did sing, how could his voice penetrate that horrible screeching music that was pouring out of Lilla's mouth? *I can't do it,* he thought. But what he said was, "Yes. All right. Let's try."

He told Skyla to take Visser and make their way to safety inside the caves.

"I won't leave you," Skyla started.

"Get Pima," Ryder begged her. "Make sure Pima's safe. Visser will know the way."

Skyla gave him one last look, then ran to Visser and pulled her to her feet. When Ryder finally saw them disappear into the rocks, he nodded at Falpian, and together they crept toward the edge of the lake.

"As soon as she hears us singing, she'll know we're a threat," Falpian warned. "She'll try to kill us where we stand."

"Wonderful."

Ryder leaned against a tree, trying to ignore the pain. He wasn't aware of the precise moment when he started to sing, only knew that his voice followed Falpian's into song as if on its own. Pictures from his own life and his friend's began to swim before him: Mabis and Farien, Pima and the Baen girls from his dreams. Falpian was by his side, lips moving. Still, their song was blotted out by Lilla's.

A thick snow was swirling down now from the clouds above Lilla's head. Falpian gripped his arm, and Ryder knew they had to sing hard or die. He didn't try to ignore his pain anymore, but felt it instead, sang it into his song.

The world came into sharp focus, and Ryder's vision expanded like a bubble, encompassing more and more. He could see the fish sleeping under the lake. He could see the seeds sleeping under the snow. The world hummed with music, was made of music, just as the Baen believed. Every rock and tree on the mountain was bleeding song. *This is what I am, isn't it?* Ryder thought. *I'm not a farmer. I'm not a sailor. I am this.* He felt his song grow stronger, and Lilla's head snapped up.

Go for Lilla first. Falpian's thoughts were clear, and Ryder understood their logic; they should attack Lilla first, and then worry about the gormy men. But Falpian didn't have a little sister in the caves, small and vulnerable, wondering why her family had abandoned her. Ryder could see the creatures now. He saw the whole mountain from high above. It would be easy. The monsters were meant to obey a singer's orders. *Come here,* he commanded. *Come back.*

Something struck his body like a blow, and he was thrown backward. Ryder rolled over onto the ground, fighting for air, his singing stopped. Lilla faced them now from the security of her tiny island. The snow in front of her was whirling down, whirling down, but it never seemed to reach the ground. Ryder tried to take a breath and sing again, but something had stopped his throat; there were cold fingers around his heart, squeezing.

Falpian was still singing, but his song was much

different now. Ryder could see him running from spot to spot, trying a note and moving on. Ryder thought he understood. The little island was the best place to sing from, but it wasn't the only place. Ryder clutched at the ache in his chest. He tried to haul himself, but he could barely move now.

Suddenly a sharp sound came ricocheting off the cliffs, and Lilla fell to her knees as if pushed. Falpian had found the right spot. The pressure in Ryder's chest subsided and he breathed deeply, the cold air like needles in his lungs. He crawled toward Falpian, leaving a trail of smeared blood on the ice. The next thing he knew, Falpian was pulling him to his feet.

"What can we do?" Ryder cried. "She's too strong!"

"Sing!"

Ryder took a breath and tried, but his voice was barely a whimper. Despite the frigid air, sweat streamed down his face. Lilla was up and singing again. The sounds were vile, an abomination. Suddenly Ryder knew what she was doing.

"Does that look like . . . ," he began, pointing at the column of snow that towered above them. They watched in horror as it twisted and bulged. Two long strands detached themselves from the body, and far above them, the top of the column resolved itself into a blank and pitiless face. The other creatures were tiny by comparison. They were not gormy men. No. This was his mother's nightmare. This. This was the Gormy Man.

The creature stretched out its long arms to the air. It tightened one rough fist, then another, as if to test its newborn body. Behind it Lilla collapsed, folding into the snow—her spell was finished. Suddenly Ryder felt himself moving, sliding out toward the great creature. Desperately he clawed the ice with his fingers, but couldn't get a hold. He grabbed Falpian's arm, but his friend was moving too. The creature was attracting them, pulling them near as if it were a magnet and they were flakes of iron.

"Watch out!" Ryder called.

A great tree by the side of the lake had uprooted itself and went careening over the ice toward the creature, dirt trailing behind its huge root. Ryder and Falpian dove out of the way. The thing reached out to it, and the tree became a part of its great snow arm. All around the lake, the tops of trees were bending toward it, quivering with attraction. Snow and debris came hurtling from all sides. Impossibly, the Gormy Man was getting even bigger.

"Look!" Falpian said. At the other side of the lake, the smaller gormy men were returning, emerging from the trees.

"It's no use," Ryder said. "We can't fight them all." A log was sticking up out of the ice, and he grabbed hold of it. Falpian held his hand in a tight grip, but Ryder could feel his glove starting to pull off.

"No," Falpian said. "They're here because you called them. We can command them. We can use the smaller ones to fight . . . that!"

Aata's vow, Ryder thought. He couldn't sing again, couldn't. He glanced at his leg—it was dark with blood. But when Falpian started, he took a deep breath. As he began, the thought that he might not live through the day came rushing toward him. He was dying. Life was coming out a hole in his leg. Somehow this gave him the strength he needed, because there was no need to hold anything back. It would all be over soon. He would be over soon.

How full of magic they were. He and Falpian could stand now, their voices stronger than the beast's attraction. They stood side by side, willing the smaller creatures at the Gormy Man. Easily it swept them aside and came toward the singers. The great tree that was its arm swung down, cracking the ice, but Falpian pulled Ryder aside just in time. More gormy men emerged from the woods, the last of them now, and Ryder and Falpian willed them to the battle. The Gormy Man sent them flying into the trees. They came apart like children's snowmen, but they re-formed, swelling up out of the ground to attack again.

Ryder turned his attention to the giant itself, thinking that perhaps he could control it as he did the smaller ones. *Die,* he commanded as he sang. *Die. You are gone. You are nothing. You are not.*

For a moment he thought he saw its body waver, but the creature was too strong. Lilla had poured every drop of hate she had inside it—twenty years of anger, twenty years of guilt and madness in the dark. This thing had her cunning, somehow; it had part of her intelligence. Ryder felt it as he sang and was horrified.

The Gormy Man swept out its arms, and the smaller creatures were drawn in. Their bodies flew toward it and came apart on impact. Then they were gone, incorporated into its immense body. Ryder was sure he saw the thing smile and cock its head exactly as Lilla would have done. It took a step toward him, and the ground shuddered. Still singing, Falpian and Ryder backed away. *We'll be dead in moments*, Ryder thought.

Go stand in the river. Why was Falpian thinking that?

Go stand in the river. It wasn't Falpian. It was his mother, his mother's voice. And then Ryder remembered. He'd stood in the river with Dassen, and the creatures couldn't follow.

Water, Ryder thought, willing Falpian to understand. They should focus their energy on the ice, not the creature; they must start the river flowing again. On the mountain they had used wind to blow the bits of the creatures away, but water should work as well. They shared a glance, and their songs changed at exactly the same time.

Crack! A fissure traveled out across the lake, splitting

the ice between the creature's legs. *We can't go to the shore,* Ryder thought to Falpian. *If we do, it will follow.* He and Falpian backed away, moving toward the place where the lake narrowed to river.

With a mighty booming sound, part of the waterfall collapsed, raining splinters of crystal onto the lake and ripping a dark hole in the ice. The creature lurched backward. Ryder and Falpian pressed their advantage, willing the ice to shatter.

Ryder saw Lilla stand up, seeming dazed. She stared at the black water that spurted over the falls and into the widening crevice. Great groaning sounds were traveling out across the lake and down the river. With a thundering crack the rest of the waterfall came crashing down, spewing great chunks of ice. Lilla fell to the ground again as the colossal Gormy Man stumbled back.

"No!" she wailed.

The Gormy Man slipped backward into the water. Ryder saw its arms flailing, its huge arms churning the water. Lilla screamed with rage. The creature went under, and when it came up again it had lost half its size. For the first time, Ryder heard it make a sound—a painful keening like the crying of a child. When it went under again, it didn't come back up.

Ryder started to limp toward the echo site. Neither he nor Falpian were singing now, but their song seemed to go on without them, reverberating back and forth over the cliffs and across the valley.

"Get off the ice!" Falpian screamed behind him. "It's breaking up!"

Every step sent pain jolting through Ryder's body, but he saw that Lilla was staggering toward the rocky island, and he wasn't going to wait to see if she had any other spells she wanted to try. He reached down and yanked the dagger from his leg. For a moment the world went white before his eyes. He used every bit of his strength to cling to consciousness and kept going, holding the bloody dagger out in front of him.

At that moment the lake made a sound like the lowing of a huge animal. Underneath Ryder's feet, the ice started to shift. He fell, dropping the knife. The next thing he knew he was in the water. He was in the water, and it was cold, fatally cold.

Ryder came up gasping and saw that Lilla was in the water too, but she was far away, flailing her arms. He saw her go under.

At the edge of the lake, a dog was barking loudly. Ryder tried to call for Falpian, but the cold had stolen his breath. He slipped under the water, remembering that he had had a dream of drowning once.

His pain was receding. The light was receding. He was sinking and all was quiet. Beautifully quiet. *This is true too,* he thought, *this deep silence. The witches are right about that.*

We live between the two great silences: the silence that existed before the world began, and the silence that waits for us at the end of all things. They are the fabric the Goddess used to make the world.

He wondered how the world could be both sides of a coin at the same time: silence and song. He'd have to ask the Goddess about that. When he was dead. It wouldn't be long now. Ryder could see the Goddess swimming toward him with powerful strokes.

The Goddess certainly is ugly, he thought. *She looks like a big, wet dog.*

CHAPTER 27

RAIKEN'S FARM

Ryder opened his eyes and smiled, burrowing further into thick, warm blankets. He was alive. The air was sweet with the smell of dried hicca stalks that were the stuffing for his bed—or rather, the stuffing for the large burlap sack that was serving for a bed. The dog didn't seem to understand that the sack was just big enough for one. All through the night he had gone from Falpian to Ryder, flopping down lovingly on one or the other, unable to choose between them. Now he lay crushed next to Ryder, half on the sack and half off, with his belly to the air and his legs splayed. His broken tooth gave his face a lopsided look.

Ryder pulled his arm out from under the covers to rub Bo's belly. "Good dog," he said. "Good boy."

He heard the front door of the tavern close quietly and sat up. There were no windows in Dassen's storage room, but through a crack in the plank wall, Ryder could glimpse the tavern keeper's heavy shape, making his way to the barn. It was just before dawn, but Dassen was going out already—searching for Mabis, as he did every day. Ryder felt a twinge of guilt; he should be going too.

"Something I should know about you and my mother?" Ryder had asked the day before.

"Well, your Fa was your Fa, if that's what you're asking," Dassen had answered. The idea that he wasn't hadn't even occurred to Ryder, but he hid his surprise at the comment. "No," Dassen continued, "it's just the old story, hardly worth telling. Two best friends love the same wild girl. She picks the one, and that's that."

In the tavern courtyard, Ryder heard the jingling of a harness as Dassen led his pack pony to the road. The truth was, Ryder didn't want to go with him. He was afraid of what they'd find. But he told himself that Dassen wouldn't have let him come in any case—Ryder wasn't well enough yet.

Gingerly he lifted his covers and looked down at his thigh. The day before, Dassen had allowed him to take the bandage off. It was an ugly scar—twisted and puckered with the stitches still in. Dassen had sewed him up with waxy string while Ryder lay on one of the tavern tables, but he barely remembered that—thank the Goddess.

On the other side of the storage room, Falpian slept. Their minds were so close now that it was hard to stay awake while Falpian dreamed. Ryder yawned.

And then he was by the sea again, sitting near a great rock with Bo at his side.

"Falpian dreams of this place a lot," Ryder said, but the dog only looked out onto the water. The two little girls had come to wade again, wearing blue to mourn their brother. Their long hair was unbound now and black as dye. Where the ends of their hair touched the water, they left black stains on the sea.

From out of the sea came a head, then a face, then the body of a man. He looked in every way like Falpian, the same slender frame, the same pale skin, the same black eyes. His clothes were perfectly dry.

"You're not Falpian," said Ryder.

The man came to sit next to him on the beach, and Bo lifted his chin for him to scratch, as if they knew each other.

"This is where I drowned," he said. "They never found my boat."

Ryder nodded. The sea breeze blew through his hair. "People say that as long as you remember someone, they're still alive."

"It's a lie."

"I know."

The man looked out toward the waves. "Falpian will never know if he is remembering me correctly, or if he's just making me up. And he'll never know if I drowned on purpose, if I drowned myself because I knew we weren't talat-sa."

"Did you?"

The man shrugged. "There's no way to tell. I'm not Farien. This isn't Bo. We're just ideas that Falpian has. I am a memory, and every day I fade."

A white seabird flashed by, and Ryder turned away for a moment. When he turned back, he was alone but for the dog. He felt a hollowed-out sadness inside his chest, but he didn't know if the feeling belonged to him or to Falpian.

Bo lifted himself up on his front legs, yawned, and settled back down into the warm sand. Ryder stroked the top of his head. The dog's eyes were closed, but his ears were cocked back, listening.

"When we were on the ice, I thought I heard my mother's voice," Ryder said. "I kept expecting her to appear. I kept thinking, why doesn't she come back? If she's still alive, why isn't she here? Bo, I think my mother . . ."

The dog moved over and put his head on Ryder's knee.

Ryder woke again at Skyla's knock. "It's the dog," she said, poking her head through the door. "He's in the kitchen, and Dassen's hired girls won't go in when he's there."

Falpian held his covers up to his neck. "They just have to call him," he said. But of course, they wouldn't; the hired girls were terrified of Bo.

"I think he's eaten all the butter," Skyla added.

Falpian rolled off his sack bed as soon as Skyla was gone and began looking around for his clothes.

"Ash on your face," said Ryder. He knew they were both thinking about their dreams, but neither wanted to talk about them.

Falpian rubbed his cheek. "Beard. Haven't shaved in days." He picked some leggings off the floor and quickly pulled them on, jumping a little to keep his balance.

"Shaved?"

"My face." He found a shirt in the corner, gave it a few sniffs, and put it on. "I asked Dassen for a razor the other day, but he just stared at me like I was going to slit his throat with it. Forgot you people didn't cut your beards."

Falpian was out the door before Ryder could respond. Just when he thought he was beginning to understand his talat-sa, Falpian would blithely reveal something incomprehensible like that. Cut his beard?

A moment later Skyla slipped into the storage room, wearing a plain brown dress borrowed from the blacksmith's wife. She sat down on the floor next to Ryder's bed, hugging her knees. It was so cold in the storage room that Ryder could see her breath, though he was perfectly warm under his blankets.

"I was thinking . . . I might go back today," she told him.

Ryder sat up again, surprised. Skyla had returned to the coven once already; he knew she'd had a long conversation with Sodan, but she hadn't told him what they'd said. "Really? You mean, to the coven? But you haven't been wearing your reds."

"Oh. Did you think . . . ?" She paused, looking at her feet. Mabis used to hug her knees in just the same way, Ryder noticed. "The villagers—they've known me all their lives, but if I'm wearing reds, I can't get a word out of them—they just start bowing at me and praising Aata."

"Since when do you care what the villagers think?"

"I don't!" Skyla pursed her lips. "It's just . . . We've always lived so far away from the valley. I just wanted to see what I was missing for a few days." She smoothed the rough fabric of her dress as if it were a fancy gown she would regret giving up. "But I always knew I was going back."

"In the catacombs," he started carefully, "it seemed like you had changed your mind about being a witch."

"I know, but so much has happened. . . ."

Ryder couldn't hide his disappointment. In his mind, he'd started to formulate a plan to rebuild the cottage. After all they'd been through, he wanted them all to be together. It was odd: Seeing the tomb of Aayse had made Mabis want to leave the coven, but it made Skyla want to stay.

Falpian entered, pulling Bo by the scruff of the neck. "Bad dog!" he scolded. Bo barked a complaint and sat down in a corner, licking butter from his paws.

"He's just bored," Ryder said.

Since they'd come to the village, Bo had only been allowed out in a fenced-in paddock at the back of the tavern; Ryder and Falpian worried there would be trouble if he were free to roam, that a villager might do him harm out of fear. Although Ryder and Skyla had explained many times that Falpian was a friend, that he and Bo had helped to destroy the monsters, Ryder wondered if the villagers really believed it. He wanted to shake them, even Dassen sometimes. He kept expecting them all to see the Falpian that he knew. But all they saw was a Baen.

"Ryder!" Dassen's gruff voice boomed out from beyond the storeroom door. "You up?" Every muscle in Ryder's body went tense. The tavern keeper shouldn't have been back so soon.

The door swung open, and the look on Dassen's face was devastating.

"Oh Goddess," Skyla said, pressing her fingers to her lips, guessing what was coming.

Dassen didn't speak at first, but he leaned into the doorway as if he needed it to keep him up. "It's Farmer Raiken," he said finally. "He found a body frozen in the river this morning."

"Lilla?" Falpian asked.

"No."

Ryder felt the same cold, clutching feeling in his chest that he'd felt when the black witch had tried to stop his heart. "But it could have been Lilla," he said, his voice shaking. The last time they had seen the black witch she was in the river. Ryder was sure she must have drowned, but they hadn't found a body. "Lilla and Mabis looked alike."

"I knew her, Ryder," Dassen said. "I knew her hair."

Skyla gave a cry that was half moan, half sob.

"I want to see her," Ryder said.

"No. You don't."

"Where is she?"

"Still in Raiken's barn. We weren't sure . . ." Dassen had to stop and take a breath. He looked to the floor. "We weren't sure where we should take her, you see. We didn't know if she should be buried in the village graveyard or in the catacombs with her ancestors."

Ryder hesitated. Mabis had once said that she lived her life in between the two places—halfway up the mountain and halfway down. But they couldn't bury her where the cottage had been. She'd be all alone.

"The graveyard," Skyla said, with a certainty he couldn't muster. "She'd want to be with Fa."

* * *

The villagers were rebuilding, but every time Falpian turned a corner, conversations died and the sound of axes on trees, hammers on nails, faded to silence. In the center of town, he passed a knot of women murmuring together at the well. He nodded and gave them an overlarge smile, but they didn't return the greeting, and their cold eyes followed him until he was out of sight. Falpian knew these villagers, that was the odd thing; he knew their names, and, if he thought hard enough, sometimes even their secrets. But they didn't know him.

He could feel Ryder. As he walked the snow-covered road of the little town, he could feel the weight of his grief. It was a weight he recognized too well. Falpian let it pull him toward the river. His talat-sa stood at the top of an arched bridge, looking out at the mountains. Below him, children played on the ice.

"I'm so sorry about your mother." Falpian came up beside him and leaned out over the rails. They could see the white humps of the planting hills and the base of the mountain, but the top of the mountain had disappeared, enveloped in clouds.

"Thank you."

"Do you want me to leave? I know you want to be alone."

"No." On the frozen river, children stared up at them and whispered.

"I came out to see if the villagers needed any help,"

Falpian said. "But . . . I don't think they want help from me."

Ryder turned to him. "I hope they weren't—"

"No, no. They were very polite."

Ryder knew he was lying. It was becoming more and more difficult for them to hide things from each other. Information passed back and forth between them without Falpian even noticing; conversations they didn't have when they were awake were simply postponed to their dreams.

"They don't know you the way I do," Ryder said.

"No one does."

For a while they stood silent, talk unnecessary. The children went back to their games. With his eyes Falpian followed the frozen river as it curved through the planting hills to a small farm just visible below the line of clouds. Ryder was looking there too. It was Raiken's farm, Falpian understood in a flash, where the body of Ryder's mother had been found.

"She must have gone to the river in the end," Ryder said softly.

Falpian nodded. "To save herself."

"Or to find maiden's woe. No way to tell." Ryder's face twisted with grief. "How can she be dead, Falpian? There's still so much I need to say to her."

Falpian wasn't sure what he should say. Why did knowing grief himself not make him any better at knowing how to help? He said nothing, but Ryder didn't seem to mind. It began to snow—petal flakes that drifted lazily, unsure where they wished to land, blurring the view of the farm and the river.

"You've been worrying," Ryder said, changing the subject.

Falpian nodded and drew his coat closer around him. "I'll be crossing the border soon. There are a lot of people in the Bitterlands who don't want war, and some of them are very powerful. I have to make my father's plans known to them before it's too late."

"Will talking to them be enough? Enough to stop an attack?"

"It will be. Once I make it known what he tried to do. No one will follow a man who tried to kill his own son."

Ryder frowned, blowing on his gloved hands. "I don't know if I like that idea. Your father will think you're a traitor. He'll think you've switched sides."

"There are no sides," Falpian said simply. Someone had said that to him recently, but he couldn't remember who.

Ryder rolled his eyes. "Yes, yes. But does your *father* know that?"

Falpian hesitated a moment. On the ice, the children squealed with laughter, throwing snowballs. "No. No, he doesn't."

"He'll make a dangerous enemy. I hope you remember

that. I wish—" Ryder broke off in midsentence, but Falpian knew what he was going to say.

"You can't come with me. It's not safe for you in the Bitterlands, and you have Skyla and Pima to think about."

"I know." His voice was steady, but Falpian saw him clutching the railing of the bridge in frustration.

An image of Ryder's sisters drifted thought Falpian's mind. Ryder was thinking about them, worrying about what would happen to them now that their mother was gone. Falpian wondered if he would still see these pictures once he went back to the Bitterlands, or if they would fade. He decided he'd miss them.

Something white whizzed toward them. With a smack, a snowball caught Falpian in the forehead. "Ow!"

"Dirty blackhair, dirty blackhair!"

He clutched his head.

"Come here and say that, you little pustule!" Ryder cried, leaning out over the rail of the bridge. Below them, a boy stood waving. A few other children stood farther away in groups or giggled behind the trees at the side of the river. "I'll make you eat that snowball!"

"Ryder," Falpian murmured, "it's nothing. He's half your size."

"Witches are going to get you!" the boy said, jumping up and down and pointing. "They're coming to get you, blackhair! Look!"

Falpian turned. A party of witches had emerged from the clouds, red blossoms on the snowy path. Some had pack ponies laden with goods. The children pointed and shouted; then, all at once, they scurried away, calling to their parents or anyone else who would listen that coven dwellers were coming to town.

"I'll go back to the tavern," Falpian said.

"No! They're not really coming for you, you know."

"I know." But in spite of Ryder's words, he turned and started down the road.

I'll leave today, Falpian decided. It was no use putting it off any longer. The things he had to do in the Bitterlands were too important to risk staying, no matter how much he might want to.

The witches' procession filed slowly toward the village. At the very end, four people were carrying a litter painted red. The person on top clutched tightly to the sides as it lurched and swayed. *Well, well,* thought Ryder, bemused. *Sodan has finally decided to see where his breakfast comes from.*

Something little and red detached itself from the party and came scampering toward him down the road—a small person. "Hey, Ry-der!"

With a thump, she fell headfirst into the snow, and Ryder started forward, but she picked herself up again without a cry and started running again. They met at the end of the bridge, and Ryder swept her up in his arms.

"Pima!" he said, squeezing her tight. "Sweetlamb."

"I went through the catacombs," she said. "But I didn't see a dead body." She sounded disappointed.

"Didn't you?"

"Yulla made me shut my eyes. It smelled like pee."

Ryder laughed.

Two witches came forward now, his cousin Yulla and Aata's Right Hand. Ryder was surprised to see that the younger witch was wearing red, not white. There was something cloying about Yulla's expression, a look of pity and solicitousness that grated on him. He guessed that she knew about Mabis.

"We met Farmer Raiken on the road," Yulla explained. She glanced at Pima and shook her head, telling him that his sister didn't know.

Ryder held Pima tight and nodded. "Later," he mouthed.

"Sodan would like to speak to you," said Aata's Right Hand. Shyly she brushed her fingers against his shoulder, and Ryder knew she was trying to be kind. "But perhaps you'd like to join us later. We are going to lead prayers at the village shrine."

"I'm not very good at praying." She looked even better in reds, Ryder thought. The color brought out the crimson in her lips—but it was hard to look at her without wondering whether, if it weren't for her, his mother might be alive.

Pima wriggled out of his grasp and ran to hold Yulla's hand. "You should come pray, Ryder," she said sagely. "It would do you good."

Ryder shot a glance at Yulla. "Maybe later," he said.

He bowed. Pima and the two witches took off toward the center of the village, but a few moments later, Aata's Right Hand came running back. She stood, breathless, at the top of the arched bridge and called down to him.

"I want you to know that I will spend my life trying to atone for what I've done. I'll never throw the bones again."

Ryder was taken aback. "That's your choice." The word "atone" made him feel uncomfortable. It reminded him of Lilla.

She turned, looking disappointed.

"Aata's Right Hand!" he called, before she had taken a step.

"Marisat," she corrected.

"What?"

"It's Marisat. My name. I'm not the Right Hand of Aata anymore."

"Oh," he said. "Well, I thought I should tell you. That vision you had, about the lake and the maiden's woe. It was a true one."

She froze, looking down at him, and Ryder was sure he

could see the rosy color leave her cheeks. "Why would you say that?"

He thought she'd want to know, that he was saying something kind, but she didn't seem to take it that way. "Because it's true."

He turned away, but she came slipping down the curve of the bridge and caught his arm. "I'm going home," she insisted. "To Dunes. To my father. No one can teach me there."

"Then go, for Aata's sake."

"How can I? If what you say is true . . ." Her grip tightened on his arm. "How could you just say something like that to me like it's nothing?"

He shook her off. "I'm just telling you what I know."

"But everyone hates me in this coven!"

He began to realize what he'd done. The covens had no boneshaker. And no one knew better than Ryder how much they needed one—the Baen were restless over the border. "I'm sorry," he said more gently. "I didn't see it. You're right, you shouldn't leave now, not if there's a chance you can learn. Can you speak to Sodan?" Marisat just gaped at him, shaking her head. "You . . . did say you wanted to atone. . . ."

Her eyes widened. For a moment she stared at him so hard he thought she'd slap him, then she looked to the sky. "Oh Goddess, I did say that, didn't I?"

* * *

The party of witches arrived, and for a while there was much excitement. Villagers came to greet the visitors and ooh and aah over the pack animals laden with stores. Ryder was amazed. They seemed to treat it all like a great gift, when really they were only being given back what they had grown themselves.

The red litter was the last thing to make it down the mountain. Of course, the villagers knew it was Sodan, and they stood around at the village side of the bridge, talking in hushed tones. Word had gotten around that Sodan had come for the express purpose of speaking to Ryder, and so they stared at him and kept their distance, as if he'd suddenly caught a case of the scabs. Ryder crossed his arms and waited and tried to pretend that he didn't care what Sodan had to say.

The litter stopped right in front of him. Four witch bearers, three men and one woman, set their cargo down into the snow. One of them handed Sodan a stick, while another helped him rise, shakily, to his feet. Ryder had to stoop to look into his face. Sodan's eyes were gray and red-rimmed, and he had a long, white beard that fell softly over his red coat.

"You know Visser, I believe." The man's dry voice was nearly carried away in the cold wind. Visser, who had been walking beside the litter, nodded curtly. She carried no gear, but held a sword clutched to her chest.

Ryder nodded and gave the witch's bow. "Is that the Baenkiller?" He thought he'd lost it in the snowslide.

Sodan nodded. "Marisat knew where it was." Ryder saw him rub the small of his back with his hand.

"Shall we speak in the tavern, sir?" He felt guilty for assuming it was pride or disdain that kept Sodan from visiting the village; clearly, the journey down the mountain had been a trial. "Dassen will have a fire on by now, and we could return his sword at the same time."

"No, no," the old man answered. "I must go to the shrine in a moment." He nodded at the knots of villagers at the other end of the bridge. "I fear that no one will join the prayers if I do not come. Visser will take the sword. She has a favor to ask of the tavern keeper."

Visser scurried away, the sword in her arms, avoiding Ryder's eye. Ryder tried to imagine this man bending his body into the witches' prayers.

"You know why I am here," Sodan said.

"I do?"

The coven leader smiled, and Ryder caught a glimpse of intelligence and humor in his round gray eyes. "What would you guess?"

"Oh. I suppose you want me to join the coven."

"I do indeed."

"Absolutely not."

Ryder turned to the group of gawkers at the other end

of the bridge. "He's come to ask me to join the coven, and I've refused!" he shouted. "If you really want to know!" The villagers looked away and tried to act as if it was just coincidence they were standing around at that particular spot.

Sodan was smirking at him when he looked back. "A shame, when both of your sisters live on the mountain. . . ."

"One of my sisters," he corrected. "Skyla can do what she wants, but Pima is a temporary visitor. When I rebuild my farm, she will come and live with me."

Sodan was taken aback. "A cruel blow for Yulla, I fear."

"My baby sister is not a tithe for Yulla to steal."

"To raise a child alone, at your age . . ."

"I have brought down the Gormy Man," he said sharply. "I can raise a child."

"The latter might prove to be the more difficult." Sodan sighed, leaning heavily on his stick. "How easily this problem would be solved if you were to live in the coven, and your whole family could be together." The man was not above wheedling, Ryder could see. To his surprise, he found himself wavering.

Sodan took advantage of the hesitation. "Now that we know what the chamber of spells can do, we cannot ignore it. It must be studied. Someone with your knowledge of singing would be invaluable to us. Skyla has already asked permission to study the catacombs, and I have agreed."

"Skyla?" The idea shouldn't have surprised him. He remembered the look of wonder on her face as she gazed around the tomb of Aayse. "But neither of us can read the spells."

"I can, and I have agreed to teach her."

"You read Baen?"

"I taught your grandfather."

His grandfather. The man was always coming up, though Ryder knew so little about him. Sodan could tell him more. The caves could tell him more. He was sure they held countless secrets about his family history, about magic, about the Baen. Briefly Ryder let himself imagine the life Sodan was offering. It wasn't what Mabis had wanted for him, that was sure. He thought of the farm his father had worked so hard to build. The forest would overtake the ruined buildings; the planting hills would be covered with grass. But Ryder couldn't pretend he was a farmer. The Goddess wouldn't take back her gift. In front of him Sodan waited patiently. Ryder had the uncomfortable feeling that Sodan had been waiting patiently for him all his life, knowing he'd end up wearing red sooner or later.

"And when the caves are studied, will we be allowed to share what we have learned with the villagers?"

Now Sodan was the one to hesitate. "The situation is complex, Ryder. The villagers wouldn't understand."

Ryder hissed, suddenly exasperated. "You people. You're like thief spiders squatting on your hoard." Even before the words were out, he knew he had gone too far.

Sodan's face grew red under his beard—a man like this heard few insults, Ryder guessed. He looked to his bearers, who stood a little ways off. Ryder was certain he would call to them at once and depart, but to his surprise, Sodan took a deep breath and swallowed his anger. It occurred to Ryder that Sodan must want him very badly.

"I have had to bear your family's arrogance over many generations," Sodan said. "And I will tell you, it doesn't get easier."

"We prefer to call it strong will," Ryder said. "And . . . I'm sorry. I was rude."

They stood without speaking for a while as the cold wind picked the snow up off the ground and swirled it around their feet. Still Sodan didn't call his bearers, didn't leave for the village shrine.

"Perhaps," Sodan began, "at the discretion of the elders, some knowledge could be shared with the village. . . ."

Ryder was amazed he had the power to get concessions out of the leader of the coven. He looked to his feet, frowning. "I won't be a boneshaker, if that's what you're thinking."

Sodan shrugged, agreeing, but Ryder could see the old man was hoping he'd change his mind eventually. Maybe

Ryder should change his mind. About everything. He might be happy in the coven. He could be with his sisters—and why shouldn't he be the one eating the tithe instead of working for it for a change?

Part of him wanted this, he realized with a start. Part of him really did want to use the gifts the Goddess had given him. Suddenly he felt a stab of loss for Kef—how he would have laughed. Everything about the idea did seem to make sense. Except that for the rest of his life he'd be singing alone. But that couldn't be helped.

"Sir," he said hesitantly. "This will sound mad, I know, but if I do come to the coven, is there some way our people and the Baen could share the knowledge I find?" Sodan smiled indulgently and shook his head. "Not the spells, not anything dangerous, but the history. Our people lived together once—the catacombs prove that. They made magic together and were buried next to each other and probably married, too."

Sodan nodded. "Yes. I think it was your grandfather's dearest wish to have lived during that time. It was a golden age. The covens were places of learning. And refuges as well, for Baen women forbidden to use magic. Their loss was our great gain, it is true, and their descendents are still among us, still contributing to the covens. But those times were long, long ago."

"Can't people make a golden age come again?" Ryder

asked. "Falpian—he already knows about the caves. Maybe someday he could come back here and help translate."

"Ryder," said the old man, very gently. "You do see that no one in the Bitterlands can know about the existence of the echo site, or about the chamber of spells." The look on his face was strangely tender, and he put a frail hand on Ryder's arm.

"Of course. You don't need to worry about Falpian. He'll keep our secret."

Sodan kept staring at him with his deep, kind eyes, as if willing him to understand something he didn't want to say aloud.

All at once, the blood seemed to drain to Ryder's feet, and he pulled away from Sodan's touch. "Just what kind of favor is Visser asking Dassen to do?"

CHAPTER 28

THE BITTERLANDS

Ryder burst through the door of the tavern. "Dassen, stop!"

Falpian was pressed into a corner, and the tavern keeper had his sword upraised, but between the two, Bodread the Slayer was snarling like a wild beast, his long body tense and slung low to the ground. Broken crockery and smashed chairs littered the floor. Skyla knelt on top of one of the tavern tables, her eyes frantic. Visser stood behind Dassen, muttering something.

"Bo, stay back!" Ryder cried. Bo drew back against Falpian's legs, but the dog's eyes were still fixed on the sword. "Dassen, whatever that witch is telling you to do, don't do it."

Visser glowered at him over her shoulder. "Don't interfere," she said. "Dassen, it is the coven who asks you to do this. In the name of the elders and of Sodan and of every witch who ever lived on the mountain, I ask you to kill this man."

Ryder came up to the other side of the tavern keeper, stepping over the remains of a broken water jug. Gently he laid a hand on his arm. "Dass," he said. "I've got only one name to ask you by. And I think you know whose it is." Dassen shot him a tortured look. "Please. You always believed my mother, even when she said unbelievable things. I know that killing this Baen is wrong. I know it. And I'm asking you to believe *me* this time."

Slowly the Baenkiller dropped to Dassen's side. Visser gave a hiss of frustration.

"You all right?" Ryder asked. Falpian nodded, but glanced fearfully back and forth between Visser and Dassen.

"No matter," Visser said. "There are a hundred others in the village who will finish this task at a word from me."

It was true. Ryder thought furiously. He should have realized earlier that Sodan couldn't let Falpian across the border with what he knew. "Yes," he finally agreed. "That's why Dassen and Skyla are going to keep you here until Falpian and I can get away."

"What!" Visser's eyes darted to the door of the tavern, but Skyla was off the table in a moment, standing between Visser and the exit. Visser glared. "Skyla, think what you're doing."

"I'm sorry. I'm very sorry." She pointed to Falpian. "But he saved us all. You were there. You saw that Baen and my brother risk their lives for us. . . ." Visser made a dash for the door, but Skyla grabbed her by the wrist and held tight. "Oh, by the red, I truly am sorry, but I can't let you go."

Visser struggled to free herself. "I will have Sodan remove you from the coven! You should ask Dassen for work in his kitchen, Skyla, because you will have nothing else. All your dreams of being a witch will come to nothing!"

Skyla blanched, but she squared her shoulders, imperious as a queen, and didn't let go of Visser's hand.

"Sodan won't do that," Ryder told her. "He needs boneshakers, and until he's sure you don't have the gift, he won't let you go. Don't make Sodan choose between the two of you, Visser. It might be you who ends up scraping plates in that kitchen."

Visser gaped at this, her face scarlet, but she couldn't seem to find a retort. Ryder turned to Dassen.

"Where are your hired girls?"

"Gone for the day. But Ryder, I can't hold a witch captive. She's an elder, for Aata's sake."

"I'm sorry, Dass. I know what I'm asking you to do. I know there will be consequences." Nervously Ryder looked to the window of the tavern, but there were no villagers in sight—everyone had probably gone to the village square to pray with Sodan. "You'll be discovered soon enough, but try to keep her in the storage room for as long as you can. Falpian and I will go through the forest and cross the river below Raiken's farm—I think I can keep us from being seen."

Dassen shook his head and cast his eyes to the ceiling. "For your mother, Ryder," he muttered. "I do this for your mother." Reluctantly he took Visser by the arm and led her away.

Ryder took his sister's hand. "I want you to know that I'm proud of you." He spoke quickly, checking the window all the while. "Whatever stupid things you've heard me say about witches, I'm proud you're one of them. I hope you do grow up to be a boneshaker."

Skyla stared at him. "Me? But you're the one with the gift."

"I'm . . . going to use my gift a different way."

A cloud crossed her face. "Wait." She glanced at Falpian. "You're just taking him to the border, aren't you? You're coming back." As Ryder hesitated, she grasped at his shirt. "No. Not again. Not to the Bitterlands—you can't!"

"Kiss Pima for me. Try to make her understand."

"*I* don't understand! Aata's sake, Ryder. You—your leg. You're not healed."

"She's right," Falpian said, staring at Ryder, as shocked as Skyla.

But Ryder had made up his mind.

Even the trees were white. Frozen fog had rimed their trunks and branches with frost. Falpian and Ryder had entered the clouds. Somewhere ahead was the border marker, but Ryder couldn't see it. All he saw was the fog and the white trees looming up like ghosts.

Behind him, Falpian was breathing heavily. The way was steep and they were both tired. "I can make my way from here," he said. "It can't be far." His voice was muffled by a scarf.

Ryder gave a faint laugh but didn't lessen his pace. "You could have made your way from the village. Saved me this whole trip." He glanced worriedly behind them, but because of the fog, there was nothing to see. Dassen would have hidden their departure for as long as he could, but by now Ryder was sure the village had been alerted.

"I'm serious," Falpian said. "You can't come with me. You won't be safe in the Bitterlands."

"Neither will you. The witches might cross the border to keep you from telling what you know. We're better off if we stay together."

A note of fear entered Falpian's voice. "Do you think they will?"

Ryder hesitated, then lied. "No. Probably not."

Behind them, the smudge of sun grew lower in the sky. For a while the only sounds were those of their breath, and their steps, and the *shush* of their walking sticks digging into the snow. Sometimes Ryder caught a glimpse of Bo between the trees, a quick, pale shape. The dog traveled with them, sometimes ahead, sometimes behind, always on guard. Ryder marveled that such a big animal could be so quiet, appearing and disappearing without a sound, as if he were made of fog.

"Think what you're doing," Falpian said, breaking the strange, muffled quiet. "I . . . I know how you feel. All the time we were at Dassen's, don't you think I was trying to think of a way for us to stay together? Together we are so powerful—but the Baen will give you the same reception the Witchlanders gave me."

"I have a gift," Ryder said. "And I've decided not to waste it. I'm going to learn to sing."

"Ha!" Falpian said. "You think you'll find a singing master in the Bitterlands? You think any Baen will teach you?"

"I'm talking about you, fool. You're going to teach me."

"Oh."

"I see it!" Ryder cried, before Falpian could say anything more. Ahead of them was the flat table of land where the border marker was. They took the last distance at a run.

When they got to the border, Ryder's legs crumpled underneath him. "We shouldn't stop," he managed to say, but he sat panting in the snow without getting up, the cold air shredding his lungs.

"Your leg," said Falpian. A few red spots were beginning to seep through Ryder's leggings.

"It's nothing. I think a stitch has come out. Give me your arm." He got to his feet. "We can't assume they won't follow. We'll have to travel all night, if you can make it."

"If *I* can make it?" Falpian laughed.

Ryder edged forward toward the place where the mountain fell away to the Bitterlands. There were fewer trees on this side; he should have been able to see the dizzying descent down to the gorge, but there was nothing but white blankness. It would be dangerous traveling in this weather, especially after sunset. Ryder knew from their previous climb that there were places where one wrong step could mean a deadly fall.

"Let's go," he said, but his talat-sa was still standing next to the border marker, blurred by the swirling fog.

"Ryder," Falpian said. "They'll kill you. Do you understand? My people will kill you."

"Lady Melicant," Ryder answered firmly.

Falpian gaped. "How would you—oh. All right, she's a friend of my mother's, what about her?"

"Lady Melicant has Witchlander servants."

It took Falpian a moment to see what he was getting at. "Oh, no. No. That's different, Ryder. They were loyal and followed her to the Bitterlands during the war. Nobody has *new* Witchlander servants."

"We'll say you saved my life in the snow, and now I'm bound to you as your faithful attendant."

Falpian snorted with laughter. "And everyone will immediately think you're a spy. And that I'm a dupe for not seeing it. No. It makes convincing the lords not to go to war all the harder, don't you see? It's too dangerous!"

Ryder stood firm, arms crossed. "Falpian, you're going up against a man who's already tried to kill you once. Yes, taking me with you would be dangerous, but our singing together is our greatest weapon. Leaving me behind would be even more dangerous."

"It's wrong," Falpian said. Ryder watched as a realization dawned on Falpian's face. "And you know it! Even you think it's wrong for you to come—you're thinking it right now!"

Ryder let out a sigh of annoyance. He hated this link they had sometimes. There was no privacy in it. And he'd thought sharing a cramped cottage with his mother and sisters had been bad.

"Yes," Ryder agreed. "It's wrong." Without warning, his voice started to quaver, though he tried to stop it.

"Somewhere above our heads there is a handful of stars that say I am meant to be a witch. They say, 'Ryder lived happily in the coven with his sisters and worshipped the Goddess until the end of his days.' And you know, a part of me really does want that. But I can't figure out a way to have it and be sure you stay alive."

Falpian threw up his hands in frustration. "But I'm not asking for your help to stay alive! I don't want to keep you from your family and from your . . . boneshaking destiny!"

Ryder took a breath and kept his voice calm and firm. "I'm going with you because the thing you have to do is too important. If Sodan sends someone across the border, you might not last the night without me. And if your father decides to try to kill you again to keep you quiet, you're better off with me than with just a humming stone. That's the way it is. You're stuck with me."

Falpian cast his eyes to the clouds. After a long moment, he said, "I'm not going to convince you, am I?"

"You already know you're not."

"Goddess help us."

Ryder laughed. "Wrong one. You're Kar, remember?"

Falpian pursed his lips, frowning. "We should at least sing. To know if they're following. To know what we're up against." Ryder shook his head. "You did just say you wanted to learn to sing, didn't you?"

"Yes, but . . ." Ryder couldn't think of a reason to object. Singing would give them a vision of the whole mountain, and they needed to know if Sodan had sent an army after them, or one lone hunter, or no one at all. "After we sing, I never know how I did it. I can never really believe it happened."

Ignoring Ryder's hesitation, Falpian took off his pack and dropped it in the snow. "Stand over here," he said. "Where it's flat. We'll start with something we know." He clapped his gloved hands together briskly. "Come, come! I'm the singing master, remember?" He grinned wickedly. "And you're my loyal attendant." Ryder rolled his eyes.

The key of rocking waves. The song of the sea. *This is where we met,* Ryder thought as he began to sing. *Not at Stonehouse, but here.* Before the chilling day, they had both, for different reasons, been dreaming of the sea. Was that how their minds had found each other?

Pay attention, came Falpian's voice in his mind. *Watch your tones, servant.* Ryder was going to regret giving him this role.

Around him, the world came into focus. Ice crystals glittered in the fog, each one suspended in the air like a tiny universe. Ryder was dazzled, as he always was when he sang. It seemed to him that there was a pattern there, if he could only see it. It seemed to him that some great mind might calculate the distances between each crystal, drawing invisible lines between them, and from them extrapolate the past, present, and future of all things under the eyes of the Goddess, and of Kar.

Then Ryder let his mind see beyond the fog, let it rise into the air like the smoke of his breath. He could see down to the shoulder of the mountain where their two little bodies stood. He could see the snow-covered trees. He could see Bo making wide circles around them, keeping them safe. He could see the way in front of him and the way behind. And everything was clear.